ROMANCE LOVERS ARE FALLING FOR THE SONS OF DESTINY

"Jean Johnson's writing is fabulously fresh, thoroughly romantic, and wildly entertaining. Terrific—fast, sexy, charming, and utterly engaging. I loved it!"

—Jayne Ann Krentz, *New York Times* bestselling author of *Sizzle and Burn*

"The magical land Johnson creates is a whimsical treat, and the brothers are a joy to behold. Readers will look forward to more in the Sons of Destiny series."
—*Booklist*

"Cursed brothers, fated mates, prophecies, yum! A fresh new voice in fantasy romance, Jean Johnson spins an intriguing tale of destiny and magic."
—Robin D. Owens, RITA Award–winning author of *Heart Fate*

"What a debut! I have to say it is a must-read for those who enjoy fantasy ar̶ ... eager-ly look fo ... hnson can't writ ... *Reviews*

"Encha ... nan make f ... A delight ... *view*

Novels of the Sons of Destiny by Jean Johnson

The Flame

JEAN JOHNSON

BERKLEY SENSATION, NEW YORK

THE BERKLEY PUBLISHING GROUP
Published by the Penguin Group
Penguin Group (USA) Inc.
375 Hudson Street, New York, New York 10014, USA
Penguin Group (Canada), 90 Eglinton Avenue East, Suite 700, Toronto, Ontario M4P 2Y3, Canada
(a division of Pearson Penguin Canada Inc.)
Penguin Books Ltd., 80 Strand, London WC2R 0RL, England
Penguin Group Ireland, 25 St. Stephen's Green, Dublin 2, Ireland (a division of Penguin Books Ltd.)
Penguin Group (Australia), 250 Camberwell Road, Camberwell, Victoria 3124, Australia
(a division of Pearson Australia Group Pty. Ltd.)
Penguin Books India Pvt. Ltd., 11 Community Centre, Panchsheel Park, New Delhi—110 017, India
Penguin Group (NZ), 67 Apollo Drive, Rosedale, North Shore 0632, New Zealand
(a division of Pearson New Zealand Ltd.)
Penguin Books (South Africa) (Pty.) Ltd., 24 Sturdee Avenue, Rosebank, Johannesburg 2196,
South Africa

Penguin Books Ltd., Registered Offices: 80 Strand, London WC2R 0RL, England

This book is an original publication of The Berkley Publishing Group.

PRINTING HISTORY
Berkley Sensation trade paperback edition / December 2008

Library of Congress Cataloging-in-Publication Data

Johnson, Jean, 1972–
    The flame : a novel of the Sons of Destiny / Jean Johnson.—Berkley Sensation
trade pbk. ed.
        p. cm.
    ISBN 978-0-425-22405-2
    I. Title.
    PS3610.o355F57   2008
    813'.6—dc22

                                                                    2008037185

PRINTED IN THE UNITED STATES OF AMERICA

10 9 8 7 6 5 4 3 2 1

ACKNOWLEDGMENTS

Do you realize I have yet to receive a single complaint for putting in these acknowledgments? In fact, I have actually been told by a handful of people how neat it is that I thank people in print. Well, duh! Without them, my writing would be crappy! Writing is usually a solitary craft, but it is almost never done in a complete vacuum. I thank you, the person holding this book, for taking the time to read these acknowledgments and learn these names (well, okay, these online screen names), because these people do help me ensure that what I write is worthy of being read.

Pern_Dragon cold read this one in spite of her busy schedule, so she definitely gets a hug for her input. Grand Poobah gets a hug, too, for helping me with the back cover copy of this book. (That's the one part of novel writing I don't like: trying to summarize everything into two to three paragraphs, ugh!) And of course, Alexandra, Alienor, Stormi, and NotSoSaintly deserve huge snuggly hugs with chocolate-covered bribery for tirelessly polishing my prose. O.o Shiny!!

As always, come visit me at: www.JeanJohnson.net, where all are welcome. Or if you're over eighteen and want to join the mostly benign chaos . . . er, creativity found at the Mob of Irate Torch-Wielding Fans—who are even cooler in person than they are online—feel free to contact me through my website.

Enjoy!
Jean

ONE

The Seventh Son shall he decree:
Burning bright and searing hot
You shall seek that which is not
Mastered by desire's name
Water shall control the Flame

Koranen sat on a stone bench placed in front of a stone table set in the middle of a broad circle of paving stones. It was the safest place for him to be. Arms folded, shoulders hunched, chin tucked onto his wrists, he watched his family and their new handful of servants bustling around him. Ignoring him.

There was another bench on the opposite side of the smallish, round granite table and space for a chess game or some other amusement on its surface, but no one joined him. For one, everyone else in the castle-like palace was too busy to sit down at the moment. They were all rushing about, either to help Mariel plant newly imported herbs in the Healer's herb garden, or they were hurrying from wing to wing of the sprawling palace, taking advantage of the warmth of early summer to cut off a few hundred yards of traveling from one point to the next. For another . . . no one wanted to get near him right now.

Frustration—for a fire-mage—was not a comfortable thing to be around if one wasn't a fellow Pyromancer as well. The source of that frustration . . . well, Kor didn't want to think about it. Thinking about it only made it worse. Last night, he'd thought about it during dinner when one of his six sisters-in-law had eaten her dessert a bit . . . sensually . . . reminding him that he didn't have, and couldn't have, a woman in his life to do that to *him* instead of her fork.

Everyone *said* they forgave him for instantly turning his dining chair to ash, dumping him on his sooty backside. But the fact that his chair had been warded against fire, yet had combusted anyway, was reason enough to avoid the frustrated man. Not an excuse—everyone liked him; there was no doubt of that—but reason enough.

Twenty-four years old, and still in exile. Joy. Roughly four years had passed since he and his brothers had been dumped on Nightfall Isle, banished there by the Council of Katan just for the suspicion of being the eight brothers spoken of in a famous Seer's ancient prophecy. Roughly one year ago, the first of his sisters-in-law had been brought to the island, setting that prophecy in motion. One by one, his brothers' verses in the Song of the Sons of Destiny—a thousand-year-old prophecy made by the famous Seer Draganna—were each coming true.

First Saber, the eldest, had fallen in love, proving his verse wasn't nearly as disaster-filled as the Council of Mages had originally feared. Then Wolfer had reunited with his childhood friend, falling as well. Then Dominor, Evanor, Trevan . . . even Rydan, the most reluctant of them all, more so than even Saber had initially been. The only ones left now were himself and his slightly younger twin, Morganen. But Trevan and Rydan had fallen for their women *months* ago . . . leaving Kor alone and thus frustrated.

And hot. Kor was almost ready to sleep in the cinders of his forge-fire, since even his fire-warded bedding was threatening to scorch with the heat of his frustrated dreams, despite the spells woven and embroidered into the hems of his blankets and sheets. Groaning, wishing the light, cool breeze wafting through the garden would pick up a little more, Koranen buried his head in his arms, shutting out the sight of two pretty Katani housemaids they had hired. Not that he could have touched either of them even if he hadn't been a frustrated Pyromancer. They were only interested in each other, as in *interested* in each other, and wouldn't have given him the time of day, even if he didn't run the risk of burning them literally with his interest in them.

There were more servants running around. A year ago, servants on the Isle would have been unthinkable, and female servants would have been put to death, by order of the Empire of Katan. Now that Nightfall was an incipient, independent kingdom, the only person left in exile was himself, and only because he couldn't, daren't, touch anyone. The memory of reddened, blistering handprints on tender, rounded flesh still haunted him, though it had been years since he last tried to touch a woman intimately.

"... I don't care, Alys!"

His ears twitched, picking up Kelly's hushed voice as she hurried along the path behind him.

"I *know* I should invite her to our kung fu sessions . . . but I just can't *stand* her outside of a business setting. And she still doesn't strike me as the sort of woman who'd shut up and actually let anyone teach her something, let alone *me* . . ."

Ah, yes, the ongoing, occasional catfight between incipient Queen Kelly and incipient Mayor Amara . . . Though "mayor" wasn't so much a possibility these days as a near certainty. They now had more than three thousand people on the island, outside of the core that was their growing family. *And not one of them an Aquamancer* . . .

His verse in the Song of the Sons was the easiest to interpret: *Water shall control the Flame* clearly meant that he, a Pyromancer,

needed an Aquamancer in his life. Not a single one from the continent of Katan had volunteered to come, however. Dominor thought
the Council of Mages was putting pressure on them to avoid the
island, to prevent the brothers not only from completing the Prophecy, but to prevent them from somehow successfully turning their
incipient kingdom into a real, Gods-approved one.

So far, they had about twenty minor generalist mages, three of
whom were skilled in construction magics, two Healers with three
apprentice herbalists, and a former female sailor who could whistle
up a wind on cue, but little else. All the rest of their new citizens
were non-mages. People who had neither magical power nor social
status like most mages had in both the lands of Natallia and Katan,
commoners who just wanted to start a new life. The brothers were
screening all of the incoming settlers with Truth Stones, making
sure to weed out the lazy, the shiftless, and the troublemakers, but
the majority of people who wanted to move here were those who
hadn't nearly as good prospects anywhere else.

"Mikor, stop playing with those worms and finish digging the
holes for the *facemint*, please."

That was Mariel, Healer and wife of Evanor, fourthborn of
Kor's seven siblings. Kor had stopped letting her son into his forge
in the last month, because he couldn't always guarantee that he
wouldn't be too overheated to be around. Kor liked her, since
she was motherly, friendly, and down-to-earth, and he liked Mikor,
because the lad was curious, friendly, and still a bit starved for male
role models. The forge was an exciting place for the boy, but not
necessarily a safe one.

Alys, who had walked past with Kelly, was married to the secondborn of his brothers, Wolfer. Serina, married to Dominor—Ev's
twin and the thirdborn brother—was hardly ever seen these days,
since she was currently the Guardian of Koral-tai, a nunnery on the
far side of the Eastern Ocean. She was also the Guardian of a powerful wellspring of magic hidden in that nunnery . . . and Dominor
was now the Guardian of a similar wellspring concealed right here

on Nightfall. There was a way for the two of them to cross the vast distances between each other's wellsprings, but it was more common for Dominor to visit Serina than the other way around—something about her faring better in her current delicate condition on that side of the world.

Amara had married Trevan. She was prickly, prideful, and used to being in charge . . . as was Kelly. The two women butted heads more often than not, but when they *did* agree on something, they could move mountains together. Most of her time, Amara preferred to work with Trev; the two of them could be found babbling about this or that new idea every bit as often as they could be found kissing in some quiet corner.

Koranen felt his skin flushing with warmth. *Don't think about kissing . . . Don't think about it . . .*

Rydan and his wife, Rora, weren't often seen, either. Then again, Rora was different enough that she would be in danger if any newcomers to the island found out about her specialness. Rydan was also a night owl by habit and preference, so it was no hardship for either of them to be elsewhere when most sensible people were awake.

Apparently Kor's next-eldest brother had hidden himself in the night to avoid the irritating pressure of the many emotions radiated by his siblings—a strange thing, but there it was. Koranen was tempted to become nocturnal, too. At least that way, he'd only have a single courting couple to avoid, rather than the dozens that cuddled around him each day. It was *sort* of like Rydan's ongoing emotional irritation, only in Kor's case, it was sheer sexual frustration. Anytime he saw a happy, romantically inclin—

Briiiingding. Briiiingding.

Jerking his head up, Koranen flicked open the faceted lid of the silver and gold cryslet clasped around his left wrist. Peering into the specially enchanted scrying mirror, he frowned at his twin's face. "Morg? What do you want?"

Morganen's aquamarine eyes looked disgustingly bright and

cheerful, before he pulled back far enough for the rest of his face to be seen. "You'll want to make your way to the council chamber as quickly as possible. I have some wonderful, incredible news!"

The image of Morg's grinning face blinked out, replaced by the normal reflection of his own. Frowning, Koranen snapped the lid shut, fingering the cream-colored stone embedded in the oval top of the communication Artifact. *Why would Morg call me to a council meeting? Is this about the lightglobes I make? Did Dominor and Serina arrange for another shipment of comsworg oil from Natallia?*

Aware that the seats in the council chamber weren't warded against heat, Koranen planted his hands on the table and focused his power. After a few moments, the scent of heated stone filled the air, and his body felt reasonably cool. Hopefully, safely so. Standing, he moved away from the table, calling out to the trio of ladies and youth a few herb beds away. "Ladies, Mikor, the table over here is extra hot. Don't touch it for at least an hour."

The plump, curly-haired Healer lifted her hand in acknowledgment before turning back to her plantings. Her dark-haired son glanced briefly at the table in question, then shook his head quickly. Mikor had already burned himself in Koranen's forge and knew better than to be tempted into touching whatever the Pyromancer warned about. Satisfied he would be heeded, Kor headed for the main trunk of the Y-shaped north wing.

Stepping in through the door nearest the council room, Koranen paused, eyeing the walls of the corridor. He knew the magical, scene-changing paint wasn't exactly controllable; it randomly flickered from scene to scene, some in slow motion, some at lifelike speed. Today, this particular little hallway off the main corridor showed a slowly billowing image of a raging forest fire, all oranges and reds and blacks.

It's nothing personal . . . nothing to do with me. Shaking his head, he tightened his personal wards, muttering, and strode for the main corridor. The walls and ceiling of that corridor showed a mist-veiled forest, visually damp and cool by comparison with its pale grays and dark greens. In contrast, the walls of the council chamber, when he stepped inside, were filled with the slightly blurred, slow-fluttering wings of butterflies . . . what could be seen of the walls, of course.

Maps of the island had been drawn and pinned to the painted stones, and chalkboards in cheval frames settled in place beneath the high, narrow clerestory windows along the top of the outer wall. Lightglobes—crafted by Koranen himself out of sand, comsworg oil, and other ingredients—sat in wrought iron stands at intervals, glowing brightly enough to dispel any lingering shadows, making the place look cheerful. The floor had been softened with strips of old carpeting salvaged from storage, and the V-shaped council table, normally a polished, age-darkened brown, was covered in sheaves of paper, proof that this had become the hub of castle activity.

Saber was already there, rib-length blond hair pulled back in a braid to keep it out of his face as he leaned over ledgers and papers. As firstborn of the brothers, and the former Count of Corvis, it was his job to manage the prosperity of the island. That meant keeping track of the imports and exports, the usage of the land and its resources, and the skills of the incoming settlers. He was talking with a matronly woman named Teretha, a former Baroness of Natallia whose lands had been overrun by the Mandarites. She had come to Nightfall Isle with a batch of refugees vetted by the nuns of Koral-tai and had proven herself an apt judge of how and where best to reclaim the old, jungle-swallowed orchards and fields here on Nightfall.

Wolfer was also in the room, apparently discussing with his twin and Teretha the migration patterns of the two deer herds that roamed the island. The big, muscular man had let his wife cut his plain brown hair shoulder-short with a little bit of layering, which allowed it to fluff out around his head, making him look shaggy. Alys referred to it fondly as his "wolf look," which was appropriate, since Wolfer preferred to take that form when he spellshifted his shape, but Koranen privately thought it made his second-eldest sibling look more like a *jonja*. A runty *jonja*, since the fierce, long-tailed, bear-like creatures were usually at least twelve feet tall when they stood on their hind legs.

Kelly entered after a moment, sporting a grin. Alys trailed in her wake, laughing about whatever had made her friend grin. Kor had known the mousy, often shy Alys almost all his life, for she had been a childhood friend of his family; he approved of her increased confidence and independence now that she was free of her unpleasant kinsmen. Kelly . . . well, the freckled outworlder was still a bit fiery-tempered at times, but she was a good-hearted person and brilliant in her own peculiar, outworlder-raised way.

Next to enter the room was Amara. The black-haired beauty quirked her eyebrow at Kelly, and the redhead silently quirked her own. They held a brief staring contest—even a non-Pyromancer could have sensed the silent sparks of clashing dominances between the two women—and then Kelly graciously gestured toward one of the seats, which Amara wordlessly took as if it were a proffered throne. Koranen secretly suspected she did so just to annoy Kelly, since the former princess had relinquished her ties to her former homeland. No sooner had she seated herself than Morganen came in through the door, levitating an oval mirror and an easel-like stand.

"Is Dominor coming?" Kelly asked him.

"No, but Rydan and Rora are, and Evanor, too."

The brown-haired Teretha finished up her business, murmuring a greeting to Alys, who was in charge of managing the palace animals. That included a placid, happy herd of dairy cattle and the infamous, vicious Nightfall chickens . . . which no one else in the castle was willing to feed, on pain of a terrible pecking. Alys' stoic bravery was almost legendary among the farmers and fowl-tenders who had come to populate the island. The former baroness had already proposed a "chase the chicken" contest for would-be warriors to undertake as proof of their bravery before being accepted as guards in training.

Koranen wasn't sure it was entirely a tongue-in-cheek offer, either. Saber—not the strongest mage on the island by any means, but undoubtedly the best swordsman—had countered that it would be more of a final test for elite warriors to take and pass. From the looks of it, Kelly was taking the idea at least half seriously.

A flash of light blond hair drew Kor's attention to the door. Evanor entered, holding the panel open for Teretha . . . then quickly catching and holding it again for Rydan and his wife. Both of them were in rumpled dark clothes, with shadows under their eyes, mussed hair, and smothered yawns. Rydan, whose hair was as black as Amara's, grunted wordlessly at the greetings from the others. Rora, her hair as plain a light brown as Morganen's, merely yawned, slumped into the chair offered to her, and sagged against Rydan's shoulder as soon as he was seated at her side. Kor wasn't sure, but he thought he heard a tiny snore from the former Aian woman.

The dark look Rydan shot at his youngest sibling prompted Morg to smile. "Relax, Rydan, you'll get to go back to bed in a few minutes . . . *if* you can sleep." A flick of his hand closed and locked the doors into the chamber. A stroke of his fingers activated the mirror, connecting it not to Dominor down under the mountains to the north, but to a strange chamber they had last seen back in the midst of winter.

Strange, rippling bubbles of energy sat atop thin stalagmite pillars in a cave-like chamber. Pastel hues shimmered across the room, lighting up the age-weathered face of a slender woman in her eighties, possibly her nineties. Her white hair had been cropped short enough to show off her ears, and her body was clad in supple, fitted leather stitched in abstract patterns of pale and medium gray. Her hand lifted, stroked the edge of the mirror on her own side, and she smiled and spoke, seaming her face with even more wrinkles.

"Greetings unto Nightfall. Which one of you is my colleague?"

Koranen's ears twitched. Like his siblings, he had partaken of Ultra Tongue almost a year ago, a combination of spell and costly potion that allowed any spoken language to be translated by the mind of the drinker, allowing them to hear and speak in another language as if it were their own, only accented. The accent of this withered, short-haired woman was sort of a drawl, with extra vowels in some of her words.

"I am Guardian Rydan," his black-haired brother spoke. Rydan's voice was as gravelly as his chin was beard-shadowed. It was not quite as deep as Wolfer's, but it was clear he was still half asleep. "Though I Guard a different Fountain these days. Guardian Dominor now watches over Nightfall. You're Guardian Sheren."

"Got it in one. A pleasure to meet you face-to-face, as it were."

"Have you recovered from your poisoning?" Kelly asked. At the older woman's curious look, Kelly quickly introduced herself. "I'm Kelly, incipient Queen of Nightfall. These are Saber, my husband, and some of his brothers: Wolfer, Evanor, Koranen, and Morganen. Plus my sisters-in-law Alys, Amara, and Rora. We all helped to defend your Fountain, along with a couple more who aren't here at the moment."

"My thanks for that. And my apologies for the Council of Menomon being royal pains in the tailfins. I actually finished recovering over a month ago, but the unmentionables were being rather stubborn about keeping our city isolated . . . until that isolation started causing serious health and environmental problems. Which is why I've been allowed this connection, having convinced them to let me talk with you.

"Menomon is . . . isolated. We need two things to survive: freshwater, and fresh air. We can extract some of the water and air we need with Artifacts and spells, but Artifacts break down over time, and spells have to be recast frequently. Before the Council insisted that my Fountain be sealed against the rest of the world, we got some of our fresh air and freshwater through the Fountainways it was connected to . . . but when it was cut off, the water grew stale, and the air grew foul. We could get freshwater from the sea, but it turned the local waters excessively salty as well as stale, and that has caused our crops to fail and driven away the herds of fish we depended on. Cutting off trade also means we've started running out of stockpiles of foods.

"Since we're all adults, I shall speak frankly: The city of Menomon has been strapped over a barrel by the Council, and *shilonked* half to death. But I've always had fair dealings with Guardian Rydan and Guardian Serena beyond him. I've also been told by my primary apprentice, Danau, that your island hosts the fabled Desalinator of Tanaka Zhou Fen, a powerful Permanent Magic capable not only of purifying seawater into freshwater, but extracting the salt as well, to keep it from concentrating too much in the water that remains behind.

"The Council is willing—however grudgingly—to open trade with Nightfall. And, if necessary, to act as a trade facilitator between you and the kingdoms of Shattered Aiar and other places that the Fountain of Menomon connects to . . . if you'd be willing to trade fresh air and water with us, and would allow a delegation from the Aquamancy Guild of Menomon to visit your island to study the Desalinator, with the intent to replicate its magics for ourselves."

Aquamancers. Koranen was glad he hadn't taken a seat at the table or leaned against anything; the flash of heat that passed through him at that hopeful thought would have scorched the seat of his chair at the very least. As it was, the moment he saw Alys fanning herself and the others looking a little warm, he struggled to contain his not-so-figurative burning enthusiasm at the idea. *Don't think about it, don't think about it, don't think . . .*

"Trade is well and good," Saber told the woman on the other side of the paired mirrors, "but you were told what we also want: an intact, complete, legible copy of the Scroll of Living Glory . . . and copies of any other scrolls or tomes dealing with the Convocation of the Gods, how to create it, how to regulate it . . . everything."

"Of course, giving you access to study the Permanent Artifact that supplies *us* with freshwater runs the risk of possibly doing something that would ruin it," Kelly added. She quickly lifted a hand, forestalling any protest. "I'm sure your Aquamancers would take great care not to damage it, but it is a risk. Three of the four processors already don't work. We don't need the fourth one to fail.

"You want to study it? That's fine with us . . . but we want the desalination plant to be fully functional before any of your Aquamancers will be allowed to return home with plans for constructing your own. It's to your benefit to do a thorough job," she pointed out, "since they'll have had three times the practice in reconstructing it . . . but that's what we want."

"Technically, that's not *all* that we want," Saber cautioned his wife, "since we do want trade, but these are our opening offers."

Koranen cleared his throat, catching his eldest brother's eye. Sweat was beginning to form on his brow from the bottled-up heat within him. He wanted to make absolutely sure that those Aquamancers made it to Nightfall soon, before he went mad with too many years of unfulfilled desire.

"That is to say, we have *one* more thing, in that opening offer," the golden-haired magesmith amended. Sheren folded her arms across her chest, her expression skeptical, as Saber continued. "We want complete copies of everything you have concerning the Convocation of the Gods, including the Scroll of Living Glory. We want the Desalinator to be fully repaired and fully functional before your Aquamancy Guild team will be allowed to leave this island and re-create a new one for yourselves . . . *and* we want your best, single, female Aquamancers to be members of that team."

He glanced at Koranen, who quickly piped up, "Send at least five of them. You can send more than that, but at least five of them should be single, female, and definitely of courtship age. I don't want to see grandmothers, and I don't want to see children."

Sheren shifted her hands to her leather-clad hips, leaning closer to her side of the mirror-scry so she could peer through to the Nightfall side as if it were merely a window. "You are the one making this demand? Whatever for? Don't you have enough women to court locally?"

Kor tried not to flush too much. He kept his answer short and to the point. "It's a matter of Prophecy. Single female Aquamancers of courtship age . . . or we have no deal."

Sheren's age-whitened brow lifted even higher. "Really?"

"I have no idea what *shilonking* is, and somehow I don't think I want to know," Kelly said to the Guardian of Menomon, "but I do know you don't have much choice in the matter. Suffice to say the ladies in question will be treated with due courtesy, and nothing will happen to them that they do not agree to do of their own free will. You have my royal word on that."

"Sounds more like I need *his* word on the matter," Sheren quipped, flipping her hand in Kor's direction.

"Trust me; he'll be on his best behavior," Kelly retorted. "I know where he sleeps at night."

That made Sheren laugh. Cheeks seaming with mirth, the Guardian grinned. "You make me wish we had more people like you in charge over here, instead of the unmentionables we're stuck with. I can spare you *four* single female Aquamancers of suitable age. But that's it for Aquamancers. The rest are needed for all the problems the Council's head-in-the-surf attitude has caused us. They'll leave in the morning and be there within about a week."

"Why not have them step across the mirrors?" Kelly asked. "Or through the Fountainway, if you're too far for a mirror-Gate?"

Guardian Sheren shook her head. "It wouldn't work. Coming to live among us, people don't have too many problems. But going back to other lands, and going too quickly, without being slow and careful . . . It's not a good idea."

"You're underwater!" Kelly exclaimed, startling the others. "You're talking about decompression sickness, getting the bends, aren't you?"

Sheren blinked, then smiled. "You're a clever one. Not many people know about Menomon's existence, let alone that it's submerged. Don't let the Council know that you know, or they'll turn paranoid again."

Koranen felt a trickle of sweat run down his back beneath his rune-stitched tunic. As the discussion moved more and more toward the reality of Aquamancer ladies actually coming to Nightfall, of his verse in Seer Draganna's Prophecy coming true, it was getting harder to contain his magic.

"Why would you want to keep it a secret?" Amara asked her. "For that matter, why live underwater at all? I'd think it would be terribly hard to grow enough edible food, let alone get enough air to breathe, like you said."

"We keep it a secret because this city can only support so many people. An influx of visitors, whether for trade or for curiosity, would put a strain on our resources. As for *why* we live down here . . . well, newcomers usually wind up here because of the catch-spells set up long ago to save sailors who were drowning in our part of the Sun's Belt Reefs."

"And you are undoubtedly reclusive, because some of those rescued souls turn out to be unpleasant sorts," Amara observed. "Like Xenos, the mage who poisoned you."

"Yes—how did you know his name?" Sheren asked shrewdly, narrowing her gray eyes.

"Because he was chasing me," the black-haired shapeshifter stated, though Koranen knew it was her sister the mage had been after, not her. "He wanted power, in any shape or form. I'm a princess of the Shifting Plains, and he thought he could wrest the secrets of my people from me. We were on a ship that was being pursued by another vessel—one that he had probably hired to give chase—when we were pushed south by a storm and ran into the reefs. It certainly wasn't my intent to send him to plague you instead, just a bad piece of luck."

"Well, good riddance to slimy rot. Speaking of which . . . there's a little caveat attached to our own side of this devil-ray bargain," Sheren told them, grimacing. "The Council wants to round up and send off all the sailors and passengers that were rescued from the same shipwreck that the mage Xenos was on. They've all been questioned under truth-spell, and none of them means harm to either myself or the city of Menomon as a whole, but the Council doesn't want to associate with them any longer. So you're getting refugees.

"The sailors will probably be able to find passage back to their homeland, Amaz, but there's a handful of traders with some of their salvaged goods, some priestess from the north, and a pair of mages. In particular, the Council wants to get rid of the mages, so they're foisting them off on you. If you don't want them yourselves," she added, "they'll all be coming with enough money to buy passage to someplace else; I browbeat the Council into giving them that much in recompense for being tossed out. But we don't want them back. So that's the other reason they'll be taking a week to get there, what with the trade goods and all."

Saber glanced at the others briefly. "You might want to advise them that there's an import tax for all goods brought to Nightfall. And if you want to open trade negotiations, it sounds like this group will be large enough to guard an additional shipment . . ."

"Well, Guardian Rydan still owes me a big pot of honey—what, you thought I'd forget about that?" Sheren quipped. "A little poisoning only slows my body, not my brain. Let me consult with the Master of Stores over what we can spare, versus what we need. Though I can tell you that fresh vegetables and fruits are on the top of that must-have list."

Koranen tuned out the negotiations. That was Saber's specialty. At this point, it would all be about trade goods, not Aquamancers, which meant he was no longer needed. That was a good thing, because the thought of women coming to the Isle—women he could *touch*—had him tightening his self-control to contain the emotions stirred by that possibility.

Slipping out the council room door, he kept himself contained all the way to his forge, tucked at the base of his tower along the outer containment wall of the palace grounds. His tunic was warm and damp with sweat when he pulled it over his head; his trousers weren't much better. Stripping down to the loincloth spun on the mainland from the rare, fire-resistant strands of stonefiber, he hitched himself up onto the rim of his forge pit and lay back on the coke cinders, grounding his magics into them.

Within moments, they glowed with yellow orange light, sizzling whenever he shifted, and droplets of sweat fell from the protective shelter of his skin. Wriggling a little to get more comfortable, Kor braced his left foot against the rim of the forge and cupped himself through the scrap of stonefiber covering his groin. *Lady Aquamancers . . . water-women . . . naked and curvaceous, and protected by Prophecy . . .*

He was a normal, heterosexual young man, at least in regard to his fantasies. Everything about his body functioned more or less normally—the thought of touching a woman, of caressing her skin, cupping her breasts, tasting her lips, all of that aroused him. Exactly as it should. The problem came when his passions were roused by the real thing, not the mere thought of it. Searing a woman's breasts with his hands wasn't good—and that he had done it twice still haunted him—but his verse in the Prophecy swore he'd be able to touch a woman *if* she was Water to his Flame. Everyone interpreted that to mean the woman being an Aquamancer, as he was a Pyromancer.

And oh, how he wanted to finally be able to touch a real woman! He did have a special Artifact, a glass bead enchanted to project the sight, sound, and feel of a woman with all the appropriate responses when she was being tumbled—the product of lengthy experimentation by his brother Trevan and assisted by the newly formed Companionship Guild, which consisted of professional wenches—but it wasn't the same. There was no scent or taste to the creation, for all that it was visually and tactilely accurate.

The bead was currently up in his quarters, so he couldn't exactly activate it here and now, though he was quite aroused. Biting his lower lip, Koranen stroked himself lightly, teasingly, through the crinkly fabric of his loincloth, wanting to enjoy the hope burning literally within him. Soon, his wouldn't be the only hand safe enough to bring him pleasure . . .

The mere thought of a woman being able to touch him—being *willing* to touch him—was enough to draw up his flesh, tighten his stomach, and spill his seed. Flames billowed up around him as he climaxed, obscuring his vision for a moment. Panting, Kor draped his other arm across his forehead, both still damp with sweat despite the yellow-hot glow of the cinders supporting him. One release wasn't enough; he was still thick with desire that boiled beneath his skin. *I wonder if I should summon the bead . . . I'd better. Might as well pour out the heat I generate into the coals and use the heat to make something as soon as I'm done playing with my birthing-day present.*

Gods—how am I going to last a whole week, waiting for these women to arrive?

Lord Consus of Kairides had a headache. This was not unusual, of course; ever since the Councilor for Sea Commerce had answered a scrying-call in the Hall of Mirrors at the capital and discovered a woman had been allowed onto Nightfall Isle—when no women were to have been allowed among the Corvis brothers on pain of death at the time—he invariably suffered a headache. These days, it was around twice a week. The Healers he had seen advised him it was stress, prescribed calming drafts, and advocated a bit more in the way of exercise, particularly for a man of his middling years. But the source of the headaches remained: the Nightfall brothers, formerly the Corvis brothers.

Today, it was the last of the shipments destined for the eight brothers and the Baroness of Devries. Instead of residing in the capital, he was here in Orovalis City, primary port of export to the incipient kingdom, just so that someone could officially examine every single chest, barrel, and crate to calculate the costs of their contents for export taxes. When the first shipment had been heavily taxed, Lord Saber—former Count of Corvis and eldest of the brothers—and that pale-haired woman, Lady Serina, had protested heavily that the original accounting was biased in the extreme.

Arguments had flung back and forth: The Empire of Katan would not accept a Nightfall-based estimate of the goods' worth, and the Nightfallers wouldn't accept the prejudice of the Katani lackeys. Finally, the youngest brother, Morganen, had stepped in and offered Consus as the arbiter. The Empire had been suspicious of his motives until the mage had pointed out that it was Consus who had kept a cool head and a reasonable attitude during the Council's visit to the Isle a few months ago. Lord Saber had grudgingly agreed after a bit of whispered persuasion, the Council had scrutinized their Councilor for Sea Commerce thoroughly before concurring it could be considered within the bounds of his official duties . . . and now the headache was entirely his.

Thankfully, they were halfway through the last shipment. The foreman at the warehouse gestured for two of his workers to open up another of the narrow, ward-wrapped crates supposedly containing mirrors from the Devries estate. The man's stomach rumbled loudly, and he grimaced at Consus. "After this one, mind if we break for lunch?"

"Yeah," one of the workers grunted, hauling on his pry-bar. "I'm so hungry, I could eat this crate!"

The lid wasn't budging. His coworker tapped him on the arm and pointed to the end of his tool, which was off its mark by half a finger length. Readjusting the tapered tip so that it slotted under the sealing runes, he pushed down much more successfully.

"Yes, yes—as soon as you get this thing open, you can go have your break." Consus wasn't feeling very hungry himself, but that was mostly because of his headache. The banging of hammers as lids were pried off or pounded back into place and the creaking of protesting nails as they were pulled and pushed this way and that hadn't helped his stress.

"How about we take a break *before* we open it, milord?" the foreman countered, gesturing the two workers away from the crate. "That way it won't be sitting open while we wander off."

"Fine. Whatever." Pinching the bridge of his nose, Consus waved the others away. "Go on; have your meals. We'll meet back here in one hour."

Grinning, the two workers dropped their pry-bars onto the paving stones of the warehouse with careless clangs that made Consus wince and grimace.

"Are you coming, milord?" the foreman asked when Consus didn't move.

"Go on ahead. I need peace and quiet for a few minutes if I'm to get my head to stop pounding long enough to quell my stomach. Not that I've been able to eat well, ever since that debacle on the Isle."

"Ah, yes, headaches don't mix well with hunger, whether they're caused by a physical pain or a political one," the man returned sympathetically. He clapped Consus on the shoulder, making the Councilor flinch. "They tend to induce stomachaches instead. If you want soothing food, avoid the Trenching Wench, the one just down the street. They have a new cook who thinks pepperfruit are a gift from Jinga Himself."

"I'll keep that in mind."

Left alone, Consus found himself a perch on a crate filled with old clothes. As the quiet settled around him, broken only by the distant sounds of commerce and traffic in the streets beyond the stout stone walls of the warehouse, his tension slowly eased. Until a voice spoke nearby, startling him.

"You might want to advise them that there's an import tax for all goods brought to Nightfall."

What? Jerking his head up, Consus looked around, but there was no one in the warehouse with him. Plenty of trunks and chests and crates, even a few barrels, but no other human being. The voice continued, male and familiar, though distorted, as if the person were speaking from the bottom of a metal barrel.

"And if you want to open trade negotiations, it sounds like this group will be large enough to guard an additional shipment."

The voice . . . was coming from somewhere near his feet?

Puzzled, Consus stood up, stepped over to the crate, and peered at it. Another voice, a woman's this time and unfamiliar to him, answered in a language Consus didn't know. Peering at the crate, he suddenly realized the sealing wards were gone. The workers had pried the lid open far enough to end the wards protecting the thin, flat crate's contents.

"*Brousu shedodu,*" Consus commanded, curling his fingers in the air over the crate. The lid pried up and out of his way with a *creeeee-aaaak* of protesting nails . . . revealing an *active* scrying mirror. Or rather, a double-mirror, one made from two looking glasses framed in a sideways figure eight, the mathemagical symbol for infinity. The sinuous frame was as polished as the two round mirrors themselves, almost as reflective. One side showed a very familiar figure, Saber of Nightfall, former Count of Corvis. The other showed an elderly woman in scandalously tight leather clothes with ridiculously short-cropped hair. Normal scrying conversations sounded as clear as if the person were right there, but this mirror had an odd echo to it, and the images weren't perfectly clear; whatever this mirror was, it was some sort of secret spying Artifact—Consus was sure of it. Mainly because neither person reacted to *his* appearance, leaning over the mirror lying on its back inside the crate.

The woman continued to speak in a language the Councilor didn't know, but from Lord Saber's replies, they were discussing setting up trade negotiations. Including a rather incriminating comment. "*And if you choose to buy from Katan through us, we can cut you a deal through some . . . free traders . . . we know. Otherwise we'd have to raise our own prices to cover Imperial export taxes.*"

Evading export duties, are we? Not that he was terribly surprised; a lot of people attempted to do so. The trick was in catching them and slapping a fine stiff enough to make them think twice about ever doing it again . . . and then watching them closely enough to make sure they didn't succeed if they *did* try again. It didn't always work, but it worked more often than not. *Strange that this mirror should activate just when they're discussing something that directly affects my office.*

The communication ended after a few more rounds of half-intelligible negotiations, leaving the mirror to reflect the rafters of the warehouse ceiling. Consus sank back onto the crate of clothes, pondering what he had seen. *A mirror that spies on others . . . even though I'm fairly sure the mirrors they're using are warded against casual scrying. Most are, these days. Why would . . . ? Where did this crate come from?* Leaning forward, he peered at the markings. *Barol of Devries, this was one of his belongings. Why would Barol of Devries want to spy on the Corvis brothers? I thought that was his father's obsession, not his, if the brothers are to be believed.*

The reflection of the warehouse rippled and wavered, then resolved into another pair of images. He recognized the dark-skinned face of Lord Thannig, Councilor of Prophecies, but didn't recognize the dark-skinned woman he was speaking to, though she was clad in the raiments of a Priestess of Kata. Again, the view and the voices were distorted, as if he were peering through a layer or two of finespun veils or listening from the bottom of a well.

"Our research confirms it. This is the last Prophecy of the Seer Draganna waiting to be fulfilled, the last Prophecy by a strong Katani Seer."

"It is strange that the Gods haven't sent us strong Seers in the last two hundred years. We've had a few Prophecies pronounced here and there from lesser Seers in recent years, but none so prolific as Draganna."

"In the last two hundred years?" Thannig asked. *"Who was the last strong one? I thought that was Grendel of Felinchat, three hundred years ago, not two hundred."*

"Duchess Haupanea."

"Who?"

"Oh, come on; you should remember her! Nea of Nightfall, the last Duchess of Nightfall, before the Shattering of Aiar destroyed her as well as her duchy?"

Thannig made a scoffing noise, wrinkling his nose. *"Nea of*

Nightfall, a great prophetess? She only made fifty-three Prophecies before she died!"

"Our records from the Temple Keepers on Nightfall showed that she *actually made closer to two hundred, though most of them were locally focused and quickly fulfilled, at first. More to the point, from the age of fifteen to the age of eighteen, her prophetic ability was noted to be gaining rapidly in strength, distance, and duration . . . and as you should know, Councilor,"* the priestess chastised him, *"Seers don't reach maturity in their visions until their midtwenties, unless they specifically concentrate on channeling the Gods' will through meditation and daily devotions in order to force an early maturation. When her parents drowned at sea when she was only sixteen, she had a duchy to run. Naturally, her Seership matured more slowly . . . but it still showed signs of eventually being quite powerful."*

"Yes, but more than half of those who 'claim' to be powerful Seers tend to be proclaiming their own visions, not the Gods', especially when they say they've been meditating to mature their powers." Thannig snorted. *"That much* my *department has proven time and again. Still . . . you've intrigued me. My office should have copies of these files. Please send them to me as soon as possible—if she was known for* local *Prophecies, then this Duchess Haupanea may have Prophesied more than just the Curse of Nightfall. His Majesty will be eager to learn of anything that could give him and the rest of the Council leverage in dealing with the Nightfall upstarts."*

"I'll send them in exchange for a certain favor . . ."

The link faded midsentence. Consus stared at the mirror, waiting for it to do more, but it remained quiescent. There was definitely something strange about this Artifact, if it could scry on its own, without any prompting from him. Something dangerous, too, if it could spy on his fellow Councilors. But he didn't want the Council to know about this just yet; trade negotiations with Nightfall were finally proceeding smoothly, and an Artifact this potentially dangerous would only make things bad again.

Nor did he want the Nightfallers to have access to a mirror that would allow them to spy upon Councilors, either. The safest place for it would be in his own possession. All Lord Consus wanted was a smooth-running, profitable Empire. Enmity and war with the incipient island kingdom wouldn't be either of those things.

Working quickly, he disguised the mirror with a concealment charm, then levitated it up over his head, high enough that the torso-sized mirror wouldn't bump into anyone in passing once he was out in the streets. He would take it to the house he had rented and hurry back with one of his own personal mirrors. Nothing that was pre-enchanted to connect to Imperial mirrors, and he'd wipe all previous personal connections from the looking glass so no one would be able to trace it back to him, but he did need a replacement for this one.

He had a rectangular mirror he could spare that should fit into the crate, and he could simply restore the lid to its near-closed condition. He would have to hurry to finish before the others' lunch was through. It looked like he would be missing his meal, but that was already a given; worries and secrets added on top of stress simply made his stomach knot all the tighter.

If I keep stressing over my work, I'll waste away to nothing . . .

TWO

The laughter of the others faded when Danau stepped into the crew salon of the *udrejhong*. It faded first, and faded fastest, among the two Menomonites in the room, Chana and Reuen. They were the two who caught sight of her and quickly looked away. Chana even went so far as to tuck an imaginary lock behind one of her dark brown ears—imaginary because, like most Menomonites, she had cropped her bleached hair so short, it stood up in thumbnail-length spikes.

Reuen—Danau's own cousin, if a couple generations removed—averted her brown-and-red-striped head as well. The foreign priestess Ora took in the way the other two eyed her and lifted her brows, but otherwise said nothing. She was polite and charming, widely traveled and well educated, but more of a listener than a speaker.

Danau always felt like the young woman was a lot smarter and wiser than she let on, that those green eyes *saw* things that other people just didn't. But the priestess, her long blond hair pinned in a coronet of braids around her head, said nothing. Not even a greeting, though she did at least meet Danau's gaze. In a way, that was an indictment against her, for not opening up and trying to make Danau feel welcome despite the others' shunning of her.

The Amazai tea-trader Cammen Del Or was the last to finish laughing at whatever jest had been shared. His dark eyes glanced at Danau, swept down over her short, lean body with male appreciation, and he gave her the same friendly smile he had always given her. Danau tried to return it, but it was hard in the face of the others' snubbing. Shoving her feelings aside, she addressed them.

"We've sighted the island in the far-scryer. Chana, I want you to be the one at the helm in half an hour. I know it's not your turn, but your time with the Wavescouts means you're good at negotiating shoals and other surface hazards. Our hosts gave us some maps of their coastline, but they admitted the maps are crude at best, so I want you and your experience in place. Reuen, go tell the others we should be arriving within three to four hours and that now might be a good time to begin packing up their belongings."

"I'll be there," Chana dismissed, not moving yet from her sponge-chair.

"Whatever you say," Reuen agreed, getting up out of her chair, then added under her breath, "*Udrezero.*"

Danau almost swallowed it down, as she usually did whenever someone insulted her like that—it was true, but it was still an insult to point it out. And normally she wouldn't have discussed business in front of someone who wasn't going to be among them for much longer. But this wasn't Menomon they were headed for, and her cousin's attitude had to stop. "Reuen."

Her cousin faced her, arching one of her brows. "What?"

"This is a diplomatic visit. Not a Wavescout patrol or a rescue mission. Everything that the four of us do will reflect upon how these Nightfallites view our city and our people as a whole. Whatever my . . . *social* reputation is, I am still Rank 10 in the Guild, the one person with a chance of mastering and duplicating what we seek to study. I am the leader of this group. I will do nothing to jeopardize our chance to study the Desalinator . . . and I will not allow you or the others to do anything foolish, either.

"You might want to consider treating me with the deference and *courtesy* I am due . . . or I will send you back to Menomon rather than have you ruin our reputation with another careless, thoughtless comment like that. You may think what you like, but you will not *say* it. If I must remove you from this team, you just might be sent back *without* the comforts of the *udrejhong* to protect and shelter you."

"Danau, I was just—"

"—I trust I have made myself clear." Danau did not make it a question. She held Reuen's gaze until the other woman dropped her eyes, then stepped back into the corridor, giving the other Aquamancer plenty of room to leave. Waiting until her cousin was out of sight, Danau moved off a few steps, then turned and slumped quietly against the bulkhead. *Gods . . . why can't I have the same social skills as everyone else? Why can't I be social like everyone else? Ama-ti is the only one who ever shares a joke with me—the rest all think I'm the joke!*

"Um . . . what's an *udrezero*?"

Reuen hadn't shut the door to the *udrejhong*'s crew salon. The questioner was the tea-merchant Cammen. Danau listened as Chana answered him.

"Well, you know *udre* is the Menomonite word for underwater, right?" the Aquamancer offered. "It also means under or below."

"Yes . . . and?"

"*Udrezero* means below water temperature."

"I don't get it."

Chana explained, a lilt of laughter in her voice. "It means *ice*, landman. Because that's how cold she is. Surely you've noticed the icicles? Or do you have a thing for being *frostbitten*?"

Danau winced, preparing to shove away from the wall and return to the rudder room. Cammen's voice distracted her.

"If this is how she's treated by the rest of you, maybe she has a reason for being cold. Maybe she just needs the right man to thaw her. A patient man."

"You'll be a patient—of the Healers—if you even try. She doesn't just socially freeze out people; she *literally* freezes them. You'd have more luck with a real icicle. Certainly you'd have more luck with a real woman. Like me."

Memory assaulted her. Danau stared at the far wall, trying to banish the image of Jiore, the first and last man to try being with her. She had bloomed late, focusing more on her education than on boys through most of puberty. The marriage deadline of her twenty-fifth year had seemed to still be ages away when she finally noticed boys and settled on Jiore as her first love interest. He had been a Wavescout, one of a crew assigned to work with the newer members of the Aquamancy Guild, showing them how to pilot their subsurface vessels and how to sail them up above the waves on the longer-range patrols.

Their first kiss had been on the surface, with blond streaks in his brown hair glinting in the sun and his brown gaze appreciative, even a little amused, when their lips had parted. It had been a hot day, and her kiss had literally been refreshing, or so he had said before kissing her a second time. They had taken things slowly—Wavescout work required a lot of time and attention—but eventually, they had wound up in his quarters back down in the city, both with a whole day free and ready to try lovemaking.

And he really had tried, had done his best to excite both of them, even holding off while each of them excited themselves, since too much touching had led to too much coldness. Jiore had approached her when both of them were ready for copulation . . . only to shrivel up within moments of success. Rushing off to the Healers, exactly like Chana had said.

Danau had literally frostbitten her would-be lover. The Healers had been able to restore functionality after a day's worth of healing, but her would-be lover hadn't been impressed. In his bitterness over being injured in the first place, he hadn't kept the story to himself, trashing her reputation socially.

Her only refuge had been her Rank in the Guild and its value to the city. It meant submersing herself in her work, becoming renowned for her effectiveness, her efficiency, her skill. How ironic it was that her reputation as an Aquamancer was a cold source of comfort when the end of the day came and she was faced with her lonely, solitary bed each night. Cold *was* the only word for it. She didn't stay long in bed if she could help it.

It's better that way, Danau reminded herself briskly, pushing away from the wall. *I've seen dozens of couples form and then break up. Romance is temporary. The only satisfaction that lasts is the kind that comes from praise for a job well-done and the request to do more. I will do this job just as well as I do the rest, and that will be that.*

It was a lonely way to look at the world, but then she didn't have much choice.

Squashing the faint, lingering urge that wanted her to join the others, to ask what joke or jest had been so funny before her presence interrupted the mood, Danau returned to the rudder room. The *udrejhong* was skimming along the surface on fast-pumping jet-fins, using its retractable sail-fins to add wind speed to jetting speed, but the jets were what provided the most speed. If they were nearing a shore, they would have to watch out for kelp forests to ensure the intake scoops didn't clog. Manning the far-scryer was a task she could do without having to be *socially* acceptable, first.

They're coming today they're coming today they're coming today they're coming today . . .

Koranen couldn't get that refrain out of his head. From the moment he woke up, all through his morning chores, breakfast, sword practice, and even spending the rest of the morning kilning yet more of the blue faience roof tiles they were using for the new buildings in the city, he couldn't stop thinking about the fact that the Aquamancers were due in port today.

It was awfully hard to wait. He couldn't eat with the others, but took his plate and glass back out to the stone gaming table in the herb garden instead, just to be on the safe side. He was also hesitant to wear his cryslet, for fear he'd melt it out of sheer anxiety. Not that fire was the only thing Koranen could produce; a true Pyromancer controlled cold as well as heat. It was his job to enchant the cold storage cupboards, and in the summertime he often chilled the others' drinks with just a touch to their glass.

When he was agitated, however, it was hard to pull heat *into* himself when it kept wanting to escape.

After his lunch, he hurried up to his rooms in the southeast end of the eastern palace wing and nervously groomed himself. Four of his six elder brothers, Dominor, Evanor, Trevan, and Rydan, had wrought changes in the water-piping system inside the palace. Now some of the refreshing rooms that had bathtubs also had the option of a Natallian-style rain-shower.

It was a fairly clever invention, a horizontal pipe with perforations. The flow of water was controlled by a simple lever, one much like the levers used to control the water's temperature, rather than the cork stoppers stuck in the spigots. Trevan swore he was working on a lever system for water control to replace the corks they currently used, since a lever was just as easy to use, but didn't run the risk of disappearing or needing replacement like the corks sometimes did.

As soon as he was naked, Koranen twisted the lever for the water all the way to the left and made sure the one for temperature was still turned all the way to the right, letting pure, stone-chilled water flow over his body. For one brief moment, he sucked air through his teeth from the shock of it. Then heat poured out of his body, sizzling the water into steam. He had to enspell the refreshing room window open just to be able to breathe after only a few minutes, but literally boiling off his inner fire helped leech away some of his inner turmoil.

They're coming today they're coming today they're coming today . . .

When the water no longer sizzled, he grabbed a scrubbing cloth and rubbed it in the nearest pot of softsoap. He loved the dominant scent, sandalwood. It was rare in Katan, his former homeland, though it was common enough in Natallia. This had an added spice to it, something called *clovan*, apparently from the exotic Five Lands of the Dragon Empire.

It was one of his birthing-day presents, from Alys. The others had given him equally practical gifts: clothes from Kelly and Evanor, rainbow pearls from Serina—a rare, rich prize outside her former homeland—shipwreck-salvaged coins and glass from Amara; a set of new pillows from her twin, and so forth. Saber had given him re-forged tools he had accidentally melted; Dominor had copied books from the Koral-tai nunnery archives on old Pyromancy spells.

Somehow, Morg had dug up a book of tales about the legendary Painted Warriors of Mendhi, men and women who could somehow channel magic through special markings on their bodies, despite not being born with enough magic to be considered mages. Kor had a secret weakness for tales of high adventure, which his twin helped him to indulge—not an easy chore when Nightfall was still relatively isolated from the rest of the world, even with the recent increase in trade. But Trevan's gift . . . well, it was the most practical of all.

They're coming today they're coming today . . .

With the water still steaming around him, he scrubbed every inch of his body, trimmed the nails of his hands and his feet, scrubbed his teeth with a brush, and spell-shaved his jaw. Then fretted over whether or not these incoming Aquamancer ladies came from a culture that preferred bearded men instead of the clean-shaven ones found in the Empire of Katan. Nightfall was supposed to be its own kingdom, which meant developing its own customs, but that was a process that took time. Kor and his brothers had been Katani citizens for a lot longer than they had been independent, after all.

Too late now, he thought, grimacing through the steam as it intensi-fied for a moment around him. Shutting off the rain-shower, he didn't bother reaching for a towel. The heat still escaping his body dried his skin and most of his hair in the short amount of time it took him to climb out of the stone-carved tub and walk into his bedchamber.

Tapering back his powers, Koranen used the comb from his vanity, untangling and smoothing his rib-length auburn hair, since it had a tendency to fluff up when heat-dried. Some of his brothers had trimmed their hair back to shoulder length to keep it cool and manageable for the coming heat of summer, while others were let-ting theirs grow long; personally, he liked long hair, though it was bothersome at times to keep it from tangling. Once it was smooth and straight, he quickly plaited the front bits out of his way, checking in the mirror to make sure the part between the two thin braids looked straight before fastening them with a binding spell.

A sniff of his arm proved the scent from the softsoap still lin-gered, making him smell clean and spicy without being overpower-ing. Trevan and Dominor—the two brothers most competitive where women had been concerned, back when they had lived on the mainland—had both agreed that choking a woman in a cloud of scent, however pleasant, was almost as bad as choking her in a cloud of unbathed sweat. But thinking about sweating made him nervous. Calming himself with a few deep breaths, Kor opened the wardrobe and pulled out one of the formal outfits Kelly and Evanor had made for his birthing-day gift.

Debating between the dark green and the dark red outfit, Kor donned a fresh stonefiber loincloth while he decided. His brothers preferred undertrousers, but stonefiber only came from the main-land in a cloth form, not a thread form. The one time he'd tried to wear stitched undertrousers while working in his forge-fire, the stitches had turned to ash, leaving the pieces of fabric puddled around his naked feet. Instead, with just a thin stonefiber sash knotted around his hips to hold up the loincloth, there was no need for flimsy stitches that could fail at any moment.

More important, the loincloth had no magic infused into it to make it fire-safe; stonefiber was naturally heat resistant. Some of the things he forged were delicate to enchant, and it was just better to avoid excess aura resonances at those moments. His regular clothes were enspelled against heat, which sometimes meant he had to strip them off before beginning a particular enchantment. The clothes Kelly had made had been enspelled by his siblings against burning, but then, they were for formal occasions, not for forge-work. And he knew he looked good in both the red and the green . . .

Annoyed with his dithering, Koranen grabbed the green outfit. The dark green would make his hazel eyes look more brown thàn green, but otherwise it was a good color for him. Red would make his eyes look more green than brown, but his hair blended in to the fabric, and he wanted it to stand out.

The trousers were a bit more fitted than the usual mainland fashion called for, and he had to spend a few moments in front of the mirror with his hands tucked down the waistband, getting his loincloth to lie just so underneath the soft silk so it wouldn't rumple too much. Rather than the usual sort of weave, Evanor had crafted the fabric in a finespun knit, so it didn't bind too much as it clung . . . but it did cling to everything from waist to ankles, meaning wrinkles showed. Kor wasn't the fashion hound Dominor was, but he wanted to look his best today, and that meant no wrinkles.

The red outfit had long sleeves on its undertunic, but the green one had a sleeveless undertunic. Ambient temperature didn't matter much to him, but he supposed if he was going to show off the muscles in his legs, he should show off the muscles in his arms, hence the green. Pulling it over his head, he checked the mirror; old memories of a younger Saber and Wolfer flexing their muscles for the castle maidservants made him flex his own arms and shoulders for a moment. He grinned at his reflection.

Digging into his wardrobe, he brought out his jewelry casket and found a couple of armbands to don, checking out how they looked against his biceps in the mirror. They didn't look too bad, really, though when he switched jewelry, the thinner bands looked better than the thick ones. The thick ones looked too ostentatious. A little bit of wealth was needed to show a woman how well a man could provide for a family, but a lot of it just looked like bragging. It was Dominor—the most competitive of his brothers, amusingly enough—who had warned him against bragging too much around women. Apparently the gentler gender was just contrary enough to like a man who was provably competent, but who didn't tout his own successes excessively.

The hem of the new tunic was a little short. Tugging at it in dissatisfaction, Koranen tried to cover the bulge at his groin. He suspected Kelly was sneakily trying to show off his masculine wares to the prospective Aquamancers with this particular style. While he *wanted* to attract the ladies, he wanted to do so in a polite way, not a blatant one . . . because, again, they would want provable competency, not bragging. The thought made him very nervous, since he had only practiced his competency in theory, and only recently at that.

The fabric wasn't going to magically grow another hand-span, however. Giving up after a few more dissatisfied tugs, he buckled a black dyed belt in place and tugged on matching black boots, birthing-day gifts from Wolfer. All of the brothers had exchanged gifts as well as the wives among them. Koranen's gift to his siblings had been as fun and easy as blowing bubbles—in specific, blowing bubbles in molten glass. His brothers and sisters-in-law had received bottles, glasses, bowls, tubes, and even tempered crystalline blades to use in their various tasks.

They're coming today . . .

His final gift—from Trevan—had initially been a new work apron, fashioned from a single piece of carefully cut stonefiber, custom-ordered and imported from Katan. But late that evening, Trevan had slipped Kor the large glass bead which now sat prominently on his pillow. The lighter redhead had enchanted it with a new version of a sexually responsive illusion-female, one fashioned with actual recordings of proper feminine responses. The two of them had tried a few months ago to create an illusory lover for companionship, but that had been before they had access to professional wenches.

The original attempts had failed due to illusions that just didn't respond realistically, and the two men had been ready to give up. But then Amara had come to the island with her twin, ending Trevan's solitary nights. Kor's had continued, even after settlers had started arriving; unlike his brothers, he *couldn't* touch a real woman, yet. He had been forced to tend to himself, until his birthing-day.

The new illusion responded quite well, thanks to the cooperative efforts of their newly established Companionship Guild, headed up by the professional wench Cari and several of her relocated mainland colleagues, both female and male. Originally the name of the guild was to have been the Wenches Guild, but after a bit of consideration, and some consultation with Kelly, Cari had decided to make the name sound more respectable. Not to mention the quality of services proffered. As a result, she had recruited carefully from the mainland, picking those who not only enjoyed their work, but who prided themselves on pleasing their customers in more than just the basest of ways. True professionals, in other words.

Two of those professionals, a man and a woman, had consented to being recorded interacting together in order to create a "training instructor" for him, an illusion-woman capable of withstanding Koranen's heat, since a flesh-and-blood woman could not yet do so. His birthing-day gift had given Kor some confidence in how to touch a woman, but still, it wasn't quite the same thing as a *real* woman. No scents, no flavors, just sight and sound and feel.

Just the thought of smelling a real woman as he held her, of practicing with her all the things the illusion-courtesan had shown him, had him feeling distinctly warm underneath the collar of his brand-new tunic. Koranen struggled with his thoughts and the temperature they raised. *Maybe another cold shower is in order.*

Briiiingding. Briiiingding.

The noise was faint, but distinctly the sound of his cryslet being scry-called. Frowning, Koranen looked around his room, then hurried back into the refreshing room. There it was, on the counter by the sink basin; he didn't remember bringing it in there, but he had been so distracted of late, he wasn't surprised he had lost track of it. Fitting it onto his wrist, he flipped open the lid. Trevan's green eyes gleamed up at him from the mirror embedded inside the lid.

"Well? What are you waiting for?"

"What?" Kor asked, confused. "Waiting for what?"

Trevan grinned at him, white teeth gleaming with the light of the sun. Kor caught a glimpse of the harbor past his elder brother's ear. "They're almost here!"

The refrain in his head, *They're almost here* . . . became a sudden, *They're here!*

Slapping the cryslet shut without even bothering to reply, he raced for the door out of his suite . . . and nearly bounced off the solid, age-grayed oak panel before he could yank it open. Then dashed back for the sleeveless overvest that went with his fancy dark green outfit. Struggling into it as he ran up the length of the southeast and eastern wings toward the donjon at the center of the castle, he realized it was inside out and fumbled it around.

When he reached the donjon, ringed all the way around by tiers of balconies, he leaped straight over the second-floor railing, shouting a word of power. Heat rushed up around him, slowing his fall, though he still landed with a *thump* that jarred him, but didn't prevent him from thrusting forward into the western wing of the palace, waist-length vest—right side out, this time—flapping as he ran.

Bursting into the courtyard between the two westernmost wings, Koranen heard a sharp whistle and saw his twin sitting on the bench seat of a mage-cart. The horseless vehicle had been fitted with padded bench seats along the sides of the wagon bed, and instead of steering reins, the vehicle had been refitted with a rudder-like wheel. Strangely enough, it wasn't the Artificing-minded Trevan who had managed it, but Morganen. Koranen supposed it was because of his constant communication with Kelly's best friend back in that other world, the one named Hope. That world was filled with unusual, imaginative Artifacts—all the more strange for how they had been created without magic to empower them.

Grateful his twin was waiting to give him a ride, Koranen leaped up onto the bench seat, quickly smoothing his clothes in place as Morg engaged the vehicle's propulsion spell with a press of his foot on the acceleration lever. The wagon didn't jounce over the weatherworn flagstones as badly as most of the others did, prompting Kor to give his twin a look. "A rudder-wheel, and a cushioning charm?"

"Springs and a cushioning charm—and an improved braking system, one made with a higher grade of friction-heat wards on the cork pads. We can take the switchbacks at a faster rate," Morg told his twin, grinning as he sent the cart speeding through the opening in the compound wall and rattling quickly down the first slope toward the western harbor.

He, too, was dressed in his finest; his trousers and long-sleeved undertunic were a light blue that brought out the color of his aquamarine eyes, though his sleeveless overjacket was a darker purple. Koranen hadn't considered mixing up his own outfit like that, but he didn't think the dark red and dark green of his clothes would look as good together. As they reached the first corner and Morg pressed on the brake lever, Kor grabbed at the sides and back of the bench seat.

"Sorry," Morg offered. "Kelly wants us to come up with something called a seat belt, to hold the riders in place, but Evanor hasn't had time to card-weave the belt part, and Trevan and Saber are still working on the latching mechanism. Hope sent over several drawings of how it works, but they just haven't had time to work out the necessary shaping spells."

"So little time, so much to do," Kor muttered, clinging to the seat as they rolled down the slopes to save time for when he had to lean into the turns. He wanted to ask Morg why *he* hadn't worked on the project yet, but his twin continued.

"We're getting the last shipment of Devries crates today, too, according to the scrying Saber got from Captain Thorist this morning. They finally received clearance from our favorite Councilor of Sea Commerce to load everything aboard the ship."

"Good—on the one hand, I feel guilty about taking time off from work to escort a group of ladies," Koranen admitted, leaning into the next turn. They had to hug the right side of the road as another cart rattled up the hill, this one driven by one of their newly settled farmers, several cages of clucking and cooing doves loaded into the bed of his wain. "On the other hand . . . it's about damned time we got the last of our things. And *past* time for the ladies to arrive!"

"Temper," Morg cautioned him as his twin radiated tangible heat with that vehement statement. "Remember, it's not *guaranteed* that one of these Aquamancers will be the right woman for you. But with four of them, there's more of a chance than you've had so far."

"But one of them *could* be the woman for me," Koranen argued.

"Which means three of them *wouldn't* be the right woman for you. Which means *you* have to continue to be careful around all four of them. No testing them with a sudden flare-up of Pyromancy," his brother ordered him. "One might withstand it, but the other three would be burned, and you don't know which one you'd be testing first."

Reddened, blistering handprints on soft, undeserving curves surfaced in his mind. Two sets, each inflicted a few years apart, but distinctly unpleasant for the woman concerned. Kor winced at the memories. "I *know*. Believe me, I *don't* want it to happen again."

"Just have patience. The right woman will make herself known at the right time—and, contrary to myth and legend regarding Prophecy, it isn't always when you first meet her," Morg added, turning the steering rudder at another switchback corner. "Just look at Big Brother."

"Which one?" Kor snorted. At Morg's questioning look, he explained. "It's not just Saber and Kelly who took time to warm up to each other. They struck sparks off each other from the very beginning, and it took them a literal dousing in water to learn to get along . . . but Wolfer and Alys knew each other for *years* before they realized they were meant for each other—well, before Wolfer realized it, at any rate. My point is, *I* don't want to have to wait that many years before I can get tumbled!"

Morganen laughed.

Once they reached more level ground, it didn't take long to encounter the outskirts of their growing little city. Most of those outskirts consisted of clear-cut fields seeded with wheat and other grains left to grow somewhat wild while they waited for more settlers to arrive. Koranen knew they had more wheat waiting in one of the old salt-block warehouses, but he couldn't yet imagine needing it with so few people on hand to harvest so much. The young blades carpeted the gently sloped hills, making everything look fuzzy green, until one reached the pale gray granite walls and blue tiled roofs of the harbor city.

Which still doesn't have a name, Kor realized, frowning. *We're all just calling it the harbor, or the city . . .* An amusing thought made him chuckle. *We should probably just throw up our hands and call it Harbor City.*

"Hope had a strange request."

Roused out of his musing, Koranen glanced at his twin. Of all his brothers, he tried not to tease Morganen about having to take such a long time courting Kelly's outworlder friend. Of all of them, only Morg had to wait even longer for a tumble than Kor did. Though at least his twin had experienced it a few times before their exile. "Oh? What did she ask?"

"She wants wheat. Pound for pound, in exchange for everything we've been bringing over here . . . and everything she'll be sending. Within the next few weeks. Looking at the fields, here, made me think of it."

"*Wheat?*" Bracing his hand on the edge of the bench, Kor twisted to stare at his twin. "What does she want wheat for? Doesn't she have wheat in her world?"

"She does. She wants it to redress the balance between the two universes. She says it's been bugging her for some time. Dirt was the first suggestion, but it carries too much in the way of living organisms—bacteria, worms, insects—so she finally came up with the idea of wheat.

"I can understand her point of view," Morg added as they approached the section of the city where buildings were still being constructed. "The imbalance *would* need to be addressed somehow. We've already taken Kelly out of her world, and all the impact she would have had upon it—perhaps not as much as one might think, considering she would have probably died in that fire, but there was a slim chance she could have escaped and survived, found someone else to marry and have children with . . . Taking Hope out of their world, too, imbalances everything all the more."

"But . . . wheat?" It seemed a bit too prosaic to Kor.

"Apparently her region is having problems with insects and drought depleting their crops, and she thinks a new strain of wheat might help counteract some of that. More important," Morg stated, "her realm doesn't believe in magic and doesn't know that other universes exist, so wheat is the most innocuous trade one can make."

"Maybe it'll help, but to just have a bunch of bags of wheat suddenly appear—wouldn't that rouse their suspicions?" Kor asked his brother.

Morg shrugged, slowing the cart so as not to hit a cluster of children playing at the edge of one of the plaza squares Amara had arranged in the city's plans. Mikor, Mariel's son, was dashing about among them, his dark, curly hair bouncing as he played tag with the children who had come with their parents to the Isle. "She says the farmers over there sometimes get bags of experimental grains given to them for growing in test-fields. Sometimes they're even offered the bags for free. In turn, the farmer reports back on how well the new grain does, trying his or her best to cultivate a viable breed . . . but sometimes records get lost, or mixed up, and a farmer just ends up with free bags of seed to sow."

"I suppose that makes sense . . ." Kor trailed off as he spotted the new docks lining the harbor. There were only six long piers stretching out into the waters of the western cove, but there were three transport vessels, plus a pair of fishing boats off to the southern end of the bay, apparently being worked on; the rest of their small fishing fleet was taking advantage of the good early summer weather to cast their nets in deeper waters. Two of the vessels looked Katani, and one had the slanted yardarms of an Aian ship "Which one is theirs? The Menomon ship?"

"Relax, it's not at the docks, yet."

Kor glanced at his twin. "It's not? But, Trevan called and said it was almost here—I almost broke my neck racing out of the palace!"

Turning the rudder-wheel on the modified wagon, Morg drove it toward the northernmost dock. "If you'll look to the north end of the cove, you should be able to see it in a moment or two. It's also coming faster than expected; I was only alerted to its presence at the farthest edge of my own wardings a few hours ago. I think Trevan called for you to come down when the ship crossed the middle wardings, the ones the cryslet towers project."

Not the least surprised that his brother had extra wardings of his own laid around the island and its waters, Kor craned his neck, peering that way. He had to shade his eyes against the afternoon sun shining in the north-northwest part of the sky, but finally spotted an object that didn't look fishing-boat shaped near the edge of the bay. An object that was strangely shaped for a ship, and moving visibly faster than a ship—a normal, nonmagical ship—usually moved.

"Magic-propelled?" he asked his twin. Of all their brothers, Koranen knew more of what his twin could do than most, though not everything by any means. Sometimes his twin kept secrets within secrets. Suffice to say, he was fairly confident Morganen had an answer and had gained the answer the moment the ship broached whatever wards his twin had placed around the island.

"It's some form of Aquamancy I'm not that familiar with, yet—it looks like it works on some sort of water-thrusting principle, like the jet-boats described in one of Hope's books," Morg dismissed, carefully turning the wagon around on the flagstones at the edge of the water before flipping the reverse lever and backing the vehicle up the long, broad planks of the northernmost dock.

Morg meant the how-things-work tomes that the woman had shared across the Veil between their worlds. Koranen had read some of them, able to decipher the foreign language thanks to his dose of Ultra-Tongue potion. Aside from some intriguing new ways of creating light and heat, and an even more intriguing way of chilling things through special, mechanically compressed and expanded gases, there hadn't been much that was new within the volumes that pertained to his work. Technology wasn't quite like Artificing, for all that some things—like cryslets and their counterparts, *sell-fones*—were translatable and thus replicable.

The books she had sent across reminded Koranen of something his brother had just mentioned. Until the ship drew closer, it would at least be a distraction to ask about it. "You said Hope wanted the wheat to address her crossing over, and the stuff she'd already sent, but it also sounded like she would be sending more things across. What sort of things, do you know?"

"She said something about some seedlings and younger trees for an orchard, as well as some personal belonging she didn't want to part with—a *lot* of wheat, in other words," Morg admitted, steering carefully with just one hand. He grinned at his brother. "She's certainly given us a lot of things to think about. This new wheel modification works a *lot* better than the steering reins ever did when backing up, doesn't it?"

Koranen had to admit it did; not once did they wobble off course more than a hand-length at most, and that mainly due to the uneven spots in the dock. Stopping the vehicle, Morg dug into one of the three small pouches slung at his waist. Kor blinked at the comb his brother held out to him.

"Here, give yourself a last-minute grooming. Did you remember to scrub your teeth after lunch?"

Rolling his eyes, Koranen jumped down from the bench and walked to the end of the dock, behind the wagon. He did his best to avoid the strands at the front which had been woven into plaits as he combed his hair, though the wind occasionally gusting across the cove didn't help. "*Yes*, I scrubbed my teeth. I did it while I took a rain-shower. I bathed, I scrubbed, I trimmed, I primped, I picked out one of my nicest, newest outfits—how do I look?"

Morg studied his twin from head to toe and back, and shook his head. "You're not my type."

Kor shoved him for that.

Morg shoved back. "Relax—seriously, you look *good*. Respectable. The perfect representative of Her Incipient Majesty . . . which is *very* good, because you'd be stuck as our representative anyway, considering the dictates of Prophecy."

Rather than shoving his brother, Kor stuck out his tongue. He handed back the comb with one hand and shaded his eyes with the other again. The strange ship was now closer, and clearer. "It looks like . . . a fish? With sails?"

"They do live a very strange life to begin with, if their city lies deep underwater," Morg pointed out. "With no reports of docks spotted on the surface by any Katani sailors over the years, maybe they have to make their ships fish-shaped just to be able to maneuver underwater. Who knows what sort of pressure-wardings are built into their vessels—plus air retention and freshening charms, and methods of maneuvering, and things we can't even guess at, yet." Morg, peering at the ship alongside his twin, frowned softly. "Does it look like it's floating on its fins to you?"

"Yes, it does—there's some sort of pod at the base of each fin," Kor said, pointing. "You can see them by the way the water breaks over the front of each one and crests to either side. Gods . . . now I'm getting nervous."

Morg grinned and clasped him on the shoulder, giving his twin a brief squeeze. "Relax. You'll do fine. You don't need to be nervous. In fact . . . I just realized your soon-to-be bride probably *will* be one of these four women, which means things should be looking up for you. *I*, on the other hand, am about to turn into a nervous wreck."

At that, Kor peered at his twin, arching one of his auburn brows. "*You* have reason to be nervous? And why do you think one of them *will* be my Destiny?"

Leveling a sober look at his brother, Morg arched one of his own brows. "Hope was talking about sending her belongings *here*, Brother. She's the other world's equivalent of a low-level Seer. She *knows* things, though she doesn't know how, or much of what— there's very little magic flowing through her world, though she does have some of it in her veins. If she finally thinks it's time for her to pack up and come across, when all along she has refused to do so . . . *that* means she has *sensed* it is almost time for her to come across. Which in turn means the end of all those intertwining Prophecies is drawing near. Which makes *me* nervous!"

"Why would you be nervous?" Kor asked, confused by his twin's troubled outlook.

"Because we still don't have all the Names of the Gods!" Morg reminded him sharply. "We may have a promise from these Menom-onites that they're bringing a copy of the Scroll of Living Glory . . . but *how* am I going to help pull off a miracle of Convocation-sized proportions if we *don't* have all the Names of the Gods?" he demanded, spreading his arms expressively before letting them flop at his sides. "I may be powerful, but I'm not *that* powerful!"

"Morg . . . the Gods *will* provide," Koranen offered, seeking a way to comfort his twin. "They wouldn't have allowed you to bring Kelly to our world, with all her strange outworlder notions of how worship should work, if They didn't agree to her thoughts and ideas. They certainly wouldn't have answered when she Rang the Bell, declaring us independent from the mainland. We *will* have all the Names of the Gods by the hour that we need them. Somehow."

"Yes, but the Gods are more inclined to help those who have helped themselves to their utmost and can do no more. What if there's more that we can do and I'm missing it?" Running his hands through his hair, Morganen grimaced at the tangles his fingers encountered. He dug out his comb again and smoothed his long, light brown locks, then plaited them back from his face, fixing the end with a bit of leather thong pulled from another of the pouches slung around his hips.

"One worry at a time," Kor reminded his brother. "First, we need to greet these people, and get them processed and settled. Then we need to get our hands on the Scroll of Living Glory. *Then* we'll know exactly what is needed to re-create the Convocation of the Gods, and how quickly we'll need to gather those names— speaking of processing, did you bring a Truth Stone? We're supposed to be getting shipwreck refugees, as well as the Aquamancer ladies."

"No, but there's a casket of them in the Dockmaster's office," Morganen replied, poking his thumb over his shoulder at a building centered between the four docks. "Besides, Augur usually handles that."

"Then go fetch the Dockmaster!" Kor prodded him. "You know the rules as well as I do; they're not allowed to petition for residency until they've passed all the questions about their intentions. Besides, only the Aquamancers are our guests. The rest might want some wagons or something to take themselves and their belongings up to the inn while they await either residency or transport off the Isle, and that's also one of Augur's responsibilities."

Rolling his eyes, his twin complied, trotting up the length of the broad, sturdy wharf. Morg could have stayed and called the other man with his cryslet, but Kor suspected his twin didn't want to stay around an increasingly nervous Pyromancer. Already, the air around him was beginning to feel a little warmer than it should. Aware of his leakage, Koranen sternly locked down his magic and faced the incoming ship, which was now halfway across the large cove.

The sails on the top of the fish-shaped ship made it look rather like a sword-snout fish, though the "snout" of this ship wasn't nearly as long or as pointed. They were currently angled to catch the north-easterly breeze, but as he watched, the ribs of the sails slowly collapsed, turning inward to align along the spine of the vessel. A glassy bubble at the front of the metallic ship covered the areas where the eyes and nostrils of an actual fish would be; now that the ship was closer, he could just make out what might be figures inside, figures that moved and did things as the ship slowed, angling his way.

Kor tugged on the too-short hem of his tunic once again, then resettled his embroidered, waist-length vest and adjusted the fit of his armbands, needing something to do now that he no longer had conversation with his twin for distraction. He was as ready as he was going to be. All he had to do was wait for his Destiny.

Any moment, now . . .

The ship, magically driven water splashing and gurgling as it rushed through the pontoon-like pods keeping it afloat, finally drew up alongside the dock. At the same moment, Morganen came back with the bald-headed, brown-skinned Dockmaster; with them came a cluster of settlers who doubled as dockworkers, fish gutters, carpenters, and anything else that needed doing in the harbor part of the city. Augur nodded a polite greeting to Koranen, but before either man could speak, the ship hissed and sank a bit into the water. A moment later, a longish, oval crack in the metallic hull appeared, levering itself out and down until it *thunk*ed against the dock, forming a more or less level boarding ramp.

A figure appeared in the opening. She was . . . short. Undeniably a female, given the very close fit of her blue leather trousers and shirt, but she was visibly shorter than Mariel, who barely reached Koranen's shoulder. This woman's hair was also short. Distressingly short; if a single one of those auburn curls was longer than his thumb, Koranen would eat his own loincloth. Her blue eyes swept the dock, her expression somewhat wary, then she moved down the length of the ramp until she was a single step from the dock. A leather satchel had been slung over her head and across her body, the bag resting behind her back, and there was a knife hilt visible at the top of one boot. The knife was inlaid with mother-of-pearl, but otherwise she was plainly dressed.

"Can you understand me?"

His ears twitched as she spoke the words, but that was simply the side effect of Ultra Tongue working its translative magic. Koranen glanced to his side. Morg merely smiled, and Augur—apprised of the importance of this visit—gestured for him to take the lead. Stepping forward, he gave the woman a bow.

"I understand you completely, as will most of our residents. Welcome to Nightfall Isle. I trust you are a member of the delegation from the city of Menomon?" he inquired as politely as he could.

"Danau, Rank 10 Aquamancer of Menomon. And you?"

Her tone was brisk, but not entirely unfriendly. Koranen offered his hand, wanting to touch her, to see if he safely could. "Koranen, Pyromancer and Lord Secretary of Nightfall."

She ignored his hand. "A pleasure. And these are?"

"My brother Morganen, Lord Mage of Nightfall, and Dockmaster Augur, plus several citizens of Nightfall. They are here to help process the incoming refugees Guardian Sheren said would be arriving with you," Koranen stated, keeping his hand extended in offering. "I am here to be your personal liaison while you are on Nightfall; I know as much about the desalination plant as any of my brothers."

Her gaze fell to his fingers, then looked away, stepping onto the dock without touching him. "Your assistance will be appreciated. I would like to disembark the refugees and see that they are settled before progressing to the rest of our business; they aren't accustomed to living in such small quarters and are eager to leave the *udrejhong*. Will this be our permanent berth during our stay, or would you prefer that we move the ship to some other anchorage?"

"Uh . . . Dockmaster?" Koranen asked, deferring the question to the older man.

"We aren't in a hurry to move your extraordinary vessel just yet, though we are expecting some ships with traders and immigrants in a few more days. Arrangements can be handled later, if it becomes necessary. For now, you may tie up to the dock," Augur said smoothly. "As an officially recognized diplomatic vessel, your docking fees have been waived, though there is still an import tax on trade goods, since I was informed only the Aquamancers are to be accounted as official envoys."

"Our mooring and anchorage are done by spell, since we don't always know what depth of sea we may be in, nor what kind of damage we could cause through carelessness." Turning, she called back through the opening in the side of the fish-shaped ship. "Reuen, begin disembarking the passengers. Chana, assist her. Ama-ti, the manifest."

Brrr, Koranen thought, as he caught glimpses of a woman with short, red and brown hair in brown leathers, a brown-skinned woman with a shock of blond hair in cream leather, and a blue-haired woman in green and blue leather. *Efficient, and undeniably polite, but emotionless. Too efficient.*

He eyed the woman who came out of the ship, the one with green eyes and the shock of short, blue-dyed hair. Her leather garments were cut with a mixture of blue and green that complemented her coloring. She also seemed friendlier than the first woman, flashing her teeth in a friendly greeting at both him and the Dockmaster.

"It's a relief to know we'll be able to understand each other," the blue-haired woman stated. "I was never very good at translation spells. I'm Ama-ti, Rank 8 in the Guild." Without hesitation, she clasped hands with Augur, then with Morg, and finally with Kor.

Morg cleared his throat with a tiny cough just before Kor accepted her outstretched hand. Reminded—and annoyed by the reminder—Koranen carefully did not test her reaction to his proximity with a little flare of his powers. Instead, he locked them down and bowed over her fingers in a courtly and entirely nonmagical way. "It will be my pleasure to be your liaison while you are here."

The other woman, Danau, snorted at that, but otherwise didn't comment. Instead, she gestured at the people emerging from the ship, naming each one briskly.

"The first passenger is the Priestess Ora from the distant land of Arbra. Following her is Zella Fin Rin, an Amazai mage, and behind her, a Mornai mage, Yarrin Del Ya," Danau introduced, gesturing at a blond woman with pale skin, a dark-haired, deeply tanned woman, and a blond man with skin somewhere between their two shades. Following them came two more men with tanned faces close in shape and duskiness to the second woman. More people began filing off the ship as well, most of them carrying sacks of belongings. "Behind Mage Yarrin is Captain Terroc Val Suor, rescued from the wreck of the Amazai ship *Tashiel*, and his second officer . . ."

THREE

❦

Danau perched uncomfortably on the padded bench of the magic-propelled wagon. Menomon had a number of magic-propelled wagons—the city had known very few horses over the centuries, let alone other beasts of burden—so that wasn't the source of her discomfort. It was the man seated next to her, playing with the wheel that guided the cart up the hillside, that made her uncomfortable.

He was tall, muscular, charming, affable, intelligent, handsome . . . everything she had learned to avoid. Yet he refused to be avoided. For one, he was their appointed liaison. For another, he seemed very determined to personally connect with all of them—the Aquamancers, that was. Danau felt her stomach knot with resentment as he laughed at some witty quip of Chana's regarding the thick foliage they passed and how it compared to the kelp and sponge forests near Menomon. She still remembered the conversation she had held with that other fellow that had met them, the aqua-eyed one named Morganen, months ago.

Back then, the Nightfallite mage had implied that single female Aquamancers were required to visit because of some sort of matchmaking prophecy. If this Pyromancer was paired so blatantly with her fellow Aquamancers, and was so blatantly interested in meeting and getting to know each of them, then the prophecy no doubt centered on him . . . which meant someone was supposed to be matched with him. If she hadn't been the strongest single female Aquamancer in the Guild—the strongest Aquamancer, period, and the second-strongest mage in the city next to Sheren herself—she wouldn't have been sent on such an important mission.

She wouldn't be here, seated next to him, struggling to hold on to the edges of the padded bench so that the swaying motion of the vehicle at each corner didn't bump them together . . . because he was too handsome, too charming, too *warm* . . . and she was too cold by comparison.

Chana, Ama-ti, and Reuen weren't the only ones occupying the bench seats lining the back of the wagon. The priestess had requested a chance to pay her respects to the incipient queen of this land, as had the female of the two surface mages, Zella. The male, Yarrin, had decided to stay down in the city and "partake of surface delights," as he had put it. The captains of the two wrecked vessels had also decided to stay in the city, to start inquiries about finding some means of passage back to Aiar for themselves and their remaining respective crews.

One other person chose to join them in heading up to the Nightfall palace: the tea-merchant Cammen. He occupied the last space in the back of the wagon, along with one of his spell-sealed tea crates piled with the others' belongings down the center of the wagon bed. The Menomonite Wavescouts had agreed to search for and rescue those crates shortly after his arrival in the city, in exchange for a ten percent cut culled from however many they had found bobbing up on the surface. It had worked, too; the enthusiasm of the Wavescouts for that much tea had wound up recovering most of his lost cargo.

Aian tea was just as highly prized in Menomon as anywhere else in the world, if not more so for its rarity. Danau guessed the trader wanted to discuss the potential for trade negotiations with the incipient queen of this land, despite the very tangible hazards of shipping anything across the Great Reef at Sun's Belt—trade was trade, after all. Even the Council of Menomon had been forced to admit how valuable trade could be over the last few months, let alone profitable.

The wagon rattled over a bump in the road, making her cling more tightly. The Nightfallite Koranen muttered an apology, swinging the vehicle around the last bend. Aiming it at the broad gates of an even broader wall, he drove the cart into a large compound of yet more of the ubiquitous gray white granite and blue roofing tiles used by the locals.

"And here we are: Nightfall Castle, also known as the palace. You can see it very clearly right now, but if you ever look in this direction from the city and cannot see it, that's because the defenses may have been activated for one reason or another. It'd be nice to not have enemies, but it's an inevitable fact of life." Braking in front of a set of doors between the two wings of the stout palace, he jumped down from the driving bench and hurried around the horseless front of the vehicle, holding out his hands. "Here, let me help you down."

Danau stared, dismayed, at the strong, capable hands he lifted in her direction. She couldn't even remember the last time a man had offered to touch her. As much as she wanted to accept the proffered courtesy, she didn't dare; his fingers were too nice-looking to risk damaging. Swallowing, she looked at the palace, avoiding his gaze. "No, thank you."

"I'll accept your help," Chana drawled, holding her dusky arms out over the side of the wagon as she twisted to face him. Koranen, glancing one last time at Danau, shrugged and moved to the end of the wagon. A man clad in light blue linen came up and was directed by the redheaded man to take the Aquamancers' bags to the southeast wing, second floor. The tea-trader picked up his crate of tea himself as soon as he jumped down.

Danau climbed down on her own as their host helped the Amazai mage, Zella, from the back of the cart. Like the trader, the dark-haired mage had left most of her belongings back at one of the inns down by the harbor; this was a courtesy visit for her, Cammen, and the priestess, a trip to pay their respects to the local impending queen. Unlike the other two, the priestess Ora had no luggage. She had clothes—fresh changes of clothes, different outfits on different days visible beneath the omnipresent, hooded black robe she wore everywhere—but Danau had yet to see *where* the woman kept them, without any bags or trunks for storage.

The blonde Arbran accepted Koranen's help out of the wagon with a polite smile, but otherwise didn't try to flirt with him, unlike the Aquamancers. Zella, Danau noted, looked about as brisk and efficient as she herself tried to be, and she took comfort in the fact that she wasn't the only female in the group to resist the redhead's affable charm. Even if she didn't want to resist it, she had no choice.

"This way," Koranen directed them. "Her Majesty is eager to meet you all." He started toward the door, then paused and gave them a wry smile over his shoulder. "Oh, and don't mind the paint on the walls. It moves."

It moves? Danau wondered, following him inside. *What, does it reach out and grab visitors like the exploring tendrils of an octopus?*

She saw what he meant as soon as they entered. The walls were covered in a painted version of swirling clouds, driving rain, and flickers of lightning. Someone had enchanted the pigments to reproduce a thunderstorm, though disconcertingly, there was no thunder to be heard, just the white blue streaks of electricity writhing briefly across the purple gray clouds lining the corridor. If brightly rapped lightglobes hadn't been placed in brackets at evenly spaced distances, the effect would have been gloomy.

The lightglobes were something one of the Councilors had asked Danau to look for, in trade goods. They had managed to grow a number of suncrystals large enough to bring daylight down from the surface, just to keep their plants, animals, and people healthy over the centuries, but it took a long time to grow the crystals. Making sure the coral of the reefs didn't grow over the absorption ends of the long shafts was an equally time-consuming process. Suncrystals also lasted for centuries once grown, unlike the mere handful of years a lightglobe could last, but they weren't portable like the lightglobes were.

The storm scene changed when they were halfway down the hall, first misting over in a gray fog, then fading into a view of horses running very slowly up and over the crests of low, golden hills. It was sufficiently distracting that Danau almost missed their entrance into a large, balcony-ringed, octagonal hall. Slightly worn red velvet had been laid out across the flagstones of the floor, connecting the four main hallways, and angling into the corners to the northwest and the northeast, where colorful, glazed windows let in the summer sunlight.

Even if it was age-worn, it was an impressive display of wealth. Velvet was exceedingly rare in Menomon, so rare that most of it was used for trim, not for a whole garment. This much velvet could have bought three seats on the City Council, two *udrejhongs*, and a balcony home overlooking the rainbow corals on the east side of the city. Of course, that was in Menomon, where the fuzzy fabric was rare and therefore precious. Here, it didn't seem rare at all, if they could afford to use it as a mere pathway for people.

The extraneous runners led to two low dais platforms, Danau noted. The one immediately to her left held a broad, aquamarine padded bench seat, heavily carved and covered in gold leaf. Above it hovered a delicate-looking coronet, proof of the incipiency of the kingdom of Nightfall. The other dais, across the hall, held two ornately carved chairs; they were also gilded, but padded in deep blue, not aquamarine. They were also empty, just like the bench. Their guide slowed, coughed with a little blush, and gave the others a sheepish look.

"I *did* call ahead and let her know you were coming," Koranen muttered. Two figures hurried up behind them, one tall and black-haired
with the heart-shaped face of an Aian woman, the other medium in
height with strawberry blond hair, her freckled face more oval.

The tall one was clad in shades of blue, and the shorter woman
wore shades of purple, and like everyone else on the island Danau
had seen so far, their outfits differed from each other. The black-
haired woman was clad in gathered trousers and a laced vest-bodice,
while the redhead wore fitted pants much closer to the Menomonite
style, and a corset laced over a short-sleeved top. Then again, this
was only an incipient kingdom, undoubtedly too young to have de-
veloped a distinct fashion sense.

"Ah, good, you're right on time. Alas, I am late, but then I've
been having a very busy morning, so I'm lucky I'm even here. Welcome to Nightfall," the strawberry-haired woman asserted in a
friendly voice, smiling at them as she moved around to stand between them and the dais without the crown. "I am—"

"—*You!*" the black-haired woman shouted. Danau twisted to see
whom she was glaring at. For a moment she thought it was the
blonde priestess, but it was the dark-haired mage, Zella. The older
woman flinched, but lifted her chin slightly, even as the newcomer
growled and seemed to grow larger, moving toward her target. "I'm
going to *kill* you!"

The redhead got there first, stepping between them with a deft
twist of her body and a hand planted on the other woman's stomach.
"*Amara!*"

"She killed members of my Family!"

"If *I* have to control my temper, *you* have to control your temper.
And we do *not* attack people without *proof* of their wrongdoings. We
will be civilized about this and do things the *legal* way. Go fetch a
Truth Stone," she ordered, shoving the woman back a step when the
taller woman didn't move. "*Go. Fetch. A Truth Stone.*"

Growling, teeth bared, the black-haired woman spun and strode
out of the hall.

Spinning to face the Amazai mage, the redhead planted her hands on her hips. "*You* are causing me a lot of trouble, whoever you are. You will be questioned under Truth Stone, and if she has a legitimate grievance against you, then you will pay for your wrongdoings, one way or another. If you resist being questioned . . . or worse . . . you will pay for that as well. Your best bet is to be completely honest in the next few minutes and hope to God that you're innocent, because I really don't want any problems between you and her messing up our deal with Menomon!"

"She's Amazai, not Menomonite," Danau interjected quickly. "She said she wanted to come pay her respects, so we let her ride up here with us."

"Then I take it *you're* the Menomonites?" the woman asked, lifting a hand to flick it at Danau, then Ama-ti, Chana, and Reuen in turn, each of them clad in fitted leathers. "I apologize for not being able to greet you more properly, but I suspect Amara will insist that we take care of this little problem first."

"You're the incipient Queen," Zella finally said, her tone smooth, though her chin was lifted slightly. She looked like she was clinging firmly to her dignity, despite the accusation flung at her.

"Ladies, gentlesir, this is Queen Kelly of Nightfall," Koranen introduced quickly. "Your Majesty, these are Danau, Chana, Reuen—no, sorry, Chana has the blond hair, Reuen the red and brown—and Ama-ti of Menomon. We also have Ora, a priestess of Arbra, and Cammen, an Amazai tea merchant . . . and the lady here is Zella, an Amazai mage. The lady who was here just a moment ago is Amara, Mayor of . . . of Harbor City."

For a moment, humor twisted the mouth of the queen. "We haven't officially named it yet, have we? We'll have to look into correcting that."

The black-haired woman, Amara, strode back into the hall before anyone could comment. She strode up to the queen, glared at Zella, and slapped a white, rounded disc into her liege's hand. Then folded her arms across her chest and faced the older woman, glaring fiercely. Queen Kelly turned to the Amazai mage, disc in hand.

"Please don't resist. Scrubbing blood out of the carpets is rather annoying. Take this disc in your hand and state that your name is . . . oh, Banjo the Clown, or something."

Zella held out her hand, and when the Truth Stone was dropped into it, curled her fingers around its edge. "My name is Banjo the Clown." Uncurling her fingers, she displayed the black imprints they left behind. As soon as they faded, she gripped the white marble again and began speaking. "My name is Zella Fin Rin, and I am a member of the King's Advisory Cabinet of the nation of Amaz. As such, I have the rank of an official envoy."

Amara started to say something, but Kelly held up her hand. The white marble of the stone was unblemished when the magewoman flexed her fingers, proving her words. "Your words are true. So far. Do you have knowledge of the incident of which Amara accuses you?"

Pausing for only a moment, the older woman flexed her fingers around the Truth Stone. "I do."

Plucking the stone from her grasp, Kelly thrust it at the black-haired, golden-eyed, growling mayor. "Then let's hear Amara's accusations—the truth only, if you please. I'll not have any false words spoken on *either* side of this matter."

"*Fine.* This woman approached the Family Whitetail, of Clan Deer, when we were making trade on the edge of the Shifting Plains. She said my sister was a 'national treasure' that 'had' to go with her to Amaz. That my sister's birth was a sign from the Gods that Aiar would be made whole. Naturally, we refused to let her go; she was Shifterai and belonged on the Plains, not with a bunch of foreigners. We made this woman go away, but then she came back with hired bandits and attacked, trying to *steal* my sister from us— and in the attack, some of my cousins were injured, and some even *died*! I want this woman to *pay* for her crimes! I demand blood-right!"

Flinging the unmarked stone at the Amazai, Amara folded her arms across her chest, scowling. Zella caught it against her chest, then gripped the disc. She didn't wait for Kelly to question her, but lifted her chin proudly. "I do not deny I went to the Shifting Plains. When I discovered her sister, I knew it was a sign from the Gods that the might of the Aian Empire would be restored, and that the place to do it was Amaz, which had knowledge her people didn't have. In their ignorance, they were dooming their Empire. I had to do *something* to restore our nation's glory. And . . . I do not deny I hired mercenaries to kidnap her. But *no one* was killed—and I *have paid* the blood-right for the injuries that *did* happen to Family Whitetail!"

She tossed the disc back, showing it was pure white.

"You have not paid it to *me*," the mayor growled. "Because of *you*, we were forced to flee the Plains when you attacked a second time—and *that's* when people were killed! I saw my own cousin cut down by one of your pet mages!"

She flung the stone back. Danau was reminded incongruously of *panka*, a ball-and-paddle game that was popular among the children of Menomon. It was played with fish scapulae for paddles and the shell of a sea urchin enchanted to bounce when struck, and the play of the shell-ball was so quick, watchers had been known to strain the muscles in their eyes and necks.

"I wasn't involved in that attack, and it was *proven* to Clan Deer that I wasn't involved when I came back to the Plains to pay a king's fortune for your sister to come with us. Only you and she had fled when someone *else* attacked. If you had let her come with *me* in the first place, none of your people would've been harmed!" Zella argued, displaying the unblemished truth of her words. "And I'm *still* authorized to pay a king's fortune for her safe passage to Amaz!"

"Well, it's a little too late for that!" Amara snapped back. "My sister is *dead*!"

The Amazai woman gasped, her tanned skin paling a little. "You . . . you lie! I heard a rumor on the docks that this place is seeking to re-create the Convocation of the Gods. That you intend to manifest all of the Gods so that their followers can discuss problems and concerns face-to-face. Your sister is key to this goal—she cannot be dead!"

Danau and the others watched as Kelly grabbed the Truth Stone from her hand. "When Lord Trevan found her, shipwrecked on our northern shore almost half a year ago, she was *alone*."

Displaying the white surface, Kelly silenced the protest the older woman was trying to make. Tossing the disc at Koranen, who caught it deftly despite the suddenness of the move, Kelly planted her hands on her hips.

"I have no idea why you think her dead sister is connected to our efforts to resurrect the Convocation. It is clear to me, however, that while you didn't want anyone killed, you still deliberately tried to kidnap my mayor's sister, forcing the two of them to flee their homeland and indirectly causing the loss of Amara's sister," she added. "While I cannot deny that our mayor is a competent addition to this island and that I am grateful for her using her organizational skills on our behalf these days, I cannot let your presence continue to agitate her.

"I suggest you return to the harbor and find a ship headed back to the mainland or something."

The Amazai mage turned to the black-haired mayor. "Where did she die?"

Amara folded her arms more tightly across her chest. "*I* think it best if you left, too."

"*Where* did she die?" Zella repeated stubbornly.

"In the belly of a giant shark, somewhere between the shipwreck and here. Now, are you going to leave, or do I get to escort you into the bay?" the mayor asked.

"Amara," the redheaded queen chided. Two men entered the large chamber from a side hall. One had hair a little more coppery than Kelly's; the other had hair the color of old gold. They approached, curiosity on their faces. Danau realized after a moment that both men looked like Koranen.

"*A*-mara?" Zella asked, looking more thoughtful than stubborn. "As in, you're a Princess of the Plains? Shifterai shapechanger?"

"Yes, I am. What of it?" Amara asked belligerently, and this time Danau knew she wasn't hallucinating; the woman *did* grow another inch in height, towering a hand-length above the Amazai mage.

"I have something of yours, I think. I recognized it among the items salvaged after the storm wrecked both ships. I was going to send it back to the Plains, once I had reached dry land . . . but if you're a shapeshifter, then it most likely belongs to you. I will give it to you, along with my apologies for the loss of your sister. As soon as I can hire a ship to take me back north, I'll be out of your way."

"What could you possibly have of mine?" Amara scoffed.

Zella shrugged, folding her arms across her own chest. "A pectoral was found in the debris. I knew that Shifterai shapechangers wear them to proclaim their prowess, so I claimed it with the intent of eventually returning it to the Clans. I'm not a complete barbarian, and I do know the value your kin place on such things. It's with the rest of my belongings, back down at the inn."

"Lord Trevan, why don't you escort your wife and this woman, Zella, back down to the city so she can give Amara her missing pectoral . . . and then ensure that she gets on the next ship headed to the mainland?" Kelly asked one of the newcomers. "I'm sure Orovalis City over in the Katani Empire will have at least one ship willing to head north for the right price. They're a much busier port than our Harbor City. Oh, and Lady Mayor . . . no harming her, unless she deliberately breaks the law while on Nightfall soil."

Danau was glad she wasn't the incipient queen. The glare Mayor Amara aimed at the freckled woman was rather intense. The red-headed man—Lord Trevan—intervened by gesturing both women back toward the western corridor. Sighing, Queen Kelly turned back to the others.

"Well, now that I've delegated *that* into someone else's hands . . . welcome to Nightfall. I am Queen Kelly, and this is my husband

and consort, Lord Saber. Cammen, you are a tea merchant; is that correct?"

"Yes, Your Majesty," the trader agreed, giving her a polite bow, tea chest still clasped in his arms. "Perhaps I could brew a pot for all of us, as a way to soothe our nerves after what just happened, as well as providing you with a chance to sample my wares?"

The blond-haired man who had arrived with the redheaded one nodded politely. "As the one who handles most of the trade arrangements, I think that's a very good idea. I haven't had a decent cup of tea in nearly five years. Come, I'll show you to the kitchens." Consort Saber, the golden-haired man, gestured back the way he had come. "We have started holding a midafternoon meal in the summertime, since supper is after sunset, which means eighth hour at this time of year. We call it *tiffin*, in honor of the Moonlands habit of the same name."

"Moonlands?" Cammen asked as they walked away. "The fabled, mythical land of dragons and rainbow pearls?"

"Yes, but not so fabled as you'd think, considering one of my sisters-in-law comes from there . . ."

"And that leaves us with just one, aside from the Menomon delegation." Queen Kelly sighed, turning to the blond priestess. "Do *you* have any startling pronouncements for me to deal with, or a civilized trade suggestion to make?"

Priestess Ora smiled and curtsied. "A few suggestions, but they can wait. I came to pay my respects to an incipient sovereign . . . and to ask you a question. I, too, heard the rumor down in the city, something about the Convocation of the Gods. Is this true? Are you really trying to reinvoke the Convocation?"

Kelly sighed and threw up her hands, letting them flop at her sides. "You and everyone else . . . *Yes*. The crown floating over there—coronet, whatever—was invoked when I Rang the Bell several months ago, swearing upon the Names of *all* the Gods that I would make this place a viable, thriving, independent kingdom. *No*, we don't know everything there is to know about invoking the

Convocation, but the crown's clearly tangible presence itself is proof that the Gods think we can pull it off.

"Unfortunately, it's been slow going. We only have a handful of months left in which to pull it off before the Katani Empire comes charging back, intent on slaughtering and imprisoning us all for the temerity of existing. Now, is there something I can do for you?"

The Arbran priestess smiled again. "No, but there is something I can do for *you*."

Kelly wasn't the only one to eye her askance. "We don't worship the God of Arbra yet, though once we pull off the Convocation, you'll be welcome to hold services for anyone willing to attend. And you're welcome to bless anyone you like, but I understand it works best if the person you're blessing also worships the same God."

Ora grinned. "Arbra has a Goddess, not a God . . . and I am merely *from* Arbra. I am technically not one of Her priestesses."

That confused Danau. This was another game of verbal *panka*, and she drew in a breath to speak. Her cousin Reuen beat her to the question.

"If you're not a priestess of Arbra, then who are you a priestess of?" Reuen asked.

"I am a follower of the Dual One, the God Darkhan and Goddess Dark Ana, ordained years ago through the holy magics of the Empire of Darkhana. I merely *live* in Arbra . . . when I am at my home. I've been traveling a lot, lately," she explained.

"Some of it inadvertently, I'm sure," Queen Kelly observed wryly, but not unkindly. "Still, if you want to practice your Darkhanan worship, you can. But you are the first person from either of those two places on the Isle, so don't expect anyone to attend your services, save out of curiosity."

"That's alright. I'm not here to preach," Priestess Ora explained. "I'm here to help you."

Kelly gave her a skeptical look. "Right."

And the game of panka *goes on*, Danau thought, bemused yet somewhat entertained by this new exchange.

"I speak the truth. My Goddess told me to find and assist the people that would resurrect the Convocation. You are attempting to resurrect it; therefore, I must help you." Ora paused a moment, then gestured in the direction the trio had taken, then at the circlet. "To be honest, at first I was following that woman Zella, because I over-heard her saying she knew what it would take to resurrect the Convocation, and that she had found one of the necessary pieces to the puzzle. But if the Gods Themselves think you can do it, I'd rather spend my time and effort in helping you. Partly because They think you can do it . . . and partly because you seem more ethical than her. At least, so far."

"Well, I'm glad to know we seem more ethical, but I still don't see how you could help us," Queen Kelly told her. "We don't even know what will be involved, so your assistance—however kindly meant—might end up being futile."

Danau cleared her throat. The sound, though small, drew the attention of both women. Facing the freckled queen, Danau gave her a slight bow. "As requested, Your Majesty, I have brought you a copy of the Scroll of Living Glory. I transcribed it myself at Sheren's request, in case you had any questions about the accuracy, or are unable to read the original language."

Just for a moment, Queen Kelly exchanged a rather odd, wry look with her Lord Secretary. Sighing somewhat heavily, Kelly held out her hand. Danau pulled her satchel around to the front and pulled out the scroll. Handing it over, she waited as the freckled queen untied the ribbon holding it together, unrolled the sticks a little, and blinked at the writing inscribed on the tough, durable sharkskin parchment favored in Menomon. The incipient queen paled after a few moments, then flushed, scrolling farther down through the list of steps. Nibbling on her lower lip, Kelly scrolled all the way to the end, then rolled up the last bit of parchment with unsteady hands.

"Charming. Just . . . *charming*! All these months we spent wait-ing . . . and the task is nigh *impossible*," Kelly muttered, grimacing.

"I could have told you what you needed to do," Ora interjected gently. "After I was *geased* by my Goddess, I traveled to the Great Library of Mendham to find the records of how it was done. The hardest task will be to find the place where your mayor's sister died and release what is needed from its anchoring point, but I have ways of tracking that sort of information down."

Comprehension dawned. Danau stared wide-eyed at the two women, as Kelly rounded on the priestess.

"Her death is no concern of yours! And frankly, it's the most current list of all the Names of the Gods that is our biggest worry! We have at most a handful of months to gather them all, in a world that doesn't have *jet planes*!"

What do black-colored fields have to do with the Names of the Gods? Danau wondered. Still, she had to make an offer. The Council was very clear on how important the Desalinator project was for the future of the city. *That is, now that they've finally acknowledged they mucked things up, cutting us off from all our external freshwater, air, and food supply sources for the last several months.*

"Your Majesty, if you need a fast ship to go looking for the place where the mayor's sister died, I am authorized to place our *udrejhong* at your disposal. Provided that we do get to examine the Desalinator fairly soon, of course," Danau said. "Our city needs a reliable source of freshwater . . . which is the main reason why we are here, in exchange for bringing you that scroll."

"You'll get to see the Desalinator first thing in the morning. The question is, is your ship fast enough to travel to all the continents of this world?" Kelly retorted dryly.

"Your worries are unnecessary, Your Majesty," Ora interjected calmly. "The Names of the Gods are being gathered as we speak. That shall be my contribution to the Convocation."

"Gathered?" Kelly repeated skeptically. "As we speak? That's a neat trick, considering how you're standing right here."

"I am not working alone in this matter," the priestess returned calmly, unfazed. "As soon as I heard of the woman Zella having found the . . . the rarest ingredient, if you will . . . I contacted my fellow Witches and directed them to scatter across the world. They have been busy finding every place of worship they could and recording the Names worshipped therein. That list has been growing for an entire year, and it has been double-checked frequently for new additions. Particularly in Aiar, where new kingdoms are still forming themselves out of the chaos left in the wake of the old."

Turning to Koranen, Kelly exchanged the scroll in her hands for the Truth Stone she had passed to him earlier. Before she finished turning back, Ora had her hand out, ready to accept it. Kelly dropped it into the other woman's palm and waited.

"I am here to assist in the resurrection of the Convocation, at the behest of my Goddess. I have directed my fellow Darkhanan Witches to scatter across the world, collecting the Names of all Gods and Goddesses currently in worship, and have compiled the most accurate, up-to-date list you will likely find within the time constraints you mentioned." Uncurling her fingers, she displayed the whiteness of the stone.

Kelly planted her hands on her hips. "Well, that's nice to know, but I wasn't born yesterday. Goddess or no Goddess, I think you want something, you and your fellow Darkhanans. Are you here to steal the Convocation out from under us, to gain the political and social power that would come with its re-creation?"

Ora met her gaze levelly and gripped the marble disc. "No. I have no interest in the political or social power that could be gained by commandeering the Convocation of the Gods." To Danau's surprise, the Truth Stone remained white when displayed. Ora continued, flexing her fingers to show her honesty. "Obviously I cannot speak for all of my fellow Darkhanans, but they have indulged me with my quest to gather the Names of the Gods, and will follow my lead."

"Then what do you want? What do you get out of this?" Kelly asked her. "What is your price? And don't tell me you don't have one. Hundreds of Witches mobilized to travel all around the world—that's *not* a cheap undertaking."

Ora shrugged. "Simply that I need to be at the Convocation."

Danau wasn't the only one to snort in skepticism. The outlander priestess took it in stride, however. Her tone remained steady, her expression calm.

"I need to stand before the Gods and tender an . . . apology . . . for something that I did. I am *geased* to do so—compelled by the will of my Goddess to complete this quest—and my fellow Witches know this. It is why they are assisting me, despite the expense. If you want the Names of the Gods, you will have to swear a vow on this very Truth Stone that you will let me be the first petitioner at the Convocation."

The two women held each other's gazes for a long moment, then Kelly plucked the unblemished disc from Ora's palm. "You can be the *second* petition at the Convocation. The *first* one is getting the Gods to swear Their protection to Nightfall as an official, Patroned kingdom." She displayed the unblemished stone, showing her words were true, then tossed it back at Koranen. "You make me curious to know what could possibly require an apology to all the Gods of this world, though."

Ora didn't change her expression by much, but it was enough to make the granite blocks beneath their feet look soft by comparison. Kelly wisely didn't press the point. She shrugged it off.

"Whatever. Get me proof of the list, and I'll write a script for the inn you're staying at to provide you with free lodging during your stay. Though you'll still have to pay for your sustenance," Kelly warned the other woman. "We have limited resources on the Isle, since we still have a limited number of ways to produce food. And you *do* realize that if that list isn't the most up-to-date version when we do get around to invoking the Convocation, we might not be able to honor this bargain?"

"Darkhanan Witches have a way of communicating quickly among themselves, regardless of the distances involved, and ways of tracking down information accurately and reliably. If you can give me two days' advanced notice, I can get you the most current list possible," Ora promised. "I can assure you that, save for a few in-cipient kingdoms which we have been keeping an eye on for the last month, we are confident we have found every center of worship around the world."

"Out of curiosity . . ." Ama-ti interjected tentatively, drawing attention to her blue-haired self, "just how many Gods and God-desses are there?"

"Not including the incipient, as yet unproven ones? There are . . . three hundred and fourteen so far," Ora related after a quick pause for thought. "Including the ones worshipped by the underwater realms, such as Menos, God of Reefs, and Althea, Goddess of Waves."

Danau knew there were at least five other underwater cities around the world, or there had been, back when Portals still worked, allowing quick and easy transit of vast distances; the archives kept by the Guardians of Menomon through the centuries held records of them, though most were too far away to travel to these days. The City of Althinac and its Patron Goddess was one of them. That this blond stranger knew of it was impressive, for Althinac hid itself for the same reasons Menomon did.

"That must be some apology, to mobilize so many colleagues. I hope you don't mind if I hang around to hear it?" Kelly quipped.

"You may listen, when it comes time to offer it. Until then . . . it is not something I would care to discuss. But I do have one other suggestion to make. When it comes time to gather that . . . rarest . . . ingredient, I think I should be on hand for that particular ritual," the priestess offered. At Kelly's skeptical look, Ora plucked the scroll from Koranen's hands, rolled it open a bit, and pointed to something on the page. "In specific, *this* part."

"*That* part," Queen Kelly echoed, eyeing the parchment dubi-ously.

"Yes. The Darkhanan priesthood actually specializes in such things—it is a technique used in conjunction with some of our Heal-ing practices. With my assistance, the process will not be nearly as risky, or as traumatic, as it may currently seem." At Kelly's dubious look, Ora gave her a wry smile. "I have enough experience to know when someone is lying *without* needing a Truth Stone in his hand. Or a Truth Wand, or any other verification spell. I don't blame you for lying, but I would think carefully about attempting that particular step without my help."

Plucking the scroll from her hands, the redhead rolled it shut and handed it back to the silently watching Koranen. "And why should I accept your help? Because you're *geased* to help me?"

"That, yes, and because it's the right thing to do."

And we're back to the panka *game*, Danau decided wryly, wishing she had some of her favorite food, breaded shrimp, to nibble on as she switched her attention back and forth between the two women. The whimsical thought reminded her that it had been several hours since her last meal. *I wonder when that tea will be prepared . . .*

"You have to make an apology before the Gods Themselves, and you're trying to tell me you know what the right thing is to do?" Kelly asked skeptically, hands going to her hips.

"Sometimes—just sometimes, even when you're doing the *right* thing—unintended accidents will happen. And sometimes you have to shoulder some of the blame for them, even if they were truly accidental and utterly unintended. An *honorable* person makes that apology, even if the problem was beyond their control, and for the majority of it, the fault of another," Priestess Ora chided her.

"But you're *geased* to making that apology. That sounds like you're being forced, to me," Kelly pointed out.

"The *geas* is merely an official seal of approval from my Goddess regarding my quest. It ensures the cooperation of my fellow Witches in my task," Ora countered calmly. "Which, I remind you, is currently being applied to your benefit."

"You know, this could go on all day, I'm sure . . . but we *do* have guests to get settled," Koranen interjected.

Disappointed at the ending of their entertainment, Danau watched him tuck both scroll and disc back into the arms of his queen. *Ah, well . . .*

"How about I go show these ladies to the quarters they'll be using while they're here, and give them a chance to freshen up before
the midafternoon meal is served? That way the two of you can discuss this matter all you like, and the rest of us can get some work
done," he finished.

Kelly arched one of her strawberry blond brows at him, but didn't
protest his incompletely disguised chiding. "You're quite right, Koranen. Please do see to their comfort. You are their liaison while
they're here, after all. Ladies," she added, turning to address the
Menomonites, "my apologies yet again for such an unconventional
welcome to the island. Normally we're a lot more organized . . . Ah,
hell," she muttered, glancing down and catching sight of blackness
forming under the touch of her fingers. Wrinkling her nose, she
corrected herself. "Alright, normally we're a lot more *congenial*, even
in our many moments of chaos—and I am definitely going to get rid
of this before I perjure myself again.

"Suffice to say, things *should* calm down and proceed more
smoothly . . . provided we don't get any more surprise arrivals, visitors, interjections, or commentaries within the next few days. Ladies, Koranen, I'll see you at *tiffin* . . . which, thanks to our trader
friend, will also be an 'afternoon tea.' Priestess, if you'll come with
me, I'll arrange for someone to drive you back down to the city."
Giving a polite nod to Danau and the other three, Kelly gestured
for the blond priestess to precede her back through the western corridor.

"This way, ladies," Koranen stated, gesturing with one arm in
the opposite direction. "You'll be quartered in the southeast wing
on the second floor. My own quarters are on the same floor, so if
you have any questions or concerns, you'll know where to find me at
night."

Now that the show was over—however confusing and yet
entertaining—Danau pulled her mind back to the main reason they
were here. "My first question regards the Desalinator. Her Majesty
said we could look at it tomorrow morning. Why not tonight?"

"Oh, Gods," Chana groaned under her breath. "Danau, we just arrived. Can't we rest and relax for a few hours, first? Not to mention, this is *supposed* to be my sleeping shift!"

Even Ama-ti nodded at that.

"Fine. We'll look at it tomorrow. But we'll do it bright and early, so get plenty of rest," Danau ordered. She turned back to Koranen and gestured. "Well? Lead the way."

"*Udrezero.*"

The whisper was so quiet, she almost didn't hear it . . . almost. Spinning on her heel, Danau glared at the other three. Or rather, two. The blue-haired Ama-ti wasn't the sort to say things like that. Unfortunately, Danau couldn't tell which one of the other two had said it, since both Reuen and Chana gave her stoic, stubborn looks in return, neither budging an inch, and neither tattling on the other by so much as a blink.

Letting her disapproval show in the stern set of her face, Danau arched one brow, silently daring either of them to repeat the insult to her face. When they carefully didn't meet her stare, she turned back around and gestured for their liaison to lead the way. Behind her, Ama-ti cleared her throat.

"I have a question . . ."

"I'm here to answer it," the Lord Secretary replied. "What would you like to know?"

"Why are there two daises?" Ama-ti asked, gesturing as Danau glanced back. "Does this land have two queens, or something?"

Koranen grinned, as if she had made a joke. "Oh, no. Trust me, one is all we can handle. No, the first dais, to the northwest, was put there simply because we had a group of people that arrived from the eastern shore, and it made sense to lead them up to the throne," he explained, turning to walk backward as he talked, so he could gesture, indicating the various directions. "We built the second one in the northeast corner for two reasons.

"Since most of our arrivals these days come from the west, we decided to move the dais so that visitors didn't have to make a sharp turn when entering the donjon hall. And the other reason . . . well, there *is* a crown floating over the bench throne, and it won't budge until Nightfall is formally recognized as a full-fledged kingdom, which makes it awkward to conduct any of our official business in the meantime without bumping into it."

"Like the column you're about to run into," Chana advised him, her tone droll. It was as if neither she nor Reuen had made that comment to Danau. She grinned at the auburn-haired man as he quickly spun, making sure he didn't hit the support pillar holding up its part of the balconies ringing the large, domed hall. "That's better," the blond-dyed Aquamancer added. "I'd hate to see such a nice backside accidentally bruised."

The man blushed. His shy smile seemed to make the early summer afternoon warmer, even for Danau. She didn't want to be affected by his charm, but it was there all the same, making her sigh. Rubbing the back of his neck, he gestured wordlessly down the eastern hall with his other hand, facing forward and leading them onward.

"Anyway, that's why it's there. Any more questions?"

"I'd like to know about the palace. It looks a lot older than the city," Reuen observed.

"Oh, it is; the original city down at the cove was mostly made from wood and was swallowed up by the jungle after the Shattering of Aiar forced everyone to flee—we had a Portal that didn't quite get shut down in time," he explained. "The island was originally a duchy, and the last duchess to rule it was a Seer. She predicted the need for the Portals to be shut down across the Empire of Katan, but in true bureaucratic inefficiency, the Council of Mages over on the mainland decided to shut this one down last . . . and they didn't quite make it.

"The duchess managed to transform most of the energy into a Curse—which is now being fulfilled—" he added, "but it caused most of the desalination plant to shut down. Which is why you're here, to hopefully find a way to revive it. We're just barely keeping up with the watering needs of the city as it is, even with all the cooling and heating pipes recycled back into the filtration system."

"Cooling and heating pipes?" Danau interrupted, confused. Koranen stopped and gestured at the walls around them.

"The palace was built out of thick blocks of the local granite, as much to make it slow to heat up in the summer as to give it many of the defensive qualities of a castle. It has high ceilings to let the heat of the day rise, and fireplaces in most of the chambers for heat when it gets cold in the winter," he explained. He scratched his head and shrugged. "I think I remember reading the donjon and the four main wings were built around eight hundred years ago, with some extensive remodeling around either four or six hundred years ago.

"The previous castle that stood within the compound proved to be too small for the duchy's needs within only a couple hundred years after the Desalinator had been built. So they razed it and built the main portions, the eight-sided donjon with its four main wings. Then the four-armed version was deemed too small again, so they added on the splits at the ends, turning it into an eight-armed complex.

"My twin says there are some spells bound into the stones themselves, keeping it in excellent repair for its age," he added, reaching out and patting one of the painted walls. "But otherwise there isn't much magic inherent in the building itself. If you get too hot in your quarters, please let one of us know, and we'll cast a temporary cooling charm; otherwise the only temperature control comes from the mass of the stone itself. Thermal spells have come a long way since this place was remade, but we haven't had the time to alter the building itself, just some of the plumbing."

The view in this corridor was of long, lithe, burrowing animals somewhere between a squirrel and a ferret, only with short, stubby tails. They popped in and out of holes dug in grassy, arid fields around the Menomonites and their host, and did so at a realistic speed. Ignoring the one that ran beneath his hand—no doubt used to the effect—Lord Koranen continued.

"As for the buildings down in the city, when we picked an architectural style for the new buildings, we chose stone for the columns and beams because one of my older brothers is particularly good at working with it, and we ran pipes up through those stone beams and underneath the floor. Cool water in the summer takes the heat out of the rooms, and warm water in the winter provides heat without the need to cut down all the forests for fuel—not that we don't have a lot of fuel right now," he added with a touch of humor, "considering how much reclamation we're still doing out there.

"But anyway, the water that flows from the Desalinator into those pipes has been rerouted back into the Desalinator to recycle it. One of my other brothers, Dominor, managed to trace most of the waterways serviced by the desalination plant, though he's not an Aquamancer by trade. He also figured out where the sewage goes; it flows from the refreshing rooms to a collection tank somewhere under the Desalinator, where it's processed. The water is separated out and sterilized, and the remaining matter is mixed into the blocks of algae and plankton extracted along with, and separated from, the blocks of salt the system produces.

"Because so many people are now living on the Isle, we've had to rethink how much water can flow into the buildings for cooling needs, and where it flows to from there, in order to ensure an adequate supply of drinking water. It was thought that if we rerouted the non-sewage water back into the system through the sewers, it would spare whatever energy supply is being used by the desalination spells, at least until the four of you can tell us what needs to be fixed.

"Of course, if we can get the Desalinator functioning at a higher capacity, we can increase our commerce in salt and fertilizer blocks, and allow more people to migrate here," he explained. "We have names of people who want to settle here listed on scrolls that could stretch the length of this hall, laid end to end . . . but we've put them on a waiting list prioritized by their ability to contribute to the island's economy balanced against how much potable water we can extract from the system."

"What about rain?" Ama-ti asked. "You make it sound like the Desalinator is the only source of drinkable water on the island."

"The island does get rain, but not enough to support the droves of people wanting to move here," the Lord Secretary said. "Whatever rain we get is needed to keep the plants of the forests and fields hydrated, particularly now that we're reclaiming old patches of farmland from the jungle. Hence the need to recycle anything that isn't rainwater to be used as drinking water."

"We use a system that sounds somewhat similar to deal with our own sewage," Danau said, nodding. "We use it to cull fertilizer for our plantation caves, since it's hard to get good dirt that isn't saturated with coral sand and salt, while the extracted water is used in the fields to keep the plants healthy. I've studied that system, as has Reuen. We should be able to extrapolate from that point of familiarity at least something of how the Desalinator works."

"I have a question," Chana offered, tucking her hands behind her back. The movement pulled her shoulders back and pushed out her leather-clad chest coquettishly. "You said you have more than one brother?"

"Yes, there are eight of us," the Lord Secretary told her. "I'm the seventh, of four sets of twins."

Chana wrinkled her nose at that, and Danau could understand why. Menomonite women were encouraged to have children, preferably female children, since far more male sailors were lost overboard in the treacherous waters of the Sun's Belt Reefs than female ones. But four sets of twins would have taxed any woman's body. The thought didn't deter the dusky-skinned woman for long.

"I understand that you people requested single female Aquamancers for matchmaking purposes," she stated. "Would that mean you and several of your brothers are single? And hopefully as handsome as you are?"

Again, he blushed hotly. Danau resisted the urge to roll her eyes at such blatant flirting. She wanted to assert that they were here for business only . . . but they weren't. She had known about this . . .

interest . . . in single female Aquamancers months ago, back when that other young man they met on the docks, Lord Morganen, had talked with her through the Fountain. That was before the Council had ordered her to close down all communication with the outside world from the Guardian's Fountain.

He recovered his composure with a quick clearing of his throat. "Six of my brothers are happily married, and the seventh—my twin, you met him on the dock—is spoken for. The matchmaking in question refers solely to me. Which is why I'm your liaison, so that we can all get to know one another."

Reuen planted her hands on her brown-clad hips and gave him a coquettish look of her own. "Is this sort of like a reverse of Menom-onite ways? One man gets a handful of women here in the land of Nightfall, instead of one woman getting a handful of men?"

"Uh . . ." Mouth sagging and eyes widening, first he paled, then he flushed. Koranen finally cleared his throat. "Uh . . . one man and one woman is the usual, *normal* way of things . . . or did you just mean courting opportunities?"

"In Menomon, the ratio of men to women is around five or six to one," Danau explained briskly. "That ratio has improved over the years, thanks to an equal number of male and female births, but with the intermittent influx of mostly male sailors, it hasn't ever completely equalized."

"*One* man, *one* woman. That's the tradition up here," he asserted, flushing again.

Chana laughed. "I'm not sure just *one* man could satisfy me properly . . . though you're welcome to try!"

Reuen chuckled, and even Ama-ti grinned. Danau flushed, uncomfortable at their behavior. *She* couldn't, daren't, flirt, and she knew it was sour envy that made her want to tell the others to stop wasting time and get back to business. Worse, if she said *anything* at this moment . . . she knew it would tempt either Reuen or Chana into making a rash comment that would make her lose face in front of this Nightfallite official and open herself to further barbed teasing.

Giving them a blush and a shy-looking grin, Koranen gestured down the hall. "We'll see . . . and in the meantime, I'll show you to your quarters so you can freshen up. *Tiffin* will be held in less than half an hour—Her Majesty complained that we weren't using minutes as well as hours, but prior to the Ringing of the Bell, we didn't really *need* minutes. We've dug out and refurbished several old clocks from the attics, and you'll hear the carillon bells from the cupola over the donjon ringing out the hours and their quarters, but only during daylight hours. Mainly because Her Majesty sleeps directly underneath the bell tower.

"But supper is served at eighth hour in the summertime, round about sunset, which means *tiffin* is held at about four in the afternoon . . ."

FOUR

◦❊❊◦

*W*ell, that *went rather well*, Koranen thought as he closed the door to his suite. Pleased with the much better evening he'd just had, compared to the afternoon, he headed for his refreshing room, intending to wash up and head to bed. Despite the turbulent start, things had settled down during the *tiffen* meal and had progressed smoothly for the rest of the day.

Dominor hadn't been available for questioning—Serina was close to her due date, so the thirdborn brother was spending most of his free time at the Retreat at Koral-tai. Since they still had the pair of twinned mirrors connecting the palace to the nunnery, it had only taken a small amount of effort to ask him where he had put his observation notes on the water and sanitation pipeways, and to combine them with notes made by Amara, Rydan . . . and Rydan's wife. Who was thankfully still sticking to Rydan's side as he clung stubbornly to his preferred nocturnal lifestyle.

It had meant sending a servant to Rydan's northern tower on the outer palace wall with a covered platter of food, rather than risk either of them attending supper. Until that Zella woman was completely off the island, and the motives of that priestess Ora had been examined under Truth Stone, it was just easier to keep the very-much-alive Rora safely out of sight. Thankfully, neither of them minded all that much. Having anticipated just that possibility, Kelly had decreed a curfew each night; residents were to be in their homes by eleventh hour each night and were not to stir outside until dawn, which at this time of the year was near fifth hour of the morning.

It presented an undeniable air of mystery to the new residents, but the explanation was simple, and remarkably truthful at the same time: While the new citizens of Nightfall slept safely in their beds, major magical enchantments were undertaken to erect the stone skeletons of each new building. With non-mages tucked out of the way, no one would run the risk of walking into a major enchantment zone at the wrong moment and ruining it, or worse, being injured by their carelessness. That explanation seemed to do the trick, thankfully.

The lack of two brothers and their wives at the dining table had been made up for by all the rest, plus the tea-trader. At least, for the afternoon meal. The stimulant had lent itself well to the rest of the afternoon as most of the Aquamancers had settled down to business, at the lady Danau's insistence. Stripping off his tunic, his boots, and his socks, Koranen dampened a washcloth and ran it over the sweatier areas of his body, his feet, armpits, chest, and nape.

All but the blond-dyed one, Chana, had spent the hours between *tiffen* and supper poring over the Nightfall notes in one of the salons in the west wing, located near the map room that had become Amara's office in the palace. Flow rates, surface tensions, ambient temperatures, and other terms had been passed around the table. When Chana joined them for the evening meal, looking rested but sleepy-eyed, she listened to the others discussing their preliminary findings and ideas, with a smile curling her lips and sly little glances cast in Koranen's direction.

Now that he was over the shock of how *short* their hair was . . .
Koranen could admit she was quite lovely. Her face was more heart-
shaped than the oval he was used to seeing, but she was just as
deeply tanned as a northern Katani woman, and just as confident of
her self-appeal. *Nice brown eyes, dark lashes . . . I guess it would be difficult to dye those without risking her sight, but I wonder, does she dye the
hairs down below, as she clearly does the ones up above? And wouldn't that
be a sight to see?*

A moment later, as he splashed his face with water from the sink,
the image of *blue*-dyed nether-curls assaulted his imagination. It
was the woman Ama-ti, lightly tanned and unnaturally colored.
The thought made him choke. Koranen wasn't so sure he wanted to
see *that* on a woman's body. The illusion-woman that had been recorded for his use was of a lightly tanned brunette, whose hair was
as natural in hue down below as it was up above. It was a normal sort
of thing to see . . . but then, so was the hair on the professional's
head.

*But these Menomonite women aren't into natural-looking hair. The
Aquamancer Reuen has red-and-brown-striped hair; does that mean she's
striped down below? And is the lady Danau's hair a true, natural auburn
like mine, or is it merely a masterwork of dyeing? For that matter, what
insane social despot declared that Menomonite women had to have such
short hair?*

A knock at the door to his suite interrupted his musings. Hastily
scrubbing his damp face and chest with a towel, Koranen snatched
up his tunic and hurried out to the front room. The knocking came
again, louder and more impatient sounding. Abandoning his attempt to get his tangled shirt straightened out and pulled over his
head, he left it dangling from one arm as he opened the door.

It was the blond Aquamancer, Chana. Surprised, Koranen blinked
at her, then peered past her as movement caught his eye, glancing
down the hall in both directions. All four ladies had been given
rooms across from his, and two of them had been drawn to their
own doorways, Ama-ti and Danau. The one called Reuen wasn't at

her doorway, but then her suite, like Chana's, was one of the end ones.

Both women saw him in his half-dressed state, muscles flexing as he glanced to either side. Both also saw their fellow Aquamancer step right up to him, bold as she pleased, and loop her arms over his shoulders. Her move brought their bodies together, distracting Kor from everything but the willing female pressing her leather-clad self into him.

"Let's talk about this matchmaking business, shall we?" Chana purred, dark eyes gleaming with interest, as she stepped even closer, forcing him back a step. Her opposite hand slid down his arm, sliding off the folds of his embroidered tunic, until she caught his hand in hers and pulled it around to her backside. Her fingers deliberately cupped his around the curve of one buttock and then gave them a squeeze. Silently ordering him what to do.

As he tentatively gripped her bottom on his own, she slid her other hand up into the hair above his nape, angling his head down to hers. Their mouths met, and Koranen sensed everything this time. Not just the feel of her lips, not just the look of her lashes as they fluttered shut, not just the sound of her soft moan . . . but the feminine scent of her mingled with her leathers, and the slightly spicy-sweet taste of the pastry she had selected for dessert teased and mixed with the fruit he had chosen.

His illusion-woman didn't have smell, didn't have taste, and the differences went straight to his head . . . and straight to his loins. Gathering her closer with both arms, lifting her onto her toes—she was a little short next to him—Koranen returned her kiss with heady enthusiasm. He wanted to devour her, to press every curve of her lovely body against every muscle of his own. This was a *real* woman, not an illusion, a wriggling, willing female who was unabashedly groping him.

A door *thump*ed shut, jarring him back to reality. Blinking, pulling his head up, Koranen looked over the top of her short blond curls. Ama-ti still lounged in her doorway, smirking at the two of them. It was the prickly Danau who had closed her door on the scene he and Chana had made. A scene Chana was still making. He'd removed his lips from hers, so she pressed hers to his throat. It felt good . . . It felt very good, and he closed his eyes for a moment, blocking out the sight of the other woman, as he succumbed to his rising passion.

"Menos, you're so hot," Chana moaned, stroking and rubbing the muscles of his chest, his waist. She nipped at the base of his throat, a move that would have aroused him further, save that her words were an icy shock to his lust-clouded thoughts. A reminder that if she thought he was *hot* . . . she might not be the right woman.

It was made worse when she dragged one of his hands to her breasts, clearly wanting him to touch them. Memory assaulted him, making Koranen jerk back reflexively. She clung for a moment, tilting her head back, a confused look clouding her face. Kor flushed, struggling with the needs of his body versus those of his conscience.

"What? Why did you stop?" the Aquamancer demanded, frowning at him.

"I . . . I think we should go a little more slowly," Kor offered awkwardly, uncomfortable with the war going on between his mind and body.

"Why? Don't you want me? Isn't that why I'm here?" Shifting her hand, Chana cupped him through the front of his trousers.

Koranen hissed a breath through his teeth; her touch was unexpected, bold, and delicious. He could feel each one of her fingers curving to gauge and caress his flesh through the spell-embroidered silk of his trousers. He could also feel his magic rising within him, heating his skin. Struggling to contain it, he watched her frown softly and pull back from him.

"Are you alright? You feel . . . kind of hot," Chana offered. Her look of disappointment and confusion at the ending of their kisses shifted to a look of concern. "Are you running a fever?"

Removing her hands from his groin and his waist, he gently pushed her back a step. "I think I should go see one of our Healers, in case I am coming down with something. I'm sure it's nothing contagious," he added, carefully skirting the border between a hedge and an outright lie, "but I don't want to cause you or the others any harm.

"Besides . . . Nightfall courtship customs may be liberal, but I'd rather get to *know* you ladies first." *I can't believe I'm saying this*, Kor thought wryly. *But it is the truth*. Body aching with need, he added, "There's a lot more to a relationship than romping in the bed—however pleasurable—and those are the things you have to take the time to discover." Catching one of her dusky hands, he lifted it to his lips for a brief, light, and hopefully not too heated kiss. "I'll see you in the morning, yes?"

Sighing, Chana dropped her hands to her hips. "I was hoping to see you in your bed long before morning. But you do feel a little warm. Can I at least see you in my dreams, tonight?"

"All four of you can see me in your dreams tonight, if you like—we won't know which one of you is Destined for me, if any of you, until we've all had a chance to get to know one another," Kor offered as smoothly as he could.

"Who says we have to be each other's Destiny?" Chana countered, moving forward to loop her arms around his neck a second time. "Why not just go straight for a roll in your bed?"

Trying not to grimace, Koranen removed her arms before she could gain another hold. She was like one of those multilimbed sea creatures that liked to grapple things, a squid or an octopus, something of that ilk. "Because I might be ill? Go on to bed, and we'll see how I feel in the morning."

Mouth pursing in a pout, she let him back her up into the corridor. Releasing her wrists, Koranen stepped back and closed the door between them. Then opened it, snatched up the rumpled green tunic that had lodged partway in the door frame, and shut the stout panel again. Swaying forward, he leaned his head against the copper-cast sigil hung on the wood, one of several anti-fire sigils scattered around his quarters.

The ones he had made for the rest of his family were designed to protect them while they slept from the threat of a fire. These were designed to protect all the things in his rooms from himself. Letting the metal soak away some of his heat, he waited for the ache in his loins to subside.

I didn't actually burn her—thank all the Gods for that—but she did *feel me heating up. Somehow, I don't think she's the right one. The Water to my Fire.* Disappointment made the lingering hints of spicy-sweet on his lips taste a little bitter. Padding back into the refreshing room, he discarded his tunic in the laundry bin on the way.

Resuming his place at the sink, he used his teeth scrubber and a bit of mint softsoap to scour his mouth, rinsing it several times while trying to think only of what he was doing at that moment, and not of the faint scent of female that still clung to his skin. Another pass of the damp, cold washcloth cleaned most of the lingering sweat and smell from his flesh, and by then, he was calm enough to put himself to bed.

For a moment, as he settled beneath the rune-stitched sheets, Koranen debated activating the illusion-bead sitting on his nightstand. He decided against it, though. Chana seemed rather bold and forward; she might decide not to take "no" for an answer and come back to see him again, and he didn't want to get caught using the illusion to relieve his needs. Not to mention he could still recall how she had stimulated all five of his senses when they kissed, though not vividly enough anymore to cause him problems.

He just didn't want to compare the illusion with the real thing, not so close to each other. *Not if it looks like she might not be the right woman for me . . .*

Ah, well. One woman sort of struck from the list, with three more to go. The redhead doesn't seem all that friendly, and certainly is not interested in me, but the striped one was eyeing me close to the way the blonde did, and the blue-haired one seems charming and sweet, though she didn't

say all that much outside of business . . . She should give lessons to their
leader in how to be efficient without being distant and prickly.

I wonder if her nether-curls really are *dyed as blue as her hair . . . ?*

Danau woke with a gasp, sheets and blankets rumpled around her
lower legs, skin tingling with the frosted glitter of sweat. Having
left the curtains open so that she would awaken promptly at dawn,
the light of one of the moons—Brother Moon, judging by the
strength of the glow—allowed her to see each unsteady puff of
breath that misted up from her lips. Shuddering, she closed her
eyes, trying to recapture her dream.

An abdomen. *That* abdomen. The one she had seen Chana plastering herself against so shamelessly last night. For such a slender,
normal-seeming man, Lord Koranen of Nightfall had a remarkable
amount of definition to his body. Each ripple of muscle had made
her want to shove the other Aquamancer out of the way so that *she*
could be the one touching his stomach . . . even though it would no
doubt end just as badly as her attempt with Jiore.

Rubbing the frost from her naked flesh, Danau groped for the
covers and pulled them back into place, curling up on her side as she
huddled under the blankets for warmth. She had been forced to dig
into the chest at the foot of the bed for extra bedding, since she was
always cold at night. Though in that dream, at least for a little while,
she had felt deliciously warm. Normally, it took a scalding-hot bath
to make her feel that warm. But while she did warm up, her brain
was now wide-awake, struggling with various thoughts.

She supposed it was appropriate, since she did remember being
in a bathing tub at one point in her dream. There had been mounds
of bubbles and a fistful of the soft manta-ray chamois Menomonites
tended to use for their undergarments. It was a strange dream, for
all it had been an erotic one, because she had been more focused on
scrubbing the leather and foam together, using the rippling muscles
of the Lord Secretary's stomach, than on that stomach and the man

attached to it. Danau remembered a corner of her mind yelling at her to *look* at him, to look up into his eyes and acknowledge that he existed, that he was more than just a gorgeous stomach . . . but she kept scrubbing her damned underwear against his chest in the dream, determined to do her laundry.

Sheren would have a grand time dissecting that *one*, she thought, missing the pragmatic, elderly woman. It didn't matter to the Guardian if Danau was a social misfit, when the Aquamancer was the closest thing Sheren had to a future replacement. The Guardian believed Danau *could* refine her self-discipline enough to manage the vast forces emanating from the Menomon Fountain. Most of those energies had been tamed long ago, bound into the maintenance of the city, so it wasn't as if she would have a lot of unfocused energy to wrestle into submission.

Unless something went wrong, of course. That was the catch. If things ran smoothly, Danau *should* be able to contain the energies. If they didn't . . . she could get hurt. Unfortunately, Menomon was short on powerful mages at the moment. The woman Zella had almost qualified, except she had clung palpably to her homeland on the surface . . . and now it seemed she possessed some rather grand ambitions.

Twisting onto her back, Danau shifted her arm over her eyes, blocking out the moonlight. She had read the Scroll of Living Glory, copied it with her own eyes and hands, and knew what the Amazai mage had been looking for. Or rather, who. A Living Fountain. All Fountains were once contained in the body of a female mage, a singularity point that spilled untamed magic into the world from where it built up in the Dark, the place spirits went as they journeyed from life to the Afterlife, realm of the Gods. Upon that mage's death, the Fountain detached itself and within a matter of hours would lodge itself in a physical location.

The Scroll of Living Glory outlined the only exception to that rule. If the singularity were detached and bound during an admittedly disturbing ritual into a special object, it could be used on a second Fountain to open the Gateway to the Gods ... and that meant re-creating the Convocation of the Gods.

The Convocation, held once each four years back before Aiar had been Shattered, had been a grand occasion. Each God and Goddess was called forth by Name to appear in the mortal realm and directly address the petitions of Their worshippers and Their worshippers' neighbors, for just one half turning of Brother Moon. The old records had spoken of weeks of celebrations both before and after, and of the worldwide cessation of hostilities.

For all that the roughly two-week period of the Convocation was short, it had created a means of resolving interkingdom conflicts, ending many of the costly devastations of battles and wars. It also made whichever kingdom hosted the Convocation the most politically powerful nation in the world.

Fortuna, according to a brief side note in the Scroll, had been the first host of the Convocation of the Gods, until the special crystal housing the mobile Fountain had been damaged and destroyed. But that had been in a year outside of the Convocation, in a location that wasn't the capital of their nation. Fortuna had survived that lesser shattering and had rebuilt itself into a powerful, enduring nation. Aiar, on the other hand, had been shattered beyond redemption because whatever it was had happened during the Convocation, which was held in the heart of their capital, and it had released the energies of two Fountains, not just one.

The Amazai mage, Zella Fin Rin, clearly wanted to try to resurrect Aiar's damaged glory. *Or perhaps she just wants to create a new glory for her homeland, Amaz. The sailors all said it was one of the few principalities that survived the Shattering and turned itself immediately into a kingdom, maintaining its social and economic stability. Certainly we benefited from their continued attempts to trade with Katan, since the sudden lack of functional Portals made sea trade more profitable than ever, if just as risky as before. With the Amazai reputation for culture and prosperity, I can see why it would be considered a good candidate for hosting the next Convocation.*

It was even more ambitious for the Nightfallites to want to resurrect the Convocation. Knowing what she knew, Danau guessed
this sister of Mayor Amara had been a Living Fountain. *Or maybe
still is . . . ? Queen Kelly only said via the Truth Stone that Lord What's
His Name, the lighter redhead, found the mayor alone upon their northern shore. She could have been temporarily separated from her sister at
that point, and merely reunited with her later.*

*Not once did either Kelly or Amara state that she was actually dead
while clasping the Truth Stone . . . so my guess is, she is alive, whoever this
sister is, but that she is currently in hiding somewhere. Which is a very
wise place to be,* Danau acknowledged. *Unless they've already extracted
her Fountain, if she indeed carries one? But then why would they need the
Scroll of Living Glory, which deals mostly with the removal and containment of the Fountain?*

You do realize this isn't really your problem, Danau, she chided herself after a long moment of quiet thought. Removing her arm from
her face, she tucked it under the bedding and snuggled onto her
other side. *Your problem lies with the Desalinator . . . and you need your
rest if you're to make serious headway when you see it in the morning.
Time to practice your meditations,* she ordered herself, closing her eyes
as she did her best to banish the memory of those taut, masculine
muscles, and the bizarre urge to wash her undergarments against
them.

Thumping her pillow into better shape, she firmly pushed it out
of her mind. *It's probably just because of something I ate. I'll have to request some fish in tomorrow's meals, just in case an excess of land-meat
causes nightmares . . .*

"These markings, here, beyond the outskirts of the city," Danau
said, shifting the stacks of maps between her and the mayor, Amara.
"They're just sketched in, but if I trace them through these two
maps . . . they look like they might have connected to the piping
system at some point, though they only seem to flow outward, not

inward. That would be consistent with irrigation systems, but I'd need to be sure. The old pipes might have backwashed a lot of dirt into the system, causing clogs that may have contributed to a reduction in capacity. Do you know what they were used for?"

"I'm not the one who knows the most about the old fields. I've been focusing more on the city proper," Amara returned. The black-haired, golden-eyed woman smothered a yawn behind her hand, blinked a bit, then frowned thoughtfully. "This map here—Baroness Teretha was working last week in this sector; the mapmaker's signature is the name of one of her assistants, I think. I know she complained about broken ceramic pipes being dug up along with the roots of the stumps they were spell-excavating, resurrecting old roads through the nut orchards or something. You'll need to speak to her."

Nodding, Danau wondered privately why the mayor and her incipient queen didn't seem to get along very well. Frankly, Danau found the long-haired woman easy to work with; Amara was methodical, intelligent, and interested in functional results. A hard worker, like herself . . . unlike her cousin Reuen, who was falling asleep over her plate of scrambled eggs, and Chana, who was so late to breakfast, she hadn't even shown her face yet. Their host, Koranen, looked reasonably awake, though he was toying with his food, eyeing Reuen, Danau, and Ama-ti thoughtfully.

Seeing that Amara and Danau had stopped talking for a moment, Ama-ti cleared her throat. "Um . . . I don't mean to pry, or tread on a delicate subject, but . . . that thing the mage-woman spoke about, a pec . . . something? What is it, exactly? I was on freshwater duty when the salvage teams went out to recover goods from the ships that month, so I never saw what was found."

"A pectoral is a special kind of collar," Amara explained, setting down her fork so that she could gesture at her upper torso. "It forms a sort of circular cape across the sternum and shoulders and is a sign of rank among the shapechangers of the Shifterai. For each pure animal form a shapeshifter can make, they add a row of decoration to indicate the beast in question. Mine is, or was, a particularly broad pectoral, more like a cape or a mantle than a necklace, but then I have the ability to form many pure shapes, so it had many rows."

"Rows?" Danau inquired.

"Well, for example, if a shapeshifter can form three animals—a horse, a dog, and a falcon—he would have three rows of decoration on his pectoral, one row of each being a motif of horses, dogs, or falcons. Of course, with only three shapes and three rows, it would look more like a thick, flat necklace than a cape," Amara admitted, shrugging, "but it would still lie flat across the collarbones, instead of climbing the neck like a choker. The Centarai—they are the horse breeders of the Centa Plains and our cross-kin—they use choker necklaces to denote rank, ones that go up from the base of the throat, and not out across the shoulders like ours do."

"Cross-kin?" Reuen said.

"There was a group of Shifterai who refused to behave in a civilized manner that were exiled and sent off the plains, early in our history," Amara explained briefly. "The survivors eventually civilized themselves, settled among the Centarai, and interbred. Every once in a while, they'll beget a shapeshifter son, and when they do, they bring that son to the Plains, where we'll take him in and give him training and a place of his own. In exchange, we usually give them one of our non-shifter men to take back. That makes us cross-kin."

"If a pectoral denotes rank and shapeshifting power, I'm surprised you're not wearing it now," Kelly observed from her seat at the end of the table. Her tone was light, but Danau saw Amara bristle slightly.

"I chose not to wear it because Zella *wanted* me to wear it. I might be grateful to have it back, but I'm not going to do anything to please that woman," Amara asserted tartly. "I'll wear it when *I* want to wear it."

"Amara, I'm not . . ." The freckled queen sighed. "Look, I'm as proud of your shapeshifting ability as you are. And frankly, a little bit envious. But mostly I'm pleased and proud of your skills. If you ever wanted to wear it, I'd be happy to see you in it. That's all I'm saying."

Some of the tension between the two women eased. Danau decided it was like watching a puffer fish swimming around; the mayor inflated at a hint of threat and deflated when that threat was disproved. *And here I thought I had a prickly existence . . .*

"I'll save it for a special occasion. I'm a Nightfaller, after all, not a Shifterai. I don't *need* to wear it every day."

Kelly choked on her drink at that. Coughing, she cleared her mouth and smirked. "That's the wolf trying to tell the sheep it's now a grass eater. You'll always be Shifterai, and you know it!"

"Maybe, but I'll be Shifterai. I won't be *a* Shifterai," Amara retorted primly. "Now, if you'll excuse me, I'm expected down in the city shortly."

"That reminds me," Koranen interjected quickly. "What are we going to *call* the city? We've just been calling it 'the city,' or 'the harbor.' So what *do* we call it? Harbor City? Something else?"

Blank looks were exchanged around the table. Finally, Kelly shrugged. "Harbor City, I guess. What do you think, Amara?"

The mayor wrinkled her nose a little, but her expression was more one of rueful amusement than distaste. "I'm not really the one to ask, since the Shifterai only have the one permanent city, and it's Shifting City, or just the City for short."

" 'Harbor City' is straightforward," Saber offered. He was Kelly's husband, if Danau remembered correctly, a large, muscular, blond man. "It describes what it is and what it does. That works for me."

"And best of all, we don't have to remember to start calling it something else," the other one Danau had met, Morganen, quipped from his seat next to Koranen.

"Harbor City it is. Make up some sort of official naming ceremony, Amara," Kelly directed her mayor. "We'll formally name the city, hold a little ceremony, make it a citywide party—we could even formally install you as the mayor of Harbor City, and give you a chance to wear your collar-thing!"

Amara laughed at the gentle teasing. "Alright! Harbor City it is. We *should* have some sort of symbol prepared for the city, before the ceremony—like the silhouetted sunset flags that represent Night-fall, with the paint that changes its color."

"I've been thinking about that, actually," Morganen said. "I think I can come up with some sort of harbor setting, something painted with static buildings in the background and ships sailing back and forth across the cove in the foreground . . . ?"

"I like it. Work on it," Kelly directed him, fluttering her hand.

"It'll have to be in a couple days, though. Hope wants bags of wheat sent across," Morganen said. Danau didn't know who he was talking about and started to tune out his words, disinterested, until he added, "She wants the balance of mass and energy between the universes addressed within the week. Particularly as she'll be send-ing over several more items very soon."

Universes? Plural? Danau stared at the young man. He didn't look like much; somewhat handsome with those aquamarine eyes, about the color of the water around the Sineffi atolls to the east of Menomon, but with plain light brown hair pulled back into a tail and ordinary brown clothes with only a bit of age-worn trim around the edges. *He doesn't look powerful enough to open a gateway between different worlds. He looks more like a harvest-mage, ready to force-grow plants for food, but little else.*

Even more oddly, his auburn-haired twin had grinned at his words, though the Lord Secretary wasn't actually looking at any-thing other than his food. Then the focus of his hazel eyes darted up and out, touching upon Ama-ti and Reuen, before shifting to meet Danau's gaze. A moment later, Chana strolled into the room, stretching dramatically and smiling at everyone.

"My, what a beautiful morning it is! I've never slept on a bed stuffed with feathers before, though I've heard they're quite comfortable. And I'm happy to report that they are. Thank you for your lovely hospitality," she added to the others, seating herself at the end of the table. Winking at Koranen, she grinned when he blushed.

For a moment, Danau suffered a sting of envy, remembering how Chana had disappeared into Koranen's bedroom last night. She had slept on a feather-stuffed bed with a partner, while Danau had slept with odd dreams all alone. Suppressing the urge to chide her fellow Menomonite for her excesses, she confined herself to a simple statement of fact.

"Hurry up and eat," she directed the blond Aquamancer. "We have a long day ahead of us."

Slanting Danau a brief, annoyed look, Chana sighed and accepted the bowls of food being passed her way.

For all that he was flattered by Chana's continued attempts to flirt with him, pleased by Ama-ti's congeniality, and intrigued by Reuen's sophisticated air, Koranen was glad for the distraction of the desalination complex when he braked the cart. Bracing one arm on the rudder-wheel, he gestured with the other at the nine looming, octagonal, ornately carved and columned buildings. Bodies were moving back and forth between one of the outer buildings and the largest structure in the center. Carts rattled over the paving stones, laden with huge, coffin-sized blocks of either pristine white or brownish green in one direction, and empty as they rattled back the other way.

"There it is," he told them. "The main one in the center is the warehouse, and the outer ones are the processors, four pairs of them. Only two of the outer buildings are in use at the moment. The one over there brings in seawater through a system of grilles and grates that filter out undesirable objects, and the other, the one everyone is using, puts out fresh drinking water and blocks of salt and algae.

"Your foremost priority, ladies, is to figure out how to produce *more* drinking water," he added. "Whatever you do, *don't* break the part that still functions. We'd have to evacuate the island in a hurry if you did, since we don't have any sort of backup supply."

"What about rainfall?" the fourth person in the cart asked. Since Chana had immediately claimed the spot on the driver's bench next to Koranen, Danau had silently climbed into the back with the other two, and let them do the talking on the ride down. Or rather, the flirting. Looking as if the thought of flirting had never once crossed her mind, she added, "The abundance of plant life I saw on the ride down here suggests a steady supply of rain."

"Most of the time it only rains intermittently, and it rains lightly," Koranen said. "In fact, it mists more than it rains, usually in the early mornings. It's enough to keep the plants healthy, but if we start putting up catch-basins, we'll lose the best water source for our crops. Once a month or so, we get drenched from a storm, but the land is hilly enough that the water tends to run straight off into the sea when it does rain that heavily. We also get more rain on the east side of the mountains than the west, but the flatter, more farmable land—and the one good spot for a deep-water harbor—is on the west side. Even if the best beaches are to the east."

He didn't bother to add that one of the reasons the plants were so healthy was their proximity to the Fountain of Nightfall and its radiant energies. Magic radiated from animals, flowing to plants like sunlight flowing from the sun; the plants absorbed the radiant energies, growing stronger and healthier, and the animals then ate those plants, growing stronger and healthier in turn. Since a Fountain produced copious amounts of magic, whatever grew nearby was invariably much healthier and more abundant than it should have been, given its resources.

"You said the one in the middle is the warehouse?" Chana asked. When Koranen nodded, she shook her head slowly, admiringly. "It looks as big as the palace. Bigger, even!"

"Yes, and no. The Y-tips added on to the original castle wings make the palace bigger in terms of overall length—in fact, the ring of trees surrounding this place is probably about the same diameter as the guard wall around the palace—but the warehouse is a solid octagon, like the donjon at the heart of the palace, only much bigger," Koranen admitted. "The palace doesn't contain as much space, since it has four chunks of garden bitten out of its sides. And there are five floors to the warehouse, compared to only four in the palace . . . if you don't count any attic space."

"The amount and size of the blocks I can see going into the warehouse doesn't equate to the size of that place," Ama-ti observed, frowning thoughtfully. "It wouldn't even be filled by four times the amount of salt and algae, if this is the standard rate. The old records spoke of the Desalinator filling anywhere from five to ten ships a day, plus burdening multiple caravans passing through the old transcontinental Portals."

"That's because only *one* of the sluice-gates still works. Each of the four output buildings has eight sluice-gates," Koranen told them. "It's not four times the output; it's *thirty-two* times the output. Of course, to me, it doesn't seem like the sluice that *is* functional is operating at full capacity, though it's as wide-open as we can make it," he added. "But then I freely admit I'm not an expert in hydromagics. Shall we take a tour of the two functional processing buildings? Or would you like to see the warehouse first?"

The others looked to Danau, who opened her mouth, closed it, then said, "Warehouse. I think we need to get a feel for what the Desalinator's capacity *should* be . . . though normally I'd rather start from the beginning of the process, not the end."

"True, but you have a good idea. If we're aware of what it *should* be doing, then we'll have our eyes opened to what it *is* doing and where the differences may lie," Chana agreed. Shifting her weight, she jumped down from the bench seat in front, not waiting for Koranen to assist her down.

Climbing down from the other side, Koranen was grateful for her display of independence. Part of him was grateful the brown-skinned, blond-haired woman could settle down and get to business without much of the fuss or tension between her and her auburn-haired leader—much like the tension between Amara and Kelly, sometimes. Part of him was grateful to avoid the opportunity to be groped in public. At least he was back to his older, plainer clothes, a pair of brown linen trousers and a sleeveless light blue tunic that fell halfway to his knees; last night's outfit had proved to be no real impediment to being groped.

Being groped by a willing woman was wonderful; he didn't deny that. In fact, Kor had enjoyed it, up until the moment she had commented on how hot he felt. But groping wasn't something one did in public. Especially as he had three more women still waiting to be tested. It would be difficult enough to flirt experimentally with Ama-ti, Reuen, or even the uninterested Danau without making Chana upset that he wasn't more eager to pursue *her*.

However did Trevan juggle all those women, all those years ago? Koranen wondered wryly, watching as the petite Danau directed her taller companions to start taking measurements. If any of the fifth-born brother's bed partners had ever felt jealous over the others, the lighter redhead must have somehow smoothed things over before Koranen had heard anything about it. *Or there may have been a conspiracy of quiet around the Virgin Brother on that particular subject, so as not to upset me by talking about one of them enjoying an excess of something I couldn't have . . .*

It wasn't as if his other brothers hid such things from him, though there hadn't been as much to hide as one might think. Saber had been too busy taking over the county after the death of their father to dally very often, Wolfer had been busy helping him, Dominor may have competed with Trevan, but the rest of them had found willing ladies only when they could find the time between helping their eldest brother, finishing their magical educations, and establishing their trade skills.

The four Aquamancers had pulled odd objects—crystals, wands, and sextant-like things—from the satchels they wore slung over their heads and shoulders. Ama-ti looked like she was measuring the height of the building somehow with her sextant. Reuen was pacing out the width between each of the eight support columns flanking the outer edge of the nearest side of the warehouse, trailing a length of ribbon she had attached to one of the pillars.

Chana was sketching the designs carved into the nearest wall on a tablet that was sort of like one of the slateboards his sister-in-law Serina loved to use. Her board was made out of what looked like polished white marble, and she had what looked like a grease pencil in her hand instead of a stick of chalk. Off to one side, Danau was slowly pacing, staring at the ground and her hands with equal measures of intensity, gauging where she was versus the movement of what looked like crystal-studded dowsing rods in her fingers.

Every once in a while, the other three women called out a semicryptic string of numbers and words, which Chana dutifully noted on her board. Peering over her shoulder, Koranen could see it was very much like one of Serina's shrunken chalkboards. With a caress of her deeply tanned fingers on the edge of the frame, the Aquamancer was able to shift whatever she was working on to one side, so that she could write her notes on a clean, unused section, much like a mage shifted the focus of a scrying mirror.

This is exploring the warehouse first? They haven't even gone inside yet!

The thought amused him. Of course, he *knew* what they were doing, more or less. They were literally measuring the size, shape, design, and magical aura of the building, no doubt in order to re-create it. Koranen had heard of certain departments in the Katani government using similar methods to maintain the older, more important buildings in the capital and elsewhere, but the closest he'd come to seeing such things had been the occasional local building project and the efforts of the road crews to keep the roads in good repair.

Eventually, they moved inside. Realizing the measurements would go on for a while more, Koranen detoured into the section of the giant warehouse that contained the bags of sand they had dredged up out of the bottom of the sea and stored for their casual

glazing needs. Hefting one of the bags over his shoulder, Koranen
moved himself to a spot where he was out of the paths of the workers, away from anyone who might accidentally stumble into him, yet
still within view of the four women, and settled the bag at his feet,
untying the neck so that he had access to its contents. Then he
twisted off the cryslet slung around one wrist and tucked it into a
pouch at his belt to keep it safe.

When he had first learned to make glass, Kor and the other apprentices had learned to add powdered limestone and potash made
from trees and sea plants, just to make the glass easier to melt. An
advanced technique used the white, rust-like powder that could be
obtained from lead, along with a little limestone; it made the glass
more expensive to create, but it produced a beautiful, crystalline
glass with a lower melting temperature. The purest glass, however,
was simply the result of melting high-grade sand at extremely high
temperatures.

Now that his magics had fully matured, Koranen didn't have to
rely on additives to lower the melting temperature of the sand.
Instead, he just scooped up a double handful of the plainer silica
stored in the bag and went to work. Slow, deep breaths in and out
helped him to focus his magic. With it came heat, and plenty of it.
It was usually easier for most mages to turn their magic into heat,
though it was often a struggle for them to change heat into magic.
But just releasing a lot of heat didn't make a Pyromancer. Control of
heat did, including keeping things cold.

Koranen was so used to working bare-handed like this, he didn't
even have to mutter any mnemonic words. A thought was all it took
to set up a ward between his forearms and the rest of the warehouse.
The ward didn't just create a translucent, silvery-misted bubble around
his hands to keep others from overheating if they came near. It also
focused that heat, reflecting it back into his hands and the sand they
cupped, reducing how much of his own inner energies he had to
spend to melt the material. The bubble-ward was his own invention,
and it was responsible for his ability to melt pure sand so readily.

In fact, it didn't take long for the clump of sand to finish bubbling and slumping into a glowing, orange yellow goo, maybe a slow count to one hundred. Carefully scooping it all into one hand, Koranen dampened the temperature, pulling enough of the heat back into his body that the melted mass solidified and turned a dull reddish orange. Shaking out his free hand, making sure it was cool enough to touch other things, he picked up the bag and moved to the next section of the warehouse, following the Aquamancers as they shifted around the inner perimeter of the building.

Making glass flat enough for windowpanes would be difficult without a high-polished stone table to spread the melted goo against, but he could easily make hand-shaped objects as he moved around, following the Menomonites—in fact, blowing shapes in molten glass was as easy as blowing bubbles in diluted softsoap. Even if there weren't an export value in blown glass goblets, bowls, and flasks, there *were* more than three thousand people now living on Nightfall, and someone would need a bottle or a pitcher.

Frankly, if the energetic young mage *didn't* have something to do as he followed the quartet around—something productive and useful—Koranen knew he'd start to resent the demands their presence were making on his time. Even Kor, inexperienced as he was, didn't think it would be a good idea to alienate a potential future bride out of sheer boredom.

FIVE

He was doing it again. The orange yellow glow of molten glass wasn't exactly distracting, but she could see it out of the corner of her eyes as she worked, and it kept drawing her attention to his hands. Flexing and twisting, molding and shaping, they pried and pulled, pinched and plucked. He lifted the glass to his lips, blowing another bubble as though the scorching-hot material was no more dangerous than saltwater candy. The golden glow altered the color of his lilac shirt, bringing it oddly closer to the rich red brown of his hair.

The rods in her hands nudged and shifted in their balancing cups, indicating another potential ley line of energies. Annoyed at herself for sponge gathering instead of paying attention, Danau returned her focus to her dowsing work. This was the fifth building they had entered, the second half of the second pair of processing plants, which housed a freshwater tank. It should have been filled to capacity, yet was as dry as a desert, just as its companion saltwater tank had been.

Of course, they knew part of why some of the sluices in the functional freshwater building didn't work; those sets of lattice halls connected to one of the dry saltwater tanks. From what the Nightfallites had said—or Nightfallers, as they called themselves—filling that holding tank had only produced salt water, tainting their fresh supply. Of course, the eight brothers confessed they had only tried that once a few years ago, and they didn't dare try the trick now just to discern the underlying cause, not with so many people dependent on a scarcely adequate water supply. But that was alright; if they could fix two of the nonfunctional tanks, they could fix all of the nonfunctional parts.

Unlike in the two buildings that did work, the dowsing signals in this one weren't strong. The first of the row of crystals studding the top of each rod barely lit, indicating a channel that had been built for the purpose of conducting magic, but which—like the tanks—was empty. By carefully crisscrossing the area, Danau was able to dowse its direction, calling out the coordinates to Chana as she moved. Not unexpectedly, some of these ley lines dipped down the ramps that the salt blocks emerged along. They had dipped down into the sluices for the latticeways in the other freshwater building, after all. The two paths connected to the sluiceways via the lattice halls, tunnels filled with networks of rune-carved pipes that formed the straining system—salt to the left, algae to the right, water up the middle, that sort of thing.

In the functioning pair of buildings, Danau had made the choice of directing her fellow Aquamancers only to observe things passively and to avoid probing directly with their magics. The system was complex enough; she wasn't entirely sure what might cause it to stop functioning at this point. It was also showing some signs of age and wear, though as a Permanent Magic, it had been enspelled for a certain amount of self-repair.

Reuen had supported her quickly enough, pointing out that if they probed one of the nonfunctional buildings and broke something in doing so, it wouldn't stop production of drinking water for the locals. They would also still have two more buildings to examine and compare against both the damaged and the functional ones if they did break something. It was just as well. Based on a rough triangulation of the other ley lines dowsed so far, magic wasn't just supposed to flow from tank to tank between the lattice halls; it also flowed inward, toward the warehouse.

Which doesn't make sense . . . unless . . . unless it flows outward?

Danau stopped in her tracks, thinking things through. *These tanks are deep, four floors deep. There would have to be thick bulwarks to support the water pressure . . . and the distance between the ring of outer buildings supports that fact, even pierced as they are by four sets of tunnels to a side . . . but that's still a lot of water to process. A lot of water processing takes a lot of energy. What was the power source for this place?*

"Danau!"

The sharp call snapped her out of her thoughts. It came from Ama-ti. Normally the blue-haired young woman was soft-spoken, but there was a trace of emotion in her voice, one that lay somewhere between annoyance and bemusement. It took Danau and the others a few moments to find her, for the blue-haired Aquamancer was standing in the holding tank—standing in one of the sluiceways, in fact.

She had traded measuring the physical aspects of the buildings— once this set had proven identical to the previous pair—for tracing the water flow, using a slightly different set of dowsing rods than the ones Danau wielded. But those rods weren't in view at the moment. Her short hair was visibly damp, darker than usual, and plastered to her head, as were her manta-ray leathers. Her satchel was still dry, but then most Menomonite bags were enchanted to remain that way.

Danau frowned as she peered over the tank railing. There was no water down there, and yet the younger woman was plainly wet, though at least she wasn't dripping anymore. Come to think of it, she hadn't seen Ama-ti for a while. The sight of a glowing wisp of light bobbing over Ama-ti's shoulder confirmed that the younger woman had gone spelunking without telling anyone.

"I know you didn't want us to disturb anything physically, but I went into the dry tunnels, expecting to either be blocked by the filtration system, or at least end up in the empty pool in the other building . . . but I stumbled into a side tunnel and wound up in the functional one instead. So I traced the sluiceways," Ama-ti called up to her. "They *all* interconnect. Each saltwater pool connects to one of the four freshwater pools, and vice versa. There are even sets of latticeworks in the tunnels waiting to be used. The only thing they don't do is connect salt water to salt water, and so forth."

Chana shifted her greaseboard out of her way. "I walked those dry tunnels myself! I didn't see any side tunnels. There weren't *any* openings at all!"

"They're not *open* tunnels—it's some sort of membrane-barrier," Ama-ti explained, gesturing behind her. "It's like the water-walls in Menomon, only they're opaque. I stopped to rest against the wall before heading farther into the tunnel . . . and I realized after a moment that my elbow had sunk *into* the wall. It took a lot of effort, and I doubt I could have made it if I weren't a Rank 8, but there *are* side tunnels . . . and they *do* process water. Or they *could*.

"I'm not completely sure, because I've never encountered one this stiff before, but I think this is a variation of our hydrostatic barriers—it *should* be flexible enough to pass through, either by water or by an Aquamancer's aura, but this one could have stiffened with . . . I don't know," Ama-ti offered, shrugging helplessly. "With . . . disuse, dryness, and old age, maybe. Or it could simply require a higher-ranked Aquamancer to pass through it—which could be why *you* didn't sense it, Chana. You're a Rank 6."

"So, you want me to come down there and survey it for myself, since I'm a Rank 10?" Danau inferred.

"Well, you have repaired most of the water-walls in the City in the last few years," the blue-haired woman pointed out. "If any of us would recognize a hydrostatic variant, it would be you. There's one more thing—the tunnel I 'fell' into, it's filled with water . . . but it's salt water, from beginning to end. The latticeworks *should* be drawing off the algae and the sodium so that the near end, the one closest to here, is freshwater . . . but it's not doing its job."

"Why would they run channels to the other processors?" Chana asked, frowning. "Never mind ones that don't work."

"Repairs." The succinct interjection came from Koranen. He had finished shaping small pitcher-flasks and was now working on what looked like a glass flower. "That's what I'd do, if I were the person building this place. I'd want to be able to shunt water out of a particular tank for cleaning, or divert it from the lattice halls for repairs, or shift water around for whatever purpose, but I wouldn't want to stop all production."

"Well . . . that *could* explain why, with just one sluice open, it's not operating at its fullest capacity," Chana offered, checking the notes on her greaseboard. "Fullest capacity would probably include additional water coming in from secondary tanks."

"But that doesn't explain the salinity of the water at the near end of the tunnel, never mind why it isn't pouring water—fresh or salty—into the basin here," Reuen reminded him.

"Maybe the desalination spells just ran out of energy?" the Pyromancer offered, shrugging. "It happens all the time on our heating taps for our sinks. Particularly if they're left running, like when someone forgets to cork the faucet when they're through washing their hands," he added matter-of-factly.

His hands finished pinching the flower into shape, some sort of rose-like creation, petals curled back in full, glassy bloom. A mutter of magic, and he tossed it over the edge of the tank, where it spiraled slowly toward Ama-ti, gleaming under the light pouring down from the clerestory windows ringing the tiered rings of the dome roof over their heads. For a moment, Danau enjoyed the falling, artificial flower . . . then envied its creation, because it wasn't meant for her.

"Here—a present for you, for finding something new about this place that my brothers and I hadn't known."

Even viewed from a quarter of the way around the huge, round tank, Ama-ti's white teeth gleamed. She caught the glass flower in her cupped hands and aimed her smile at the redheaded man. "Thank you! It's beautiful."

"No more so than you. Than *all* of you," Lord Koranen clarified, shifting his gaze to the three women up by him.

His hazel eyes met Danau's last. For a moment, she fancied that he had saved the best view for last . . . but pragmatism set in. *He probably saved the least-liked for last. I haven't encouraged him, and I cannot encourage him. These Nightfallites . . . Nightfallers might not insist that I leave if I injured him accidentally, but I just can't take that risk. Not until I know how to re-create this place, or at least have gained enough understanding to re-create some sort of variation on it.*

Shoving aside her feelings, Danau lifted the dowsing rods in her hands. "I'll come down there, and you can show me the first spot, but then you'll have to come up here and trace these ley lines in my place. If they're as linear as they appear to be, some of them seem to cross directly underneath the warehouse, and I want to know if that's because they merely follow these hidden lattice passages, or if it's something else, something different—and don't forget to take them down into the tunnels when you're through up here. I want every thumb length of this place dowsed. There's far too much processing going on to not have *some* sort of power source.

"I want that power source found. I want to know why it's not working and what it'll take to get it replicated as well as restored—you can play with your flower later," she added, unable to help herself. "Right now, we have work to do."

She didn't have to hear them say the word to know it was on Re-uen and Chana's minds, based on the brief, dark looks they aimed her way: *Udrezero. Well. Let them think it all they want. I am the best Aquamancer in the Guild, married or not, and we have a job to do.*

Tucking the dowsing rods into her satchel, Danau crossed to the ladder nearest Ama-ti's position. The wave-like rungs were mounted at four different spots around the tank and were in remarkably good repair for something several hundred years old. It occurred to her as she descended to the passage Ama-ti stood in that she couldn't see any outlet pipes. Pausing halfway down, she looked up.

"Chana? Make a note for us to look for hydrostatic barriers along the dry tank walls. There *should* be outlet pipes for transporting the desalinated water to various parts of the island, but I don't actually see any."

A small, petty part of herself took pleasure in the sound of Reuen smacking her forehead. Danau had never understood why Reuen disliked her so much, since the only thing Danau excelled at was being a more powerful Aquamancer. Her cousin had good looks; men flocking to court Reuen in the hopes of being one of her future husbands, and enough power and skill on her own to be a competent, praised Aquamancer. But it was still satisfying to hear the red-and-brown-haired woman castigating herself.

"Menos! I didn't even *notice* that. I'll start cross-checking the wet tank's pipe placements with the dry tank in just a moment, since I'm almost done with my measurements."

Get your mind back on the job, Danau, she ordered herself, swinging from the ladder to the recessed ledge Ama-ti occupied. The blue-haired Menomonite touched her briefly, making sure she didn't fall off the ledge.

"Thank you; I'm ready," she said as soon as she had caught her balance, allowing Ama-ti to withdraw her fingers. Danau usually kept her magic under control, but it was simply easier to make sure people didn't touch her for very long, in case she chilled their fingers accidentally. It was just one of those things that she had to do. "Now, show me where this membrane is . . ."

"Chana tells me you're avoiding her."

Koranen looked up from the glass fish he was shaping. Reuen had climbed back up the ladder at some point and now lounged against the wave-motif railing circling the empty tank. She had positioned her body in a way that showed off her slender but shapely curves and gave him a hint of a smile.

"I wouldn't say *avoiding* her, so much as giving the *rest* of you a chance as well. I don't know which one of you—if any—is Destined for me," Koranen said, shrugging. "The only way to find out is to give each of you a chance. Chana is . . . forward. I can admire a woman who knows her own mind. But then there's Ama-ti, who is charming and sweet. That can be a good quality in a woman, too. And of course, there's you."

"Me?" she asked, moving closer and lounging a little more coquettishly. Her fingers traced along the railing. It made Koranen wonder how they would feel against his skin.

"You seem . . . sophisticated," he chose his words carefully, seeking a way to define her prevalent qualities. "Intelligent."

"And here I thought I was pretty." She mock sighed, moving another step closer. There was a light in her blue eyes, and the way that they dipped to his lips made him think she wanted to kiss him.

Koranen quickly looked around the hall, but Chana and Ama-ti had both stepped outside, no doubt intending to visit the nearest of the refreshing rooms built into the corners of the octagonal warehouse. The petite Danau wasn't back yet from her tunnel explorations, which meant the two of them were alone together. Mindful of the still-hot glass in his hands, he cooled it with a thought, stepped back, and set the hand-shaped fish on the ground by the other glass objects he had made.

Shaking out his hands to dissipate any lingering heat, Koranen moved back in front of her. "I think you're very pretty. I'm not accustomed to such short hair on women, or in such unusual colors, but it does suit you somehow."

Reuen ran her fingers through her thumb-length locks, giving him a wry smile. "Short hair is practical when you have to dive through water-walls half a dozen times a day in the course of your work."

"Ah—because the water would tangle it around you," Koranen realized, comprehending the problem. "But why not just put it in a braid? That's what I do when I have a lot of work in the forge and I don't want my hair in my way."

Reuen reached up toward his long, auburn strands, then hesitated before actually touching them. She lowered her hand. "That's because you work in a dry environment. Going into and out of water all day long . . . Well, if you don't wash and dry your hair every single time, if it's long, it'll *stay* wet. And if it stays wet, then it'll molder. Literally."

That thought made him wrinkle his nose. "I've never had that problem myself, but then I usually dry myself with a thought, even if my hair is in a braid. I can concede your point, though. Short hair would be more practical than long if you work in water every day."

The Menomonite woman smiled up at him. "Almost everyone in Menomon has short hair, so I find your long hair to be rather . . . exotic. I like it. In fact, I want to run my fingers through it. May I?"

Koranen nodded quickly, not about to deny her request. He liked the thought of being touched, but more than that, he liked that she *asked* before touching him, where Chana had simply grabbed. *Maybe this is the one*, he thought, shivering a little at the prickling sensation caused by Reuen's nails lightly stroking through his auburn strands. *Gods, Trevan was right: Having your hair stroked and combed is quite sensual—maybe she'd like it, too?*

There was only one way to find out. Lifting his own hands, Koranen lightly raked his fingertips through her dye-striped locks. She hummed and narrowed her eyes in pleasure, the corners of her mouth curving upward. That reminded him of his earlier thought that she might want to be kissed. Shifting his hands to gently cup her head, Koranen tipped her face up to his.

She met his mouth willingly, sighing and leaning into him. Here he was, kissing the second woman in as many days, and she tasted just as great as the first, though there were no hints of dessert on her lips. The midafternoon meal had been ages ago, supper wasn't quite ready, and so the only thing she tasted of was herself. It certainly didn't take either of them long before they were literally tasting, lips pressing and parting, tongues touching and sliding.

Feeling her fingers sliding across his scalp, tugging on strands of his hair, Koranen deepened the kiss. Her soft moans encouraged him. Gathering her closer, he slid his arms down her back, pressing their bodies together. Soft, supple leather, resilient curves, warm with a floral-musky scent that spoke of softsoap and woman . . . Kor felt himself beginning to heat up and knew he should scale things back, to take this moment slowly, but she just felt too good in his arms.

Their mouths met and parted, met again . . . Then she pulled back, making him open his eyes in time to catch her wincing. His arms relaxed reflexively, letting her pull back. Just as he feared, she fanned herself as she spoke. "You feel rather . . . *hot*."

Dammit!

Biting back his frustration, Koranen released her completely, stepping back to put insulating space between their bodies. "Sorry. We'd probably better not do that again."

Reuen stared at him for a moment, her expression uncomprehending. Then understanding dawned in her blue eyes, widening them. "*Oh* . . . You *literally* get hot for a woman, don't you? That's why you think you need to court an Aquamancer, to be the water that douses your fire!"

Blushing, Koranen nodded. Self-consciously, he raked his fingers through his hair, neatening it. "Chana said I felt hot last night while she was kissing me. And now you felt it, too. I don't think either of you will be the right bride for me. Which means it might be one of the remaining two . . . or it might not be any of you. Nothing's guaranteed, but I do have to try. I just don't want to hurt anyone while doing so."

Her look of comprehension, even sympathy, turned shrewd in the next moment. Almost sly. "Actually, I think I might know of the perfect woman for you . . ."

Bemused, Koranen arched a brow in silent query.

Reuen smirked and trailed one of her fingers down his chest, then pushed him back a little. "You just relax, and let me take care of everything. And *go slow*. She's rather shy, and doesn't like being rushed in a relationship. Take the time to get to know her and fall in love with her before you bed her. But I've known her pretty much all my life, and I think she'd be *perfect* for you."

"Perfect," Koranen repeated, torn between doubt and hope. "Which one is she?"

"Why, Ama-ti, of course!" Reuen offered with a soft laugh. "You don't think a woman—sorry, a *person* as sexless as Danau the Great would be excited by anything other than her work, do you? That's all she lives for, and all she cares about. *You* need a woman with at least *some* passion in her veins, not to mention all that sweetness you've already seen." Patting his chest, she gave him a warm smile. "Let me take care of everything. You just plan on courting Ama-ti. Nice and slowly, *don't* rush anything, and definitely don't hurry to kiss her. She's a bit shy about that sort of thing—she wants to make sure it's true love before she'll swim into a man's bed."

"I hope you're right," Koranen muttered, hope overtaking his doubt. "I've been looking forward to meeting the right woman for me for a very long time, and I plan on making her very happy when I do."

Chuckling, Reuen patted him on his chest one last time, then moved away. "I think I'll go visit the ladies' refreshing room, and see if I can have a private chat with Ama-ti about possibly dating you. Maybe you should see if there's a restaurant in this brand-new city of yours worthy of an intimate dinner for two," she added over her shoulder. "I know for a fact that Ama-ti *loves* land-food—that's what we call anything that's not fish or shellfish, in Menomon."

Nodding, Koranen immediately wracked his mind for such a place. There were only a few restaurants that had opened down in the city, no more than half a dozen at most—if that—where one could sit down, though he'd seen at least a dozen brazier carts doing a brisk trade at the edges of several construction areas. Unfortunately, he couldn't guarantee the quality of any of them, not even the carts. Not when he and his family continued to fix and eat their meals at the palace.

Pleased at having Reuen's help, he grabbed another handful of sand and focused his emotions into magical heat, melting the granules quickly. *Maybe I should make her another glass flower, since she seemed to like the first one. An orchid, this time . . .*

Lagging behind the others as they returned to their quarters before supper, Danau discovered unpleasantly that a small bit of rock had somehow managed to find its way inside her boot. It required pausing next to the second-level balcony of the large chamber at the heart of the palace, so that she could brace her hip on the edge of the stairwell entrance and unlace her shoe. It made no sense to get a rock in her shoe when she was indoors, but she supposed she had picked it up outside. From there, it had no doubt worked its way painlessly down to the edge of her foot, where it finally proved an annoyance big enough to notice.

And there it is, a tiny speck blown out of all proportion. Particularly when comparing its annoyance factor to its size, she thought wryly as a broken bit of pebble no bigger than the dot made by a quill pen fell from her boot. She couldn't even hear the noise it made as it bounced on the granite tiles lining the balcony floor, it was that small.

In the next moment, her straining ears twitched, hearing words coming from one of the levels above, accompanied by approaching, echoing footsteps.

"Haven't you told him yet?"

"No. I haven't."

The second voice she recognized as belonging to the incipient queen of this place. The first, as the man spoke again, Danau guessed to be Queen Kelly's husband. They were speaking in hushed but emotionally charged tones, but the acoustics of the chamber allowed Danau to overhear.

"Kelly, you *have* to tell him. If we're going to have any chance . . ."

"How do I tell him *that*? That he has to do *that* to her? Frankly, I don't think he's going to take it very well, and I'd really rather not see him in a towering rage—can you honestly tell me that he *wouldn't* get upset?"

"Then tell *her*," Saber argued back, their voices shifting as they moved around the upper curve of the donjon. From the way the voices cleared up, but lost volume, they were moving away from her. "It's *her* life on the line, not his."

Ah. That's what they're talking about, Danau realized. *The Scroll of Living Glory. So the sister* did *survive, and is carrying around a Fountain inside of her. And—like her sister—she apparently married someone on the island. Probably yet another of these ruling-family brothers, since there are eight of them, and they're speaking of this fellow with familiarity . . .*

"I don't even know if *she'd* take it well," Kelly pointed out dryly. "I don't know if *I'd* take it all that well, though from what that priestess was telling me, it sounds like it might actually work."

"They have to be told. *Both* of them. That woman Zella may have sailed to the mainland, but she's not the only one who would come looking for trouble. The sooner they know, the sooner they'll realize it has to be done. I don't *like* it, but it has to be done. And since you're the one that wants the Convocation, you're the one that'll have to face them both as *you* explain it."

"Saber . . ."

"*Do* it," the unseen male ordered. "No more arguing or stalling. And you'll do it tonight."

"Yes, dear."

That *was interesting*, Danau thought as their footsteps faded. It was an intriguing glimpse into the dynamics of Nightfall politics. *Queen Kelly comes across as a confident, in-charge type of woman, the kind who makes up her own mind . . . but it seems her husband can definitely dictate a few things to her. If I ever have to coax these people into doing something in Menomon's favor, I'll have to make sure to convince him as well as her.*

Tugging her shoe back onto her foot, she tightened the laces around her ankle, knotted them in place, and headed up the eastern corridor. The others had disappeared up the hall while she had fiddled with her foot, and they hadn't heard the cryptic conversation. But as she strode into the southern half of the two eastern wings, she heard Chana and Reuen laughing. Danau tried not to listen, but the sound of her own name being spoken made her slow and pause at the doorway of her cousin's suite.

"And Danau doesn't even know?" Chana asked, laughter palpable in her tone despite the closed door between her and her eavesdropper.

"*Ama-ti* doesn't know," Reuen answered. "I just have to make her an amulet to ensure she safely ensnares *all* of his attention—a good-luck charm, as it were. I do want them to have a happy life together, after all."

Chana snorted with laughter, though Danau couldn't see why that comment was so funny. *They must be talking about Ama-ti and the Lord Secretary, and the matchmaking thing.* She frowned in thought, quietly opening the door to her suite. *I thought he was courting Chana. Or that she was courting him, one of the two. I guess not. Figures—she's the kind to just grab the nearest good-looking man for sex, and he* is *handsome. She didn't sound brokenhearted about him dating Ama-ti, though . . .*

Pity, she snorted silently. *Chana deserves a broken heart—they claim that I'm cold, but those two are colder still. It actually makes me glad I'm not trying to pursue a man. I, at least, know better than to subject him to physical cruelty. Those two make emotional cruelty an art form . . . and they revel in it. If they weren't such good Guild members, I'd have objected to their presence on this team.*

Turning her attention back to their conversation, Danau discovered the thought of Ama-ti entering into a relationship with their auburn-haired host made her uncomfortable. She was honestly happy for Ama-ti, who was one of the few Menomonites who went out of her way to avoid mentioning Danau's unfortunate social problem. They weren't close friends—Danau didn't have any close friends, though the blue-haired Aquamancer and the Guardian of Menomon came closer than most—but at least Ama-ti was friendly and open-minded. The younger woman deserved happiness in her life, for her kindness. If that meant netting good husbands, Danau would be happy for her.

But . . . the redheaded foreigner was quite the catch. Pyromancers and Aeromancers were very rare in underwater cities like Menomon; he would be honored by most of her people if he came back with Ama-ti to live in Menomon. Plus he was handsome, intelligent, talented, charming—even his occasional blushes over Chana's and Reuen's occasional bold comments only made him all the more interesting.

Distracting, rather, Danau reminded herself firmly. *You don't let distractions interfere with your job. You need to find more of those thickened membranes. They were certainly easier for me to pass through than for Ama-ti, though* easier *isn't the same as* easy, she admitted to herself, ducking into the refreshing room to use the facilities. *I think they did "dry out," causing them to solidify. They're not exactly like our water-walls back home, but they* are *a variation of the hydrostatic barrier principle.*

The question is, are there other such barriers elsewhere around the complex? I still can't figure out how all those lattices were empowered, after all. There has to be some sort of empowerment Artifact. One central unit, or four units, or even thirty-two of them, one for each of the lattice halls. A lot of those runes on the lattice filters looked like they included self-repair spells. The system should have repaired itself, if damaged . . . but it hasn't. Which *strongly suggests the power to enable those repairs is missing.*

I need to talk to that baroness they spoke of, Teretha, about the network of pipes that drained the process water to houses and fields. I should also look through any local historical records for this place—there may have been some sort of disaster that broke the pipes, draining the Desalinator. I do know it stopped working when Aiar Shattered and the local Portal nearly destroyed the island. Did the destruction of the Portal cause a physical explosion, a magical one, some combination of the two? If I can learn exactly what happened, that could help quite a lot.

I'll send the others out into the field after talking to this Teretha woman. They can survey and map the old and new pipe systems while I swim through whatever old records might exist. That would get her away from the Lord Secretary and her colleagues. It usually worked best if she avoided seeing romantic interactions, so that there was less chance for her to feel sour with envy, or worse, despair.

"Finding the pipes isn't going to be a problem," Baroness Teretha informed the four Aquamancers and their Pyromancer escort. "Finding how they originally *lay* in the ground—that might be a problem. The forest out there is a real tangle. We pull up shards of old pottery pipes all the time, usually when we're clearing a field and we dig a stump out of the ground—the uprooted trees leave gaping holes that we have to backfill with dirt extracted from the roots, so we have to filter out the shards of pottery when we do so. Most of it was buried below plowing depth by at least a couple feet, but some of those trees have dug down deep."

"Were they water pipes or sewage pipes? Could you tell?" Ama-ti asked, looking up from the maps spread out on one of the flat tables in the map room of the palace.

The baroness had come up to the palace to make her report over supper, giving the Menomonites the perfect opportunity to quiz her on the old network of pipes across the island. Koranen had yet to find an opportunity to speak privately with the blue-haired Aquamancer, since they had finished their survey of the desalination buildings just before supper and had come down here immediately afterward. He supposed he could wait until the next day, but the thought of her maybe being the right woman for him was too exciting to dismiss.

Cultivating as much patience as he could stand, he listened to the others discussing yet more of the technical aspects of Aquamancy. Not that it wasn't interesting, but it wasn't forge-work, so it wasn't his area of expertise. Without that expertise, he had few opinions to offer, which meant he was stuck listening to their conversations, rather than participating.

"Water. They're too small for sewage," the baroness dismissed. "These are more like irrigation pipes and some larger conduits that fed the hamlets and farmsteads. We do know where some of the main trunk lines run—they're large, stone-carved pipes, big enough for a man to walk through, but you'd be able to tell from the look and the smell if they ever ran sewage, even after two hundred years."

"Back home in Corvis County, we always sunk the sewage system as deep as we feasibly could, at least five or six body lengths," Saber offered. "That way, if there was a break in both the drinking and sewage pipelines, it wouldn't taint the drinking water. We've always done it that way in Katan. Since this was a Katani duchy, I wouldn't think the sewage lines are that different, which means they won't be that close to the surface."

"I wouldn't think *any* sensible, workable system would have been built so that there was a risk of wastewater mixing with the drinking water," Chana said wryly. "But they still should be found and checked. As a lower priority, of course."

"We can just dowse for the main pipes, since those are the important ones," Reuen offered. "All the extraneous outlets from the main pipes will have to be tracked and sealed until needed, of course, but first we have to find the main conduits. Smaller side pipes can be rebuilt and reopened as needed, but if we can get the Desalinator functioning, we don't need to turn the island into a swamp caused by a lot of water leaking into areas where the pipes are no longer intact."

"While you're doing fieldwork tomorrow, I'm going to dive through whatever old records can be found. Not just the origins of the Desalinator," Danau said, "but what happened when the system failed, back during the Shattering. My instincts are telling me there is a power source to this thing that is no longer functional. Otherwise the system *should* be able to repair itself and function properly when you run seawater through the dry lattices."

"I'll leave a note for our historian to find as many relevant texts as she can in the palace library for you," Saber offered. "And Morganen can whip up a batch of Ultra Tongue for you to drink in the morning, so you can read whatever you find. A lot of it is in old Katani, which might be difficult to read otherwise."

"Good. I'm used to doing research, so I should be able to assist your historian with the searching tomorrow, once I can read the language."

"She actually prefers working at night, when it's quiet and she doesn't have to socialize," Saber temporized. "But she's good at digging up information, and you should have everything you need by morning, so it won't slow down your research efforts."

"So long as I have access to enough records to puzzle out what may have happened, I'll be happy," Danau returned. "Please thank her for her work on our behalf."

"I'll pass that along."

Finally—it looks like they're breaking up for the evening! Koranen turned to the blue-haired woman at his side, seizing the opportunity to speak with her, even though they had an audience. "So, um . . . Ama-ti . . . I noticed a new restaurant in the southern part of the city the other—"

BOOM!

The flare of light accompanying that crack of thunder—glaring through and rattling the panes of the high, narrow windows at the top of the map room walls—was so bright, it blinded and deafened Koranen. Before he could recover, lightning flared again, rattling his bones from the concussive fury outside.

On what should have been a clear summer night.

Blinking madly, Koranen looked at his eldest brother and said—or mouthed, he couldn't even hear himself—a single name. *"Rydan!"*

Saber, his face paler than the third and fourth flashes could account for, mouthed a different name, his gray eyes wide with fear. "*Kelly!*"

Both men abandoned the map room at a scrambling sprint, and both men took the fastest, nearest door out of the west wing, scrambling for the northernmost tower along the outer wall. Koranen could feel his skin prickling with charged energy, half static, half magic—he could see Saber's golden hair fluffing up and out, as it flapped from the wind the magesmith created as he ran.

Abruptly, while they were still several yards from the nearest staircase to the ramparts . . . the lightning *stopped*. Only the dying echo of thunder remained as it rolled away from them. Koranen nearly stumbled from the shock of it, while Saber put on a burst of speed, leaping the steps four and five at a time as soon as he reached them. He slipped and banged his knees near the top, cursing loudly, but still scrambled forward.

Catching up to his eldest brother, Koranen helped haul him upright and pushed him ahead, along the ramparts to the door into Rydan's tower. They burst into the gong room, so named for the summoning gong that hung in a black-lacquered stand in the center of the otherwise sparsely appointed room. It wasn't the only thing occupying the chamber at the moment; Saber immediately aimed for his wife, who was on her feet and apparently unharmed, though the freckled hand raking through her strawberry blond hair trembled visibly.

Koranen swept the rest of the room with his gaze. He spotted his sixthborn brother sprawled across the floor near the outer wall, apparently unconscious, given the unmoving, untidy sprawl of his black-clad limbs. But not dead, thankfully. Rydan's wife, Rora, crouched next to him, patting his cheek in an effort to rouse the black-haired mage. Confused, Kor returned his gaze to Kelly, who was shakily reassuring her husband that she was all right, patting Saber's arm with her free hand.

It took the seventhborn brother a moment to realize what was in her other hand. A mirror. In specific, a familiar mirror, one of the two remaining mirrors they had forge-cast to reflect back the magics of one of their previous enemies almost a year ago. It had been intended to fling the death-magics of Broger of Devries back into the madman's face, but apparently Kelly had used it just now to defend herself from her brother-in-law's rage.

The lingering, deafening effects of the abrupt thunderstorm faded, allowing Koranen's hearing to clear, which meant he caught Kelly's explanation midsentence.

". . . he'd react badly, and since I've been carrying around one of these spare spell-reflector mirrors ever since they were made, I made sure it was already in my hand, just to be on the safe side—and no, you're *not* allowed to kill him. It was an *accident*. At least, I'm sure that under more normal circumstances, Rydan wouldn't be trying to kill me," she added in a voice somewhere between unsteady and resolute. "But he didn't fling the lightning at me; it just happened. And I cannot and *will not* blame him for getting upset! I'm also not going to allow you to hurt him just for doing what *you* would have done—for what you *did*, in a way."

"What *I* did?" Saber demanded. "What do you mean, what *I* did?"

"Did you, or did you not, kill Alys' cousin in a fit of protective fury when the Council of Mages came to this island?" Kelly challenged her husband.

Deciding the two of them were capable of working out their argument on their own, Koranen crossed to his other brother and sister-in-law. Rydan groaned, muscles flexing—then his eyes popped open, and he struggled to sit up, worry etched on his pale face and despair in his voice. "—Kelly!"

"She's all right," Rora quickly soothed him. "She's perfectly fine. Are *you* all right?"

He looked up at his wife, with her light brown hair and green eyes, clad in gray clothes cut in a similar fashion to Kelly's—and lunged up at her, wrapping his arms tightly around her. She *oof*ed at the pressure of his grab, but otherwise didn't protest. Instead, she stroked his black hair, holding him and murmuring soothing sounds into his ear. Comforting him as he spasmed and shook in her arms, muttering what sounded like *No, never, no* under his breath.

Rydan was *crying*. Koranen felt a bit awkward, faced with such an intimate, emotional embrace. Meeting his gaze, Rora jerked her head slightly, silently, toward the rampart door still standing open from their abrupt arrival. Catching the hint, Koranen rose and crossed to the other couple. Saber was holding Kelly, comforting her and drawing comfort from her. Kor suppressed his envy over both couples; instead, he silently shooed his eldest brother and his first sister-in-law out of the tower with just a few gestures. Saber resisted for a moment, then guided Kelly out of the tower.

They got as far as the bottom of the steps, then Kelly muttered something too shaky to be discerned, and crumpled onto the bottom two steps. Saber quickly sat beside her, pulling her close and holding her again as she trembled in what had to be an aftershock reaction. Koranen had to leap over the railing and drop a body length to the ground, since they covered the bottom two steps, but it wasn't that far.

It was, however, necessary. The middle-aged baroness, the younger Aquamancers, and a couple of curious servants had managed to follow them as far as the flagstone-paved edge of the northern courtyard. More people could be seen approaching through the evening gloom, though there weren't many in the palace complex to be summoned by the unexpected sound-and-light display.

With their incipient queen having an adrenaline reaction and her consort husband comforting her, it was up to Koranen to diffuse the understandable curiosity of the others. Donning his most affable smile, he spread his hands and subtly herded the others back from the bottom of the steps. "Nothing to worry about, ladies, gentlemen, just a magical accident—ah, good, Lady Mariel, you're here. If you'd check on Queen Kelly, then go up and check on Lord Rydan, it would be appreciated. I don't think either of them really

needs a Healer, but it's always better to be cautious than caught un-
awares."

"But, what happened?" Baroness Teretha asked.

"It was just an accidental buildup of magical energy—my brother
Lord Rydan is renowned as the 'Storm' for his ability to draw upon
the power of lightning and convert it to magic," Koranen explained
smoothly, as much for the wide-eyed servants as for the baroness,
who was a minor mage herself. "He probably just had one of those
moments where his control slipped while doing so—I myself have
occasionally sneezed and found myself setting things on fire entirely by accident. It doesn't happen often, and usually a mage isn't
so powerful that it's a bad thing, but at our level of magic, the effects can be a little more intense. Especially if it's unexpected."

Behind him, he could hear the plump, curly-haired Healer hum-
ming one of her bruise-mending tunes, and knew she was attending
to Saber's step-mangled legs. The magic-imbued tune was familiar
by now, thanks to the brothers' near-daily sword work practices.
Koranen cleared his throat and gestured for the others to return to
the nearest wing of the castle. He would have to ask Kelly what had
happened later, but for now, his curiosity would have to remain un-
satisfied.

"Since the excitement is over, we can now go back to what all of
us were doing, yes?"

SIX

❧

❦ot an obtuse woman, the former Natallian baroness quickly
took over, offering the four Aquamancers around her a
chance to look over the expansion plans she had charted, to show
which water-pipe systems should be looked at first for priority in any
repair and restoration efforts. The servants wandered back to the
palace, leaving only Evanor. The slender, light-blond mage quickly
squeezed past Saber and Kelly, however, following his plump, petite
wife back up the rampart stairs.

Watching them go, Kor wondered how any couple, one so tall
and one so short, could manage to kiss each other comfortably, but
then recalled how Ev and Mariel did it. Usually the two managed by
finding the nearest step for her to mount, so that their heads were
closer to the same level. *Danau would need at least two steps, which
would make it hard for her and anyone courting her to get physically close.
Not that anyone would want to get close to her, as prickly as she is . . .*

That is not *nice of you, Kor,* he chided himself, realizing the direction his thoughts were headed. *Rydan was just as prickly in his own*

way—Gods, what would be the odds of her having the same problem he suffered, of being attacked magically by the emotions of everyone around her? Injured by things she has no control over . . .

The thought made him shudder and feel a lot more sympathetic toward her. *The others aren't exactly friendly to her—maybe if I'm friendly, if I show that I'm safe to be around, she'll thaw and relax a little? It worked with how Kelly was treating Rydan, before Rora told us all what his underlying problem really was . . .*

Behind him, Kelly was finally speaking again, explaining what happened. Explaining the first part, that was, which hadn't been easy to hear with so much nearby thunder still ringing in their ears the first time around. Koranen kept an eye on the courtyard to make sure the others were out of eavesdropping range, while doing so himself.

"I knew Rydan wouldn't like what the Scroll of Living Glory says has to be done to extract the Fountain from his wife. So I took the spell-reflecting mirror with me, just in case. Not that I thought he *would* use his powers deliberately, but I'd rather be cautious, you know? And he *was* upset. Rora was shocked beyond words, and *he* went into a towering, nearly wordless fury—"

"—And that's when he struck at you?" Saber growled.

"No! That's when the lightning struck all around the tower. *He* didn't strike at me . . . but he was like . . . like a big *Tesla coil* . . . It's a machine-thingy that deals with high-voltage electricity—a *mechanical* version of a lightning-generating spell. It's one of those things that, sometimes, if you get too close to it, it'll spark at *you* instead of its receiver coil," Kelly explained roughly. "He had these little streamers of electricity, miniature lightning, trickling out all over his body. I brought up the mirror out of reflex, because I didn't want to accidentally get struck.

"The irony of it is, I think *that's* what triggered the streamers to turn into an arc, maybe drawn by the magic in the mirror. Since that *is* what the mirror does, isn't it?" she reminded her husband. "It draws in magic, channels it inward, funneling it away from the wielder, and then flings it back outward again at its caster. And that's exactly what happened. Lightning sparked from him to the mirror in my hands, and then the mirror zapped him right off his feet.

"Frankly, I was more concerned that *I'd* accidentally harmed *him*, rather than the other way around. But he was still breathing, if knocked unconscious. Possibly from the fall more than the lightning, since I've seen him playing with lightning like Koranen, there, plays with fire."

Blushing, Koranen carefully kept his back to the couple seated on the stone steps. Back when they were younger, before Rydan had turned sullen and moody from his undiagnosed affliction, the two of them used to amuse themselves by dancing their primary affinity around their fingers, Rydan with miniature lightning, and Koranen with little flamelets. Saber had given them hell for it back in Corvis, when they had needed to hide Kor's pyromantic abilities and Rydan's affinities for electricity from the Council of Mages, two of the defining signs of the Song of the Sons of Destiny, the Curse of Eight. But they had eventually been uncovered.

After they had been sent into exile on Nightfall, the trick had fallen a little flat for a while, until Kelly and the other ladies had started entering their home and their lives. The children on the Isle, including Mariel's son, Mikor, found his little flame-finger trick fascinating, and it was a quick, cheap form of entertainment. It also didn't hurt to show them little bits of magic, or to explain the amount of discipline and study that had to go into learning how to control such things. Certainly it kept most people from being afraid of him, which had always been one of Koranen's chief concerns about his affinity for fire. But the first verse of the Song had contained a Curse, and once they knew the Corvis brothers looked like the subjects of it, the Empire had forced them into exile.

Kelly continued with a sigh. "Anyway . . . it was an accident. I'm sure he didn't mean it, and I'm utterly grateful that this mirror didn't explode like the last one did. Morg may have done a marvelous job of reattaching my finger, but I'm still leery of losing another. So, presuming Rydan wasn't badly injured, you're not allowed to thrash him.

"I left a copy of the scroll with them—Rora had it last," she added. "Rydan started freaking and sparking, so she grabbed it from him to read it for herself. When he wouldn't calm down, I brought up the mirror, and, well . . . bang! Once they've both calmed down, I'll just ask *her* to read through the ceremony and tell her what the Darkhanan priestess told me, about how she can help bring Rora back to life."

"—*Back to . . . ?*" Whirling to face them, Koranen choked back the words, hating the way his voice had broken. He was twenty-four years old, not fourteen, after all. Double-checking the courtyard to make sure it was empty, Kor hissed at Kelly. "Back to *life*?"

"Yes, well, you didn't get to read the Scroll, did you?" Kelly muttered glumly. She braced her elbows on her knees and her chin on her hands, leaning against her equally unhappy husband. Her gaze was focused more on the horizon than on Koranen, though she continued to answer his question. "That's the hitch in our little plans. The *only* way to extract the Fountain from a Living Host is for that host to die.

"There's no way around it. The Scroll says that Rora's powers will automatically defend her if mortally threatened by an outside force. And since *some* recorded accounts of Living Hosts mentioned their Fountains lashing out and protecting them from their attackers in some rather unpleasant ways, the only person who could safely kill the Living Host is the Guardian melded to their Fountain, which means *Rydan* has to be the one to kill Rora."

"No wonder he was so upset, he lost control of his magic," Koranen muttered, sympathetic. It wasn't difficult to imagine the kind of havoc he himself could wreak if something rendered him upset enough—they'd be lucky if a spell-reflecting mirror *could* protect any bystanders from a sudden blast of overwhelming heat. Shivering at the unpleasant thought, Koranen shook his head. "I know he wouldn't want to hurt you, but you're very lucky he *didn't* hurt you."

"He'd have cause, though I'm only the messenger bearing the bad news." Kelly sighed. "There's a set of spells, one that gently slows and stops the heart, and the other that can maybe revive the host as soon as the Fountain drifts free and is captured and placed in a special vessel prepared for it . . . but apparently the revival spell doesn't always work. Actually, it sounds like the magical equivalent of certain medical techniques in my world. Which don't always work, either, though they're fairly reliable these days. The priestess had a bit to say about that."

"And I'd like to Truth Stone her about it, before I'll believe it," Saber scoffed. "Even if it were true . . ."

"I *did* use one. She's telling the truth. It makes sense—as much as anything in this world makes sense—and it makes for the best chance of reviving Rora," Kelly argued, though her heart visibly wasn't in it. "I wish it wasn't necessary, but if we're to have any chance of keeping Katan from having every legal right to come here and try to wipe out the lot of us in a very ugly battle . . ."

Koranen jiggled his hand between them, recapturing Kelly's attention. "Since I was busy escorting the Menomonites around, care to explain to *me* what she told you?"

Kelly rubbed her forehead, nose wrinkling. "I don't know if I can, but I'll try. It was a long conversation . . . The priests of Darkhana, whom they call Witches for some strange reason, carry around these *souls* inside of them. They're usually the deceased spirits of former Witches, who when *they* were alive, had carried around spirit advisors of their own, and so forth back into the mists of time. Darkhana is like one of the oldest, most stable nations next to the Empire of Fortuna, apparently.

"Anyway, because of this connection to the dead, they have this ability to go into the Dark, which is supposed to be the transition zone for spirits as they leave Life and journey to the Afterlife, realm of the Gods. At least, according to her people's theology," Kelly amended.

"It's the same in Katan, and in all other lands," Saber corrected. "Life, Death, the Dark, and the Afterlife are all the same; your spirit takes the same journey as anyone else's, regardless of whom you each worship."

"I meant, their theology gives them the ability to enter the Dark without actually being dead themselves," Kelly corrected. "Or rather . . . the living half of the pair isn't dead, the one Ora called the Host. The Guide is the dead soul they're partnered with, if I remember right. Anyway, one of their priestly jobs is to gently shepherd lost souls through the Dark until they can find the Light of the Afterlife. Conversely, they can use those same soul-shepherding skills to *prevent* a spirit from heading into the Afterlife. If a death is a sudden shock, that spirit is going to snap away from the body like an arrow from a bow, and they may either go straight for the Afterlife, or go so far from their body into the Dark that they can't find their way back."

"So these Witches can prevent the spirit from 'snapping' too far away and keep the soul on hand for being tucked back into their body when it comes time to revive them," Koranen stated, figuring it out for himself.

"Yes, and she says they're very good at it. The Darkhanans, I mean. And that she in particular—and her Guide—have had plenty of practice in reviving people," Kelly agreed. "He catches the spirit, while she casts healing magics on the body to make it sound and whole and ready to be inhabited again. Or as Ora put it, it's no use stuffing a spirit back into its body if the person died from a gaping hole in their gut. They wouldn't have to cast a lot of restoration magics on Rora, but they could catch and hold her spirit close at hand, ready for the revival process."

"*If* it works," Saber countered skeptically. "Even if we could get Rydan to consider the merest possibility of it, I'd want to interrogate this woman under Truth Stone myself. I don't want the Council making war with us as much as anyone else doesn't—even more so, since you and I are at the top of their pending execution list—but

I'm not going to risk my sister-in-law's life on a stranger's mere say-so. Or—forgive me—on your word alone. I have to *see* the truth in pure white for my own eyes."

They sounded like they were going to start arguing again, though Kelly didn't look any happier about the situation than Saber did. Koranen held up his hands, recapturing their attention.

"I don't think I can help you with this one. I'll wish you luck, on the process being reasonably possible, on this priestess speaking the truth, on even so much as being able to talk to Rydan and Rora *calmly* about the subject . . . but I have my own problems to deal with. Since I can't really help you, I think I'd better go back to focusing on them."

Kelly perked up a little at that, giving him an interested, curious look. "Speaking of which, how *is* the Great Water Hunt going?"

"Two down, two to go, and the next one looks very promising, according to the last one. Reuen figured out I get rather exothermic when I'm excited," Koranen explained wryly. "She didn't *say* in so many words that Ama-ti should be able to handle me, but she did imply it. I'm not going to rush things for obvious reasons, but I am hoping to catch her and invite her out to dine at one of the, what, half a dozen restaurants down in the city?"

"Five. Three of them are in the inns," Kelly added. "Everything else is a pushcart operation, because it's very cheap to buy the supplies for a pushcart business, and extremely easy to get started. But it's also easy to get sloppy in how the food is cooked and handled. I have the Healers and their apprentices checking all the carts and each of the restaurants at different mealtimes to make sure their food-handling practices are safe—the costs of the meals are now a part of their retainer fees, provided they agree to do health inspections whenever they dine out, and the restaurant and brazier-cart owners get a tiny tax cut for feeding the Healers. So far, everyone is paying attention to the list of safety steps I had Rora spell-copy and distribute with the pushcart vendor permits . . . but there's still the danger of whether or not a particular recipe is edible."

"Can you at least recommend one of the restaurants?" Koranen asked her. "I'd like to take her to a place where we can focus on each other and not on the business of the kingdom . . . or have my family, wonderful though you all are, scrutinizing my every move as I try to court her."

That made Kelly chuckle. "Fine, fine . . . There's a restaurant on the south side of the city that's had good reviews from Healers and citizens alike. The Giggling Pear."

Kor gave her a dubious look. "The Giggling . . . Pear?"

"Apparently their youngest son named it, or something." Kelly shrugged. "It's very popular already, despite the odd name."

"Isn't that the one down by the shipyards?" Saber asked his wife, bemused. "I thought that one wasn't finished being built yet, though I've heard conflicting reports that they're also open for business."

"No, that's the Happy Flask; they've already built the brewery in the basement, since it takes time to ferment all the necessary beverages for a good seaside tavern, but they're still getting the rafters raised and readied for roofing," she explained. "Amara said they'll be ready for the tiles in two more days, so they'll probably be able to open in three or four more after that."

"The Giggling Pear it is," Koranen said before they could go off on yet another tangent. "I'm going to go catch up to the ladies and see if I can invite Ama-ti out to dinner tomorrow night."

"Don't forget, Evanor is having his first concert in the new performance hall in a few days," Saber reminded him. "I can't wait to hear him, but I also can't wait until it's over, so he can get back to work. He's been practicing with several of the musicians that moved here in the last few months, and they're finally ready to give a performance now that we have a hall for such things, but the demand for more of his music boxes is gaining strength on the mainland."

"Oh, yes, the concert! That'd be a lovely outing to take a lady to," Kelly agreed quickly, twisting and giving her husband a pointed look. *"Wouldn't it?"*

Giving his wife a wry look, Saber mock sighed and asked, "Would you like to go with me to a concert in a few days, my love? Considering you *have* to be there, to officially open it, and we've *already* planned to go?"

"Yes, but I'd love to go *with you*, and not just *go*." Leaning in close, Kelly nuzzled his nose with her own, then kissed him.

Koranen decided to leave before envy could overcome his amusement at such blatant manipulation.

"If she's gone to bed, then I'll just have to catch her in the morning, I guess. The rest of you are invited to a concert my brother Evanor and several other musicians have arranged to perform in two more days."

"Oh, don't bother asking Danau," Reuen said, a chuckle buried in her voice. "She's really not the best sort of person one could have at a social gathering."

Danau stopped before entering the map room. She had ducked out to visit the nearest refreshing room, not to go to bed. *And yet again, I am caught overhearing someone trashing my reputation.* It was made even more bitter by the fact that this wasn't Reuen saying these things in private to a fellow Menomonite. *If I didn't know yet whether or not I needed her, I'd tell her to swim back home. As it is . . . I'm going to have to discipline her.*

Stepping briskly into the room, Danau sought out her cousin and stalked straight toward her. Before she could do more than draw in a breath, *he* stepped between them. The Lord Secretary gave her a warm smile. "As you may have overheard, we're holding a musical performance in two days, and I personally would be delighted if you would agree to come."

I personally . . . I personally . . . Between the warmth in his smile and his hazel eyes and the sincerity in his voice, Danau had to stop and blink at that. He stepped to the side, turning to include the others, and that broke the daze his words had put her in.

"This will be our first real chance to celebrate anything as a community, and you'll have front-row seats, so I hope you brought your fanciest clothes. The hall is a marvel of construction. It seats two *thousand* people—a *very* ambitious project, but it was undertaken at the Queen's insistence. So there will be quite a lot of us celebrating the chance to hear the first formal performance," Koranen told them. "There will actually be two performances, but the first one is the most prestigious, obviously."

"Well, Danau, *did* you bring your fanciest clothes?" Chana asked, her tone just shy of being openly doubtful.

"I'll find something to wear," Danau replied as calmly as she could. What she *wanted* to add was, *When I peel it off your carcass and dye it a prettier shade*, but that would have been impolite. Chana's hidden barb stung. After Jiore's public denouncement of her potential as a wife, Danau had quickly learned she wasn't going to be invited out. She did have formal leathers stitched and beaded with her Guild rank and pinned down each arm with her commendation brooches, but that was for ceremonial moments, not a night at a performance hall. And it wasn't for mucking around in the innards of a malfunctioning piece of Permanent Magic . . . so she hadn't brought it. Her formal leathers were all the way back in Menomon.

I don't know where, or how . . . but I'll find something to wear—maybe someone in the city will have an outfit close to my size that they can finish quickly . . . Oh, who am I kidding? She was one of the smallest adults in Menomon, and it looked like these Nightfallers were just as tall as everyone else she'd ever seen. There was nothing physically wrong with her—magically, yes, but not physically—other than that she was simply shorter than most.

But I can at least look tomorrow morning before settling down to my research. After they've headed off to survey the pipe systems in the fields. Maybe Menos will smile upon me.

Danau woke with a gasp. Sweat frosted her skin, despite the weight of the covers piled over her small frame. Shivering, she curled up in a ball, huddling under the blankets, but she could still hear *his* voice. Could still feel *his* touch.

In her dream, Lord Koranen had approached her . . .

She was clad in her formal leathers, while he was clad in nothing but a couple scraps of white cloth and a glistening, slick sheen of non-frosted sweat. His eyes raked down her body, stripping away her outer clothes literally as well as figuratively, leaving her in her breast band and undershorts. But when she crossed her arms, embarrassed to be caught without her armor—for all that most Menomonites went swimming in their underthings, since it was far easier just to dry or change them than to dry or change an entire outfit—he caught her arms, pulled them away from her body, and stepped up against her. Only they were floating together, bodies brushing sensually against each other, as they drifted in the warm waters of the Sun's Belt Reefs.

Even now, in her bed, Danau shivered with pleasure, breasts and belly aching with the memory.

He came close to her, lips brushing her ear, and murmured, "I personally would like you to come . . . personally want you to come . . ."

There were two meanings for the word *come* in the Menomonite tongue. Danau whimpered. Her left forearm pressed over her breasts, trying to ease the ache in her nipples. Her other hand slid down between her thighs, cupping her mound. That felt good—achingly good—so she slipped her fingers between her nether-lips, which felt hot with need . . . but the moisture she encountered, though there was a lot of it, was bitterly cold.

It didn't hurt her fingertips physically—she could *feel* the cold, for all it didn't harm her—but it was a cruel reminder of *why* she couldn't do things like that. At least, not with handsome, redheaded surface dwellers. Or anyone else. Curling up into a tighter ball, Danau huddled under the bedding for warmth, ignoring the tears that dampened her pillow before freezing in crinkly hard streaks as soon as they left the shelter of her skin.

Ohhh, yes, that's good . . . Take that one off, too . . .

Sprawled on his back, surrounded by glowing coals, one forearm tossed over his head and the other curving over his hip, giving him just enough reach to tease his aching flesh as he watched the pretty Ama-ti peeling off the outer layers of her clothes. Having an affinity for fire meant having an affinity for light, and that in turn meant an affinity for casting illusions. She wasn't actually there; he was merely seeing a hazy projection of the Aquamancer standing over him, lit from below as if she really were straddling his knees where they draped over the edge of his forge.

It was an idealized projection, of course. No one but he could have stood on the rim of the forge and not been singed by the heat radiating from its coals, never mind the heat of his body. But his imagination was up to the task, for when she bent over, his flesh pulsed at the sight of nice, rounded breasts. They were probably a little bit bigger than the real things, of course, but this was his imagination, and he wasn't going to fetter it.

And now . . . the corset . . . yesss . . .

Licking his fingers, Koranen wrapped them around his shaft, switching from teasing to stroking as he imagined what Ama-ti would look like. Topless, feminine, beautiful . . . He gripped himself, rippling his fingers from near the bottom of his manhood to just beneath the head. Hips lifting a little off the somewhat lumpy cinders, he imagined her touching her breasts.

Yes, yesss! And now the undertrousers . . . !

They were Katani in style, since he didn't know any other kind, but as soon as she loosened the drawstring, they dropped down her

legs; flames roared up around him, obscuring the illusion for a moment in his excitement. Koranen didn't care; he stroked harder,
picturing her dropping to her knees over him, straddling his hips,
reaching for his shaft so that she could tuck it into that place all
his brothers swore was a warm, wet glimpse into the Afterlife on
earth . . . and yelped, flattening his erection against his stomach
under the abruptly protective grasp of his palm.

His illusionary Ama-ti had *blue* nether-curls. *Blue.* That was just
wrong!

Wincing, Koranen tried to rebuild the image of her naked body
again . . . but he couldn't get that one thought out of his head: *As
above, so below.* If her head-hair was blue, so would her nether-hair
be blue. And that was just too unnatural!

Frustrated, Koranen shifted the arm above his head to his eyes,
covering them. It was the easiest way to banish the unsettling illusion, though the thought of it still haunted him. *Gods . . . blue nether-
curls—ugh! Blond against dusky skin might not have been quite as bad, but
it's still no pairing of coloring you'd see on a Katani woman . . . and stripes
wouldn't be any better! The only one of the four of them who looks* natural
is Danau, only she's unnaturally uninviting.

*She knows she's supposed to be here for a possible matchmaking, yet she
acts like she follows the men-avoiding ways of those nuns over at Koral-tai.
We specified single women who were interested in men, so surely she* would
be interested in men. In theory, at any rate . . .

That thought amused him, it was such a wry thing to think. *In
theory. All of this is "in theory," at least until I can find my Destined
mate . . .* Body still aching with need, Koranen shrugged, both mentally and physically. *Well, if my loins want me to imagine a "natural"
Aquamancer . . . I guess I'll just have to imagine her. At least, until her
attitude turns me off.*

Let's see . . . first . . . a smile . . . It was a shy smile that his mind
conjured, but when he shifted his arm off his head and looked up,
there she hovered, floating from the waist up in the hazy waves of
heat radiating around him. Smiling shyly. *Alright . . . and then . . .*

naked shoulders . . . mm, yes . . . and those breasts—if she didn't have such handfuls, she'd look like a child, but those leathers don't leave much to the imagination, despite the way they cover her from neck to toe . . .

Mm, yes, nice breasts, very nice . . . He resumed stroking himself, pausing only to dampen his palm again, since his saliva was one of the few things that wouldn't evaporate or burn away. *I'll imagine her with dusky, tight nipples . . . and that tiny waist . . . She's so small, I could practically cover three-quarters of her waist with my hands, if she'd just let me try.*

Instead, it was her hands that slid down her waist, one of her fingers pausing to circle and tease her naked navel. Only then did the illusion finish filling out her body down to the knees, which was far enough for his needs . . . and her nether-hair was indeed natural, as reddish brown as his own masculine curls. Stroking harder, Koranen felt no repulsion as he imagined her kneeling over him. Of course, he felt nothing, since this was merely a projection of light and willpower, but the image was enough to excite him.

Ohhh, yesss . . . Play with your breasts . . . Cup and caress them . . . yes yess yessss . . .

Light and heat flared in the smithy built next to the base of the southeastern tower.

"How is your glazed ham?" Koranen asked politely. They were tucked in a corner, enjoying their meal. The evening rush was almost over, and while she had chosen the glazed ham, he had picked the restaurant specialty, breaded sea bass.

"Juicy. I don't see why they call this their third-best dish . . . but then, they *do* claim to specialize in fish," Ama-ti added, wrinkling her nose a little. "Though *specialize* isn't really the word for it, considering what Menomonites go through to make fish taste like anything *but* fish . . ."

"Sorry about the fish thing," Koranen apologized yet again. "Reuen said you liked land-food, and I just asked which of the few restaurants we have would be good to eat at. I didn't ask what the focus of their cooking was."

"Well, this *is* an island kingdom," the blue-haired Aquamancer allowed graciously. "It's very hard to get away from fish when you live in or right next to the sea. And the ham *is* very good. We don't have many pigs in the herding caverns, so we only get to slaughter and share a few bites now and again for special occasions."

"I'll admit it's not one of my favorite meats," Kor said, shrugging as he speared a couple of slices of root vegetable on his fork. "But I suppose I should consider things like pork and dove a rare treat, these days."

"There aren't any doves in the city. Nor any of the game birds. Lots of ducks and chickens and geese, though," she admitted. "Anything that was in a cage that went overboard in the rescue zone, really. Four-legged animals aren't as likely to be transported, and long-range seabirds are usually tough and stringy . . . and taste like fish."

"You really don't like fish, do you?" he asked.

"Let's just say that *everyone* has an herb box, if they have a window that faces one of the Sun Towers. Rooftops are good growing areas, too, if you can afford to buy that much soil."

"Why not trade for land-foods?" Kor asked, curious. "Why keep yourselves so carefully hidden?"

"Ever heard the phrase 'sunken treasure'?" Ama-ti returned dryly, reaching for her wineglass and taking a sip before continuing. "True, it's been several hundred years, but Menomon has been attacked before. The last time, we were attacked by a private fleet made of mercenaries and mages culled from the southern shores of Aiar. They claimed that they just wanted their merchant-patrons' lost cargoes recovered, but the truth was that they wanted *all* of the goods lost to the reefs, whether these were their lawful goods or not. And that attack was the last gasp for the Council; the invaders nearly collapsed the protective wards shielding the city from drowning or being crushed to death by the weight of the sea.

"*Nothing* is allowed to interfere with the city's safety, so the Council declared that the city had to go into hiding. We cloaked the shield in illusion-wards and sent Wavescouts to the surface to seek out and destroy all navigational records of our exact position and to destroy what references they could find on the surface to our existence. We still do our God-sanctioned task, rescuing drowning seafarers within our area of influence, giving them a place to live and so forth . . . but Menos hasn't insisted we let everyone else know that we're still down there."

"Ah. So when that mage, Xenos, was trying to take over your . . . you know," Koranen hedged delicately, since they were out in public, and one didn't speak of Fountains publically, "that also threatened the city's safety?"

"Yes. It took a while, but Sheren browbeat the Council into acknowledging our debt to you for helping us defeat him. Danau said that if you hadn't been distracting him, weakening him, she and the Wavescout mages wouldn't have been able to break through the wards he had placed on the Guardian's Hall." Ama-ti saluted him before sipping again from her goblet.

Koranen flushed a little at the mention of Danau's name. He felt guilty, sitting here with Ama-ti, getting to know her with the purpose of courting her, when he had stroked himself to a very satisfying climax last night to thoughts of a different, red-haired Aquamancer, not this blue-haired one. But he was here with her, and enjoying her company.

She had chosen a set of leathers that, while still unornamented when compared to the slowly emerging Nightfall fashion, were still lovely. Her pants and tunic were stitched in triangular, somewhat diagonal stripes of light and dark blue; they brought out the green of her eyes, especially as the lighter stripes were more of a light turquoise. Compared to the mostly Katani or Natallian fashions around them, she looked a bit exotic.

Certainly she looked every bit as good in her leathers as Baroness Teretha did in her ribbon-trimmed tunic-dress and tights. Koranen had noticed her when they entered the restaurant; she was apparently being wined and dined by that blond man, the Aian mage who had come ashore with the Menomonites. He might have stopped by their table to say hello, but the couple had been seated in the far corner of the room and seemed to be deep in intimate conversation.

At least the mage Yarrin was acting intimate, trailing his fingers in patterns over the back of Teretha's hand. Kor could just see the now-dreamy-eyed expression on the older woman's face. She had started out looking somewhat skeptical and now looked rather doting.

He must be as good at seduction as Trev is. Well, if she doesn't mind flirting with a younger man, all the more happiness to both of them, Kor silently allowed. *I do wonder what compliments he could give her to put that dazed look on her face, since she's normally a very practical-minded woman . . . Oh! I should compliment Ama-ti on her clothes, shouldn't I? Trevan says women like it when a man notices her clothes.*

"I like your garments—they look lovely on you," he managed, hoping he didn't sound like a fumble-tongued idiot. Knowing he had to add more, he offered, "They're very different from Katani and Natallian fashions, and, um . . . I kind of like it. On you."

She smiled and blushed. "Roje made them for me. He's *so* talented—he's the best leather-tailor in the city, with half the Council begging him to dress them, and the other half impatiently waiting for his mourning period to be over. But he's promised to marry *me* and has held to it for over nine months despite . . . What?"

Koranen carefully closed his mouth, swallowed, and tried to find his voice. "*Marry* you? But . . . I thought . . ."

"What's wrong?" Ama-ti asked him, setting down her fork, a look of concern clouding her face.

"We requested *single* Aquamancers. I'd think that *wouldn't* include betrothed ones," Kor managed to say, keeping his voice low to ensure this conversation stayed private, too.

She gave him a blank look. "So? I don't see what the problem is."

"How can I consider marrying you, if you're engaged to another man?" he clarified.

"Well, I'll admit Roje can be a bit temperamental when he's in one of his creative moods, but his past co-husbands never seemed to mind," she returned blithely.

"Co . . . husbands?" This was making less and less sense to him. Kor stared at the Aquamancer, confused.

"Well, yes. It's the law. Unless there is a sound medical or magical reason, or the couple was married originally back in their surface life, the surface woman adamantly refuses to marry any others . . . *and* pays a hefty fine," Ama-ti added, "all women in Menomon must take on at least three husbands, if not more, and must marry the first one by the age of twenty-five. I'm twenty-four, which is Chana's age, and Reuen is twenty-three. The other two have more time than me, but I'm looking for co-husbands who can get along with Roje.

"Roje was one of five, before his first wife died—she was a Wavescout, which is a tough and sometimes dangerous profession. He's still in the middle of his mandatory three-year period of mourning, so you'd have at least a year and a half before he'd come along as a second husband, but the ban only exists to give the unmarried men a better shot at snagging the available women during those intervening years."

Sitting back in his chair, Koranen stared at her, stunned by the thought of being only one man among a handful. Katani culture—which he was still very much steeped in, despite Nightfall's declaration of independence—stressed one woman and one man, period. Even the Empire's Patron Deities, Jinga and Kata, stressed that two-people-only relationships were the best way to go. The Gods of the mainland to the west of Nightfall tried to remind Their people that same-gender couples weren't anathema, and that the Katani people weren't supposed to persecute and ostracize them, but Nightfall had been populated by a majority of male-male and female-female pairings who just couldn't live happy, productive lives under so much social disdain . . . but they were still only two-people couples.

It was a very foreign mind-set to try to contemplate.

Except there's one loophole, he remembered after a moment and shook his head slightly. "That's presuming I'd be traveling to Menomon, where Menomonite law reigns. If we stayed here on Nightfall, the rule is that there are two people in a marriage. No wives with three husbands, or husbands with three wives."

"*Not* return to Menomon?" It was Ama-ti's turn to look dubious.

Koranen picked up his wineglass as she continued, a wineglass he himself had made a month ago, if he remembered right. Ama-ti looked as floored by his statement as he had felt about hers. She prodded at her food, but set down her fork after a moment, still taken aback.

"And only *one* husband? I have never understood surface dwellers in that regard. How can only one man satisfy a woman's needs? If she's lucky, he can service her twice, maybe three times a night when he's young and hearty, while she can go five or six times quite easily, once she's warmed up!"

Koranen choked on his wine. Around them, the volume level of the other patrons' conversations dipped.

"How can a woman *not* need three or four husbands in her bed?"

Face burning, Koranen saw one of the server lads hurrying their way, the same one who had brought them their plates of glazed ham and breaded fish. He looked to be about eighteen or nineteen, and blushed as he approached, clearing his throat. "Milady . . . if you please . . . this is a *family* restaurant. Such conversations are . . . well, not meant for younger ears, yes?"

Ama-ti blinked, then blushed. "Sorry . . . my apologies. Your culture is very different from mine, and I should have remembered that. We will be more discreet."

"Thank you." Bobbing a bow, the youth hurried away again.

Well, that was awkward . . . three *husbands? Mandated by law?*
Koranen suppressed a shudder at the thought. But he also couldn't
let her statement pass unchallenged, despite the family-friendly am-
bience of The Giggling Pear. "A man who cannot satisfy his woman
is a man who has failed to acquire the proper education in such matters," he murmured quietly, leaning forward so that only she could
hear his words. "I may not have a wide variety of experience, but I
have had a thorough education."

*Thanks to Trevan's advice over the years, and the Companionship
Guild, and the clever little illusion-based instructor they helped him
create . . .*

That put a sly look on his date's face. Bracing her elbow on the
table, she leaned her chin on her palm and briefly fluttered her
lashes in his direction, though she was careful to keep her voice low.
"I *suppose* I could change my opinion of such things, *if* you were to
give me a proper demonstration of this . . . education of yours?"

Puzzled, Koranen eyed her. "I thought . . . Reuen said you should
be courted slowly. Which is something I find I'm inclined to do
anyway—a real relationship is one where the couple gets to know
each other outside of the bedclothes, as well as within them. And it's
not as if you can fix the desalination plant overnight, or you would
have mentioned that by now, I'm sure."

"No, we can't. We still don't know what powers it. But you have
Danau working on the problem. Ever since . . . um, well, in the last
eight or so years, she's gotten very good at her job," Ama-ti said,
cutting into her ham again. "She takes a great deal of pride in doing
the best job possible, and she's the most powerful Aquamancer in the
Guild. Not to mention the second-most-powerful mage in the city,
which irks a lot of people on the Council . . .

"Anyway, if anyone from Menomon can figure it out, it'll be her.
Because if she can't, you'll have to search far and wide for a more
clever Aquamancer, and the next-nearest large pool of them that I
know of is in the city of Float Pierce, off the Bay of Sand and Stones,
far to the northwest."

"I'll keep that in mind, though I hope she *is* clever enough to figure it out. A few hundred more citizens, and we'll have to start putting out rain barrels and provoking my sixthborn brother into whipping up a few storms a week just to fill them with enough drinking water."

Glad they were back to a safer—and somewhat saner—topic, Koranen steered their conversation back toward her work, wondering if the blue-haired woman across from him was worth overcoming the clear cultural differences that had just been revealed between them.

"*I*'*m sorry, milady, but we just don't have anything ready-made in your . . . exact size . . .*"

It figures, Danau thought in disgust, and not for the first time. Her disappointment had been a refrain in her head ever since her trip down to the city. She had been ambushed by work as soon as breakfast was over, with no chance to go down the hill to look for anything. *Anytime I try to prove I still have worth as a woman, someone ruins it for me.*

Well, alright, it's not their fault the tailors in this land don't have anything adult-styled yet cut for an almost child-sized body. There was that one tunic that was actually pretty, a festival garment one of the tailors had brought from somewhere . . . Guchere, that was it . . . but it wouldn't accommodate my breasts. And I'm not such a sexual eunuch that I'd cut them off just to fit into it!

Reaching the door of her suite, she flung it open, then slammed it shut behind her. Or almost slammed it; catching the edge a finger length from the frame, she stopped its momentum, then shut the door quietly. *No need to let anyone know how frustrated I am. The only dignity I have left is my dignity. Even if I have to wear a sack tomorrow night, I'll go to the damned concert, and I will have a good time!*

Now, focus on your work, she ordered herself sternly, shoving her feelings back into their usual compartment. *Somewhere in your mess of notes from today is the information you need.* Pulling out the chair at the table by the windows, she settled herself in front of her stacks of notes. She had abandoned her work after the midafternoon meal with the strange name, *tiffen*, and supper wasn't for another half hour, which meant she could probably make some headway. At this point, *any* work would be headway, however small, mainly because there was so much of it to wade through.

Aside from briefly glancing through the material to make sure it contained information that might possibly be useful, she had done more magical copying than actual reading. Seven hundred seventy-four years' worth of notes on the Desalinator, in fact—and three of those years contained transcriptions of the preplanning stages. Not that there was much of the latter, and much of that hadn't been preserved with the best parchment-salvaging spells, but there was a letter that had been preserved with three of what looked like seven sheets listing components that would be needed. Or at least, the number scrawled in the corner of the third readable sheet looked like a seven; there may have been more at one time, but that was all the sheets she had.

Other records were lists of production rates for various eras over the last eight centuries. Having been given a host of scribal supplies— it was very good of these Nightfallers to fund and supply her and her fellow Aquamancers' needs—she drafted a graph on a broad, blank scroll and enchanted a pen to start marking down dates and rates, plotting them for an eventual graph. While she wasn't an Arithmancer, she did have a solid grasp of mathemagics, thanks to her training in the Guild.

One of the things she had copied was a list of all the Guardians' names; she knew there was a Fountain on the island, and it was quite possible that the Fountain was, or rather, had been the power source for the Desalinator. *If something happened to sever the magical connection between the two, it should be simple enough to reconstruct the old channel, or enchant a new one, to resume power. I'll have to make an inquiry in that direction.*

Another thing I'll have to do is go back over the spellgraph Chana made of the dimensions of all nine buildings. Everything is very symmetrical in the outer buildings from what I can tell, but there is that one room in the warehouse which might have been a manager's office at some point. I know I wanted to check the thickness of that back wall, since it seemed like the room was a little shorter than it should have been.

Not to mention I don't even know if the Guardians of the local Fountain were supposed to maintain the Fountain's energy needs or not. Which wouldn't be the sister, but a statically anchored one, since they have to have one if they plan to open the Gateway to Heaven for the Convocation. If the Shattering of the Portal disrupted the flow of power—

—A knock at the door disrupted her. Quickly scrawling a reminder to investigate the records of Guardians below her note to investigate that wall for possible secrets, Danau rose and crossed to the door. Opening it, she found herself confronted by the smiling face of Lord Koranen's brother. *Morganen, the Lord Mage of Nightfall. I wonder what that equates to, in Guild Ranking terms.*

"Can I help you?" she asked, wondering why he would want to talk to *her* of all people. And why he was carrying a wooden chest. Aside from meals and their dockside meeting, she really hadn't interacted with him. "Is it time for supper? Or . . . ?"

"No, no, you haven't missed supper, and I don't mean to bother you," the light-brown-haired man stated quickly, still smiling at her.

It was a little odd to be smiled at. Danau didn't know what to make of him. "*Why* are you here?"

"Well, I have something for you. May I come in?" he asked, gesturing past her at the sitting chamber.

Stepping back, Danau held the door for him, then closed it. Gesturing for him to pick a seat, she followed him, expecting him to head for the padded couch, or one of the stuffed leather chairs. Instead, he walked right past the furniture and entered her bedchamber.

Taken aback, Danau trailed after him. *Gods . . . he doesn't expect me to take him on as a husband, does he? I know his twin is looking for a wife and that the other six are married, but I can't take* either *of these*

*two! Menos—how do I turn him down politely, without making every-
thing a hundred times awkward?*

Setting the chest on her vanity table, he unlatched and opened
the lid. Danau hastily wiped the dismay from her expression as he
glanced her way. He smiled slightly, almost shyly, as he spoke.

"I have a friend," Lord Morganen stated as he worked, pulling
out a bundle of fuzzy, dark cloth. "She's . . . well, she's an outworlder,
but though her world is very different from this one, she's something like a Seer in her land. And when I opened up the connection
between the Veils this afternoon, she had *this* waiting. She said it
was for you. At least, I'm presuming it's for you, since you're the
only 'little redheaded one' I currently know."

An outworlder . . . Seer . . . me? Befuddled, Danau eyed the bundle of fabric in his hands. "What is it?"

"A dress . . . I *think*. It's cut in an outworlder style, but it doesn't
seem to have any sleeves or shoulders, and it has one of those weird
zipper-fastener things—you pull up or down on the little tab to
open or close it, if I remember right," he said in an aside, eyeing the
garment dubiously. "She also said I'm to have you try it on, and
check to make sure it fits. Of course, I'm not the tailor my brother
Evanor is, but even so, I'm not too shabby with a stitching spell or
two." Pausing, he cleared his throat, then unrolled the dress a little
and gingerly fished out scraps of fabric.

Danau realized belatedly the fuzzy, dark blue green material in
his hands was *velvet*—a very rare commodity in Menomon. Some of
the scraps looked like they were made of silk and lace, which were
seen only slightly more often than velvet; plus someone had fashioned leggings out of some sort of very fine gauze. It was difficult to
tell *what* the material was, either a weave or a knit or maybe something entirely new. Danau only knew that the leggings were made
from something sheer and either black or dark gray.

The wealth wadded so carelessly in his hands staggered her. Fabric was only ever encountered as debris salvaged from wrecked ships;
growing plants for their fibers was considered a waste of precious

soil, when food crops were far more necessary. She also realized the scraps were undergarments, cut somewhat similar to the sparse, practical Menomonite style. No one would make such things so frivolously, however—it was madness, when even the smallest scrap of finery could be used instead as decorative patches or trims. Linen and cotton, maybe, but not silk or lace.

Handing over the dress and the scraps, the Nightfall mage gave Danau a moment to realize the lumps rolled into the middle of the dress were a pair of odd, sculpted shoes covered in matching, plush velvet. Clearing his throat again, Lord Morganen displayed the spool he had fished from one of the pouches slung at his waist. "She, um, also suggested you would need thread-of-copper, for stitching runes. Luckily for you, my brother Evanor makes his own. I don't know which runes you'll need, though, and Evanor is better at needlework than I am, so if you can't do it yourself, just ask him, and he'll be happy to oblige.

"Of course, that'll have to wait until after you've tried on the garments, since I'm supposed to size them first, and that could interfere with any protections," he told her.

"Size them?" Danau asked, distracted by the soft, fuzzy feel of real velvet against her skin.

"From, well, the undergarments out."

That made her quirk her brow skeptically. Only one man after Jiore had dared to try to see her without her clothes, but she had figured out quickly that he'd just wanted to gawk at the living *udrezero*. *Once was more than enough, for that.* "You'll tailor my undergarments and get paid in a free thrill at the same time?"

Morganen blushed. "Um, no. Definitely not. I'm in love with someone else. All other women are like sisters to me, particularly when compared to her. And you're as safe in my company as if you *were* my sister. So . . . Sister," he added with a slight bow, "if you would don the pieces of the outfit, we can see how much of it needs tailoring to make you look your best. With luck, we can get it done in the next quarter hour, so we won't be late to supper."

Taken aback, Danau stared at the fuzzy cloth in her hands, and the metallic thread in his. Thread-of-copper was the best medium for stitching thermal wards. Most of her clothing was discreetly stitched along special ribbons stitched underneath various hems, to minimize outward signs that she was different from others. Even her bedding back home was embroidered at the corners with thread-of-copper to ensure that a stray dream didn't cause accidental damage. "Your . . . friend . . . knew I would need this?"

The light-brown-haired mage shrugged. "She just knows these things. They call it *sigh-kick* abilities where she comes from. An odd label, but then, it is another universe. They don't have a lot of magic in her world, but she *does* have Seer-like powers. I've found it's best to just follow along when she goes into one of her 'you must do this' trances. So . . . will you let me help you look beautiful? I'll presume it's for tomorrow night," he added. "That is when you'll be dating Koranen, right?"

"What?" Danau almost laughed; she was caught off guard by that. "No. I don't date. Ever. But . . . thank you for the dress. I didn't bring anything appropriate."

"You turned him down?" Morganen asked her, brows rising in surprise. "But . . . why?"

"He didn't ask."

"But you *were* invited to the performance, right?" the Nightfaller wanted to clarify.

"Not for my presence alone. He invited all of us," Danau explained. "A group outing."

The Nightfaller mage folded his arms across his chest, rubbing briefly at his chin. "Odd . . . Well, he might realize his mistake in not making himself clearer by the end of tonight . . . or at least, one hopes he will . . .

"Go on. Go get dressed," he directed her, changing the subject. Then flushed again. "Um . . . the thing with the ribbons in it is apparently some sort of belt for holding up the leggings. The rest of it should be self-explanatory. I hope. I mean, you *are* both smart and pretty, but . . . well, with my heart already taken, you're not my type, so I'd really rather not have to help you put them on. Nothing personal, but . . ."

But I'm not anyone's type, she thought, somewhere between wistfully and bitterly. She was careful, though, to shield her magic tightly so that frost wouldn't damage the costly materials in her grip. Only for this beautiful, expensive dress would she contemplate going out in public. Nodding, Danau retreated toward the private refreshing room included in her suite. "I think I can figure things out. I'll, um, be back in a few minutes. Though I really *don't* date anyone."

"Perhaps. But sometimes it's good for us to step outside of our normal ways of doing things." He gave her a warm, encouraging smile. "If nothing else, hearing Evanor perform in full voice *is* worth the trouble of dressing in your best. He's a Song-mage, and he'll be backed by a full troupe of musicians tomorrow night, so it should be spectacular. Go on; try it on . . ."

SEVEN

T he Barol Mirror, as Lord Consus of Kairides had come to
think of it, was very peculiar. It never activated on its own when
someone else was around, and it only activated intermittently . . .
but every time it did so, Consus found himself listening in to a
mirror-conversation that pertained to something that interested
him. If it were a random thing, it would scry upon and display random messages, but it didn't. Not all of the messages followed the
same topic—some of them followed the business of Nightfall, but
other conversations regarded his fellow Councilors.

Having finished surveying the last of the Nightfall shipments,
Consus had declared that he was tired, suffering from headaches,
and taking a break from his duties for a couple of weeks. The Council had grumbled a bit—and Consus' deputies had grumbled a bit
more, since his work-based headaches were now entirely theirs to
deal with—but since he normally didn't take breaks for personal
reasons, he was within his rights to do so. That was advantageous
for him, for not only did it give him a chance to relax; it allowed him

to spend hours in the same room as the double-paned mirror—during the same hours that his fellow Councilors most often used their own communication mirrors, no less.

It was disturbing to learn just who was involved in questionable mirror-based correspondence. He caught a conversation wherein Councilor Thera of the Department of Taxation arranged for her relatives to get certain "tax breaks" . . . by teaching her cousin exactly how to dodge the Sea Commerce taxes that were normally paid when goods were loaded onto or offloaded from the many ships plying the Katani coast. It involved the use of mirror-Gates to discreetly move cargo between a warehouse on land and a ship at anchor in a nearby bay, and then producing official government vouchers from mages for "mirror-Gate transportation" to cover *how* the packages got there, by pretending they were being carried by couriers.

Officially the government was paying itself those taxes . . . but the difference in profit went into Thera's pockets. Apparently he would have to order a covert increase of surprise inspections of anchored ships, under the guise of searching for smuggling operations . . . which this basically was. Consus couldn't move directly against Thera, not when she was the Councilor for Taxation, but he wouldn't let his office fail in its duties, either.

Other scryings contained some of the conversations Councilor Finneg held every few days with one of his relatives, grumbling and even ranting about how everyone else looked down upon him with disdain. The duke, having challenged and been defeated by that red-headed woman, incipient Queen Kelly of Nightfall, had grown a little *too* efficient at his job, heading the Department of Conflict Resolution with a level of ruthlessness that had caused the various nobles across the Empire to think twice before throwing a fit with their neighbors, or whatever reason they had used before. *No one* laughed to his face, and few talked about the incident anymore . . . but he repeatedly ranted that he knew his fellow Councilors were still *thinking* about his ignoble defeat, and calling him names in secret . . .

Consus now worried for the stability of the Empire as a whole, whenever he thought about Duke Finneg's personal stability. He didn't like worrying. The middle-aged mage wanted things to run smoothly and efficiently here in Katan. No unexpected surprises.

The Barol Mirror did help a little bit toward that—Councilor Thera was one such case—but the more he isolated himself with the mirror, hoping to catch another conversation, the more Consus realized the mirror was dangerous in the wrong hands. *And* that the Council of Mages, the ruling body of Katan, weren't exactly the right hands. Too many of his fellow Councilors were patently in politics to protect their own best interests and to extend those best interests to their best friends, not to the populace as a whole.

It would be hypocritical for Consus to claim that he didn't have his own best interests at heart: Here he was, taking time off from his duties as a Councilor just to make sense of a potentially danger-ous Artifact that could potentially cause himself trouble, either di-rectly or secondhand. Staring at the mirror now hanging in his privacy-warded study in his home back at the capital, Consus ac-knowledged that his personal interests had always been to keep himself out of trouble. But behind that lay a genuine interest in the welfare of Katan.

He had mediated that poorly ended meeting on Nightfall Isle so that neither side went to war, which would have been bad for the Empire. The former Corvis brothers, now the Nightfall brothers, were too powerful and too cohesive a group not to have caused a lot of trouble if it had come to an outright battle. He intended to step up shipboard inspections to make sure the government wasn't spending its tax earnings improperly.

He would keep this mirror out of his fellow Councilors' hands, because they would use it highly improperly . . . yet he couldn't hand it over to its proper owner, Alys of Nightfall, formerly the Lady Alys of Devries. The last of the Devries family had aligned herself firmly with the Nightfall contingent, after all. Giving them a mirror that gave them access to politically sensitive conversations—especially ones concerning the governance of Katan—would be treasonous, now that he knew more or less what the mirror did.

But the middle-aged mage couldn't quite bring himself to destroy the mirror, either. There were too many secrets being revealed, too many potential dangers to the kingdom that could be thwarted, *if* one were careful enough. Someone could use this mirror for the greater good, if *he* were ethical enough . . . and though Consus would be the first to admit he didn't do a vigorous effort at being the Sea Commerce Councilor, he did do his job as it should be done. Ethically.

This thing worries me, though, he acknowledged as he stared at the Barol Mirror yet again. It wasn't active—it was late at night; the few servants he kept had retired after a quiet supper to their own pursuits, leaving him alone and unlikely to be interrupted in his study. *Mostly, because I don't know* how *it does what it does. How can this mirror have . . . have the prescience of a* Seer?

Of course, it wasn't *exactly* like a Seer. Studying the paired circles of silvered glass, Consus sipped at his drink, a tiny cup filled with a measured portion of burgundy-hued frostwine. It was one of his few, rare indulgences; most of his personal life was as simple and uncluttered as his approach to his work, but he did have one or two vices. The rare vintage only grew in one location in the world, in some ungodly far-off place called Scoville, somewhere in the northernmost wilds of the kingdom of Arbra, as far north and east of Sun's Belt as the southernmost shores of Katan were to the south and west.

The smooth, fruity-sweet tang of the fermented wine—more potent than the brandy made from the sugar vines grown in the northwest isles off the coast of Katan, hence the small glass—stimulated his senses. He didn't drink it to relax; there were better brews for relaxing. This stuff made him think better. Or at least wilder. Sometimes that was a necessary advantage when he was getting nowhere with a particular, lingering problem.

A stray thought crossed his mind as he rolled another sip across his tongue. It wasn't an uncommon thought, but this time, it held an extra meaning. *I still don't know how frostwine got its name, or how it is made. Much like I don't know how this mirror got its powers, or how it was made . . . It doesn't see into the future, just into the present, but it sees the need of its lone observer . . .*

Shifting his attention to the bottle to serve himself another trickle, his gaze fell on the stack of books waiting to be read in his spare time. *Perhaps a mental diversion will refresh my thoughts. I've been staring at this thing for too many hours . . .*

Picking up the first of them, he smiled at the author's name. It was an Aian mage, Kerric Vo Mos, a prolific writer, albeit one whose works were rare and costly to acquire. His previous volume— and the one to hook Consus on his lively, engaging style of prose— had covered the art of postcognitive divination. For the Councilor of Sea Commerce, it was useful to know where certain goods had originated, particularly when checking cargo manifests. From there, Consus had managed to acquire five others previously published by the foreign mage.

This book, the latest, covered research into a new form of mirror-Gate travel. The author spoke of his experiments in using glazed floor panels that one just stepped upon, spoke the command word—spoken by anyone, even a non-mage—and it instantly transported the user to the desired end destination, being another of the mirrored floor tiles. Lifting the refilled cup to his lips, Consus took a sip . . . and choked literally on a sudden collision of thoughts.

Scrying the past—Kata! Coughing, he hastily set down the tiny cup, licking at his fingers as soon as his lungs had cleared, so as to not waste a single sloshed drop. *Where did I put that book? It detailed how to construct a variety of temporal scrying spells*, including *how to scry into the past for the construction techniques of any unknown, rare, or foreign Artifact! Blessed Gods, this wine seems to work every single time.*

Setting aside the book on floor-Gates, Consus escaped his chair and hurried to his bookshelves, searching for his collection of Vo

Mos books. *All I have to do is craft myself a past-scrying spell, and I can see how the Barol Mirror was made! Ah, here it is . . . good, good!*

Returning to his reading chair, Consus settled back into its cushioned embrace. It would take time, of course, and it might not answer all of his questions, but it wasn't as if the mirror was going anywhere. Neither was he, but then, he liked his life just as it was. Safe and secure. Just like that dangerous, troublesome piece of metal and glass.

The mirror activated again. This time, the image on the left was the age-seamed face of Lady Rannika of Keness-Mot, Councilor of the Archives. On the right was a moonfaced, deeply tanned man with black hair and strange marks inked on his cheeks. Consus frowned, sitting forward for a closer look. The man spoke in a garble of foreign words, frustrating him . . . but those marks *were* vaguely familiar.

"The Scroll of what? Living Glory?" Councilor Rannika asked, voice echoing out of the silvered glass in a half-muffled way. *"I'm not sure. We have over three hundred thousand scrolls in our archives. When was it written?"*

Garblegarble . . . Kata, I'm getting rather tired of this! First that old woman talking with Saber of Nightfall, and now some foreigner who . . . Mendhi! Consus bolted out of his chair a second time, crossing to the shelves containing the volumes he read when he wanted to relax. *Here it is . . . the Painted Warriors of Mendhi, mage-warriors who use skin-signs, tattoos of runes embedded in their skin that are linked directly to their power . . . Yes, the illustrations match, more or less.*

Wait. That man is from Mendhi?

He turned back to stare at the mirror, but Rannika was already fading, even as she pledged to look for the scroll in question. The other half of the mirror was back to a normal reflection of the Sea Councilor's private study. *What in the Names of the Gods was that about—and why did I get to see it? I don't normally have any interest in the Archives, unless it's to look up records of past trade values, or maybe shipboard incident rates. I've certainly never heard of a Scroll of Living Glory before!*

I am tired of not being able to understand the languages I'm now running across. I have translation pendants for Aian, and I could probably dig up and dust off some old ones for Natallian, but these people are from too far away for my liking. I think I'm going to have to requisition a dose of Ultra Tongue from the Department of External Affairs.

He winced as he thought it, but the middle-aged mage knew he didn't have much choice. *Jinga, that's going to eat up a few of my favors with them . . . Gods-be-damned Translation mages are practically bonemonkeys in disguise—they always want to suck out an arm and a leg in exchange for something like that!*

Alright. Ultra Tongue, and a temporal scrying. I can do this. Somehow.

*S*MACK!

"—Ow!" Ducking and rubbing the stinging spot on the back of his head, Koranen glared at his twin. Morganen had come up to him just after he had returned Ama-ti to her suite. "What was *that* for?"

"We need to talk—that's why."

Curious, Koranen followed Morg up the hall toward the main east wing. Not until they were halfway between the split in the hall and the donjon did Morg turn to face him. Aqua eyes met hazel, as his twin gave him an impatient look.

"You told me this morning before sword practice how you'd already tried courting Chana and Reuen, and they noticed your heat," Morg reminded him. "And tonight, you went out with Ama-ti. But Danau hasn't been asked out, yet. So when is the fourth one going to get her turn?"

"*When* I'm done crossing Ama-ti off the list, *if* I'm crossing her off," Kor grumbled, still soothing his scalp. This wasn't quite how he'd pictured his evening ending. It wasn't going to end in bed-tumbling, because he did have doubts about Ama-ti's compatibility, but then, his doubts about compatibility this time had little to do with Ama-ti's ability to survive the literal heat of his excitement and everything to do with his feelings about the Menomonites' strange, multi-husbanded culture. "I haven't found any reason to cross her off, yet . . . other than the multiple-husband thing."

"Well, you are going to play fair and square with *all* of them. That means you're going to go to Danau's quarters and let her know that she, in specific, will be your date for tomorrow night. And arrange to go out to dinner or something before the performance," Morg ordered. "You may have eliminated the other two, but you can alternate dates with the remaining pair. They'll only be here for a limited amount of time, and if you spend too much time with one and not enough with the other, your Destined bride might walk off without either of you realizing it."

Koranen eyed his brother with suspicion. "Do you know something about Danau that I don't?"

"I couldn't say."

"Morg . . ."

Morg lifted his hands. "Hand me a truth wand, Kor, for *I* cannot say if she's the right woman for you or not. I cannot say if *Ama-ti* is the right woman for you, either! Only *you* can determine that."

Kor grimaced a little, knowing his brother had a point—he was the one with the heat-control problem, so only he could test the candidacy of a potential wife.

"But since I've sent the wheat across to Hope, and she says she'll start sending across seedlings and belongings within a day or two . . . well, that suggests to me that you'll figure out which woman it is fairly quickly, which means it has to be one of the ones that are already here. But in order to do *my* job as the official matchmaker of our family," he added, touching his chest with both hands, "I have to make sure *you* consider as many possibilities as you can, as quickly as you can, so that you find the *right* one. You daren't settle for anything less."

"I *know*. But . . . *Danau*?" Glum, Koranen headed for the southeast wing. Expecting Morganen to take the northeast branch toward his own suite, he winced as Morg smacked him again on the back of his head. "Ow! Dammit, Morg—!"

"*Ask* her. *Any* of them could be your lady, but you won't know which one until you try it *with an open mind.*"

Rolling his eyes, Koranen strode away from his twin, back toward his own wing of the palace. When they first had arrived on the island, exiled and alone, the eight Corvis brothers had found and claimed this place. With each of its four main wings terminating in two more wings, there was enough room and then some; the brothers had merely spread out for privacy.

Saber had claimed it would cut down on the number of fights if they weren't forced to spend every minute of every day together, and it had worked to some extent. Learning to depend solely upon each other had forged a certain powerful unity between them; Koranen knew his brothers would back him in anything, just as he would back them. But they still got into the occasional argument, even now. Mild ones, but arguments all the same, so it was good to have space and distance from other men.

But if I went to Menomon . . . I don't like the idea of being just one husband among many. Ama-ti is charming, and sweet, and pretty . . . I might have to ask her to shave herself down below if she does dye that blue, like she does her head-hair . . . but at least she's charming and sweet.

Danau . . . isn't. Polite, I'll grant. Even formal. But charming? Sweet?

Reaching her door, he hesitated, not sure if he really wanted to spend an evening in her company. *Gods . . . Ama-ti's revelation was an unpleasant shock. But she's nice, so that mitigated it somewhat . . . except she wants to go back to Menomon and her—ugh!—second husband-in-waiting. What if Danau also has someone back home? If she refuses to settle here, if I had no choice but to either go with her or face celibacy for the rest of my life—Gods forefend—I'd have to deal with that stupid Menom-onite law and her unpleasant brusqueness . . .*

He almost didn't knock.

What stopped him from leaving, however, was Morganen's comment on how little time he might have left for finding his Destined bride. It was said, after all, that the distant Threefold God of Fate set life's events in motion, and that mere mortals sometimes had to scramble to keep up with them . . .

Right. I can do this. It's only for one night, after all . . . and she might have a good reason for being so . . . Stop that line of thought right now, Kor ordered himself. *She* is *capable of politeness and courtesy. There* is *a wonderful person somewhere in there, and I* will *find a way to bring her to the surface.*

Rapping on her door, he squared his shoulders and waited for a response. He heard some noises, the scrape of a chair, then footsteps. A moment later the door opened, and he looked down on her auburn hair. It struck him again how short she was, short enough he could have tucked her under his arm with room to spare.

Her short-haired head tilted up, blue eyes dragging up the length of his chest until they met his hazel gaze. Koranen took a moment of his own to examine her. She was clad in a faded green robe made from some kind of soft leather, a bit oversized and wrapped so that it all but enveloped her small frame from throat to palms and toes, though the belt cinched around her waist showed him the curves hidden beneath the worn material.

Danau wasn't expecting an interruption, let alone this particular one, and one still clad in the sleeveless blue outfit she had seen him wearing when he had escorted Ama-ti out of the palace earlier. In fact, she hadn't expected to see him this soon after leaving the palace compound. *What is he doing here at my door?*

She was still in two minds about wearing the splendid gown, despite the effusive, firm compliments Lord Koranen's twin had given her. It was only after she had readied herself for bed that she given in and risen again so that she could stitch runes into the garments she had been given. But though it was late, she had a duty to be helpful to these Nightfallers, and that meant answering the door regardless of the hour.

"Yes? You wanted something?" she finally asked.

"I . . . wanted to make it clear to you that I'm taking . . . that I would *like* to take you out to dinner tomorrow before the show," Koranen amended, remembering that it wasn't polite to *tell* a woman what they were going to do, but rather give her a choice in the matter.

Dream-memory flashed through her, of her undergarments and his chest, of his words murmured in her ear . . . and the way she had awakened covered in frost. "I don't date."

She started to close the door. Koranen flexed his muscles, quickly bracing the panel open with his forearm. "I know you eat; I've seen you doing it. And I know—also because I was there—that you are fully capable of eating in public. So I am asking you to come out of the palace with me and share a meal. Thirdly, I know you are more than capable of joining a conversation that wanders over a variety of topics . . . and that you can do so while you eat. Now, what in any of that could you possibly object to doing? Eating? Talking? Doing either while out in public?"

His logic was impeccable. There was one argument that could counter it, but Danau couldn't bring herself to admit her failure as a woman. She did have some pride left. But that could go two ways; she *did* have some pride. "What about Ama-ti? Or Reuen or Chana? I thought you were dating one of them?"

"Each of you gets a turn. That *is* why you are here," the auburn-haired mage stated, shrugging and folding his arms. "To be courted. By me."

"I don't date." She tried closing the door again, but it met his shoulder as he shifted his weight.

I am going to smack Morg four times more, for this, Koranen thought, masking his irritation behind a pleasant, determined smile. *Be persistent . . . Jinga's Sacred Ass!* "Yes, but you *do* go out in public, you do eat, and you do talk. I've seen you doing it with your colleagues. Am I not one of your colleagues?"

That made Danau snort. Hands going to her hips, she peered up at him skeptically. "If you ever *did* something to help out with the

Desalinator, then yes, you'd be one of my colleagues. All you do is play with molten sand."

That made him roll his eyes. "If you'd *give* me a task, I'd *do* it. I have plenty of work piling up back at my forge, believe me."

"Then why aren't you there, working?" she asked.

"Because I'm trying to get to know each of you," Kor countered. Seeing her start to withdraw again, he switched tactics, aiming for her work ethic. She hadn't once shied from her job, or anything connected to it. "And because someone in the family needs to know how the desalination plant works. Since I need to get to know you ladies for Prophecy's sake, practicality and efficiency demand that I also be the one on hand to observe your discoveries."

The corner of her mouth quirked up, twisting into a wry smile. "A practical man. So the only reason you're courting me is because . . . ?"

Koranen hated that he had to put it into unromantic words, but if keeping the romance out of the evening was what she wanted, he had to give it a try. "Because it's practical to give each of you at least one uninterrupted hour of my time. Which we can easily do over dinner. That way, if it doesn't work out between us, we can eliminate that possibility from my Destiny, and I can move on . . . and I won't have to pester you so persistently again if things don't work out between us."

Her slight smile faded. For a moment, Danau didn't see him; she just saw Jiore, his blond-and-brown-dyed hair gleaming warmly in the light of the northernmost Sun Tower . . . which had also lit his expression, one as cold as her skin. Snapping out of the memory, she shook her head. "It won't."

"But you'll still go to dinner with me?" Koranen pressed.

Mastering the urge to roll her eyes, Danau sighed. "Whatever. We'll go out to dinner, eat, and find something to talk about. And then we'll go and enjoy the concert. But that will be *all* that we do. I don't do anything else."

"But you *will* go out to dinner with me. *And* talk with me," Koranen added, wanting to confirm that part. "We *might* have more in common than either of us think, but neither of us will know until we try—you do have something pretty to wear, right? Not that your leathers are ugly or anything . . . but this is the very first concert we're holding as a kingdom, so it's very special."

"I do have something pretty—I have an entire dress made from *velvet*," Danau added, his question pricking at her pride. He might not know the significance of velvet to her people, but she knew. Still, she couldn't help retort, "The question is, do *you* have something nice to wear?"

"I think I can scrounge up something in velvet for myself," he reassured her. Relieved she had given in, Koranen didn't mind her challenge. Of course, the only velvet outfit he knew where to find immediately was an old Katani court outfit from his pre-exile days. *At least it'll be something that covers my groin, even if I have to rush it through Evanor for age-related repairs.* Pleased, he grinned at Danau. "Shall we say fifth hour and thirty, tomorrow evening?"

"That early?" she asked, her expression dubious.

"The performance is at seventh hour, so that will give us time to drive down to The Giggling Pear—I can recommend the food, at least, since I just ate there tonight—and still have plenty of time to order, eat it, and get to the performance hall. And if we skip *tiffin*, we'll definitely have an appetite."

Locked into a *date* with the enthusiastic man, whether she wanted it or not, Danau managed a smile. "That will be fine. Now, if you'll excuse me, I may not be getting as much work done tomorrow as I'd like, but I'll still need a full night's sleep."

Don't take offense at her comment—you know the work on the Desalinator is important, and I'm sure she didn't mean it to come across resentfully. She didn't sound *resentful, just matter-of-fact . . .* Stepping back from the doorway, Koranen nodded.

"Of course—um, you have a nice smile," he added before she could close the door between them. *If I can keep complimenting her, maybe she'll warm up to me.* "You should use it more often."

Danau blushed, reaching for the edge of the door. "Thank you. Good night."

"I hope to see more of it, especially over dinner—good night!" he called out just before she shut the panel between them. Convincing Danau hadn't been easy, and he still wasn't sure if a single evening of courting her would be worth it.

But . . . it's only a single night. The Gods know I really only need to hold her hand and test it with a little heat, something that would take a mere moment to test, if I wanted to risk injuring her. Spending an evening with her would be an act of kindness, and the Gods favor such deeds.

Turning away from the panel, Koranen inhaled deeply, then blew out his breath, trying to relax. He tensed in the next moment, catching a glimpse of movement through a palm-wide crack in Chana's door off to the side. The moment he shifted toward her, she closed her door. Thankfully, without slamming it. As much as he didn't want to hurt Chana's feelings by not inviting her out to dinner, he couldn't exactly court the blond-dyed woman, either. Not if she noticed his heat.

And if Danau notices your heat, too? The thought was depressing. Koranen couldn't shake it, though. *If she does . . . that would leave only Ama-ti. I don't want a wife with blue hair . . . and I really don't want to be one of half a dozen husbands. I want my own wife, just her and me . . . Maybe I should get it over with,* he thought, glancing at Ama-ti's door. *Give her a kiss, see if she can or can't stand my heat . . .*

Sighing roughly a second time, he almost crossed to her door. Something stopped him. It was a very simple thing, the squeak of a floorboard. In particular, the squeaking of a board in the suite beside him. Danau's suite.

Oh, that *would be smart—go out on a date with one, arrange for a date with another, then go back to the first and try to kiss her, when the second one could possibly hear you knocking on the first one's door . . . never mind the third who was watching us just now . . . Somehow, I don't think even Trevan ever managed to pull off something that fraught with courtship danger.*

Take yourself to bed, Kor, he ordered himself. *Or rather, back to the forge. You left scorch marks on your sheets this morning from the heat of your dreams, in spite of all your anti-fire wards . . . Gods, how am I going to sit across a table from Danau when I've pictured her naked and kneeling over me, touching herself as I watched? That'll be awkward . . . arousing, but awkward.*

Discreetly adjusting his trousers, Koranen strode for the stairs, trying not to think too much about it.

"**D**inner is delicious . . ."

I can't open my eyes . . .

"But you . . ."

Why can't I open my eyes?

"You are even *more* delicious . . ."

Danau struggled to open her eyes, to look and see what was happening, but all she could do was feel the warmth of the body pressing against her, the tickle of luxurious, exotically long hair feathering over her face . . . the nibbling of warm lips along the side of her neck, the puffing of hot breath into her ear, sending shivers down her limbs.

I can't . . . open . . .

Warm fingers brushed aside her clothes, caressing first her shoulder, then her ribs, before a thumb found the curved edge of one breast.

Ohhhh, who cares?

Wrapping her arms around her lover, Danau caressed his blessedly warm skin. She could feel one of his knees sliding between her thighs and parted them wider in welcome, though the bedcovers were in their way. And his hands, though they were teasing her ribs and her breasts, weren't in quite the right place. Sliding her fingers from his back to her chest, intertwining them with his, Danau showed the Lord Secretary of Nightfall how to caress her touch-starved flesh.

Together, they stroked upward from the base of her breasts to her hardened, aching nipples, where she showed him how to rub each peak in a tight little circle. It felt so good, she couldn't help the whimper that escaped.

"Yesss," he breathed into her ear, flooding her with more of the warmth she craved, warmth which she pulled into her passion-starved body.

"Yes!" Danau whimpered in agreement. Still teaching him how to tease her breasts with one set of conjoined hands, she slid their other pair down beneath the covers, delving both of their fingers between her thighs. She felt him enveloping her, sliding under her, warming her from below as they circled, rubbed, flicked . . . Pleasure mounted, collected . . . broke with a shuddering cry, and *now* she could open her eyes, only to find she was entirely alone in the gray predawn light, on a very hard, ungiving bed, with very stiff sheets trapping her legs.

Sliding her hands free of breast and groin, Danau felt the moisture on her fingertips and grimaced in disgust. Not over the act of pleasure—she was still a woman, and occasionally needed some sort of release—but over the hope her dream had raised within her. *Not real . . .* never *real! He'll* never *touch me like that!* Frustration bubbled up within her, until it released itself in a growl and a slamming of her fists on the bedding to either side of her, accompanying a burst of energy.

The mattress cracked and collapsed. Danau had only enough time to yelp and fling up her wrists and knees, protecting herself from the bedposts and formerly gauzy canopy as they crumbled and thumped down around her, fracturing further. She yelped again as bits of shatter-frozen wood and cloth bruised her shins and elbows, and swore as one piece of *udrezero* wood caught the edge of her scalp.

"—*Dammit!*"

The heat still thrumming through her flesh, warming her muscles and bones, wasn't the heat of a lover's body; it was the heat that had been part and parcel of the formerly room-temperature bed. Every physical, tangible thing in the world contained at least some potential heat; unfortunately, when Danau grew excited, her magic craved that heat and absorbed it from anything she touched. Today, that heat came from an innocent piece of furniture and bedding, turned so brittle from the cold that her frustrated, careless blow had shattered it.

Several years ago, that heat had come from her one and only lover, injuring him.

Failure . . . just a damned failure *. . . and* stupid, *too—there was enough thread left over, I* should *have spell-stitched containment wards for the bedding!* Blinking back tears, Danau stared up at the ceiling, trying to figure out how she would explain *this* to her hosts without either humiliating herself, or worse, letting her fellow Menomonites know. *I can't exactly hide it, either; they have servants in this place, even if only a few. One of them is bound to come in here and notice I shattered the waves-be-damned bed!*

Angry at her lot in life, Danau began shoving bits of icy, broken bed frame and shards of frost-rimed blanket out of her way. Crawling out of the wreckage, she brushed off the excess bed curtain dust, then strode for the refreshing room. Throwing the temperature lever to the far left and the flow lever to the far right, she stepped under the spray pouring down from the pipe that stuck out over the ceramic tub. Steam quickly billowed out from the water streaming over her head . . . but by the time it reached her feet, the spray had formed little frost crystals.

As she scrubbed her skin ruthlessly with a scrap of sponge and a bit of softsoap, the water spattering around her threatened to coat the bottom of the bathtub in ice. Danau struggled with her temper, focusing on clearing her mind and listening just to the pattering of water and the hissing of air through her teeth, thinking only of her breath. She might have an unnatural affinity for turning things *udre*-cold, but she was just as prone to slipping as anyone else. Now was not the time to add injury to insult.

I'm not getting back to sleep after that. *I might as well dress and go over my notes some more. There's that one span of wall that's too thick. I'll try to dowse it for some sort of hidden door, maybe another magical membrane-barrier, later today, after we've finished plotting out the main pipeways and sealing any cracks.*

Work was a safe topic. Work was her *only* topic.

I really do think there's some sort of hidden power source down there, some sort of control center for opening and closing those extra sluice tunnels—maintenance tunnels, as Lord Koranen said. Koranen . . .

For a moment, she could almost feel him in the shower with her, standing behind her, touching her as she rubbed the sponge over her cooling body. But the falling spray stung her feet and clattered noisily against the bottom of the tub. Gritting her teeth, Danau focused on just breathing and just scrubbing until the water stopped freezing as it fell.

"Yesss . . . yessss . . . *yesss* . . . !" She hovered above him, hips flexing, hands sliding, fingers swirling and cupping and pump—

"Uncle Kor?"

Koranen jerked upright, both hands quickly shifting from stroking to covering his erection. Eyes wide, he stared at the closed door of his forge while his illusion shattered and faded around him. "Wha . . . what? Uh . . . *Mikor?*"

The boy's voice came through the stout metal door, raised enough to be heard. "Good morning, Uncle Koranen! Can I come in? Are you doing something magical in your forge? Mother said I don't have to set the table this morning, and it isn't breakfast yet, so I thought I'd come out here."

His loincloth and sash belt were on the forge floor, his body was smeared with soot, and his manhood ached with interrupted need. *Nothing like . . . what did Kelly call it? Nothing like* childus interruptus *to cast a desire-dampening spell . . .* Clearing his throat, he spoke up, wanting to be sure Mariel's son heard him through the door. "Um, no, it's not safe to come in here this morning! I'll . . . uh . . . make it up to you another day!"

"You promise?" Mikor asked through the door.

"I *promise*!" Koranen swore. It was the safest way he could swear, because his body really did not like being interrupted mid fantasy.

Mikor said something cheerful in response, then said nothing else. Silence filled the forge, save for the faint hissing of the still-glowing coals beneath the mage. Koranen hoped it was because the youth had moved away, leaving him to his privacy . . . but there was no getting over the fact that his previous mood was now spoiled beyond repair.

Grimacing, he climbed out of the forge and eyed his soot-streaked limbs. Parts of his body ached from sleeping on the nut-sized lumps of cinders, and parts ached from waking up to incompletely fulfilled lust. He needed a shower, a meal, and a woman. His woman. *Gods— I shouldn't have left my birthing-day toy up in my bedchamber . . . though having her moaning in her pre-enchanted way when the boy came by would have been even worse.*

At least he had gotten enough sleep to be functional. Picking up his loincloth, Koranen slung it in place, then bundled last night's clothing together. By the time he was ready to leave, his erection had subsided, though he would have to hurry to avoid being seen skulking across the grounds and slipping up the castle stairs to his second-floor suite.

Then again, it was early, and the palace servants weren't so dedicated to their work that they would rise and begin cleaning at the crack of dawn. He hoped.

Things went sort of well; he got halfway between the stairwell and his suite door on the second floor, when the door to Danau's room opened. Koranen checked his stride, blushing hotly, but she didn't even glance his way. Instead, she turned and strode away from him, toward the heart of the palace. Then stopped, sighed, and bent over, pulling off her boot.

Koranen watched as she adjusted her sock, apparently to smooth out a wrinkle. But it wasn't her sock that held his attention. Rather, it was the sight of that beautiful, double-moon curve of her backside. Her flesh strained against the blue gray material of her trousers, showing off the supple flexibility of the tanned leather. Koranen felt rather envious of her trousers, being free to hug such a delicious piece of anatomy with impunity.

For such a tiny woman, she really has the most perfect . . .

He nearly jumped out of his skin when she stamped her foot back into her boot. Without looking back, the auburn-haired Aquamancer strode up the hall, leaving him to swallow and lower the bundle of clothing in his arms to hip level. Just in case anyone else decided to step out of their room this early in the morning. It wouldn't do to let anyone see his resurrected interest in her. Or his interest in anyone, however bold the Menomonite culture seemed to be about such things.

Hurrying to get into his suite, Koranen shut the door quietly and dropped his boots on the sitting room floor. He pitched his dirty clothes in the direction of the laundry hamper, opened the windows to let the impending steam out, and climbed into the tub, setting the water as cold as could be. First, a quick scrubbing with a sponge to get the soot off his naked hide. Then . . . a long, personal scrubbing with just the softsoap and his palms, until he sated his renewed interest in Danau, the prickly, distant Aquamancer with the perversely perfect backside.

At least here, safe in his own quarters, he wasn't as likely to be interrupted by anyone as he was when in his forge.

"An accident?" Kelly repeated, giving Danau a bemused look.

"An accident," Danau confirmed, hands clasped behind her back to hide the way her fingers had twisted around each other. "It was an accidental bit of magic, unintended, unwanted . . . and unfortunately unavoidable. I am prepared to offer the replacement cost of the bed in recompense, as well as my sincerest apologies."

The incipient, freckled queen shrugged. "Well . . . considering the state of some of the furniture in this place, old age may have helped your accidental demolition of it further along than you might think. Of course, I also have no idea how much a bed frame is worth."

Danau winced. "The mattress and blankets were destroyed as well."

"Ah. Anything else?"

Danau shook her head. "Fortunately, the accident confined itself to the bed and its contents alone . . . or I would be offering to replace the floor as well."

She couldn't stop the blush from heating her cheeks, though she did struggle to keep the air from chilling around her. Not that it would be unwelcome; today appeared to be shaping up into a very warm morning. Breakfast hadn't even been served yet, and already the Queen's family were dressing in sleeveless garments. Kelly herself had forgone the shell-skirt thing and the underblouse of her usual attire, and was clad just in a pair of trousers and a bodice-vest, her feet laced into sandals.

Danau thought it was more sensible attire than all those previous layers, but then, Menomonite fashions were often more about practicality than anything else. The Aquamancer wouldn't mind a little external heat after this morning's debacle. *In fact, a hot summer's day will be rather refreshing. Menomon's temperature tends to vary only a little. I usually have to go up to the surface with a Wavescout patrol to really feel warm.*

Kelly, who had been frowning softly in thought, finally shrugged. "What we really need right now are copper coins; the economy is a little short on spare change. How many have you got?"

"Uh . . . about forty of them? Maybe a little less?" Danau added, trying to remember just how much she had brought.

"Forty it is, then. Plus . . . ten silver. As for replacing the lost bed, we'll just have the servants move Saber's old bed into your room . . . which will be as soon as I can remember which part of the attics we originally moved it into when I was clearing out his things. When he moved up into the Lord's Chamber with me, I took over his old room for my dojo, the salle where I teach self-defense classes to my sisters-in-law." Kelly rolled her eyes. "*Some* of my sisters-in-law. I suppose I *should* open up the classes to anyone who wants them . . .

"You're welcome to join us, if you like. We usually exercise the hour before lunch, out in the west-northwest wing," she offered to Danau.

"Does that invitation extend to me?" another voice asked. Danau glanced over her shoulder; the mayor of the soon-to-be-official Harbor City entered the dining hall and stopped next to the short Aquamancer. Amara folded her arms across her chest. "Or would you rather I stayed away?"

"I'd *rather* we figured out how to get along," Kelly quipped, giving Danau another insight into the strawberry-haired monarch. "You're . . . welcome. To come. *If* you can remember that whoever is teaching *is* the teacher, and you don't waste most of that hour arguing with whoever is teaching you. Mariel teaches some of the time, too. Not just me."

Amara smiled. "I don't see a problem with that. I like her."

"And me?" Kelly asked skeptically.

The taller woman smirked. "I'm still withholding *some* of my judgment on that one."

I think she's teasing Her Majesty, Danau decided, though the evidence was dubious at best. *Menos, I'll be glad to get back under the water. The Council may be a headache to deal with, but at least it's my headache, with shoals and reefs I'm used to navigating.*

"Ah, there you are, Mayor Amara!"

All three women turned to meet the newcomer. Kelly smiled at the older female. "Good morning, Teretha."

The middle-aged woman didn't even acknowledge the redhead. Instead, she went straight to the black-haired woman in their midst. "I had a sudden idea on how to quickly clear the fields north of town, up on the plateau above and beyond the Desalinator, but it's going to take a lot of magic. I'll need your sister to meet me as soon as possible at the Ollen Farm."

Ha! Pleased her suspicions and guesses were so openly confirmed, Danau frowned in the next moment. She lagged behind the other two women, however, as both Kelly and Amara quickly scowled.

"I have no sister!" Amara snapped. From the twitch of her eyes, Danau guessed the black-haired woman was suppressing the urge to look at the foreigner in their midst.

"Of course you do! I was just telling a friend all about her. You *must* bring her to the Ollen Farm right away, so I can tell her how she needs to use her power!" the baroness asserted. "Now, *promise* me that you'll go fetch her immediately, yes?"

"I'll do no such thing!"

"Teretha . . . are you *feeling* alright?" Kelly asked, this time giving Danau the quick, sidelong look that Amara had repressed before returning her attention to the older woman.

Teretha smiled. "Never better! I need to get Rora to Ollen Farm as soon as possible."

"You are *not* yourself," Kelly stated warily. "Teretha . . . I'm going to have to ask you to go see the Healers, alright?"

"Healers?" Amara snorted. "Send her to Morganen. She's acting like she's been enchanted!"

"I think I *should* go see the Healers. I am feeling a bit stressed. I'll go see them now. I promise." Turning on her heel, the baroness strode out of the dining hall.

Kelly stared at her retreating back, then lifted her arm and flipped up the white crystal lid on her silver and gold bracelet. She jabbed at several smaller crystals. Curious, Danau held her patience, waiting to see what the incipient queen was doing. After several moments, the Aquamancer heard the voice of Lord Koranen's twin, faint but clear. Danau had seen Lord Koranen use his bracelet-thing . . . *cryslet*, that was the word for it . . . but she still wasn't entirely sure how it worked, other than that it was a miniature, portable scrying mirror.

"You rang?"

"Morganen, I need you to go chase down Baroness Teretha and cast some diagnostic spells on her, or something. She was just in here, absolutely insistent that Amara bring someone to see her at Ollen Farm, someone who *doesn't exist*."

Folding her arms across her chest, Danau kept the truth to herself. It wasn't her business to discuss the secrets of another nation, not when this particular secret wouldn't be of any benefit to Menomon. *Well . . . I suppose if this sister is a Living Fountain, then her Fountain could be put to good use expanding Menomon's square footage . . . but really, where would we expand into, without destroying the very corals that shelter, conceal, and provide for us?*

"Can it wait?" Morganen's voice countered, sounding a little strained. "Hope just started sending across a *lot* of stuff, and I'm not even sure if I'll make it to breakfast at this rate."

Sending across? What could she be sending across from an outworld? Wouldn't that unbalance the movement of the universes, if too much was shipped from one existence to the other? Danau wondered, confused.

Kelly's strawberry blond brows rose, her words echoing Danau's curiosity. "She's sending stuff across? What kind of stuff?"

"Plants. A *lot* of plants. I'm having to float them up onto the ramparts—sorry, but I *have* to go. I'll track down the baroness in an hour or so . . ."

From the way Kelly blinked, then slowly closed the lid of her cryslet thing, the connection had been severed quickly. "Well, I suppose it *could* wait . . . though she really wasn't acting like herself just now."

"She seemed rather . . . artificially cheerful," Amara said, searching for the right words. "Like she was *too* cheerful."

"She seemed to me like a pragmatic woman previous to this, but her actions just now weren't very practical-sounding, not if you're trying to hide this Rora woman," Danau offered, joining the conversation. At the quick exchange of looks between the other two women, she added, "I already figured out your sister was alive, but it wasn't my business, and it *isn't* my business. It certainly isn't Menomon's business. You can resurrect the Convocation with the help of a Living Fountain, *or* not resurrect it, however you want," she finished. "I'm just here for the Desalinator."

Amara glanced between the two redheads. "If she brought the Scroll of Living Glory for us to read, then she's probably read it herself. But why haven't I seen it?"

"Because it's your sister's business," Kelly returned firmly. "Not yours. If she wants you to read it, she'll let you read it. In the meantime, we have a city to finish building . . . and here come some of the others. This subject is dropped."

Both women nodded. Danau certainly had no problems dropping it; as she said, it really wasn't her business. Instead, she turned her attention to the newcomers. A handful of men entered the room, a couple of women trailing after them, along with a boy of about ten or so.

Lord Koranen wasn't among them. Aside from a slight pang of regret, Danau brushed aside his absence and nodded to the incoming bodies. Ama-ti had entered with the others, and Danau nodded to her before offering a newer, safer topic.

"Good morning. I think I may have found the entry point for the control center to the Desalinator, though I'll have to examine it later this afternoon. We still have the outlet pipes to finish measuring, repairing, and capping as a priority," she added, taking her place at the far end of the table from the incipient queen, since the others were picking out their own seats. "If there is a control center—and there should be—then once we figure out how to access it, we can figure out what's been powering the desalination and filtration systems, and how to revive the nonfunctioning segments. But it would be helpful to know exactly what damage to the outlying system remains in need of repair, and get those repairs started so that we *can* restart the rest of the Artifact."

"Permanent Magics may take a year or more to set up, between preparation, construction, enchantment, and empowerment, but this shouldn't take nearly that long," Ama-ti agreed. "The structure is already there, and most of what we've found looks to be sound, or at least in good repair. What we lack most of all is knowledge of the power source behind the filtration system. Once we know the ins and outs of that, the repairs should go relatively quickly."

Her words faded out as a familiar redhead strode into the room. Not from lack of vocal effort, but simply because Danau stopped listening to Ama-ti. Instead, she caught herself staring at the Lord Secretary and quickly looked down at her plate, trying not to blush. *This isn't the shower. If you start drawing heat out of nearby things, it'll be the people around you, and that wouldn't be good.*

He doesn't seem to be dressed very special, she added silently, flicking him a glance as he settled a few seats away from her. *But he did make a big deal about tonight's concert . . . so he must be planning to change before our . . . date. Which I plan on doing, too. I'll have to bathe after crawling around in old, buried pipeways anyway.*

I don't know if our date *will be worthy of that dress—I don't know what could be worthy of such finery—but even I can't resist something so fine.* Another flick of her blue eyes to the man clad in plain green, and she reluctantly added, *Or someone. However out of my reach.*

Back to your work, Danau. Back to your work . . .

EIGHT

ost of the time, the cloth wrapped around his forehead
was just for show. Sometimes he would fake a sweat for
his brothers' sake, but given how the eighthborn mage could draw
upon the ambient, loose energy shed by all living things, he rarely
grew tired. Certainly, he used his own power to gather up the excess, unclaimed energy, but merely to guide and to shape it, which
took longer to exhaust him than gathering and shaping his own inner forces.

Today, however, Morganen *needed* it for a sweatband.

First, he had to float over two thousand burlap sacks, holding
seedlings and saplings ranging from baby-sized to man-sized, up
out of his workroom to the ramparts of the great wall surrounding
the palace compound. Without damaging any of them. Then he
had to trek out into the forest-covered hills on the west side of the
island, clearing enough undergrowth to plant all those seedlings
and saplings along the middle-upper slopes.

Then he had to water them and imbue them with just enough

magic to ensure they survived the shock of being transplanted. Not just any magic, but life-force magic fresh from the source. The aether-gathered stuff might have done, and would have done . . . but these were *Hope's* plants. Ones which she didn't want to leave behind in her old world. Morganen wanted them to thrive, to be healthy when she finally came across, and to be a symbol of how he felt about her.

All of that took a lot of his magic. And a lot of his time. If he hadn't paused before leaving the palace to pack a waterskin and a couple of Natallian-style pocketbreads, loaded with meat and greens and a tangy-sweet sauce for energy, he might have been in trouble from hunger, not just exhaustion. As it was, Morg wasn't feeling too steady on his feet when he finally returned to his quarters to shower and change for the afternoon meal.

Fresh clothes and clean skin helped to revive some of his energy, but not all of it. When he finally made it to the dining hall, the light meal of salad greens and baked fish was already being served. He wasn't the last to the table, but Morg's arrival wasn't inconspicuous.

It was made worse when he slumped into his seat and braced his forearms on the table. Saber took one look at the youngest brother and stated bluntly, "You look like hell, Morg. What have you been doing?"

"Playing farmer all morning. And half the afternoon." At least the salad was mostly raw, being tossed greens and finely minced fresh vegetables. Every mage learned—either through lessons or life experience—that raw vegetables were best for replenishing lost energy. Digging into it was tiring, but it tasted good enough to elicit a moan of appreciation from him.

"Farmer?" Kelly repeated from her seat at the head of the table. "Morganen, I asked you to track down Baroness Teretha and check her for any reason that could have made her act so strangely this morning. You said you'd get to it within the hour. That was almost eight hours ago."

Dropping his fork, Morg slapped his forehead with both

hands, then dragged his palms down his face with a groan of self-disappointment. "Gods! I'm so sorry. I completely forgot about that! I'll head out as soon as I've eaten. I promise."

"You'd *better* eat," Mariel warned him. "You look like you were dragged through a defensive ward backward a few dozen times." The plump, curly-haired Healer passed a bowl of fruit his way. "Have some of this. *And* some meat. Mages cannot live on vegetables alone. It's not healthy."

Dutifully, Morganen took some of the whitefish from the platter Chana offered, though the smell made him feel a little queasy. At least he wasn't the last to come to the table. Reuen came in after a few moments, and Koranen and Danau were still missing.

As was Dominor, but then, the thirdborn brother usually joined his wife for meals these days. Given Serina was living on another continent entirely, and heavily pregnant, Morg wasn't surprised at Dom's absence. Kor was another matter. Hoping his twin was actually enjoying Danau's company—that outworlder dress was a dead giveaway as to her identity, as far as he was concerned—Morg concentrated on eating enough food to be able to cast the necessary tracking and diagnostic spells for his appointed, belated quarry.

Within a few minutes, Morg's energy-depleted queasiness faded, giving him more enthusiasm for the herb-baked sole. Just as he was lifting another forkful to his mouth, the door to the dining hall opened, and Dominor entered, surprising everyone. Ignoring the hastily offered greetings with a dismissive wave of his hand, he went straight to the Healer in their midst.

"Mariel, would you *please* come with me back to the Retreat?"

Morg was taken aback by Dominor's appearance. Normally meticulous about his grooming habits, the dark-haired man looked in desperate need of a shave and a change into something other than the rumpled, stained, blue tunic and trousers he wore.

"What's wrong?" she asked him. "Is Serina alright?"

"Oh, she's *fine* . . . if you count driving me absolutely insane with her mood swings, her crankiness, her complaints about swollen ankles and bloated feelings, and having to use the . . ." Raking a hand through his dark brown locks, Dominor gave his sister-in-law a pleading look. "Would you *please* pack up a couple weeks' worth of things and move to the Retreat? At least until the baby's born and my wife regains some of her *normal* insanities? She's asking for *you* specifically."

Mariel glanced at the others. "I'm not surprised, but . . . We can keep up with the minor injuries we've had so far on the island, but we're short a few Healers, if anything serious should happen."

"Trust me, I covered that," Dominor pledged. "The Mother Superior has agreed to send their new Healer here in your place so that we're not shorthanded. That's the one that replaced you when you came over here, isn't it?"

"Yes—why don't you sit down and have something to eat while I discuss the idea with Evanor?" Mariel suggested. She glanced at her son, who was making a face. "And with Mikor . . . since I don't think he'd want to be stuck with a bunch of nuns, far from his lessons and his friends, for the next few weeks."

Mikor shook his young head so hard, his curls bobbed around his head. "I wanna . . . I *want to* stay. I like Scholar Sarang. He makes learning stuff fun! And there's *nobody* to play with at the Retreat. Can I stay, Mother?"

"*May* I stay, Mother," Evanor corrected his next-son, who rolled impatient green eyes at the admonition.

"*May* I stay, Mother?" the youth repeated dutifully.

Morg hid his smile behind a mouthful of food. He remembered pleading in a similar manner with his own parents for special treats and special visits. That had been a long time ago, of course. It was good to have more than one generation around, again.

It also reminded him of an unspoken problem in their slowly growing family. When Mariel cuddled her son in a one-armed hug, reassuring him that she'd come back for visits or for an emergency, Morganen caught sight of the wistful look in Kelly's aquamarine eyes, and the way she bit her lower lip just for a moment. His outworlder sister-in-law glanced at her husband, who also briefly wore a subdued look.

That's another problem I hope I can find a way to resolve, Morg admitted. *Not just for Kelly's sake, but for Hope's as well. If Kelly isn't able to have children, and if it's because she's from another universe, neither will her best friend. Not that I'm eager to have children right away, of course . . . but I don't know if it's just Kelly who can't conceive, or if it's something wrong with Saber, or if it's because the balance between the universes has to be addressed first . . . like sending all that wheat over to Hope's world, in exchange for all those shade-loving bushes I planted.*

His muscles ached just thinking about it. Most of the effort had come from his magic, yes, but some of the planting effort had taken place manually, especially toward the end when he had to save his energy for empowering the plants. Mindful of his exhaustion, Morganen peeled the rind off a redfruit and composed his list of spells for locating Baroness Teretha to ascertain whether or not she really had been charmed or enchanted somehow.

Not that it's likely; true, she's not a powerful mage, but she is an experienced one. I'll take a wagon down to her home, see if she's there, first. If not, a couple hairs liberated from her hairbrush should get her tracked down fairly quickly. I'll need to take an undifferentiated tracking amulet with me . . . if I can remember where I put them. What was it, two years ago that I made the last batch? I know it was after Trevan had been bitten by that watersnake. If Rydan hadn't found him in time . . .

Catching and smothering a yawn, Morganen resolved to go to bed as soon as the concert was over. A few seats down from him at the dining table, Mariel was reassuring Dominor that she would go and pack as soon as she had finished her afternoon meal. And that she would be ready to leave for Natallia in the morning, but that she *wasn't* going to miss her husband's concert for anything. Morg couldn't blame her. Tired as he was, he didn't want to miss Ev's performance, either; there was a second performance scheduled for the next night, but there weren't any seats available.

Hopefully, whatever problems Teretha might be having wouldn't take too long for him to solve, since he still had to bathe and change.

"There, that should be the last of the cracks in this particular tunnel," Koranen murmured, stepping back from the freshly fused seam. A swipe at his face only rubbed the dried clay and lime dust around, but the kerchief he had brought had been rendered too dirty to use a couple of hours ago. He'd just have to suffer until he could bathe and change for their dinner date. Kor glanced at his companion and smiled wryly at her beige-streaked nose and brow. *Until we* both *can bathe and change.*

Catching his smile, Danau gave him a wary look. "What?"

"I was just thinking you've got as much clay smeared on you as I seem to . . . but in truth, I probably have even more, since your hair is so short and mine is so long." Sketching her a little bow, Kor added, "I concede the Menomonite point, that short hair is highly practical compared to long."

Danau found herself smiling and unbent a little. "And I concede that your skills are quite useful in this job, not just for making baubles."

Work-obsessed is right, Koranen thought, carefully not taking offense at her dismissal of his glassmaking skills. *She's probably just a little jealous that I haven't made her anything, yet. I'll have to rectify that.* Pulling his cryslet from the pouch slung at his waist, he checked the time, marked by a series of tiny, creamy white dots added around the rim. Kor grimaced. "It's almost five of the afternoon. We let time get away from us. Let's get back up to the surface and get ourselves cleaned off—dinner might be a little delayed, but we can always bring a lunch basket with us and order something we can take to the concert."

"At least it was a good day's work. And the bags and buckets are lighter than when we started," Danau said, gesturing at them. "I'll float the ones on this side, if you can get those."

Koranen nodded. His family had found a deposit of clay beneath the sea in the last few months. It wasn't the highest quality around, but when mixed with coarse sand and powdered, baked limestone, it turned into a decent mortar. It had to be mixed on the spot with freshwater, since even without heat it set fairly quickly, but with Koranen heating the paste to speed the curing process and Danau spell-sealing the water inside the paste's surface to strengthen it, neither of them had to worry about that paste falling off the curved tunnel walls within the first few moments of it being applied.

The silence between them as they walked, Kor decided, was more companionable this afternoon than it had been this morning, when the two of them had first set out to patch old cracks and seal off broken pipeways in the main water tunnels leading away from the Desalinator. Work-based conversation and cooperation had done a lot to smooth out the stilted awkwardness between them, enough that he had managed to eke out a few comments on other subjects.

The Pyromancer was fairly sure he had found the right formula to approach this particular Aquamancer: At least ninety percent of their conversations had to be work-related, but he *could* slip in one compliment or personal observation for every ten subjects discussed without being rebuffed.

Sort of like feeding some poor, starving creature; too much at once, and she only chokes on it. But a little bit doled out at a time seems to be doing the trick. She certainly is blossoming, becoming more friendly with me and not just merely civil. At least, she seems to be more friendly . . . It wasn't easy hiding his pleasure at his success. *I do believe all those years of listening to Trevan is finally paying off. Even if she doesn't turn out to be the right woman, I can at least say that I've made her happier with some deft, subtle courtship.*

Danau glanced at Koranen out of the corner of her eye. She wasn't entirely sure why he was smirking. It wasn't a big smile, just a little quirk at the edge of his mouth, but he was definitely pleased about something. Part of her hoped it was because of *her*, the part of her heart still filled with a futile hope that she could find someone to please, that she could still be a real woman somehow, instead of a sexless, frigid illusion of one. Her practical side, however, pointed out that it wasn't kind to give a man false hope for getting anywhere with her.

At least there's the dress. From what his twin said, that dress is mine to keep, even after we leave. Though I won't ever be a wife, I can at least wear a dress made entirely of velvet. There are outfits made entirely of silk back in the city, but no one else has a garment made completely of velvet. It was a petty pleasure at best, but it was hers, and she hugged it to herself for comfort. Spotting an access ladder in one of the side tunnels they had already repaired, she gestured at it.

"That one should let us out somewhere near the southeast part of the city. At least, I think. We might be messy and not entirely acceptable for a public appearance, but I'm getting tired of walking around by mage-light. And it's stuffy down here. I don't mind the heat, but I could do with some fresh air."

"I don't blame you. I could use some fresh air, too. And some greenery in my line of sight, instead of all this grayery," Kor joked. Organizing the bags and buckets into a more compact mass, enspelled to follow rather than precede him, he started up the ladder.

The heavy ceramic lid was still in fairly good repair, though two centuries of dirt had wedged itself into a sort of seal around the rim. It required a touch of magic as well as muscle to break the seal, but he managed to get it open. Thankfully, Koranen recognized their surroundings as soon as he levered the cover out of the way: a small side street not far from Baroness Teretha's house.

A small dog trotted past, sniffing and yipping at him as Koranen climbed out of the pipe, and the sounds of children laughing and a horse nickering could be heard from somewhere nearby. The air was hot and dusty, and the slight wind felt more like a smothering, warm blanket than a source of relief. Summer was his least favorite season solely for the heat it brought; he didn't need more of it in his life.

As Koranen shifted his floating bundles out of Danau's way, he spotted his twin pacing slowly up the otherwise empty street, studying the crystal-and-metal pendant dangling from his hand.

"Hey, Morg!" Kor called out. His twin looked up after a moment, glancing their way with a distracted air. "What are you doing?"

"Looking for our missing field reclamation expert. Kelly said the baroness was acting very strangely this morning before breakfast, but this is the first chance I've had to track her down," Morg told them, detouring their way. "Most of the signs I'm getting are rather faint. Which doesn't make sense, unless she's left the Isle."

Danau frowned at that. "Why would Teretha leave the Isle? She seemed very happy with her work here. A little odd and fanatic about it this morning, but . . ."

"You were there?" the Lord Mage asked her, surprise lifting his light brown brows. "What did she say, exactly?"

Danau shrugged. "Something about a new method of repairing irrigation pipes, and a definite insistence that Mayor Amara's sister be brought out to the Ollen family farm immediately—don't bother with protestations," she added quickly, lifting her hand to forestall the youngest brother's indrawn breath. A quick glance confirmed the three of them were still alone; even the dog had trotted out of view. "I already know her sister is still alive, and I know it's no business of mine why or where. Nor do I have any reason to tell anyone outside your family what I know, so the secret is safe with me."

"Then your discretion is appreciated," Morganen managed after a moment, giving her a slight bow. "But that's all she said? That Amara's sister had to go out to the Ollen Farm?"

"More or less," Danau admitted. "But she was very forceful about it, and very indiscreet about blatantly mentioning a woman who supposedly doesn't exist in front of a stranger such as myself. She also swore she'd take herself off to the Healers for examination, at your queen's suggestion . . . but I don't think she did."

"No, she didn't. Nor is she at her home. According to her house-keeper, she took one of the carts to the palace and back this morning. Traveling in a wagon scatters the stray hairs and dead skin cells a lot more than if she had walked, making such things that much more difficult to trace," the mage added, gesturing with the pendant. The crystal in the middle was actually two thin slabs of clear quartz, with a small coil of brown hair sandwiched carefully between them. No doubt it was one of the missing woman's hairs. He looked at Danau again. "Do *you* think she was charmed or enchanted somehow? Based on what you saw, I mean."

"I didn't know her for very long, but it *could* be possible," Danau admitted, scratching absently at the side of her nose. That reminded her of the mortar drying on her skin, and she grimaced. "Whatever was wrong with her, she wasn't her levelheaded self this morning. She was . . . overly cheerful and very excited. More so than some new idea should have warranted, given how insistent she was."

Memory crossed Koranen's thoughts. "Maybe she's just enthusiastic about her new swain, and it's spilled over into the rest of her life?" Both his twin and his impending date eyed him askance at that. Kor shrugged. "I saw her at the Giggling Pear last night with that blond mage that came off the boat from Menomon. They were having a rather courtly looking chat over their meal, touching hands and talking a lot. She looked rather besotted with him by the time . . . well, by the time Ama-ti and I left."

Wonderful, Koranen chastised himself, wincing internally. *Mention the last woman you dated—and the meal you had with her—right in front of your current courting project . . .*

Morg shrugged. "Well, I'll check out the Ollen Farm, see if she went there, then go look up this blond mage . . . Yarrow, was it? What do you know of him, Danau?"

"His name is Yarrin," Danau corrected. "I didn't have much contact with him since he was the Mage Guild's responsibility as a generalist mage, and not the Aquamancy Guild's. But I do know he was *very* eager to leave Menomon, even offering to let his memory

of Menomon be erased from his mind if he could be returned to the
surface. From what I heard, he all but leaped for joy at the chance to
be tossed out with the others we rescued from the shipwreck that
murderer magic-stealer, Xenos, was on. He didn't seem to have a
problem with claustrophobia or hydrophobia as far as I could tell,
but he was eager to leave. That's the most I can say about him."

"Who knows?" Koranen dismissed. "Anyway, if he was courting
her, then she may have gone to him if she wasn't at her home," he
said. "At any rate, this Yarrin fellow might have had something to
do with her enthusiasm. Though that doesn't *prove* anything was
affecting her, beyond natural enthusiasm."

"It doesn't disprove it, either—I know Kelly wrote the law to
state that all suspects are to be considered innocent until proven
guilty by law," Morg dismissed, "but he's new to the island, and we
don't know what motives he might have for courting an older
woman. One with a position of some power and responsibility. He
could just be a social climber, seizing an opportunity to gain a
baroness-lined nest, or he could be honestly interested in her, and
she in him . . . or he could be one of Amara and Rora's old enemies
from the Aian continent and has somehow influenced Teretha to
try to get him closer to his original quarry."

Koranen grimaced. "That lattermost one has an unpleasant
amount of potential in it, Brother."

"Agreed. *But* it is only a potential right now," Morganen said.
"Which means I'm going to the Ollen Farm to look for traces of her
there, and if I can't find any, *then* I'll go looking for him as my next
lead. Hopefully I'll have tracked her down in time to change for the
concert. Speaking of which . . . the two of you look a tad under-
dressed. Shouldn't you be heading back?"

"We know. We're on our way back now. See you tonight," Koranen returned politely. He gestured for Danau and her flotilla of
buckets and bags to precede him. Once she was past him, beyond
line of sight, Kor stuck out his tongue at his twin.

Morg gave his sibling an absentminded wave, already returning his attention to the diamond-shaped pendant dangling from his hand.

Even after a few days, Danau was still amazed and bemused by the variety of images the enchanted paint on the walls could project. When she entered her suite, parting company from Koranen with a reassurance that she really was going to wash and change for their . . . date . . . the Aquamancer wasn't expecting the night sky that greeted her the moment she finished shutting the door.

All of the walls in the front parlor were spangled with constellations, and the wall to the left of the doorway leading to the bedchamber had hints of an impending moonrise. With the curtains closed against the afternoon sunlight—no doubt done so by a servant to magnify the effect of the paint—the stars glowed out of the walls, leaving strange, squared silhouettes wherever the furnishings were scattered around the room.

The effect was nice to look at, but difficult to navigate, particularly now that the door was shut, leaving her in near-total darkness. Two thin beams of indirect light dissected the darkness, cast by the slight gaps in the heavy curtains covering the windows. Groping beside her for the lightglobe, Danau hesitated as she noticed a small patch of darkness interrupting one of those floor-crossing lines. *Ugh . . . I hope it's not one of those rat creatures. Rats, mice, and roaches are among the few things the shipwreck wardings* don't *rescue from drowning, and with good cause . . .*

Finding the globe with her knuckles, she rapped it sharply, blinking against the strong white light it obediently cast. And saw several more dark lumps, as the spots cleared from her eyes. Several dark, fuzzy . . . blue green . . .

Danau took one unsteady step forward, her mind struggling to comprehend what her wide eyes swore they saw. Another step . . . a third, and she fell to her knees. Eyes prickling, she crawled the last little bit of distance between her and the nearest scrap. Her hand reached out, hovered over the piece, no bigger than a third of her palm, and very, very gently touched its curling, fraying edge.

It was . . . velvet. Deep blue green . . . velvet. *Her* . . . velvet.

Frost crept over the cloth, coating it with a different source of fuzz, a coldness deep enough to match the flush burning her face. It spread out from her kneeling body as fast as her pounding heart, until she couldn't tell where it ended and the blurriness of her tears began. The dress . . . *her* dress . . .

It hurt so much, she couldn't bear it.

Her hands threatened to freeze to her cheeks. She didn't know when she had covered her eyes, but Danau sniffed and tugged her palms free, flexing them to crack and brush away the broken bits of her tears. Scrubbing at her face, she sniffed again, breath misting as white as the room.

It's Chana. It has to be her. Or Reuen. Chana—she *overheard me telling Koranen about the dress.* Rubbing at the tears threatening to freeze on her face, Danau pushed to her feet. There weren't many frozen lumps in the sitting room, maybe part of the upper bodice at most, but she didn't doubt the rest of the dress was equally shredded. Stepping carefully to the bedroom door—even she wasn't immune to the ice she created in times of stress—Danau nudged it open, trying not to add to the frost damage. Replacing the bed had been bad enough, but to have to explain the need for a new doorknob wouldn't help her current humiliation.

More pieces of dress lay scattered across the second chamber's floor. Heat flushed across her skin, and the walls and floor in the bedroom started to turn white. Struggling for self-control, Danau turned and carefully exited her suite. The door to Koranen's quarters was closed, its occupant oblivious. That was good. It was the only thing that would make this situation worse, to be *pitied* by a man.

Striding to Chana's room, Danau grasped the lever, intending to confront the other woman . . . and broke it, crumbling the chilled metal the moment she tried to use it. Gritting her teeth, she jammed her thumb against the stump of metal and focused her power into the latch. A push with her palm broke that, too, swinging the door open. Let *Chana* explain how her door came to be broken . . . if she survived what Danau wanted to do to her.

What that would be, she didn't know; it didn't help that Chana wasn't in her suite. Or maybe it did. Even the newest of incipient kingdoms held laws against murder . . . though this one might have been considered justifiable.

A quick, doorknob-breaking tour of Reuen's rooms proved that she, too, wasn't there. Which meant they were back at the Desalinator. Working. Work was *all* she had, now . . . and she would show those two exactly what *her* work could do. Face hot, breath cold, Danau strode swiftly, silently, for the nearest stairwell, ignoring the clattering of the tears that bounced across the hallway floor.

Standing under the icy-cold spray, surrounded by billowing steam, Koranen caressed himself. Hands splayed over his chest and abdomen, he smeared the softsoap lather over his skin, paying attention to his nipples and his navel. He didn't want to take too long with his shower, but a little fantasizing wouldn't hurt, and he was fantasizing that she was taking a rain-shower with him, instead of in her own rooms.

Mm, yes . . . she could rub her hands all over me, anytime . . . Wish I could've helped her bathe all this muck from her body, too . . . Trevan says making love in a bathtub is a lot of messy, wet fun . . . Ohhh, yesss—whoo, thank the Gods the water is cold tonight!

At least he had the foresight to clean his lower body first; scrubbing it now would delay him even further. Forcing himself to rinse off rather than continue his self-ministration, Koranen shut off the water and steamed himself dry, raking his fingers through his hair to detangle the clean strands. A press of his hand to the edge of the mirror frame over the sink basin cleared it of fog after a few seconds.

Peering at his face, the Pyromancer muttered under his breath while running his fingers over his chin. As soon as his jaw was spell-shaved smooth, he grimaced at his reflection, checking his teeth. A cautious huff of breath into a cupped palm proved it wasn't offensive, so he didn't bother with brushing his teeth.

Let's see . . . It's been a hot day, so I think if I wear the dark blue velvet trousers and the matching overjacket, the one with the silver trim, but wear sandals instead of boots and forgo a shirt entirely, I shouldn't be too uncomfortable—oh, hair! Braided, or loose? Loose, he decided. His hair had dried with a slight wave to it, and he liked the way it tumbled down over his naked shoulders.

The velvet outfit, when he dug it out of its chest, was creased with age. Grimacing, Koranen spread it out on the table in his sitting room and ran hot palms over the fabric, carefully smoothing out the wrinkles. A few refused to straighten, but he was running out of time, if they wanted to make it to the restaurant before the concert. It would have to do.

Wrapping a clean loincloth around his hips, he tucked it into the trousers, laced on the sandals, and belted the sleeveless overjacket in place. Since there was a pouch threaded on the belt, Koranen dug a handful of coins out of the lockbox he kept under his nightstand, counted them roughly to make sure they were enough to pay for dinner, and tossed them into the black leather bag. Donning silver armbands along with his cryslet, Koranen fluffed out his hair with his fingers and checked his reflection in the refreshing room mirror. A bit of lint needed to be brushed off the velvet, but otherwise he looked good. Ready to be tumbled in a bed. Giving himself a grin for encouragement, he left his quarters and crossed to Danau's door.

The corridor was refreshingly cool, compared to his chambers. One of his siblings must have wandered through the palace casting a cooling charm, since even the thick stones composing the palace wouldn't be able to ward off the full heat of a hot summer day. Grateful for the dip in temperature, he smoothed his hair back from his face, then lifted his hand to the aging oak panels.

A rap of his knuckles nudged the door open a few inches. Bemused, Koranen gingerly pushed it open. "Danau?"

No answer. But the sight that greeted him confused him even further. Half the sitting room glistened with beads of dew, while a large patch of floor about a third of the way into the chamber glittered from a rime of . . . frost? *Frost, on a hot summer day? Even with a cooling charm, there shouldn't be frost in here!*

White-fuzzed scraps didn't belong on the floor, either. Stepping into the room, Koranen called out her name again. "Danau? Are you in here?"

No response. His proximity to the frost melted it in floor-baring circles around his sandal-clad feet. Crouching, he reached out and picked up one of the frosted scraps. For the first second or two, he felt the chill of the fabric, then it melted away, baring the remnants of blue green velvet.

Velvet . . . from the dress she was going to wear. A dress that's been torn to pieces . . . by one of the others? By Chana? She knew Danau had the dress; she overheard us talking about it. Certainly there'd be no reason for Danau to tear a dress to pieces . . .

The reason for the shredded velvet scattered over the floor wasn't too difficult to piece together; Reuen and Chana didn't seem to like Danau very much, even if Ama-ti got along with the petite Aquamancer well enough. The frost and the dew confused him, though. Its presence made no sense.

Why would she cast a frost spell on the remnants? On a hot day like today, it wouldn't be of any use for preserving evidence—all it would do would make everything damp! Losing a fancy dress would make her upset, yes—it would make anyone upset, even me! I'm upset right now that anyone would be so cruel to her, but . . .

Koranen suddenly realized the circle of frost was melting rather rapidly. It wasn't the fact that it was melting that caught his attention, but rather the *cause* of its melting. Him. A Pyromancer. Closing his eyes, Koranen groaned softly.

Morg . . . I am going to kill you for being so Gods-be-damned secretive*!* He would have to add himself to that list, too, for being blind. *Jinga's Sacred Ass—the moment she refused to touch hands with me,* I should have known*!*

Smacking himself in the forehead scorched the scrap of velvet still cradled in his palm, wafting tendrils of smoke into the air. Rubbing at his nose to contain the urge to sneeze, Koranen cooled and dropped the fabric on the floor, disgusted with himself. *He* didn't touch people very often for fear of accidentally burning them. *He* needed a woman who could withstand his heat. *He* burned things when he got upset, unless he was very careful to contain his affinity for fire . . . which wasn't always possible when caught up in some strong emotion.

A woman who could withstand his thermal problems would have to be his opposite: a woman who *absorbed* heat, just as he *radiated* it . . . which meant getting upset would make her chill her surroundings. To the point of causing frost.

"Kata—and all the other Patrons of Lovers—I am an *ass* for being so *clueless*," he stated formally, staring once more at the singed bit of fabric before closing his eyes. "And I beg You for Your forgiveness and Your assistance in *not* being an ass any longer!"

Berating himself silently for being a mindless idiot, Koranen straightened from his crouch and padded into the rest of the suite, checking to make sure Danau wasn't there. She hadn't bothered to shower and change, he decided, noting the dry bathing tub. *We parted company, she entered her room—I shed my clothes and ducked into the shower—and she saw her dress, got upset enough to freeze everything within reach . . . and what? Ran off to cry in private? Stormed off to confront the others?*

If so, he couldn't blame her. He had a score of his own to settle with Reuen. *She* knew *Danau was a . . . an* anti-heat generator, *for lack of a better term. She had to have known! All of them had to know. So why didn't they* tell *me Danau was my opposite?*

Leaving Danau's quarters, he spotted a blue-haired head coming his way. Ama-ti. Like he and Danau had been, she was coated in smears of clay and lime from her own efforts at sealing the cracks in the main water tunnels.

She didn't seem to dislike Danau, but why hadn't she told him about this? Waiting impatiently for her to approach, Kor responded to her greeting with a nod. "Ama-ti. Why didn't you tell me about Danau?"

Green eyes blinked blankly at him. "Tell you what?"

"That she *absorbs* heat," he said carefully, reining in his temper. "That she generates cold whenever she's upset!"

The Menomonite had the grace to blush, though her discomfort didn't seem to stem from the embarrassment of being caught. "It's, well . . . it's not something one *talks* about. To have brought it up would have been cruel. I mean, she can't *help* being the way she is—you really shouldn't hold it against her. I mean, she was *born* that way. Not that it showed up until puberty, but she just can't help being a . . . a . . ."

"A what?" Koranen asked tightly, folding his arms across his chest. "Abnormal? An aberration? A freak of magic?"

Ama-ti picked her words carefully. "Socially . . . Danau is considered *less* than ideal as a woman—no one doubts her qualifications as an Aquamancer," she hastened to add. "It's pretty much the only place where she can succeed, and she does so indisputably . . . but because of her, um, her little *flaw*, well . . . she'll never have a husband, let alone the three or four a real woman is supposed to wed. No one wants what happened to Jiore to happen to them."

"Jiore?" Kor asked, wariness mingling with rising jealousy. He hadn't even considered Danau having courted another man before.

"Frostbite," Ama-ti revealed delicately, making her point with a vague gesture of her hand and a glance downward. "On his . . ."

Kor felt parts of his anatomy wince in pure masculine sympathy, before he reminded his body that he had *never* suffered from frostbite, not even in the coldest, snow-laden winters back in Corvis County on the mainland.

"Anyway, I personally thought it was very tasteless of Jiore to ruin her reputation like that, but really, what else could he do? Stay silent and let another man be injured like that, even if it wasn't intentional?" Sighing, Ama-ti shook her head and closed the distance between them. "I'm *not* trying to ruin her reputation further—I like her! And I certainly don't hold this one little flaw against her. Menos just made her that way, for whatever reason He had in mind. But if you are going to go out on a date with her tonight . . . well, you need to know, so you don't have any high expectations for how your evening will end.

"She is quite smart, and a good conversationalist, so you should still be able to have a good time." Lifting her hand, Ama-ti patted him on the arm—then jerked her hand away and stared at her fingers. Gingerly shaking them, she shifted her gaze to his face. "You . . . ah . . . Hot?"

"Very." Keeping his arms folded, Koranen glanced past her, up the corridor. "Are the other two still back at the desalination plant?"

"Maybe; they still had some work to do, so I came ahead to the palace. We *were* going to work another hour, but I thought it might be nice to take our time getting ready for the concert, so as senior-most, I called it a good day's work, and they didn't object, just said they'd finish up their last task and come up as soon as they could. Um, Koranen . . ." She trailed off, then tried again, nodding at his arm. "Your, um, heat . . ."

"Is none of your business. You have a leather-tailor waiting for you when you get back home," he added more gently as she blinked. "With any luck, you'll be happy with him . . . and with whatever other men you may choose to marry. I will not be one of them."

Giving her a polite bow, Koranen detoured around her, heading for the rest of the palace. There was no telling where the other two Aquamancers had gone, but he could guess where Danau had gone. Back to the Desalinator. Either to try to find Reuen and

Chana, the most likely culprits for the destruction of her clothes, or to bury herself in her work. The one thing she consistently focused on.

It's because it's all she has, all she can be proud of, if she's a "failure" as a woman . . . at least, according to the asinine beliefs of Menomonite society. It solidified his belief that Nightfall was the place to stay. *Ama-ti is sweet and tactful, but I'm not stupid enough to think that* flaw *is the word they use to describe Danau.* Freak *would be more accurate. Or whatever the Menomonite equivalent would be.*

Gods . . . given the way her colleagues treat her, I doubt she's had an easy life. I, at least, had my family to support and defend me, in spite of my own flaw. My brothers and I knew if word got out that I was a Pyromancer—and it did—it would convince everyone we were the Sons of Destiny that the Seer Draganna Prophesied. And we ended up being exiled for it . . . but that was a physical exile as well as a social one. After we were dumped here four years ago, I didn't have to put up with people reacting to my excessive heat anymore.

Danau didn't have that option. All this time, she's had all those people in the city knowing that she's potentially dangerous . . . and so she doesn't date. Ever. That part finally made sense. She wasn't ugly by any means, if a bit . . . *If a bit* cold *in her interactions with others,* Kor thought, wincing at his obliviousness. *She's smart, competent, educated . . . She should have had suitors lining up to court her, especially in a society where women are outnumbered by men five to one.*

His situation could have been hers, if he hadn't had the love of his brothers to shelter him. *It isn't fair! And it's no wonder she "doesn't date" anyone—well, that's going to change, because if she really is what I think she is, she's* perfect *for me . . . and I owe Morg a slap on the back of his head for hiding it. He had to have known!*

Mindful of the heat his angry thoughts were generating, Koranen focused on calming himself down. First he had to find Danau, then he had to confirm that she was indeed plagued by a problem the exact opposite of his own, then the two of them test his heat versus her cold . . . and, Gods willing, be able to touch

and kiss without him burning her breasts, or her giving him frostbite on his . . .

Right. Hopefully we will *cancel each other out. Because if I'm utterly
wrong, and* none *of these Aquamancers is meant for me, I'll probably
self-incinerate!*

NINE

❦

They weren't at the Desalinator. Wherever Reuen and Chana had gone, it wasn't to their chambers, and it wasn't around here. Frustrated, Danau emerged from the last freshwater building she had checked. Not even the heat in the air could warm her soul, though it did its best to warm her flesh.

Standing there, staring sightlessly across the compound, she debated taking the wagon she had borrowed back up to the castle to clean herself up, but remembered Lord Koranen was still up there. Getting ready to go out with her. He would expect her to be ready for dinner at a restaurant, and dressed up elegantly enough to attend the first official entertainment of these people.

In a precious velvet gown that had vindictively been torn into shreds.

I'm not going back there. I can't—I won't! Her temper had calmed somewhat on the drive down, even during the search through the buildings—now unoccupied but for a sparse crew of workers shifting salt and algae blocks into storage—but her breath started to mist again at the thought of going back up to bathe and change into plain, ordinary leathers. Humiliating ordinary leathers.

She couldn't deal with it. Memories of Jiore telling everyone and anyone that she was an icicle in the shape of a woman tore at her. The scorn, the derision—it would start all over again. She didn't know which woman was responsible for the loss of her dress, but Danau *still* didn't know enough about the Desalinator to have said whether or not she could send either of them back to Menomon in disgrace, without it potentially damaging their chances of reviving this gorgeous, old Artifact.

Gritting her teeth, Danau pushed away her feelings and concentrated on the huge building at the center of the complex. *I never did investigate that too-thick section of wall . . . I'll do that right now. It'll get my mind back where it belongs, on the only refuge I have. My work.*

Ignoring the rattling of the carts transferring blocks from outbuilding to warehouse, blocking out the curious glances the workers aimed her way, she strode into the central structure. The area she had marked out as possible former office space was in the southern part of the building. It meant leaving the warmth of the sunshine for the much cooler shade of the huge structure, but only she found that annoying. She hated being cold; it reminded her of what she was. The workers, however, clearly enjoyed it.

Shows what they *know . . . Oh, stop that, Danau,* she ordered herself. *It's not their fault you're not a real woman. You can blame Menos and the other Gods for arranging your fate, you can blame your late mother and your four co-fathers for creating your body, and you can even blame yourself for not being able to control your powers, but no one else made you what you are!*

And while you are *a failure as a woman, you are* not *a failure as an Aquamancer. Now, go figure out what's wrong with that wall!*

The size, shortness of hair, and close cut of her clothes allowed Koranen to spot Danau as she entered the warehouse. As he had surmised, she hadn't cleaned up from their afternoon trek through the pipes, looking for cracks to seal. Guiding his wagon to a stop next to another one—no doubt the one she had borrowed to get down here—he set the brake and climbed down.

It was a relief to hurry into the shade of the oversized building; the breeze gusting in through the large open doors was still warm and dusty, but the deeper he went, the cooler it became. Despite his sleeveless, shirtless, bootless state, the deep blue velvet of his outfit was just a little too warm for this particular afternoon. Sweat continued to bead on his brow, even after he escaped the sun.

For such a small woman, Danau had a long, fast stride. He didn't catch up to her, though he did at least keep her in sight. She didn't linger in the occupied areas, but instead headed straight to the cluster of smaller storage rooms in the south end of the warehouse. Slipping inside, she vanished from view.

By the time he reached the outer doorway, she wasn't in the first room, though she had lit the single lightglobe resting in a bracket next to the door. Nor was she in the second, when he crossed to that door. But she was inside the third storage chamber, past the door to the refreshing rooms that served this part of the warehouse. Hands still dusty from the clay and lime of earlier, she was running them over the wall to the left, searching for something.

Danau heard someone enter the room behind her. Not in a very sociable mood, she didn't bother to look behind her. All she wanted was to dismiss whoever it was and focus on her work. "I am not interested in company. Leave me alone."

That irritated Koranen. "We have a date."

Flushing, Danau spun to face her intruder, struggling to hide the threat of her breath fogging in counterpoint to the heat flushing across her face. It didn't help that he looked very good clad in deep blue . . . *velvet*. She struggled even harder to suppress her hurt and her anger, and faced the wall again. "I'm sorry. I changed my mind. Have a nice dinner, and I hope you enjoy the concert."

"Danau . . ."

"Go away!" Only half of her attention was on the wall beneath her fingers, but Danau still felt the difference when her right hand crossed the boundary of *something* her eyes couldn't discern. Probing it with her fingertips and her power, she added dismissively, "I am *working*."

"Why?" Kor challenged the petite woman fingering the opposite wall. He moved toward her, not about to be deterred . . . particularly when he felt how much cooler the air was, the closer he came to her. "Because someone destroyed your dress?"

Danau stiffened, humiliation flushing through her. Apparently, he had gone looking for her and spotted the carnage scattered over her floor. Gritting her teeth, she probed the stiff barrier disguised as a segment of wall. "*Yes*. Because I have *nothing* to wear. How *female* of me!"

Koranen winced at that. Ama-ti's comment about her fellow Aquamancer being considered less than perfect as a woman was still fresh in his mind, and clearly a sore point in Danau's. "I did not ask you to accompany me because of a dress, however lovely it might have been. I asked you to accompany me because I wanted *your* company."

"I. Don't. Date." Struggling against her emotions, Danau threw her frustrations into her power, trying to force what felt like a particularly tough hydrostatic barrier to respond and soften. It didn't budge. "Gods! *Open!* I know you're there! Why won't you *open?*"

Irritated by her stubborn refusal to face him, by the way she was hiding herself, her potential, in her work, Koranen grabbed her shoulder. "Danau, I am *trying* to talk to you!"

"Don't touch me!" Spinning to push him away from her, Danau felt her ankle twist and lost her balance. Expecting to bounce off the wall from the force of her arm thrusting against his, she gasped as she felt herself falling backward instead. Her push became a desperate scrabble to catch herself, clutching at his arm and sleeve.

A section of darkness had opened behind her the moment her back touched what should have been an age-faded, whitewashed

stone wall. Koranen, caught off guard by the sudden opening, lunged
forward to catch the unbalanced woman. Her desperate, wide-eyed
grab pulled him off balance, too. The pair fell, unable to stop themselves.

Koranen wrenched himself to one side as he dropped, not wanting to crush the petite woman beneath his larger, heavier frame. He
managed to avoid most of her, bruising his forearm on the floor
next to her shoulder as he twisted. Using that, he thrust his falling
frame sideways, though it deepened the bruise. Somehow, he managed his task, rolling even as he fell . . . but at the price of dropping
farther than expected.

Sharp stone steps bit into his shoulder, hip, and legs as the lack
of a level floor threatened to send him even farther downhill. Grunting in pain, Kor managed to stop his tumble with an awkwardly
braced heel, though his fall ended with a painful bruising down the
left side of his body, particularly his lower ribs. Breathless from the
pain, he had only a moment to register the dust layered on the stone
steps supporting him. Then their sole source of light winked out,
leaving them in utter darkness.

"What?—No!" Scraping sounds told him Danau had regained
her feet; they were followed within moments by the slapping of her
hands against the wall. "Open! . . . *Open!*"

The bruises down his sides didn't make him feel inclined to
move just yet. Nor did the slope of the steps. It was the thought of
her stepping the wrong way and tumbling past him down to the
Gods knew where that prompted him into action. A twist of his
fingers summoned a small but bright ball of fire. Both of them
winced from the sudden glow, but it did banish the darkness.

They were in a stairwell, one with age-cracked whitewash coating its walls. Cobwebs lingered in the upper corners, fuzzy with
some of the same dust that had gathered on the steps, and which
was now smeared in gray streaks across his velvet clothes. Sitting
up with a grunt, Koranen peered down the stairwell. It descended
roughly a floor and a half to a small landing, where it made a partial

turn and descended even farther. Beyond that, he couldn't tell where it went.

Danau slapped the wall again. Everything that could go wrong *was* going wrong, and in the worst possible way, by raising her hopes and then dashing them to pieces. First, a beautiful velvet dress had been generously given to her. Then it had been destroyed. Then she found a hidden doorway which had opened long enough to let them inside, but now it wouldn't open again. She had no idea *why* it had opened, either, or how it had opened, or how to get it to open again.

They were trapped.

Straining against it with mind and body didn't budge the stones one whit; the only thing that budged was her lungs, panting from frustration. What stopped her from slapping the wall and trying again was the frost that crept outward from her palms. Betraying her shame. Snatching her hands away, she glanced at the other redhead in the stairwell, grateful to learn his attention was focused down the stairs instead of up toward her. With effort, she managed to make her breath stop misting visibly, though she didn't quite trust herself to touch the wall again.

"I *can't* get it open."

That made him glance up at her. Levering himself off the steps, Kor mounted them. She shifted back from him, not quite shrinking from his touch. Guessing she wouldn't welcome a repeat of the struggle that had ended with them tumbling into this place, he slid one of his hands over the stones, opening his mage-senses to the wall.

Nothing. "I can't even sense anything. No opening, no difference between where we fell through and where the wall was solid . . . Nothing."

"It's a hydrostatic barrier, just like all the other ones we found," Danau told him. "I'm sure of it. It's just . . . *stronger* than the rest. It *should* respond to an Aquamancer, to *me* . . . but I can't budge it. I don't even know how I budged it in the first place, and now we're trapped down here!"

"Calm down," Kor ordered her, struggling to keep his own emotions in check. "We got in here, and we will get out again. If not this way, then some other way. Given the redundancy of all the other barrier walls you found, I can't imagine this is the *only* entrance to . . . to whatever is down there. We just have to have enough patience to find it and to figure out how it works."

"Koranen, I may be an Aquamancer, and can draw water out of the very air itself, but we don't have any *food*. If I cannot get *this* door open, what makes you think I could get any others to work?"

"Well *maybe* you should have bathed and dressed in whatever you had available, and gone out to dinner with me, instead of running away," he reminded her. She gaped at him, then reddened, scowling at him. Koranen felt the air chilling even further around her, and fought an urge to smile in triumph. *She* is *the opposite of me . . . She is, she is!*

"Maybe *you* shouldn't have come chasing me." Stepping around him, she cautiously started down the steps.

Starting to point out that if he hadn't, she might have been trapped in here *without* a cryslet to call for help, Koranen bit back the words just in time. They *were* trapped down here together . . . and that meant she *had* to spend her time with him. Slipping off his communication bracelet, Kor tucked it into the pouch at his waist. If she didn't see it, she wouldn't think of asking him to use it, and if she didn't think of him using it, she wouldn't realize he *had* a way of calling for help. That would give them time to sort out the misunderstandings between them.

"Well, I guess it's too late to change any of that," he stated instead, trying not to sound cheerful as he followed her, bringing the illusion-light with him. "We might as well go exploring, since we're stuck down here. Alone. Together."

Reaching the landing, Danau twisted to give him a dirty look. "This is *not* a date."

"Why not?"

Danau gaped at him for a moment, then threw up her hands.

"You're insane! I'm still mucky from slogging through the pipes, no one knows where we are, we're trapped down here with no food and no way out, and you think this is a *date*?"

Kor shrugged, not quite hiding his smile. "I'm with you. That's reason enough."

"You are *insane*."

"Maybe . . . but I'm still your date."

"Oh—just look for another way out! At least the air doesn't smell too stale, so we shouldn't have to worry about suffocating." Stomping down the steps, Danau followed them as they reached another landing and angled again off to the left. An octagonal turning, she noted. "Is everything here based on the number eight?"

"More or less." Koranen started to change the subject back to their date, and their powers, but something at the edge of their view caught his attention. "Is that a door, on the left side of that landing down there?"

"I think it is." Hurrying down the last flight of steps, Danau faced the wooden panel. She looked at the metal lever, festooned with age-dusted cobwebs, and recalled what she had done to the doors of Reuen and Chana's suites. "Um . . . you open it."

"I'm quite sure that whatever spiders used to occupy this place have long since died," he told her, grasping the handle. It clicked open with a thunk, and the panel swung back with a *skreel* of un-oiled hinges. The chamber beyond was large, dusty, and shadowed, despite the bright glow of his mage-light, but then, it was also quite large and cluttered at regular intervals with strange Artifacts.

The nearest one, Kor found after a reflexive check of the wall next to the door, was a lightglobe. Reaching up, he knocked on it with his knuckles. Nothing happened.

Danau groaned, unable to believe their rotten luck. His little flame-ball shed some light, but it flickered and it didn't illuminate anything beyond a radius of about fifteen feet. "Great. It's so old, it doesn't work! I hope your spell doesn't go out, or we'll be lost *and* blind."

"I *make* these," he reminded her. "All it probably needs is recharging."

Lifting the head-sized sphere from its holder, Koranen sank his mage-senses into the device. It didn't take more than two heartbeats to learn what was wrong with it: The comsworg oil infused throughout the sphere had dried and solidified. But there *was* enough residue to reignite it.

"I need some water."

Danau frowned at him. "You're thirsty already?"

"I need to rehydrate the oil in this sphere. About a quarter cup of water. If you can infuse it into this sphere . . . ?" He held out the orb.

She gave it and him a doubtful look. "Koranen, that thing is *glass*. Even I cannot pass water through solid glass."

"In my hands, it isn't solid. Or it won't be," he amended. "I can open up minuscule holes, which should allow it to absorb the water like a sponge. All you have to do is condense the moisture on the surface, and I can do the rest."

Sighing roughly, Danau tucked her fingertips around the sphere, trying to avoid brushing his skin with hers. Within moments of concentrating on her task, beads of dew misted and gathered across the smooth-polished globe. They sank into the surface, replaced by more beads, until he nodded and drew it out of her grasp.

Watching him shake the globe in his hands forced her to bite her lip, just to stifle an urge to giggle. Somehow, she didn't think he had meant he would *literally* mix the oil and water trapped inside. Laughter was inappropriate, however. There was very little that was amusing about their situation, other than watching him jostle the globe.

It didn't take long for him to rehydrate the power source inside the lightglobe. A few more shakes, a muttered trio of spells, and he thumped the ball, igniting it into a far better light source than the small bubble floating over his shoulder. It still didn't illuminate the whole of the chamber they were in, but the two sources of light did reveal a lot more in the way of details.

This *was* the control center for the Desalinator; Danau was certain of it. Thin, ribbon-like pipes of metal-webbed glass arched over their heads, dipping now and then to pass through Artifacts cast in silver and brass, stone and glass, before arcing up and out again. They converged toward the center of the room, though they didn't quite reach the center; instead, they swerved into clusters of four abreast that then dipped straight down, forming a set of bar-like columns spaced a hand-span from each of its nearest neighbors, and a double arm-span apart from the next-nearest clutch.

Some of the dust-and-cobweb-covered Artifacts those glass-and-metal ribbons touched looked like archaic variations of the ones the Guild used back home, gauges for temperature, density, quantity, salinity, mineral content, purity . . . Others didn't have a known purpose, but there seemed to be eight major groupings arrayed around the chamber, each interspersed between lesser clusters. Whatever they were for, it seemed to match the eight outbuildings of the desalination complex.

Needing to see more, Danau moved farther into the room; Koranen came with her, dismissing his flame-ball now that they had a better light source. In the middle of the chamber—the octagonal shape of the walls was just barely discernible in the glow of the lightglobe, allowing her to gauge distances—she could see an elliptical crystal mounted on the top of a spire of dusty, rune-incised metal erected in the heart of the circle formed by those pipes.

The center Artifact had to be the power source. Crystals were often used to store energy, and that crystal was almost as big as a lightglobe, for all it was faceted and clear beneath the upper layer of dust, not smooth and translucent white. Plucking the lightglobe from Koranen's palms, she headed straight for the spire. The gauges could be studied later.

Koranen frowned at her, but Danau continued deeper into the room, oblivious to his irritation. It was as if she had forgotten he existed. *I should have pressed the point of our potential compatibility* before *we found this place*, he thought, shifting to catch up with her. *She's not quite as bad as Serina can get when it comes to mathemagics, but she* does *immerse herself too much in her work.*

His longer legs allowed him to catch up to her before she reached the ring of pipes. Snatching the glowing globe from her hands, he gave her a pointed look as she spun and scowled up at him.

"Give that back."

"No."

"Koranen, I need it! I think I've found the power source for this place," Danau said, reaching for the sphere. He quickly lifted it up over his head. Given that she was more than a foot shorter than him, she knew she couldn't snatch it back. Not without practically climbing the tall man to reach the sphere held aloft in his hands. That would require touching him, and that, she could not do. "Give it back!"

"No."

"But the Desalinator . . . !"

"Will still be there when we are through talking. And we are *not* through talking." Now that they were near the center of the room, and their primary source of light was held over his head, Koranen could see more details of the chamber. There was an alcove off to one side, with what looked like the furniture for an office in its depths. If his eyes didn't deceive him, he was fairly sure the alcove contained a dusty but padded couch as well as a desk and chair. Still holding the glowing ball out of her reach, he headed that way. If they were going to get into an argument about their potential compatibility, they might as well be comfortable . . . or at least distanced from any instruments that might be vulnerable to extremes of cold and heat.

"Koranen—where are you going?" she demanded, hurrying after him.

"Somewhere that we can have a long-overdue talk." A glance assured him that she was following him. Reaching the alcove, Koranen plucked the age-darkened lightglobe from the stand on the desk, dropped the lit one in place—it brightened further from the impact—and set the spare globe between two stacks of dust-coated papers so that it wouldn't roll around.

Danau reached for the papers, distracted by the possibility that these were the plans of the great Tanaka Zhou Fen, creator of the Desalinator. Fingers wrapped around her wrists, startling her and pulling her away from the desk. "Don't touch me—and let go of me! Koranen, let *go*!"

"Why? Are you afraid I might hurt you?" he challenged her, leaning down so that their faces were close together. She refused to meet his gaze, however. "Or are you afraid *you* might hurt *me*?"

That was her exact fear. It was the reason why she couldn't look into his hazel eyes, and couldn't bear the warmth of his hands, for fear they would turn ice-cold. Danau tugged on her wrists. When that failed to free her, she tried kicking at his nearest shin. He shifted that leg out of her way, frustrating her. "Let go. Now!"

"On one condition," Koranen impulsively offered. That caught her attention, and she lifted her eyes to his. He smiled, glad he finally had the upper hand. "Kiss me."

Her mouth dropped open. "*Kiss* you? Koranen—how many times do I have to tell you? I. Do. Not. Date!"

"Well, neither do I!"

That made her gape at him again. In the next moment, she scowled and tugged at her wrists again. "Chana? Reuen? Ama-ti . . . ? You certainly fooled *me*."

"I do not date for the exact same reason *you* do not date," Kor asserted. Then corrected himself. "Well, not for the *exact* same reason. More like the exact *opposite* reason."

"I sincerely doubt that," she scoffed and aimed another unsuccessful kick at his legs. His stupid ramblings warred with her fear at being trapped; if she lost control of her power, she could literally freeze his fingers and shatter them as surely as she'd shattered those doorknobs back up in the palace. "Let go of me, or . . . or I'll start *hexing* you!"

"Danau, I *burn* women. Literally. Just like you *freeze* men!" He gave her arms a gentle shake, enough to make her glare up at him. "Did you hear me? I am *just like you.* The first woman I ever tried to touch in passion, I left handprints on her flesh. *Burned* on her flesh."

That sank past her agitation. Stilling in his grip, Danau stared wide-eyed at Koranen. "You . . ."

"*Burned* her," he repeated, holding her blue gaze as firmly as he held her arms. "I know how much it upset you to find the bits of your dress scattered across your floor. I *found* those bits still coated in frost. *You* caused that frost, didn't you?"

He burned a woman, just by touching her . . . in passion . . . Fiore . . . She couldn't look him in the eyes.

"Admit the truth, Danau. You *were* upset at the destruction of your gown, so upset that you couldn't contain your magic. *Weren't* you?"

"*Extremely.*"

The word escaped her quietly, but he heard it. Kor wanted to kiss her, to soothe the pain in that single word . . . but his back was starting to ache, protesting the difference in their heights. Again, he thought of his brother Evanor, and Ev's short wife, Mariel, and wondered how they managed the disparity.

Shifting to the side, he tugged her gently with him, backing up to the dusty couch, across from the opening to the larger chamber, and a bookcase holding several cobwebbed, dust-fuzzed tomes and scrolls. Dropping onto it made the leather beneath the grime crackle, dry and brittle with age, but there was still enough padding to cushion his fall. Another tug, this time with a twist, pulled her firmly onto his lap. Altering his grip to wrap his arms around her body, Koranen held the short Aquamancer close, ignoring how she strained away from him. Almost nose to nose, he stared into her blue eyes and spoke.

"When I realized you were upset, I left to go find you. That was when I found and confronted Ama-ti. She told me you had as much luck trying to make love with some Menomonite man as I'd had with Katani women—no running away from this!" he ordered when she flushed and squirmed in his grip. "The Gods made you *and* me to be different. Unique. Given those differences, I *think* we were meant for each other."

His words made sense. *If* they were true. She opened her mouth to question him about his claim of burning that woman in his past . . . and sneezed. Hard. Three times in a row.

Koranen wrinkled his nose at the damp spots warring with the dust smears on his sleeve. Even he was feeling the urge to sneeze from the sheer amount of neglect around them. Focusing his power, he snapped his fingers. "*Mundicarum!*"

Dust whirled off the furniture, and dirt whisked off the floor. Cobwebs ripped out of the corners as he spell-cleansed the alcove . . . and more than the alcove. A veritable cloud of grime billowed into the center of the office space, compacting into an unappealing brownish gray ball almost twice the size of his head. It tightened, hardened, and dropped as the cleaning spell ended, landing with a hefty *thunk.*

Blinking at the sphere, Kor arched his brow. His intent had been to clean the alcove, and maybe a bit of the main chamber beyond. Not the whole thing. That much cleaning magic should have left him feeling tired, yet it hadn't. How puzzling. Shaking it off as unimportant, he returned his attention to the short-haired woman in his arms.

"Look. There is an easy way to test this," he said. "Kiss me. *Touch* me. Have your wicked way with me! Trust me, I *won't* object to it."

His attempt at teasing, accompanied by a lopsided smile, didn't amuse her. The last man to reassure her he wouldn't object, *had* objected in the end. Loudly and repeatedly, to anyone who would listen. "And when I hurt you? Will you humiliate me and vilify me all across Nightfall?"

It is a very good thing the two of us will be living up here, he thought. *If I ever went to Menomon, even for a short visit, I'd be tempted to track down this Fiore idiot and give him a hands-on opinion of the things he did to hurt this woman.*

Shaking his head, Koranen gave her his word. "*I* will not do so. I will *never* hurt you. Not like that. Gods . . . I'll even take a mage-oath on the matter, if you like," he added impulsively. "I, Koranen of Nightfall, bind unto my powe—"

Danau pressed her hand to his mouth, cutting off his words. He had released her wrists in order to wrap his arms around her waist and was still imprisoning her, holding her in place, but she could do that much. The offer was undoubtedly made on impulse, maybe even a bit rashly . . . but it touched her that he *would* make such an offer at all. Oath-bindings were powerful things. If Koranen had completed his vow, he *would* have been forced to hold to his sworn words, whatever they were.

His hazel eyes regarded her steadily, watchfully, though he didn't try to say anything more. Danau realized his lips and chin were still warm under her touch. Even if she wasn't overly agitated—a little, but not overly so—his flesh should have started to grow cold by now. Shifting her fingers to his cheek, she cupped it, then slid her fingertips back to his lips.

There wasn't much difference between the two places, temperature-wise. In fact, his jaw felt a little cooler than his mouth, though she hadn't touched it before now. When she moved her hand up to touch his brow, he licked his lips, distracting her from the feel of his skin.

Kor wanted to touch her in return, but carefully refrained from doing so. She was on his lap, no longer resisting the way he was holding her, and she was touching him of her own free will. The last thing he wanted was to startle Danau into retreating from him. Or alarm her.

Or worse . . . burn her. He was *reasonably* sure he wouldn't, couldn't harm her with his passion, but the safest way to be sure was to let *her* take the lead. To progress at *her* pace. Except she was taking too long to finish exploring his face and move on to more interesting things. Licking his lips again, he said, "Kiss me."

"Kiss you?" Danau repeated, trailing her fingers down to the underside of his jaw. As short as she was, compared to him, being seated in his lap like this left their heads more or less level with each other.

"Yes. Please," he managed to add politely.

Doubt still clouded her thoughts . . . but he was still warm beneath her touch. Warm, clean-shaven, and willing to try. And polite about it. Somehow, that made her smile inside, though her expression remained mostly sober. Still, doubt remained. "Are you sure?"

"Yes." His tone was firm. Confident. And slightly impatient.

"Alright." It had been a long while since her last kiss. *Jiore . . . was eight years ago. So it's been a very long while*, she thought, sliding her fingers to the edge of his jaw. Hesitantly, still wary of her damnable magic, Danau closed the distance between their lips. A slight tilt of her head aligned it better in relation to his, avoiding the potential awkwardness of two noses meeting in the wrong place. Heart pounding behind her ribs, she touched her mouth to his.

Koranen felt a flush of heat rising within him, but not as strong as it could have been. At least, not in comparison to the tingle of excitement that skittered from lips to groin. This was the real thing, and it was unnerving and exciting at the same time. Before these Menomonites came, the last time he had kissed a real woman had been four and a half years before—if one didn't count kissing an enchanted facsimile over the last few months, one without any scent or flavor. But this wasn't the distant past, and this wasn't some incomplete illusion. Nor was it Chana or Reuen in his arms. This was a woman he *didn't* have to fear touching.

A tip of his own head gave him the perfect opportunity to gently suckle her lower lip. He followed it with a touch of his tongue, gliding it along her soft skin. Danau pulled back a few inches, blinking at him. The hand cupping his jaw shifted, allowing her thumb to graze his own bottom lip, her gaze slightly worried, or maybe disbelieving. She blinked again, then leaned in and kissed him a second, more thorough time. This time, it was her lips that parted, her tongue that tasted.

That second kiss led to a third, and a fourth. The fifth and sixth and seventh blended together; at some point, both of her hands caressed his face, then shifted into the loose strands of his rib-length hair. Koranen took that as permission to touch her as well, ruffling her short-cropped locks beneath his palms as their mouths met and mated with increasing hunger.

Danau couldn't stop touching him. His scalp felt normal beneath her fingers, his lips and tongue warm and wet as they clashed sensually with hers. And yet she wasn't suffering from the slight but persistent sensation of cold that normally plagued her. In fact, she felt increasingly warm. So warm that her leather shirt started to feel restrictive, uncomfortable.

She was too warm, yet he still didn't feel cold. There *had* to be something to this theory of his, that they were meant for each other, like two halves of a broken and long-separated whole. Pulling back from his lips, she wrestled the knot out of her belt, dropping the strip of ray-skin somewhere behind her. His hands dropped to either side on the couch. Hazel eyes wide with wonder and a little wariness, he watched her as she tugged the hem of her plain, clay-smeared tunic over her head, tossing that aside as well.

Against his will, Koranen's gaze fell from her face to her breasts. They weren't huge, but they were feminine. If he touched them, he could just envelop them in his palms and fingers and thumbs. But Kor didn't move. His hands clenched where they rested on the age-cracked leather of the couch, fisting against the urge to touch, and the memory of two different sets of reddened, blistered handprints. Caused by indulging in similar urges years ago.

This wasn't an illusion-enchanted bit of glass, composed of and protected by layers of carefully enspelled magic. This was a real woman, with real breasts made of real flesh and real blood wrapped in delicate, pale, very real skin. His favorite part of a woman's body, so very different from his own . . . and so very vulnerable to him.

Staring at them, confronted by them, Koranen felt the fire rising beneath his skin. It felt sluggish, less than it had felt back when he had awakened on top of the coals in his forge that morning, hard and aching with need. Still, he couldn't bring himself to touch her breasts, though they were right there, inches from his velvet-covered chest. Perfect breasts, tempting him.

He could not risk injuring them if his guesses were just guesses in the end. Wrong.

TEN

◦❊◦

Danau didn't know why he wasn't touching her chest, now that she had bared it. *Maybe he's not a breast man. Fiore wasn't.* Her previous attempt at a lover had been a seat man, more interested in the curves of her backside than the ones on her frontside. *But it's not fair to compare them,* she reminded herself, shifting to pluck at the tongue-and-hole style belt he wore. Below the strip of black leather, it was obvious he dressed to his left. *This is an entirely different man . . . and so far, I haven't done anything to chill his ardor, literal or figurative.*

Maybe this really will *work, between us . . .*

He didn't complain when she unbuckled his belt, letting it fall to either side on the age-worn seat. And he did rock his body a little when she tugged on the sleeveless coat he was using like a shirt; he even moved his hands to help her remove the precious velvet. Once his upper body was bare—save for the bracelets banding his muscles—Danau gingerly spread her hands over his chest.

He felt warm to her touch, very warm, and strong, and lightly furred with a sparse smattering of reddish brown hairs. Most of them gathered around the flattish ovals of his areolas, but a few straggled down toward the laced front panel of his trousers. With his hands back on the couch seat, palms braced, he seemed to be content to let her explore. Again, an unbidden comparison rose in her mind. *He's at least as muscular as Fiore was, maybe even more so. Definitely more than most male mages I know . . .*

Sliding her hands over his ribs, his pectorals, she asked, "Your forge-work . . . it gives you all these muscles?"

"Some of it. Some of it comes from sword practice."

"Sword practice?" Danau repeated, surprised. "You fight physically, as well as with magic?"

Kor nodded. He bit his lower lip, inhaling when she slid her fingers over his nipples, and tried not to flare too much with pleasure, though she didn't seem to notice his inner heat. "Yes—Saber is the best of us at physical combat, but I can beat his twin almost half the time . . . and Wolfer is . . . uh . . ."

Danau had paused her hands just below his nipples, rubbing the little pink brown peaks gently with the edges of her thumbs. "Wolfer is . . . what?"

Gathering his pleasure-scattered wits, Kor remembered what he was trying to say. "Wolfer is good enough to beat his brother about one bout out of every ten. I can beat him—Wolfer—almost three times out of every six."

"Wolfer . . . That's the big, broad-shouldered one, with the brown hair and golden eyes?" Danau wanted to confirm. At his nod, she gave the lean Pyromancer a dubious look. "I don't mean to doubt you, but he's at least half again as muscular as you. You're not weak, but strength is an undeniable factor in combat."

"I'm sw . . . swift. Faster than I look." He almost couldn't stand it; she had accidentally scraped the edge of one thumbnail against his left nipple, and it had seared him from chest to groin with a thin line of liquid fire. Kor could feel sweat beginning to bead on his brow. If she hadn't removed his sleeveless doublet, he would have been forced to shed it anyway. And yet she hadn't mentioned how hot he was.

When she shifted and climbed off his lap, Koranen didn't know if he was disappointed simply because she had stopped touching him, or because he might have grown too hot for her to be comfortable on his lap. For a moment, he could smell the familiar scent of unprotected, fire-warmed leather, and knew he'd have to get off the couch before he scorched it. But she didn't leave him; to his unnerved delight, Danau merely repositioned herself, climbing back onto the broad, padded seat so that she straddled him rather than perching sideways on his lap again.

She settled her hips on the ends of his knees, though. That gave her enough room to brace her hands on his upper thighs and lean forward. The angle brought her face close to his sternum; a slight shift of her weight swung her toward one of the nipples she had caressed. Once there, Danau paused, hesitant to proceed. Touching him, knowing that she was arousing him, was arousing her. Therein lay her problem.

This was the point where her explorations of her last lover had started to cause problems. As she stared at him, she realized prickles were rising on his chest, as well as a faint pink flush beneath the tanned hue of his skin. Disappointment flared through her. Lifting a hand, she gingerly touched his skin, expecting it to be chilled by mere proximity.

It wasn't. His chest was quite warm. Borderline hot . . . and it stayed that warm under her fingertips. Emboldened, Danau blew on his nipple. It perked and tightened, enticing her into leaning close enough to cover it with her lips. If *this* didn't chill him . . . It did elicit a groan, and she felt his body shift, heard his hands as they left the padded seat and returned again with a sort of helpless flop and a crackle of dried leather. She heard his breath catch in his throat, heard it rush out of his chest, and suckled, testing how far she could push their interactions.

"Gods!" Koranen couldn't stop his hips from bucking, though

he did confine most of the act to a rough twitch. He couldn't even look at what she was doing; it was too erotic, being touched by a real woman. Being touched by this one. Eyes closed, mouth open, he panted for breath as she sealed her lips and swirled her tongue, igniting half a hundred nerve endings crammed into a spot no bigger than his thumbnail.

A glance down showed her how much she was affecting him. His manhood strained at the deep blue velvet of his pants. Wanting to relieve some of his pressure, and reconfirm she was only giving him pleasure, not freezing cold pain, Danau plucked at the ties lacing the front of his trousers together. A whimper escaped the Nightfaller. At some point he had closed his eyes and looked like he was suffering from her touch, if in a good way.

An unfamiliar feeling spread through her—at least, not one she was accustomed to feeling around men. Smugness. *She* was making him whimper. Tugging on the laces, Danau loosened them. Again, his hands rose, then flopped back, fingers spasming as if to stop her, or maybe encourage her.

Holding so much power over a man's pleasure, being able to please his body so visibly, made her own flesh ache with need. Prying open the folds of his pants, she pulled the privacy flap aside. White fabric lay beneath, gathered between his thighs and sashed around his waist. The gathers to one side had loosened enough that she could see a bit of his shaft, pinkish red from being engorged. Another tug, and she managed to get his trousers out of her way enough to slide the fingers of her right hand between his erection and thigh.

"*Kata!*" Koranen swore, choking from her touch. Her fingers were cool, a distinct contrast to his overheated flesh. He pried his eyes open, desperate to make sure her skin wasn't blistering . . . and it wasn't, though he could have sworn *his* was, for she eased him sideways out of his loincloth, then stroked him gently, exploring his flesh. It was the single most erotic sight of his life, and the acknowledgment of that fact came simultaneously with the drawing up of his sack, warning him he was mere moments from spending himself right then and there. Sweat beaded on skin, heat flushing across his body from scalp to soles . . . yet she *wasn't* burned?

Danau was in an equal state of shock. Breasts aching, womb clenching, she was *touching* him . . . and she hadn't chilled him? Amazed, hand still stroking him, she whispered the thought uppermost on her mind. "Menos, you're so *hot* . . ."

"*GAAAH!*" Agonized, Kor shoved her off his knees. It was pure self-preservation, *her* self, and it was proven necessary: The moment she dropped free, landing on the stone floor with an *oof*, he could smell scorching leather. Thankfully, the pain in his passion-thwarted groin had curled him over; it was a simple enough matter to continue the roll, dropping onto the spell-cleaned, flame-resistant floor next to her.

"What the . . . ?"

Stunned by the abrupt shove and her subsequent fall, Danau stared at Koranen. He, too, had dropped off the couch, and a good thing, for she could see the dark brown imprint of his body where he had seared the cracked leather. She could smell the scent of burned hide and hints of smoldering wool . . . but it was the groaning, huddled ball of masculinity lying on his side that concerned her the most.

"Koranen?" Twisting onto her knees, Danau leaned over him. He was muttering something under his breath, eyes scrunched tightly shut, knees drawn up as close to his chest as his arms and his flexibility could allow. It took her a moment to realize what he was muttering.

"*Killmekillmekillmekillme . . .*"

He . . . thinks . . . oh, Gods! She smacked herself in the forehead. *I shouldn't have said* hot! *That would be like* him *saying to* me *that my fingers felt* cold! *Gods . . . Menos . . . if I didn't have to fix this, I'd be laughing. Or crying. He* is *right—we* are *meant for each other . . .*

Knowing she had to stop his miserable line of thinking right then and there, or they wouldn't get anywhere, Danau didn't bother to be gentle. She *wanted* to get somewhere with him. Eight years was far too long to suffer the embarrassment of celibacy.

Slapping him on the muscles of his uppermost arm, she stated loudly and firmly, "Koranen, you are *supposed* to be feeling *cold* right now!"

The bluntness of her words, or maybe her volume, penetrated Kor's misery. He opened his eyes, blinking. She took that as a sign that he was listening and asked him a question.

"*Are* you cold?"

Am I . . . ? It was the most ridiculous question possible; he felt so hot, he could smell the velvet of his trousers beginning to heat up, despite the thread-of-copper stitched along the inner seams in protective runes. "No . . . I'm *hot*. Don't touch me!" he added quickly as she hooked her fingers around his elbow, tugging on his arm. He clung to his knees even harder. "Stop it! I don't want to hurt you!"

"Koranen, you are being *ridiculous*. If anyone should be hurt, it would be *you*! Are you frostbitten? Did I freeze you? Am I chilling you right now, now that I'm touching you?"

He blinked, considering her words. There *was* a difference when she touched him. He couldn't smell heat-stressed fabric. Twisting his head, he peered up at her. "No . . . but . . ."

"Stop being ridiculous about this, and let me have my way with you," Danau ordered him, tugging firmly enough to roll him halfway to his back. "Don't make me force myself on you!"

The absurdity of her demand penetrated Koranen's confusion in a way little else could. It wasn't *impossible*, but it was very difficult for a woman to force herself on a man. Even more so for a woman as small as she was, compared to someone as tall and muscular as him. Rolling fully onto his back, Koranen eased his sandal-clad feet to the floor. He felt oddly vulnerable, for his shaft was still poking out of his trousers, if somewhat deflated from the idea he'd been about to blister her skin.

Threading her arm beneath his, she grasped him again. Kor choked, then shuddered, as she squeezed, rippling her fingers. Worse, she dared to ask him a question, forcing him to think through the physical sensations of her fingers on his flesh and the fire in his blood, all of it warring with years of protective instinct.

"Are my fingers cold?" Danau asked, grasping him just enough to shift his foreskin as she stroked down and up. "*Are* they?"

"Cold?" he managed, panting. The sudden reswelling of his flesh made him dizzy, blood racing through his veins, cramming to get back into the part it had just vacated "No. Cool . . . yes. Gods—!"

Danau watched him fight for breath, his gaze shifting from the ceiling to her face, then down to his groin and back. After a few more strokes, he grasped her wrist and hand, stopping her movements.

"Don't . . . !"

"Why not?" she asked, rippling her fingers around his heat, since she couldn't stroke them at the moment. A new doubt assailed her, one that had nothing to do with her magic. "Am I doing it wrong? I know I'm out of practice, but—"

"—Oh, you're doing it *right*," Koranen managed to rasp, grimacing as she rippled her fingers again. "I just . . . *Danau*! If you keep this up, I'm going to explode!"

The hint of a squeak in his voice made her feel warm deep inside. Warm and powerful, and just a little bit feral. Pulling her hand free, Danau caught *his* wrists, shifting onto her knees as she did so. While he was still frowning in confusion, she shuffled on her leather-clad knees, swinging herself around so that she straddled his upper chest, facing his loins. His upper body was broad, making her hips ache from the spread of her thighs, but it put her in a very good position to control what happened next.

One moment, he was trying to make her stop stroking him into a precipitous state of arousal . . . the next, he had an up-close view of her backside. Leather clad, since she had only removed her belt and tunic, but it was undeniably rounded and feminine. She didn't weigh much, either, though she did weigh enough that when she leaned forward, it pressed down on his chest and—*Holy Gods in Heaven!*

Koranen's head slammed into the floor as his body bucked, then bowed. Warm—wet—tongue—lips—his brain imploded, and his muscles constricted, and someone—him—yelled wildly. Fire billowed through his body, blinding eyes that rolled back up into his head. All there was in the whole of the world was the hardness beneath his heels, shoulders, and head, the weight of her body compressing his chest, and that warm, wet heaven sliding back and forth along his very needy flesh.

Worse—better—whatever—she added her hands to the mix. Cool, sweet, firm, and rippling, they added pleasure to the lower parts of his shaft in the same way that oil added heat and light to a burning brazier. His back thumped onto the floor, his hips flexed into her touch, and his arms wrapped around her hips, pinning her lower body in place. If she'd only been half a foot taller, he could have spelled away her clothes and returned the favor to the best of his ability, but even that urge lasted only a handful of seconds at most. The amount of time it took for his sack to draw up tight, for the fire in his veins to whirl down his spine, for an almost agonizing, sheer bliss to boil up out of his blood and out of his flesh, accompanied by a wordless, delirious shout.

As prepared as she could be, given how long it had been since her last, aborted chance to experience such things, Danau braced herself for the taste of him. Other women had complained in her presence of bitterness, astringency, even a cleaning-potion taste, but the hot liquid pulsing from Koranen's flesh tasted mostly of the sea. Complex, with strange underflavors, but not unpleasant . . . and very, very hot. With no sign of his temperature diminishing, despite the way his climax, his pleasure, excited her.

Easing her touch, Danau gently milked the last few drops from his flesh, then let his diminishing shaft drop from her lips. He was still mostly clad in his blue velvet pants and white loincloth, sandals strapped around his feet. As he panted beneath her, calming back down from his orgasm, she started working his pants down his hips. If he didn't freeze during *that*—and if he didn't burn *her* while doing so—she wanted to know what else they could do together.

Everything, if they were lucky.

With the fading of the inferno in his veins came an astounding clarity. Koranen didn't feel the least bit lethargic, either. Relaxed; there was no doubt about that. And sated, but only temporarily. He didn't feel the slightest urge to roll over and sleep. Instead, the Pyromancer felt the urge to cheer.

Buoyant with a grinning triumph, he let out a whoop, squeezing the hips of the woman still straddling his chest. *His* woman. *"YES!!"*

Tossing his head back and laughing as he did so, he smacked his skull into the floor. Right on the same spot he had hit a few moments earlier. Wincing at the bruise, Kor didn't let the pain diminish his euphoria. He wanted to hug Danau, to kiss her—the closest thing he *could* kiss was the inseam of her leather trousers, given their relative, inverted positions. Unable to help himself, *needing* to express his joy, Kor shifted his grip, grabbed her hips, and pulled her groin up to his face for a lips-to-leather *smack!*

Danau blinked, jolted figuratively as well as literally. He wanted to kiss *that?* A moment later, her mind reprocessed that information. *He wants to kiss* that . . . *!*

Far be it from me to stop him! Squirming free of his grip, Danau flopped onto the floor by his shoulders and unbuttoned her pants, shoving them down her legs. She flushed with embarrassment when she realized her boots were still laced in place, and fussed with the doubled-over leggings so she could unbind and remove her footwear first.

Until she noticed something happening. Around her bottom and heels, a thin patch of frost started to form . . . and the scent of heated velvet once more reached her nose. Stopping for a moment, she glanced at Koranen.

While they touched each other, neither of them had caused anything to burn or to freeze. But *separate* . . . their two unique problems remained. *We truly do cancel each other's magic. At least, the heat/cold aspects. But what does that mean for our spellcasting? Does it neutral-*

ize that part of our powers, too? Is that how we opened that door, by somehow draining or banishing the hydrostatic barrier?

It *had* vanished the moment she had touched both him and the wall, after all . . .

As soon as he realized why she had pulled free, Kor curled up into a sitting position and unlaced his own sandals, grinning madly. One of the thongs snapped, breaking the thread-of-copper runes protecting the material from his lust, but he didn't care; he could always repair it later. Much later. Shaking his feet free of the leather, he rolled onto his back, planting his heels and arching his back to clear his buttocks from the floor. That allowed him to shove his pants down his legs. A quick fumble at the knot of his loincloth, and the two pieces of fabric were easily stripped from his body and tossed aside.

Twisting somewhat upright, he braced himself on his palms and his now-naked hip. A bruised hip, thanks to his tumble on those steps, but the pain was unimportant. Koranen faced Danau as she struggled to remove her boots. *His* woman. His Destiny. Water to his Fire. His flesh might still be a bit too sated to respond immediately, but only *his* flesh had been satisfied. Hers—still partially dressed—needed to enjoy the exact same treatment, to the best of his ability.

"I think you need a little help," he murmured, smiling. At her puzzled look, he grabbed her nearest ankle and tugged the unlaced boot free. Despite the earlier heat of the day, she wore a thick wool sock on her foot. *Probably because she literally freezes without one to help keep her warm.* Peeling that off gave her enough time to finish unlacing her other boot. Koranen tugged that one off, too, letting her get her other sock.

When she stood up to step out of her trousers and peel down her undertrousers, Koranen stilled, giving her groin a wary look. With the lightglobe shining from the desk off to the left, he wasn't completely reassured until she kicked off the last of her garments, turning to the side just enough to fully illuminate her flesh . . . but there it was. Plain, dark auburn nether-curls. Neither long nor short, they looked to be just as normal in hue as the hair—however short it might be—that grew on her head.

"Thank the Gods . . ." he breathed, closing his eyes in relief. Here was one Aquamancer, at least, who didn't pervert what nature had intended.

"Thank Them for what?" Danau eyed him warily.

"Your . . . hair. Below," he added, lifting a hand so he could gesture at her crotch. "It's not dyed. When Reuen told me that Ama-ti was 'perfect' for me, I couldn't stomach the thought of her having blue hair down *there*. That would be utterly unnatural!"

Sidetracked for a moment by her cousin's name, Danau shook it off. She would deal with Reuen later. Now was not the time to get angry. "The Healers say if you're going to dye your nether-hairs, you have to be extra careful. Eyebrows and lashes are forbidden, of course, since that's too dangerous, being too close to the eyes. But then, I've never bothered with anything lower than my scalp. Just my head-hair."

"Thank the Gods for that," Kor muttered, giving her hips one last, grateful look. Then the second half of her words sank in. Lifting his gaze, he gave her a puzzled look. "You do dye your hair?"

"Yes, of course—it's very popular in Menomon, because we usually keep our hair too short to style. If you can't braid it, pin it, or coil it . . . the only decorative thing left to do with it is either shave patterns into it, or dye it different colors, and shaving hasn't been in fashion for the last two years," Danau said, shrugging. "Hardly anyone keeps their hair natural colored, let alone long, unless they're from the surface. It's a way of telling a native from a newcomer."

"Shaving . . . head . . ." Koranen eyed her askance, then shook it off. "Dyeing your hair is only slightly better than that—Menomoni fashions are *very* strange."

"It's Menomonite," she corrected, smiling. It was amusing to discover she wasn't the only one who was confused about what to

call a particular group of people. But she had to make him understand why her hair *wasn't* dyed right now. "Because my hair is dark,
in order to turn it bright or light in color, I have to bleach it. And
because it has red highlights, it has to be bleached strongly to turn
it blond and not just orange, and *that* makes it very coarse after a
while," Danau said. "So about a turning of Sister Moon ago, when I
got tired of the lighter colors but it was too damaged to dye dark
again, I just had all of it shaved off and let it grow back. When I return to the City, I'll probably get it dyed again."

Koranen stared up at her. Dyed hair was one thing, but his mind
couldn't quite grasp a woman with a shaved head. Not unless she
was terminally ill or deeply fevered, or had suffered a head wound in
need of mending. Sometimes Healers had to do that to their pa-
tients. But struggling to grasp the idea of a bald-headed wife was a
little too difficult.

Taking comfort that they would live on land, not in the water—
which would allow her to grow out her hair—he dismissed the need
for such things. "Well, I'm accustomed to naturally colored hair.
And I *like* the natural color of your hair."

A blush stole over her face at his firmly spoken words. "I like
yours, too . . . though I do think you'd look equally good in sea colors. I know I do, and we both have about the same coloring."

"Sea colors?" he asked her warily.

"Blues and greens, streaked and shaded to blend into each other,"
she explained, gesturing at her head. "You'd look even more stun-
ning, because your hair is so long—like one of the kelp forests out
in Cerulean Bay. Between the two of us, Ama-ti and I could dye it
for you, if you wanted to try."

Koranen shook his head. "I think I'll pass." Wanting to get off
the subject of hair and back onto the subject of finally enjoying the
wonderful world of sex, Koranen shifted from his hip to his knees.
He lifted his hands to her, beckoning with a flutter of his fingers.
"Come here."

Remembering their compatibility, the utter lack of frost or fire on either part when she had fondled him, Danau willingly moved to straddle his thighs. When she tried to drop and settle on his lap, however, he grabbed her hips and held her in place, keeping her on her feet. A wordless noise of inquiry was met by a grin from the Nightfaller. Lifting himself off his heels put him at just the right height to rub his smiling face against her breasts, accompanying the act with a happy sigh.

"Gods . . . knowing that I can *touch* you, without burning you—Danau, I am going to touch you *everywhere*," Kor warned her, pulling back just enough to give her a brief but serious look. "If I do anything you don't like, just let me know, and I'll try something else . . . but in the Names of all the Gods, if I do something you *do* like, let me know, as much as possible. I haven't exactly had a chance to practice on a real woman, though I've had plenty of opportunity to study the theory of it."

"That is fair and reasonable," she allowed. "If you'll give me the same courtesy. It has been eight years since my one and only other lover, and unlike you, I didn't have a Prophecy to reassure me I'd eventually ever have another lover, so I haven't even been studying the theory. All I remember are old lessons from my sexual education courses, and those were over a decade ago."

About to kiss her breasts, Koranen pulled back with a frown. "Eight years? And a decade? How old are you?"

"Twenty-seven." She flushed a little as she admitted it, though she tried not to let it bother her. "I know it's a bit old to be unmarried, but the Council ended up giving me a magical exemption from the requirement of having the first of my three husbands by the age of twenty-five."

Her confession bemused him. Sinking back on his heels, Koranen eyed her. "Huh. I'm only twenty-four. You're three years older than I am."

"Is that a problem?" Danau asked, wary.

"Well, no . . . It's just that I hadn't really thought about our ages before now." Dismissing it with a shrug, Koranen returned his attention to her breasts. The corner of his mouth quirked up. Deliberately shifting his hands from her hips to her chest, he cupped the soft curves. Then peeled back his hands for a quick check before covering them again. "Mmm . . . *perfect*. And not a single blister."

A wriggle of his fingers tickled her. Danau laughed and squirmed. Sliding his hands around her ribs to her back, Koranen pulled her back into nuzzling range, where he licked, then suckled, alternating his attention between the two peaks. *Maybe he is a breast man after all . . . ouch! A little too enthusiastic about it.*

Remembering his request for her to *tell* him whether or not something worked, Danau winced again and cleared her throat. "Um . . . they're not going to dispense milk, no matter how hard you suckle. So, um . . . lighten up a bit, will you?"

"Mmphf?—Oh, sorry," Kor apologized, releasing her flesh. The peak of her breast did look a little redder than the other one, though thankfully from suction, not from temperature. "Do you still want me to suckle them? Only, more gently?"

"Well, yes . . . and licking. I liked the licking bits," she agreed. Then she sucked in a sharp breath as he leaned close and flicked his tongue quickly over her nipple. He stopped and pulled back. Danau managed a reassuring smile. "I *really* like the licking bits."

Unable to resist a grin, he wrapped his arms around her waist and laved her whole breast with his tongue. She giggled and squirmed when he licked the underside of her breast, down by her ribs. Then gasped and squirmed harder when he lapped at her ribs directly. Within moments, he had her laughing and writhing and gasping out half-formed protests as she tried to push at his shoulders, until her knees buckled when she let out a peal of laughter.

Catching her as she collapsed, breathless from laughing too hard, Koranen laid her on the ground, looming over her on his elbows and knees as he gave her a few moments of respite. Only when she had caught most of her breath did he continue, this time capturing her mouth for a suckling kiss. She moaned into his mouth, her hands coming up to spear through his hair, tugging on the long locks, until he realized she was caressing her skin with his hair.

A shift allowed him to press kisses to her chin and throat. Between salutes, Koranen asked, "So, you like my hair?"

"It's *beautiful*," Danau confessed breathlessly. Moving down to her torso meant more of his long hair could be rubbed over her skin, and the feel of it against her breasts was intoxicating. After too many years of thinking she'd never, ever be able to do something like this, to *finally* have a lover, and a lover with long hair . . . it made her giddy with the ability—no, the *right*—to release her self-control. "It's so soft, and it tickles so nicely . . ."

Koranen pulled his head back, freeing his locks from her fingers, then dipped his head and shook it, scattering his hair across her torso. Danau moaned again, rubbing the strands into her flesh. Wanting more, she sucked in a breath when he started kissing her ribs again, but this time he didn't lick. Not until he reached her navel, where he didn't just lick, but suckled on the dimple of flesh as well. Eyes widening, she arched up into the strange, sensual attack, feeling her nerves ignite with a fire that had nothing to do with magic, and everything to do with lust.

"Oh! Oh, I *like* that! Do it again!" she ordered when he paused to look up at her, auburn locks sliding across her belly.

Chuckling, Koranen complied. Then—unable to resist—he blew a raspberry into her belly, making her shriek with startled laughter. Grinning unrepentantly, even when she grabbed and tugged on his locks in punishment, he slid a little farther down her body. That forced him to part his feet around one of the legs of the couch, one foot forced to tuck itself beneath the old furnishing so that his limbs had room to stretch out. It also put him at the perfect place to contemplate the one task Trevan always said was *vital* for a good lover to master: kissing and suckling a woman's femininity.

Kor had done this before, if only in practice with the illusion-courtesan Trevan had gifted him for his birthing-day. The illusion-woman had been fairly vocal about what to do, too, so he knew *how* to please Danau. The one thing the illusion *hadn't* prepared him for was the, well, scent of her body.

His fifthborn brother had warned him the illusion would have only touch, sight, and sound, lacking in both taste and smell, and that a real woman was a heady, musky thing. Danau . . . hadn't bathed yet. Had, in fact, worked hard enough earlier in their day to have generated a healthy sweat, even for someone who had to wear wool socks on a hot summer day to keep herself warm. So the smell beneath his nose was a bit . . . strong. Not unpleasant by any means, just . . . strong.

Trevan said some days it could smell rather strong, he reminded himself, adjusting the position of his arms and shoulders between her obligingly spread thighs. *It's not bad, but it is strong. He also said that the taste would be even better than the smell, and that to brave one meant gaining the reward of the other.*

Kata, I hope he's right . . .

Danau, waiting with carefully concealed trepidation, lifted her knees a little to ease the curve of her lower back over the hard, un-yielding floor. Jiore had liked this part, though he had jokingly compared it to lapping at an iced-cream dessert. At least, at first he hadn't minded how literally cold she was down there. *But I'm not cold in Koranen's arms. I'm* not, she reminded herself firmly. She felt him gently parting her nether-lips with his fingers, and braced her-self. *I'm not cold, and I . . . ohhh . . . Gods!*

Her body bucked beneath the first, experimental stroke of his tongue. Kor finished his swipe and pulled back a little, swirling his tongue around the roof of his mouth to spread the flavor for analysis. The corner of his mouth quirked up as he acknowledged the truth: His fifthborn brother was completely and utterly right. With the taste of her mouthwatering musk coating his tongue, stirring his blood with primal thoughts, the smell was much more tolerable.

Dipping his head, he licked her again. She shuddered, hands delving into his hair. A moment later, she raked his locks up onto her belly. Aside from the need to scrape the occasional strand out of his way—both his head-hair and her nether-hair—Koranen let her play with his mane. His focus was the soft folds between her thighs and the warm nectar that needed to be coaxed and nibbled and suckled out of her flesh.

The smell was still strong, but it blended with her taste, salty-sweet and musky; together, they wrapped around his senses, blinding him to everything but the sight of her nether-curls, the sound of her panting moans, the feel of her hips gyrating her flesh against his lips, nose, and tongue. Even though his lower body was pressed firmly into the cool stone of the floor, anchoring him as he lifted her hips to his face, he felt himself hardening, preparing for his first taste of real lovemaking.

But he couldn't stop devouring her. Her moans became cries, her quivers hard shudders, and the liquid increased from an ooze to a flood. She shouted something, bucking in his grip, then pushed at his forehead. Koranen backed off obediently, if reluctantly. He was breathing heavily, he realized, though nothing like her gulping, gasping pants. He was also hunching his hips slowly, rubbing his erection against the hard, unyielding floor.

The floor was no substitute for the real thing. However, all of Trevan's lectures and comments on lovemaking stressed that the first chance for intercourse with a woman, particularly an untried one, should be when *she* was demanding it. Both Danau's words and actions suggested she wasn't entirely a virgin . . . but she had also stated quite plainly that it had been eight years since her one and only attempt. Trevan had said that a woman who went without the pleasure of the bed for more than a couple of years had a tendency to "tighten up" inside, as if returning to a virginal state. A considerate lover took his time with such a woman. Koranen intended to be very considerate.

His petite, short-haired lover shifted, forcing him to duck as she lifted one leg over his head, twisting onto her side, while she continued her struggle to breathe normally once more. *Trevan says some women can go forever and ever from one climax to the next, while others need a few minutes to breathe and rest. And that some react in different ways, depending on the intensity of her climax. Looks like my woman needs to rest a little bit, at least for now.*

Of course, thinking about his brother in the middle of all of this was a little weird, Kor acknowledged ruefully. The corner of his mouth quirked up. *One of these days, I am going to know enough about the actual aspects of lovemaking to not have to rely on "Trevan says this" and "Trevan says that" . . . but for now, "Trevan says" most women like to cuddle after an orgasm.*

Licking his lips, savoring the last smears of her nectar, Koranen crawled up the length of her body, then twisted onto his unbruised hip, scooting himself up against her back. She jumped a little when his erection poked her buttock, but settled back against him with what sounded like a contented sigh when he did nothing more than wrap his left arm around her, tucking her close. A bend of his right arm offered his biceps as a pillow, which she accepted as well.

"I trust you enjoyed that?" he asked.

ELEVEN

◆∋C◆

The answer to that question was so obvious, and thus so banal, Danau couldn't help the laugh that escaped her. "As much as *you* seemed to."

She squirmed her hips backward into his erection to emphasize her point, then relaxed again, sighing.

"No going to sleep," Koranen ordered her when she sighed a second time. Shifting his left hand, he gently tweaked one of her nipples, making her catch her breath. Adjusting his right elbow to brace himself on the floor, he leaned over her, pressing soft kisses to her shoulder and throat. "We're not finished yet . . ."

Danau did feel deliciously relaxed, more so than she could re-member feeling in a very long time, but her mind wasn't the least bit sleepy. They were still trapped down here, she was beginning to feel both thirsty and hungry . . . and he was playing with her breasts again. The same hands that had deftly played with fire and sand, shaping beautiful, artistic baubles, now played just as deftly with her flesh, making *her* feel like molten glass. Well, there was the occasional accidental thumbnail scrape, and a few touches that could have been either firmer or lighter to engender more pleasure, but for the most part, his fingers pleased her quite nicely.

The only problem was, their position didn't exactly allow her to return the favor. The moment she decided to worm free of his embrace, he splayed his hand across her belly, inadvertently tickling her ribs on the way down. Squirming, biting her lip to keep from giggling, Danau felt his manhood twitch and harden further.

I should do something about that . . .

Wriggling free, she twisted onto her hands and knees, intending to turn around and taste him again—him, she could touch with impunity, and fully intended to do so. For too many years, she had denied her sexuality; now, Danau could do whatever she liked to a man, with a man, so long as it was *this* man. Unfortunately, she didn't get very far.

Before she could finish turning around, the Pyromancer groaned and hooked his arm around her thighs, holding her in place. A moment later, she heard him inhale deeply. It was the only warning she had before he buried his face in her folds, lapping and suckling hungrily. Caught off guard, aroused as much by his fervor as by her own pleasure in the act, Danau groaned and dropped her head to her forearms, knees spreading to give him better access.

He shifted as well, moving directly behind her, arm sliding down her thighs until he was braced on his hands and knees. Koranen devoured her until her whimpering, rhythmic moans penetrated the passion hazing his mind. Blinking, wiping at his nose to clear some of the liquid smeared over it, he managed a coherent thought. *Well, she's not begging in so many words . . . but I've heard that kind of need before. Or rather, overheard. And this is supposed to be an enjoyable position . . . Jinga, and all the other Gods, make sure I don't get this wrong!*

She was in a very good position for what he had in mind; her upper body was lowered to the floor, raising her hindquarters, but her knees were splayed and bent, lowering her hips. She was also short.

All he had to do was shuffle forward on hands and knees, and . . . Yes, he covered her torso completely with his own.

Pressing a kiss to her spine, Kor braced himself on one arm, using the other to reach for his erection. Not quite sure where to aim, he found he had to rock back onto his heels for a moment . . . which was when he saw what one of her hands was doing. Her left arm still pillowed her cheek, but Danau had tucked her right arm between her knees, and was fingering herself. Stroking her little pleasure peak with a circling, rubbing touch.

Kor blinked, distracted by the sight. *I must remember that for later . . .* Filing away the technique in his mind—Trevan said the woman herself usually knew best how she liked to be touched—he aimed the head of his shaft, rising up on his knees. Encouragingly, the moment he nudged her slit, she pressed back onto him, her fingers circling a little faster.

"Mm, yes . . . ! Please," Danau breathed. She knew it would be a tight fit, but touching herself wasn't enough. Not even being licked by him, however enthusiastically, was enough. There was an emptiness low in her belly, one which instinct said *he* could fill.

Flushing with pleasure—she *had* begged him, yes!—Koranen bumped her a few times with the tip of his erection then angled it so that it slid one way, then the other, coating the shaft. He had almost forgotten that part. *Lubrication is always important, if you want to avoid chafing problems,* he reminded himself. She felt warm and wet, and the air cool in contrast as it brushed against his dampened skin. Gritting his teeth, Kor re-aimed his flesh, braced it against her opening, and grasped her hips. Not to pull, but to guide, because *she* backed onto him as soon as he was centered, pushing herself onto him with a low groan.

Heat flushed through his body, as her flesh parted around his. He snatched his hands away reflexively, but there were no reddened marks, no blisters, no sign that it was a fiery heat. Just a passion-filled one. Sliding his hands back over her rump, Koranen grasped her hips and pulled, adding his efforts to her own. Slowly, the two of them came together, until the only thing keeping him from thrusting that last, final inch was the pain of his teeth biting into his lower lip.

Warm, tight, wet, constrictive . . . There weren't any adjectives adequate enough for this moment, other than one single word: *real.* He was buried in a *real* woman, *his* real woman, and was no longer a helpless, pathetic, power-cursed virgin. Koranen swayed as most of the blood in his head rushed to his loins, hardening him to the edge of his control. *No* . . . *no* . . . *mustn't lose* . . . *Gods! I* will *be a good, considerate lover! She* will *have enough time to enjoy this, dammit!*

Abandoning his lower lip, Koranen bit his tongue instead, using the compressive pain to counter the constrictive pleasure of her flesh. Slowly, carefully, he shifted forward, lowering his hands from her hips to the floor until he was braced on all fours over her. She whimpered a little, making him wonder if it was from pain or pleasure. Determined to let *her* make the next move, Koranen flicked his hair out of his way and kissed her upper back.

Danau felt the soft tickling of his hair slithering across her back and accepted it as the distraction it was. It had been too long, and she was too tight, and he was too large. Yet he was taking his time, long enough that the stinging was finally fading from her loins. And the soft kisses he bestowed on her shoulders were tender and sweet. This was more than just raw, experimental sex between two people who couldn't have it any other way.

This is the man a Seer said was Destined for me, she acknowledged. *This is why they asked for single female Aquamancers* . . . *and why I was born this way. I could've done without the years of humiliation and frustration* . . . *but when we return to Menomon, with this man, my* husband *at my side* . . . *exotic, handsome, powerful* . . . *talented,* she acknowledged as she felt his shaft twitch inside of her, flexing with the shifting of his weight as he flicked his hair again, allowing him to kiss the curve of her other shoulder. *Menos—did You have a hand in making him, as well as his own Gods?*

Then again, whichever deity had a hand in Koranen's existence didn't really matter. He existed, and he was hers. And right now, she wanted more of the warm, willing man dusting kisses along her nape. His care and stillness were considerate, but the stinging had faded and her hunger was back. He filled her, yes, but she needed more. Friction.

Impatient, Danau rocked a little, moving her flesh only an inch or so against his, but still an inch. She heard him inhale sharply and rocked a little harder. The sigh that escaped him was accompanied by a faint groan, letting her know her movement was acceptable. Enjoyable for him as well as for her. Rocking beneath him, increasing her vigor, Danau sought after the rest of the delights buried in the heat—*oh, Gods, the heat!*—of intercourse. There was nothing left worth thinking about, other than the feel of him finally reciprocating, finally feeding the hunger that cramped her abdomen with need.

Passion warred with self-control, churning in an agony of indecision; he had to ensure she orgasmed to be a good lover, but his own needs were overwhelming him. All he could feel was feminine flesh that felt tight, wet, willing, and *unharmed*. Enthusiastic, even. Her movements were now quite vigorous, threatening to unsheathe him. Caging her hips with his left arm, Koranen braced his right arm; that allowed him to thrust into each of her bouncing strokes. It also allowed him to twist his wrist, slipping his fingers between her thighs, circling their tips as soon as he found her turgid little peak.

Danau gasped beneath him. A few strokes, more from the motion of her body than from any effort of his own, and she tightened around him, crying out. The back of her head almost cracked into his chin as it snapped up from the force of her climax. Koranen didn't really notice; the grazing of her soft, short hair along his jaw line was nothing compared to the clamping, squeezing heat of her flesh. Overwhelming need flared through his body, burning away his self-control.

Jerking them together as deeply as he could, Kor let his passion unleash in a groan of relief. Each spasm raced from the crown of his head to the root of his shaft, searing his nerves before it pulsed physically into her depths. With each gasping inhale, he could *smell* the scents of sweat and sex released by their efforts. Dropping his head, he tongued her shoulder, needing the *taste* of her in his mouth. Needing the reassurance that Danau, unlike any mere, enspelled glass sphere, was *real*.

His woman. His. *Real*.

Head drooping, arms and thighs trembling, knees hurting from the hardness of the solid granite floor, Danau wanted nothing more than to lie down. He was still holding her with his left arm, so she sagged to her right, pulling free of his embrace. Thankfully, he let her go. Cool stone met her flesh, giving Danau an unexpected, eye-opening discovery: For the first time in her adult life, ever since the onset of puberty heralded the blossoming of her powers . . . coolness felt *good* against her passion-flushed skin.

Reluctant to let her go, but feeling as if he had drained all of his strength into her body, Koranen sagged to his left. He wanted to see her face, to kiss her lips . . . to *not* feel the bruises on that side, he discovered. Grimacing, he rose up and shifted over, settling onto his right side with a sigh. He was now behind her back. Kisses or no, he would have to heal the tenderized results of his fall down those steps before he could face her like that.

Right now, he was too sated to want to try. Still, Trevan had stressed how the after-lovemaking parts were just as important to women as the bits before and during. So, scooting back a little, he scooped his hand under her knees, rolling her legs so that she twisted onto her back. Danau squirmed a little, getting more comfortable, and once again he provided his own arm for a pillow.

At least with him on his side, his thighs folded up underneath her buttocks and her legs draped over his, they were close enough for a kiss. She returned it with a slight lift of her head, pleasing him. So did the sight of her smile.

Danau couldn't help it; she felt both shy and yet smug. Shy from being overwhelmed by what they had done, and utterly smug that they *had* done it . . . and that neither of them had injured the other in doing it. *It. Sex. Lovemaking . . .*

A frown pinched her brow. The arm she had draped across her stomach, since there was no room for her left arm between their bodies, rose enough to smack him on the hip with the back of her hand. "What took you so long to come into my life?"

The silliness of the demand made Koranen laugh. He nuzzled the side of her head, still chuckling . . . then choked on an undignified snort as someone's stomach rumbled. His, possibly, though from the blush on her cheeks, it might have been hers. "Well, I'm here now. And though I'd love nothing more than to stay here with you, naked and ready for *more*," he mock leered before sighing ruefully, "we've already missed our appointment at the Giggling Pear, and we're going to miss the concert, at this rate. We *should* get dressed and start looking for another door."

That made her frown deepen in concern. "We're going to miss the concert anyway! Unless it was something *we* did when I touched you and the wall together at the same time . . . Koranen, we're still *trapped* down here!"

"Kor," he said, earning a puzzled look. "You can call me Kor, if you like, not just Koranen. Most of my family does."

"Kor, now is not the time to be discussing nicknames," she chided him, though she did at least use the shortened name. "As fun as this was, we cannot live on lovemaking alone. And I'd really rather not die down here, especially as no one knows where we are!"

"Relax," he ordered her, cupping her far shoulder as she started to sit up. "I brought my cryslet with me; it's in the pouch on my belt. If worse comes to worst, I can call my twin, and he can find us with one of his looking glasses and open a mirror-Gate. Though I'd rather put that off until *after* we've both dressed. He may have seen me naked throughout the years, but I'd rather he didn't see you."

"You had—?" She sat up anyway, pushing his arm down to her lap. "Why didn't you *tell* me you had a way to get us out of here? We could've been free an hour ago!"

Giving her a pointed look, Koranen slipped his hand between her thighs. She sucked in a sharp breath, then shuddered, squirming against the circular rubbing of his fingers. It didn't take long before he had her flushing and breathless as well.

"Point . . . well made," Danau acknowledged, fighting against the urge to rock into his touch. The edge of his finger scraped a tender spot, making her flinch. "Watch the nails," she muttered.

"Sorry," he apologized, lifting up on his other elbow so he could kiss his way from her shoulder to her breast. She squirmed free after a moment, scrambling to her feet.

"This isn't getting us out of here. We're hungry, and thirsty, and that floor is too hard—we need to figure out what's down here, and how we got down here, and how we're going to get out of here," she added, pulling her lust-addled wits back together. Turning around, she spotted her undershorts and snatched up the soft gray leather. Before she stepped into them, however, she spotted two doors in the alcove-like office, on the wall opposite the desk. "Look—one of those has to be a refreshing room! There wouldn't be an office down here without one. At least, one would *think* they'd build a refreshing room down here, when they were building them into the warehouse and other buildings up there . . ."

Koranen wryly acknowledged that she was rather like his sister-in-law Serina. Still naked, still somewhat flushed from love-making, Danau was already back to thinking about her work. She turned to him, eyed his naked body with a gleam in her blue eyes, and dropped her gaze, blushing. Then frowned and stooped, emitting an exasperated sigh, and picked up his velvet trousers.

"Put those on! I can't think straight when you're naked!"

The garment hit him in the chest. Koranen gave her a sardonic look. "Isn't thinking a bit overrated?"

"Koranen, look at my feet. I am *frosting the floor*. If we don't get control of ourselves now, and get into the *habit* of self-control, we'll never be able to go out in public! It's only when we touch that we seem to cancel out each other's powers. I'm going to check out these doors. One of them might be a refreshing room, and the other might be an alternate way back up to the surface. Either way, your assistance would be more helpful if you weren't so distractingly *naked*."

Sighing heavily, Koranen levered himself off the floor. He didn't bother to put on his trousers, though, just dropped them on the floor by his overtunic. Nor, he noted, did she put on her undergarment, though she carried it with her as she strode to the nearest door. Following her, he conjured another small fireball, adding the extra light over her shoulder as she twisted the lever and pulled open the door.

Brooms. Buckets. Bricks of age-whitened hardsoap, the kind used to scrub floors. Dropping her head for a moment, Danau muttered under her breath about how the distant Threefold God of Fate was giggling at them from afar, then closed the door. Marching over to the other one, she opened it . . . and sagged in relief at the sight of a necessity seat positioned across from a counter with a basin and cork-stoppered spigot. Lovemaking was messy, and it wouldn't hurt to wash the seed that had seeped . . . down . . .

Menos! Eyes wide, Danau turned and stared up at Koranen.

"What?" He didn't like the shocked way she was looking at him.

"I . . . we . . . We didn't use any form of contraception!"

Koranen stared back at her, equally stunned. They hadn't . . . His instincts awakened, flashing him a vision of her slender belly rounded with *his* child. His heart kicked in his chest, a painful thump of hope—he hadn't really dreamed of having children before now, not when he couldn't even hold a woman. Before *now*.

"Oh, Gods . . . I didn't mean to . . . I'll have to . . . to wash . . ." Danau muttered, shock coursing through her veins, puffing her breath visibly as her magic started sucking the heat out of the air around her.

Catching her shoulders as she turned from him, Koranen shushed her. "It's all right, Danau. We have three competent Healers on the island. I'm sure they know ways of taking care of things. Assuming you *want* to . . . you know, stop anything from happening."

The misting of her breath had stopped. Blinking, she craned her neck to peer up at him over her shoulder. "Assuming I *want* to?"

"Well, you don't *have* to stop it from happening," he pointed out. She turned to face him, frowning, and he dropped his hands to his naked hips, absently shifting the left one so it didn't press on one of his bruises. "If you haven't noticed, you and I just coupled *because* we were Destined for each other."

Her own hands shifted to her hips, leather undershorts dangling against one thigh. One of her auburn brows arched skeptically. Koranen continued before she could do more than inhale.

"According to Prophecy, the Water that can temper my Flame is my Destined bride. Since you are the only woman who can do that, *you* are clearly meant to be my wife," he told her. "And wives and husbands can have all the unprotected lovemaking they'd like! It's only for casual romping that contraception is absolutely necessary."

"That's *assuming* both the husband and the wife *want* children," she pointed out.

Koranen felt his heart thump again. This time, it was for a far less pleasant reason. "You . . . don't . . . ?"

Heat radiated from him in his distress. Part of Danau enjoyed the warmth, while another part acknowledged that, had he been her, their breath would have been frosting again.

"Kor . . . look, for the last eight years of my life, I thought I'd *never* have another lover," Danau explained, dropping her undergarment so she could reach for his hands. Drawing them away from his hips, she held them in her own, tempering his heat. "I *gave up* the thought of having children because of it. I had to plan my life around being single for the rest of it, and I got used to it.

"That's not to say I liked the thought of being alone . . . but it's been eight years of believing I'd *never* have a husband, let alone have any offspring. You can't just reverse eight years of thinking the exact opposite of something as monumental as *that* in a single night!"

Shaking his head to clear it, Kor focused on the meaning behind her words. He clung to her hands, not wanting to let her go. Not just as his own personal heat-sink. "Danau . . . are you saying you *want* to consider—just consider—the possibility of having children? Or are you saying you *don't* want to have children, period?"

"I'm saying I have to *think* about it—and right now might not be the best time, either, even if the answer *is* yes. We still have the Desalinator to figure out, and then after we return to Menomon, we'll have to figure out how to build a second one for the City. Both things will require a lot of time and energy. And while I don't know a lot about children," she admitted wryly, "I *do* know they take a lot of time and energy. Children shouldn't be treated as . . . as a whim, something to create on impulse. Or as an accident. You can't set aside a child to work on something else like you can an Artifact."

"Well, true," he acknowledged. "But . . . wait. *Return* to Menomon?"

"Yes, return to Menomon," she repeated. "That's why I'm here. To study and repair the Desalinator, with the intent of finding a way to replicate and re-create it for the benefit of everyone back home."

Koranen winced. He had forgotten about that part. *I couldn't deny her the right to help her people. From the sound of it, they're as short on drinkable water as we are, and they have a lot more people.* Gripping her hands, he let go of some of his plans. "Fine. We'll fix the Desalinator and return to Menomon long enough to re-create it there. But then, when we get back up here, we'll be free to have all the children . . . if any . . . that we could both want."

"Get back up here?" she repeated dubiously. "But, Menomon is my *home*."

"And Nightfall is *my* home," he returned. Koranen sighed, looking down at their clasped hands. "How ironic. Here I was, hoping we'd have an easy courtship. Find the woman who douses my flames, marry her, and live happily together for the rest of our lives. Only we can't even agree on *where* to live."

Danau could concede his point, that *his* sense of home was just as strong as her own. She *was* needed down in Menomon, for all she wasn't socially liked; she was the closest thing the aging Guardian Sheren had to a suitable replacement, though she wasn't strong enough to enter the Fountain for more than a few moments at a time before the buzzing of the magic agitated her nerves too much to focus. The City relied upon strong Aquamancers to handle the delicate, dangerous balance of life underwater, and again, she was needed to help with a dozen different tasks a week. But he was part of a family fighting to establish a brand-new kingdom, with all the many needs a brand-new kingdom would have for years to come. A large, supportive family.

She couldn't abandon Menomon without a second thought, but neither could he abandon Nightfall.

"Look . . . we *don't* have to decide anything right now. Except that we *do* need to figure out and fix the Desalinator, and I *do* need to return to build one for Menomon. If you come with me . . . you *might* decide you like our way of life down there. Or I might decide I'd rather be up here, where no one mocks me for being less than a woman . . . since even if I do take you as a husband, I'll still only be able to have just the one, you.

"But if I am to give the thought of coming back and living on Nightfall a chance," Danau stressed, squeezing his hands a little, "*you* have to promise to give life in Menomon a chance, too." She managed a lopsided smile, attempting a touch of humor. "You'd certainly be very popular as a Pyromancer. I don't think we've hosted more than three or four in the entire history of the city."

Her attempt at humor helped, but her logic was too sound on its own to ignore. Koranen didn't want to leave his family just yet. Not with the problems of resurrecting the Convocation still looming over their heads. But he could compromise.

"Alright. I'll go with you to Menomon, and give your home a chance. *But*," he stressed, "we will not leave until after both the Desalinator is fixed *and* the Convocation of the Gods has taken place. I will not leave Nightfall until after it has the protection of the Gods Themselves to help take my place."

The hubris of that statement made her laugh.

He grinned, but didn't smile for long. Fixing her with a sober look, Kor continued. "Seriously, we have had too many enemies looking to bring us low in the past, and we still have a few looming in our immediate future. The Empire of Katan is still upset that we've declared our independence with a successful Ringing of the Bell, and they're positively incensed that my brothers and I are no longer exiled in forgotten, womanless exile. The Mendhites know that we were looking for the Scroll of Living Glory but were refusing to give it over until they knew if we had a Living Host . . . which my family suspects means they were intending to come and steal said Host. And that woman Zella—somehow, I don't think she's gone for good."

"I wouldn't think so, either," Danau agreed. "She struck me as rather single-minded and stubborn."

"Exactly. I will not abandon my brothers," he said firmly, if quietly. "Not while they still need me. The more I hear about how poorly your own people treated you because of the side effects of your powers, the more grateful I am to my own family for not shunning me because of mine. It would be a poor way to repay them to turn my back and walk away when they needed me most—and you'll notice that they haven't shunned *you*, either."

"That's because they don't know about me," Danau pointed out.

Releasing her hands, Koranen pulled her into a hug. She didn't even reach his chin, forcing him to stoop just to rest his cheek on the top of her head, but he endured it for her. She could endure *him*, after all. "They'll come to know you soon enough. When they do, they won't mind nearly as much as you think—remember, *we're* not Menomonites. No one is going to ostracize you just because you're a little chilly at times.

"But come—we have a refreshing room to use, and some clothing to don, and a Desalinator to explore. If we don't find a way out of here within the next hour, we'll just have to wait until the concert is over, then call my twin to come open a mirror-Gate," Kor stated. Then flashed her a grin. "I know how we can pass the time, too . . ."

Blushing, Danau buried her face against his chest, relieved to know she *could* do so without risking his skin. "Desalinator first. *Then* we can have fun."

"Speaking of which, if we don't get out of here in time, we can catch my brother's concert tomorrow night. Though we'd probably have to stand, since from what I heard, all the available seats have been sold," he allowed.

Squeezing him in return, she pulled back, sighing. "Then let's clean up and dress, and see what we can find."

This can't be right . . . Why would the trail lead to the Desalinator, when Yarrin said the last he saw of her, she had boarded a ship?

It was at the docks, looking for that ship, that Morg had finally picked up a stronger signal than before. Though calling it *strong* wasn't accurate. Frowning, Morg eyed the straining crystal in his hand. It was tugging almost straight down, but only because he was right next to the wall of the one active intake tank. *And why such a faint trail, even now?*

The crystal angled inward, and down. The door was on one of the other seven walls, off to his right. Detouring that way, Morg watched carefully as the pendant swayed. Triangulation suggested the missing ex-Natallian *was* at least near the building, though the runes still weren't flashing from proximity. The implications of that were grim. The only things that lay down at that level, gauging by the angle of the pendant and its thong, were the intake pipes bringing seawater into the holding tank.

If I'm that close, within two dozen body lengths or so of my target, the spell should have triggered its proximity aura. But it hasn't. I should have crafted the variant that could tell whether or not she was still alive, as well as how close she was.

Since this building housed the intake tank, there were no work-ers to dodge. Stepping inside, Morg muttered an enhancement charm and watched as the diamond-shaped pendant pointed off to the left and distinctly downward. Clutching the thong in his hand, Morg headed for the nearest escape ladder, iron grilles with undulating wave patterns molded into rungs. They were meant to help rescue anyone who might accidentally fall in, but in this case, would help him descend. A snap of his fingers altered the pool before he started down; climbing and casting magic were difficult when gestures were a part of most mages' magic-focusing repertoire.

By the time he reached the water, the surface had hardened until it was as solid as ice, providing a firm surface for him to step onto. Now the pendant strained more diagonally than vertically. He was headed in the right direction, but it still pointed down. But it wasn't enough to just stand on the surface of the pool. What he wanted was still several body lengths below the waterline.

A mnemonic mutter accompanied by slow, paired sweeps of his hand reshaped the glasswater spell. Stairs formed, permitting him to descend down to the level of one of the pipes bringing water in from the sea, the one the pendant pointed at. Unfortunately, he was now low enough that, though sunlight shone through the high win-dows in the walls far overhead, there were too many shadows ob-scuring his vision at this depth.

Another flick of his hand, a quick scratching of his fingers in the air, traced a glowing rune. In the golden white glow it cast, he spot-ted several lumpy shapes half blocking the grille allowing water into the tank. At first, the mage couldn't make sense of them . . . and then, horrified, he recognized toes . . . and a heel . . . and at the other end of the nearest of the objects, part of a severed knee.

He almost lost control of the glasswater spell. The walls bowed inward, splashing saline drops around him before Morg snapped his eyes shut, disciplining his mind. For a moment, nothing existed—*nothing*—but the shape of a water-lined stairwell solidified like an oversized, carved crystal. He would *not* be sick. Whoever this had been—and most likely, it had been Teretha—his being sick would *not* reverse her dismemberment.

It did, however, explain why the signal was so weak. Prying open his eyes, Morg stared at the body parts with a grim detachment. A lower leg with foot mostly intact, a bit of what might have been an upper arm, a . . . a chunk of pelvis . . . and what looked like water-darkened strands of hair. Small fish darted among the shapes, taking little bites out of the sodden, drifting flesh.

Jaw clenched tight, he reached out with a hand and gestured gently. Gingerly. The body parts bobbed, shifting position. Revealing a face. It was pallid and strangely flaccid, and parts of her nose and lips had been nibbled on . . . but it *was* the missing baroness. Those parts that should have still been attached to other parts were clean slices, not the jagged edges one would expect from some predatory fish's attack.

She hadn't accidentally fallen off a ship and drowned. Baroness Teretha had been systematically dissected. Dismembered. Murdered.

He could feel the flanking walls of water trembling along with his nerves. Tightening his grip on his will, Morg considered the implications. It wasn't pleasant, staring into those sightless hazel eyes, but he was a mage, and he was trained to think clearly even under the most difficult of circumstances. That training was necessary, because if there was a murderer loose on the island, it was possible that murderer would pick another victim.

Eyes straining into the shadowed darkness of the pipe, Morg looked for more evidence. No other body parts were visible. The male mage Yarrin *had* sworn under Truth Stone that the last time he had seen the woman was when she had walked onto a ship and that he had not harmed her before they had parted ways. It was possible, even probable, that the other . . . parts . . . were still somewhere out in the harbor, drifting and being nibbled on.

Only these bits had been sucked into the pipes. He must have picked up one or two parts being drawn into the pipes when he had reached the quay, earlier. That was why the signal was so faint; he had been tracing only a small portion of the woman . . . and at that acknowledgment, his stomach churned again.

There was nothing more he could do from down here. Turning away, Morg mounted the spell-glazed steps. His back prickled at the thought of that sightless, lifeless gaze following him, and the air in the depths of the tank felt close, stale. By the time he reached the top of the ladderway, he felt like he was struggling for breath. It was with relief that he sagged onto the age-smoothed flagstones surrounding the tank; he didn't feel sick anymore, but he did feel weak enough to tremble.

He would have to cast a scrying of the immediate past. It would take energy, but since her disappearance was within a single day, he wouldn't need a lot of special preparations. Other than the crafting of a special, sanctified mirror, of course, one formed out of a pool of his own blood. There were other methods, ones that used a normal scrying mirror, but they required time, special ingredients, and complex runes. The alternative spells required less energy to go such a short distance into the past, but they also made lengthier trips into the past easier. Only for the most distant, difficult scryings did a mage have to add blood to the mix . . . or the most impromptu.

Morganen wrinkled his nose at the thought of cutting himself after seeing *that*, down below, but there was no quick way around the necessity. Not if he was to cast the spell quickly enough to catch the murderer. The fastest of the other four or five ways he knew required at least half a day to set up the runes and process the herbs into the proper mirror-coating salves.

I can't let those . . . pieces . . . remain in the water. We know the desalination process purifies the water for drinking, because it recycles the raw sewage from the city and the palace, processing it as fertilizer ingredients for the algae blocks. But she, or what's left of her, deserves an extraction . . . and a cremation.

At least I can use the blood-mirror to extract her remains, once I'm done scrying the past. That Vo Mos book talked about all the variations a blood-mirror can be used for. I know I can't do it beforehand, since it would taint the sanctity of the mirror, rendering it unfit for temporal scrying . . . but I also don't have to have any special powders to use a blood-mirror as a mirror-Gate, not at this close of a distance. It's grue-some, but it's powerful.

Might as well do it right here, he thought, settling himself on the ground more comfortably. *The sooner I get this over with, the sooner I can forgive myself for* not *looking into this matter this morning. If I hadn't been so intent on heeding Hope's wishes, on* personally *planting those seedlings as soon as they came through the mirror . . . I might have been able to prevent this tragedy . . .*

Might. That was the painful part. A mage could only scry into the past; he could not reach through the mirror he made, could not alter what had already come to pass. That was Fate's most immu-table law. Past and future could both be seen by the right person under the right circumstances, mages for the former, Seers for the latter. But the past was the past. Only the future, immediate or dis-tant, could be changed by the will of mortal man, and he had been busy planting bushes and seeds all day.

He couldn't change what had happened, but he *would* stop it from happening again. Until he did the scrying, it was best to leave the . . . pieces . . . of the puzzle in their current places, making it easier for him to retrace their route. Afterward, he could rescue whatever he could, and see that her body was prepared for burial. If nothing else, the Natallians who had come here with the baroness would want to hold a memorial of some sort . . . as well as a trial and punishment for her murderer.

Summoning the enchanted dagger his brother had given him for a birthing-day gift more than a decade ago, Morganen lifted the spell-sharpened edge to his wrist, bracing himself for the coming pain, and the additional drain on his power.

*G*ood Gods! Panting, soaked with sweat, the exhausted mage swayed back from the mirror he had made. The hand that lifted to rake back his light brown hair from his head trembled violently. He passed it down over his face, wiping shakily at the moisture slicking his skin. *That . . . that shouldn't be possible . . .*

Gods—the blasphemy *of it all!* Sickened by what he had seen, Consus staggered back until he could reach his favorite chair. Dropping roughly into the padded seat, he blinked his eyes, then closed them. The Barol Mirror wasn't just a creation of sand and silver. Ashes had gone into its making. Ashes culled from the unearthed bones of no less than four Katani Seers.

Seers were national treasures, venerated for their intimate connection to the far-seeing hearts and minds of the Gods Themselves. To desecrate the resting spots of their mortal bones was beyond blasphemy. It was *unthinkable.* Kata and Jinga should have struck down Barol of Devries on the spot, the moment he had dug into the first grave!

And yet . . . unthinkably . . . They did not interfere. It was difficult to grasp. It was said that the Gods protected Their divine prophets. There was even that story Lord Thannig, Councilor of Prophecies, liked to tell from more than a century ago, of three would-be muggers being turned into goats simply because they attempted to rob the Seer Turilonna in some minor town down in the southeast of the Empire. *Or maybe it was sheep . . .*

The point is, the Gods do intervene to protect Their Seers. So why didn't *They intervene?* He eyed the double-looped frame of the scrying mirror. *Alright . . . so the Seers weren't alive anymore. And it's been said over and over that once the spirit departs the body, the body is nothing more than a shell. The Healers all agree; if it cannot be revived within a quarter hour of death, it cannot be revived at all. So . . . maybe the Gods* don't *protect the earthly remains of the long-departed, and They only protect the ones who are still alive.*

But one *of those bodies had been the Seer Draganna herself, greatest of all Katani prophets. How could the cemetery priests not realize her grave was desecrated?* He glanced to the side, at the unguent-smeared mirror he had used to peer into the past. Scanning more than five years into the past, focusing his will to ensure that he saw the creation steps before the mirror, his focal point, had actually come into existence, had drained him of too much power to try to find the answer to that question right now.

I'll have to let it go. I'm almost out of vacationing time as it is.

The Council was expecting him to come back to work within three days. His subordinates were expecting his return. No doubt they would attempt to pile on his shoulders everything they hadn't finished themselves. *Of course, I'll just turn around and dump it all back on their shoulders,* he thought, lifting still-unsteady hands to his face, rubbing at his eyes.

He was so tired, he almost didn't hear the opening words, voices distorted by the double-paned mirror's peculiar scrying properties. But his ears *twitched,* in that way that said the Ultra-Tongue dose he had bartered several favors for was functioning. Someone was discussing a subject of some importance to him, someone speaking in a foreign tongue.

Struggling to pay attention, Consus frowned at the brown-skinned faces that appeared in both halves of the mirror. *Moon-round faces . . . tattoos . . . Mendhites? Again? And two of them?*

"Ships Fifteen and Sixteen have been deployed since our last communication, Kon-Dakim," the middle-aged male on the left said, bowing his head politely. *"Estimated aether-distance remains at seventy-five percent of functionality, within a ten percent variance."*

"Good. And the others, Dakim?" the elderly man on the right inquired.

Consus didn't know what a *kon-dakim* or a *dakim* was, other than probably some sort of name or title. A title, he decided, rather than a name, as he had first thought; both men had tattoos on their faces, but it was the badge on each man's collar, one more fancy than the other, that suggested a rank of some sort. Unless they *were* names.

Some things just didn't translate, even through Ultra Tongue, if they didn't have an equivalent word in the receiving language.

"Ship Seventeen is ready to drop long-anchor once they have reached their aether-distance," Left Man stated. *"Ship Eighteen will head for the mainland and seek either alliance or distraction with the mainland, depending on their current standing with these Nightfallites."*

Consus lost some of his weariness. *The Mendhites are coming* here? *And they're worried whether we're allies or foes of the Nightfallers?* This *was* something that pertained to him and his office, unlike his last visit by a Mendhite in the Barol Mirror.

"The mirrors?" asked Right Man, recapturing the Councilor's attention.

"They are ready; Ships Three, Four, and Five reported some minor damage during the storm, and Ship Three lost one of its spare mirrors, but the Gate mage reports the other two are still fully functional."

"And the potions?"

"We sustained unforeseen damage in the last storm. The bottles of Mind-Bender are still intact, but one of the Lust Philtres lost the seal on its cork. Puhon Krais was affected by the unguent absorbed into the padding. He is . . . working it out of his system," Left Man stated carefully. *"Given the small dose, he should be fully recovered from the potion and its aftereffect before reaching the island."*

"Good. It would not do to have him lose control on the first female he sees. It is imperative you do not draw attention to yourselves. Even with tattoos designed specifically to aid the Puhon brothers with their infiltration, it will be difficult to pass themselves off as locals if they act too far out of character."

Tattoos? Consus thought, bemused. *Infiltration? I know they mark their bodies with runes to focus magic—is this some sort of illusion-casting rune?*

"*I will presume Gayn and Foren are taking precautions with the Philtre case,*" Right Man said.

"*Krais will not let them near it,*" the younger one stated. "*He does not wish either of them to have a change of heart and tamper with it.*"

The elder Mendhite narrowed his brown eyes. "*They swore under Truth Wand that they would capture the Living Host, kill any current Guardian, and take that Guardian's place, bringing her back to us. Do the Puhon brothers hesitate?*"

"*I believe they* will *raid this place for the glory of Mendhi, and succeed,*" Left Man returned firmly. "*But I do not think Krais is happy that his brothers were chosen to accompany him and have their own chances at succeeding. I believe he is concocting these reasons so they cannot sabotage his chance at claiming the female.*"

The *Kon-Dakim* chuckled. "*He is ambitious, like his father.*" Sobering, the elderly Mendhite fixed his scrying partner with a firm look. From Consus' point of view, the man stared at the midpoint of the air between them, so it looked a little odd, and less effective for the Councilor of Sea Commerce than it surely was for the *Dakim*. "*Make certain they understand that petty rivalry will not be tolerated. The only thing that matters is the theft of the Living Host, the death of any Guardians that may have been paired to her, and mirror-Gating her as swiftly as possible to Mendham.*

"*All three have been sent because all three have the capacity to be Guardians of a new Fountain. All three are well trained in combative magics. And all three are capable of killing whoever gets in their way, with subtlety and discretion. Ideally, they will return the Living Host to the Elders unmated and intact, whereupon a lottery will be cast for the selection of her Guardian. But the world is not an ideal place. Mistakes may happen, and she may already be mated,*" he admitted. "*Seizing control of her Fountain during the confusion may become paramount. That is why the Puhon brothers were selected, because they have the skills, the power, and the self-control to step in* if *they need to commandeer the woman.*"

"*If I think that Puhon Krais, in my carefully considered judgment, will be more of a detriment and hazard to the mission than an asset, I will remove him personally from the assignment,"* the middle-aged Mendhite vowed. *"Or Puhon Gayn, or Puhon Foren."*

"The Elders are relying upon your discretion in this matter. Above all, these Nightfallites must not succeed in restoring the Convocation. That is our Destiny."

Left Man nodded, but looked troubled. *"Kon-Dakim . . . what if they have already extracted the Fountain? By accident or by design?"*

"Your assignment would then be to verify whether both Fountains are fixed or not. If the second is fixed . . . nothing can be done, and you will have failed to arrive in time. Yet you will not have failed entirely, for you would have prevented them from resurrecting the Convocation of the Gods at the very least. However . . . you will not be returning in triumph."

Left Man nodded. Consus thought he seemed a little paler than before, though the deep tan of his skin made judging such a thing difficult.

"If the Fountain is unfixed, it must be stolen and transported, the same as if it were a girl. It cannot, however, be transported by mirror-Gate without shattering the Gate and the person transporting it.

"Either way, there is one more task for the brothers to consider: There will be a bonus if they manage to kill the would-be ruler of Nightfall, a female named Kel Ee."

"A bonus?" Left Man asked, brows rising.

"A Katanite Elder we spoke to, Dook Finneg, has requested it. If the Puhon brothers succeed in this, once the Fountain has been transported to Mendham, send Ships Fifteen through Twenty to Katan. This Finneg has promised to fill their holds with silks, herbs, and other trade goods worth twenty times their native value in our land—and the brother who commits the kill will have the contents of two of those ships entirely for his own."

It was a good thing the tattooed faces of the two men faded after that. Consus stared at the silvered glass, mentally cast adrift by what he had just learned. *Dook Finneg . . . Duke Finneg . . . is plotting to kill Queen Kelly? But . . . but that is* forbidden *by the very fact that she was the one who Rang the Bell! Katan cannot interfere directly in the attempt to make Nightfall its own kingdom!*

Unless . . . unless he thinks to claim it isn't interference, since they could simply declare a new contender for sovereign? But she Rang the Bell—and it's still a case of him offering payment for the deliberate death of their incipient queen! I have to warn . . .

Shifting to get out of his seat, Consus groaned and sank back into its padded embrace. Hands lifting to cover his face, he berated himself silently. *I cannot warn them. The Empire does not want them to succeed at acquiring a Patron Deity—Gods, a whole Convocation's worth of Patron Deities—so if I warn them, I'm helping them to fight off this invasion . . . and giving them a chance to succeed in breaking fully away.*

And yet . . . and yet, it does seem the Gods want them to succeed. That woman Rang the Bell; the Gods clearly answered her by conjuring that crown . . . I have no idea what this Living Host business is, or how a Fountain can be "unfixed," or what they mean by it, or to do with it. Yet these Mendhites seem certain it is part and parcel of the Convocation of the Gods—and what a mess that *would be, to have the Corvis brothers go from ignoble exiles to the most politically and spiritually powerful family in the whole of the world!*

I cannot betray my own nation. And yet . . . and yet, if I do not tell them that this invasion is coming . . . am I not a potential accessory to murder? To the murder of an incipient queen, even! Rubbing his hands over his face, he tried to scrub away the dilemma, but it would not go away. *The law is clear; if someone knows of a plan to commit a crime as serious as murder, yet that person does not speak up, does not act in some way to see that it is stopped . . . by their silence, they are* aiding *the murderer, as surely as if they had sharpened the knife used to slit the victim's throat! I would be almost as much an accomplice as the Duke is, for promising to reward that woman's killers!*

But if I tell them, warn them . . . they could succeed in breaking away, and that is contrary to *my duties as a Councilor of Katan. We are forbidden to interfere, as in forbidden to prevent them from becoming a kingdom; we cannot hinder them from accepting those wishing to migrate to them, and had to repeal the laws isolating them in their exile. But His*

*Majesty has also stated quite clearly that we are equally forbidden to inter-
fere in the sense of helping them. If I warn them, and so help them . . . I
would be committing treason as a government official.*

It was a horrible, headache-inducing dilemma. To stay silent
and be an accessory to attempted murder, or to speak in warning and
be branded a traitor. Groaning again, Consus slumped forward, elbows braced on knees as he kept his face buried in his hands. *I cannot decide—how can I? And yet . . . I must, for staying silent and doing
nothing is a decision, in and of itself.*

*Gods . . . is this the punishment I must suffer, for eavesdropping on the
revelations caught by a mirror crafted from the desecrated bones of Your
former servants?*

There was no answer, only an undisputable truth: The Barol
Mirror *was* dangerous, even when held by the hands of the most
well-meaning.

TWELVE

❦

Danau stared at the papers in her hands. Someone had gone to the trouble of inking preservative runes at each corner, keeping the paper soft and bleached, not brittle and yellowed. They had also placed these papers on the surface of the desk so that someone on the *far* side from the chair would be able to read them, oh, say, the moment she left the refreshing room and crossed to the desk to investigate whatever was there.

More than that, the content of these pages was astounding. This was *exactly* what she needed to know, penned in neat Katani characters that made her eyes twitch, thanks to her dose of Ultra Tongue. Behind her, the door to the refreshing room opened.

"Koranen . . . the last ruler of this place, Nightfall . . . she was a Seer, correct?"

"Yes. The last Duchess of Nightfall was a Seer," he confirmed, fingers raking through his hair to comb it a little.

"Hah-*oo*-pan-ee-ah? Hah-oo-*pan*-ee-ah?" she asked, sounding out the name scrawled at the bottom of the last sheet. Names were difficult to translate, since most were relics from eras so old, their original meanings were no longer directly associated; the best Ultra Tongue could do was provide a rough translation of the necessary sounds in her mind. "How do you say this name?"

Coming up behind her, Koranen wrapped his arms around her, dropping a kiss on the top of her short auburn hair. Peering over her head, he studied the letters. "Haw-pan-*ay*-ah. It's an older eastern dialect, so the *au* and the *ea* are diphthongs, and the accent is on the third syllable. My name is stressed on the first syllable because it's from the western half of Katan, and because it has three syllables, not four. My twin's name is stressed on the second syllable because it's more southern."

"Well, this Duchess Haupanea was *very* considerate, even for a Seer. She's written down exactly what I need to know about how the Desalinator works. At least, as a summary. She also listed where the indepth instructions for each section are found in the bookshelf over there. Clearly, she knew we'd be down here . . ." Danau flushed, but thankfully didn't frost the pages, since Koranen was holding her from behind.

"I've heard they can be that way. Or at least, Mariel's first husband was that way. Mariel says you get used to them knowing things you never told them. And it's not like they have a choice in knowing it, anyway," Kor said. "So. If Her Grace was kind enough to supply all the basics you need . . . what does it say?"

Since he hadn't taken long to use the facilities and dress, she hadn't done more than skim the papers. She took a little more time to read the details now. "Well . . . half the ribbon-pipes are testing tubes for gauging salinity, temperature, and so forth, as I suspected from the general shapes of the Artifacts out there. The other half are . . . for gauging the life-content of the water? Protozoa, bacteria, algae, plankton, tiny fish . . . anything that gets past the filtering grilles." She frowned at that, handing him the topmost page of the thin stack in her hands. "But why would the filtering grilles *let* life through, if they can weed out the larger forms?"

"Because the larger ones would gunk up the works with their carcasses?" Kor offered, scanning the page handed to him.

"According to this paragraph, most everything is extracted from the water, all save for a light matrix of certain minerals. If you distill water to its purest form, stripping out all of the minerals, you run the risk of the water latching onto *your* body's minerals, stripping them out of *you* if you drink it. If the only thing that's really needed is the salt, why produce the algae blocks, too?"

"You said Menomon was having a problem with its local salinity, right?" Kor offered.

"Yes, because we weren't stripping the salt out of the water, which caused it to accumulate in the local waters at a higher level than the local sea life could tolerate . . . Ah, of course. To prevent the system from clogging from algae blooms and so forth," she said, handing over the next page. "That's why you have to extract the plankton and such, so that it doesn't thicken the local waters . . . Here we go. How the system is powered. The spire in the center . . . Yes, that's the key to the system. Reservoir and distribution node in one . . . *Gods!*"

"What?" Koranen peered over her head at the page. Her hand was trembling, though, making it difficult for him to read the words the last duchess had written. "What's wrong?"

"The crystal is *only* for starting the system and for storing over-flow energy. *Most* of the power . . . most of the system gets its ex-tractive power from the *deaths* of all those miniscule organisms! This is . . . *blood*-magic . . ."

The horror in her voice made Koranen snatch the last two pages out of her hands so that he could read it for himself. "That can't be right . . ."

It was. But it was more than that. Koranen read it aloud to try to make sense of what the duchess had written down for them.

"*The initial empowerment of the system comes from the life force of a particularly strong Aquamancer, and during maintenance phases, only an Aquamancer's own personal life-energies can restart each section. But, once started, the system is mostly self-maintaining and only needs recharging every forty or fifty years, depending on physical maintenance needs, because the life force of the plankton, algae, and so forth is harvested by the rune-spells carved on the separation lattices even as they are extracted, dried, and compressed into blocks.*

"It is to be noted that the life force of these creatures is never once used by a mage, that the entire system can only be started by a mage who gives a substantial portion of his own life-energies to prime the system and nudge it into functioning, and that any attempt by an outside force to draw upon the magic culled from the life-energies of the dying minuscule sea life will cause that particular latticework to shut down and need to be restarted by the freely given powers of a mage . . ."

The remaining page detailed what steps had to be followed to restart the system, either just one tunnel and lattice at a time, one pair of buildings at a time, or the whole system all at once.

Danau couldn't believe it. She had hoped to bring this system back to her people, but it was a system that deliberately harvested life-energy? "This whole system . . . it's cursed!"

Koranen shook his head. "It is blood-magic, yes . . . but it's not evil. These *are* lives that would die anyway if, oh, the water was boiled to distill it and separate it from the salt and algae. You'll note how the Desalinator excludes larger, smarter life-forms. The larger stuff would give exponentially greater energy to the system, empowering and making it more efficient, but it *doesn't* do that. And the energies aren't being used by one specific mage. It could be argued that killing and eating things is blood-magic, because their lives are sacrificed to sustain ours . . . but we have just as much right to live, eat, and drink as any other form of life. This is just one other way of doing so, and our benefit from all that drained life force is indirect at best. So this system *isn't* evil, in and of itself. It's just . . . energy efficient."

Forced to concede his point, Danau sighed. It felt good—if strange—to be able to relax against him. To be able to touch him, and not have to worry about her powers inadvertently harming him.

Lifting one hand, she cupped his bare forearms under her fingers. "*Expedient*, you mean. Though energy efficient would be right, too; the amount of power required to extract the sheer volume of water this facility can process would practically require half the energy of a Fountain being dedicated to it.

"An Aquamancer of the thirteenth or fourteenth rank might be able to energize it for several days at a stretch, and do so several times in a row, but they'd probably exhaust themselves before a turning of Sister Moon had passed. *I'm* only Rank 10! I can't sustain a system like this for more than a day! How am I going to restart it, even with the help of my Guildmates?—Not that I'm *inclined* to let Reuen or Chana help. *One* of them destroyed my dress!"

That made him chuckle and cuddle her closer. "Supplying power is *not* a problem with this family, Danau. We have all of my brothers plus two Fountains to draw on."

Plucking the pages from his grasp, Danau sorted through them and pointed at one of the lines on the last sheet, holding it up so he could read over her shoulder. "See that? It has to be an *Aquamancer*. She states specifically that it must be a powerful Aquamancer who energizes the crystal. Aquamantic energies aren't the same as generic— you're a Pyromancer; you *know* that!"

"Well, maybe just *filtering* the energies through an Aquamancer will be enough to attune them," he offered.

"Koranen, when you and I touch, we *cancel* each other's power. That's how we got through the hydrostatic barrier, by cancelling the aquamantic energies holding it stiff. Unless we bring one of your brothers down here to try feeding me magic, somehow I don't think *cancelling* the energies will help the Desalinator to function better," she pointed out.

Her words made him frown. Koranen took the sheets back, finding the right page after a few moments, the second-to-last sheet. "Here it is. The duchess wrote that *only* an Aquamancer powerful enough to restart the system can get past the doorway. That only a powerful Aquamancer *can* put magic into the system, because of the 'power-flow restriction spells' that make it very difficult to *extract* energy from the system.

"If you got in here, you *are* powerful enough to restart the system, Danau. And it clearly says Aquamancer, not some powerful mage in general," he reminded her.

"But I *couldn't* get in here," Danau stated, twisting to look at him directly. "I wasn't strong enough on my own. It wasn't until *you* touched me that the barrier . . ."

She trailed off, blue eyes widening. They narrowed after a moment in speculation. Danau turned away, her attention aimed at the center of the large chamber beyond the alcove's archway. Koranen reordered the pages and set them on the desk. "If *both* of us are required to make you a powerful Aquamancer, then we can test this theory on the door up above. We can have you touch it and focus on being an Aquamancer, while having me touch it and focus on being a Pyromancer at the same time . . . and touch it singly or with the other person as backup."

"And then what? Have me touch it while you're touching me, and picturing myself as a Pyromancer? What we did was *unconscious*, Koranen. I wasn't exactly thinking about being an Aquamancer when you touched me!"

"Not consciously, no, but you *were* chilling the air in your distress," Kor reminded her, looping his arms around her shoulders. The reminder of why she had refused to go out with him reminded him in turn of why they *could* date each other, after all. But dipping his head to kiss her strained his back and his neck. Grimacing before his lips could connect, Koranen sighed and straightened. "*This* isn't going to work."

"What isn't?" Danau asked, worried that he had stopped, instead of kissed her.

"I sincerely hope this Menomon City of yours has a lot of steps you can stand on, because my only other choices are a permanent hunch in my back . . . or this." Stooping, he scooped his hands under her rump, lifting her up against his chest. Danau gasped and clutched at his shoulders, but that only brought their torsos to-gether. Despite the layers of velvet and leather in their way, he could feel her breasts pressing into him—unharmed breasts—and sa-vored the sensation, smirking at her. "Of course, it isn't nearly as dignified as standing you on a step, but it *is* more fun."

With her lips parted on an indrawn breath, she was perfectly placed for a kiss. Swooping in, Kor finished his interrupted attempt. At first she stiffened in his arms, her mouth hesitant beneath his. But as the heat of interest flushed through him, she muttered some-thing that sounded like *warm* against his lips, and melted into him. Within a short time, Koranen's hair was mussed, his overtunic was half pulled out of its belt, and he was trying to find the couch out of the corner of his eye.

He couldn't return the favor with her hair, since it was too short, and he couldn't tug at her clothing, since his hands were needed to support her weight, but he did find the broad, padded seat with the side of his knee. Her legs had lifted at some point, wrapping around his hips. A shift of his hands got them out of the way, allowing him to turn and sit down. That broke their kiss, but it wasn't a bad thing; Danau blushed and grinned almost shyly at him.

"I can touch you, can't I?" she asked, licking her lips. "I mean, *really* touch you—anytime I want . . . right?"

Koranen wasn't about to say *no*. In fact, the possibility of their missing his brother's concert entirely was not an unappealing one. Cupping her leather-clad hips in his palms, Kor met her gaze steadily.

"Danau, you and I are Destined for each other," he reassured the redhead straddling his lap. "Refusing you would be like . . . like re-fusing the Laws of God and Man. Unthinkable."

His answer reassured her, but Danau wanted more. Too many years of being mocked and jeered and avoided were warring with the truth of this one, singular man. "And . . . you *do* want me?"

With a gentle tug of the hands on her hips, he slid their groins firmly together. There was no mistaking what that lump was, or the palpable flexing of his hips, pressing it into her core. Danau flushed with the thrill of the blatant act, but she needed to know more.

"I meant, do you want *me*?" she clarified. "I know I'm not the most charming of women, and I'm not the prettiest . . ."

About to answer her with a flattery, Koranen remembered a piece of advice that one of his brothers had given him. Not Trevan, but something his twin, Rydan, had said. *Women love to be flattered, but only if it is the truth.* That observation had been made many years ago, and it had been made to a young lady who had pursued the sixthborn Corvis brother rather vigorously, despite his obvious disinterest in her. *She had been trying to get him to compliment her, and when he wouldn't comply, complained that women liked being flattered . . . and when my brother said* that, *it implied that any flatters he could have given her would be false. Which means, whatever I say to Danau* must *be the truth.*

"Danau, you are intelligent. I *like* intelligence in a woman. I've enjoyed listening to you talk about your work, and have been flattered when you've listened about mine. You're a bit work-obsessed, like my sister-in-law Serina," Kor added honestly. "But given your, well, lack of a social life until now, I can see why you'd focus most of your attention on that. With a bit of practice, I'm quite certain you can divert, oh . . . a third of that focus to pouncing on me and tumbling me into the nearest bed."

"And you wouldn't mind in the slightest," Danau agreed dryly.

"I may have been a virgin until now, but that doesn't make me *insane*," he retorted. "What sane man would refuse his one and only woman the chance to have her way with him?—And *no*, I'm not displeased with your physical appearance, either," he added before she could protest that part. "Of course, I'd love to see what you look like with long hair, but you have a pretty nose, kissable lips, a stubborn chin, and nice blue eyes. And breasts."

She quirked one of her brows. "Breasts?"

"Yes. You have breasts. I *like* breasts," Koranen said. And then wondered if he'd gone a little too far in his blunt honesty, for she tipped her head back in laughter. Shrugging mentally, he shifted his hands from her hips to those breasts, cupping her curves through the soft leather of her tunic.

At some point during her time in the refreshing room, she had managed to clean the powdered clay from her outfit, though both her clothes and herself would need a real scrubbing, not a casual enchanting. Even he needed a bath. *And, with any luck, we'll have yet another reason very soon to bathe. Preferably together.*

"Then I guess I'm glad I have them," she managed to say once she stopped laughing. Smiling, Danau wrapped her arms around his shoulders, ready for another kiss. The feel of rich velvet underneath her splayed fingers enhanced her enjoyment, but it was the warmth of his flesh, satiny-soft and flexing with muscles, that was the greater sensual thrill. She started to work her fingers under the armholes of the blue, vest-like garment—and yelped as his hip rang.

Briiiingding! Briiiingding!

"Menos!" Danau swore, jerking back from Koranen. The Nightfaller groaned, then grabbed for the pouch slung at his side. Unlatching the flap, he pulled out the gilded, silver bracelet with its hinged crystal lid.

"Yes?" Kor asked impatiently the moment he had the Artifact open and could see a face in the scrying glass. It was Kelly. "You wanted something?"

"Are the Aquamancers with you?" the freckled woman asked.

"Danau is, but not the others." Kor wanted to shut the lid and get back to the kissing and fondling of earlier, but something in the way she put that made him frown. "Wait, what do you mean, the Aquamancers, plural?"

"Well, Ama-ti is here, but we can't find the other two," Kelly said. "We were all going to ride down in a caravan of carts, but they're not in the palace. I was hoping they might be with you, but if they're not . . . then they're missing."

"They'd *better* be missing," Danau muttered, remembering the horror of finding her precious dress all over again.

She didn't feel the frigid cold anger of earlier, however, just a regular sort of ear-burning rage. Not when she was seated on her Pyromancer's lap. That realization took some of her anger away. Not all of it, but some of it. *If they hadn't destroyed my dress, if he hadn't pursued me, if we hadn't fallen into this place and been trapped here . . .*

"Well, wherever they are, either they'll meet us there, or they'll have to walk down to the concert hall," Kelly said, shaking her head. "I hope the two of you are having a nice dinner."

Koranen glanced at Danau, then dropped his gaze down the length of her leather-clad torso. The smell had been a bit strong at first, but just thinking about her taste made his mouth water. "Better than expected."

Danau blushed, remembering how he had "dined" on her flesh. *All these years of suppressing my natural urges . . . It's hard to accept I really* can *have a physical relationship. The most I've ever been able to have since Fiore was a sexless working relationship . . . But I don't want just sex,* she decided firmly as he said good-bye and snapped the lid shut again. *I want . . . I want everything. Love, romance, conversation, even just complaining about our various projects!*

"What are you thinking?" Kor asked her.

"Everything." Danau surprised herself by admitting the truth, but it was the truth, and she wasn't going to take it back. "I want everything. Talking, laughing, complaining, appreciating, helping, loving . . . everything in a relationship, not just the sex. Lovemaking is good—lovemaking is great! But I want . . . everything," she finished, shrugging awkwardly.

He grinned at her, spreading his hands. "That's perfect—that's exactly what *I* want. I want everything, too!"

Danau started to respond, only to be interrupted by the gurgling of her stomach. Blushing, she made a face and backed off of his knees, regaining her feet. "As much as we might agree . . . we really do need to work our way out of here and go find something to eat."

Disappointment warred with his desire. Knowing she was right,

Koranen sighed and scooted forward, preparing to stand. A hand touched his jaw, lifting his face. Once Danau had his attention, she leaned down and kissed him. Then wrinkled her nose again.

"You're right. The disparity in our heights *is* an uncomfortable factor," she acknowledged.

"At least when you're sitting on my lap, you're the perfect height," Kor pointed out, pushing to his feet. He loomed over her for a moment, then dropped a kiss on top of her head. "We'll work the rest of it out, somehow. Let's go try touching that doorway upstairs together. If we can do that and get it to open, then we can go find something to eat."

"And we can come back down here tomorrow to finish exploring everything," Danau agreed, glancing at the desk and the papers left to examine. A thought crossed her mind, making her frown. Pulling away from Koranen, she headed for the desk.

Behind her, Koranen rolled his eyes, wondering if she was obsessing over work again. *If she is, Big Brother Dominor is going to have to tell me how he successfully distracts* his *wife from her work . . .*

"Koranen . . . you said something about the pipes that cool the buildings in the city during the summer," she said, flicking through the pages of the summary the last ruler of the island had left for them.

"Yes, it got rerouted back into the one functional holding tank, so that more of the volume could be salvaged for drinking and bathing purposes. The system doesn't produce enough water for us to waste it carelessly."

"But that's wrong—the system has a *constant* flow rate," she told him, turning to face her lover. "We've already determined that the one functional sluiceway is operating at full capacity. Chana inserted the data we gathered into her mathemagical formulae, and the results are very clear. You can't 'recycle' the water; the system can only produce a very limited amount, because only *one channel* is still functional. It only has *enough* energy to . . . Oh, Sweet Seas of Menos!"

Her eyes had widened in horror, alarming Kor. "What? What's wrong?"

"You said you're recycling *freshwater* through the system? You're diluting the algae and plankton!" Danau exclaimed. At his non-plussed look, she flapped the papers in her hand. "According to *this*, the system has to be 'refreshed' every few decades with an influx of outside magic, because the magical energies extracted from the minuscule life-forms being turned into algae blocks aren't enough to keep the system running in perpetuity!

"Kor, if the system is recycling *filtered* water, it's gathering even *less* life-force energy from the water it's processing, and relying even *more* on that crystal node out there! Depending on how much energy is left—and after more than two centuries since the last 'refill,' I wouldn't count on it having a lot—that last latticework could be on the brink of a collapse!"

He paled, absorbing the implications. "If that lattice fails, we're *out* of drinkable water. It's summertime. In winter, we'd be better off, but we don't get more than a few hours of rain every ten or twelve days at this time of year."

Tossing the pages on the desk, Danau spun on her heel and strode for the main room. Koranen started to follow, then remembered their source of light. Snatching the lightglobe from its holder on the desk, he hurried after her. This was one instance where his height was a blessing; with longer legs, it took him only a dozen strides to catch up with her. Together, they made their way to the crystal perched on its rune-marked spire.

The faceted oval was just above head height for Danau. Lifting her hands, she calmed herself with two slow breaths, made sure her powers weren't frosting the air, and gently pressed her fingertips to the surface. Only what her fingers touched didn't feel like crystal. Frowning, she ran her hands over the facets and finally dug in a nail. "It's another hydrostatic barrier—why have a barrier on the crystal?"

"The same reason for having a barrier on the door, I'd say," Kor reasoned. "To keep lesser-powered mages from draining energy out of the system, accidentally or deliberately."

"Accidentally?" Danau asked, bemused.

He shrugged. "The first time young Mikor wandered into my forge, he'd seen me handling a bit of metal with my bare hands. When I put it down and turned my back, he touched it and burned his fingers because *he's* not a Pyromancer. Now he knows better, but now he's not the only child on the island, either, and we all have to watch for children running about, in and out of craft shops and construction areas alike."

"You can *tell* a child not to run where and when it's dangerous, but they don't always heed you," Danau agreed wryly. Looking at the crystal, she nodded. "Yes. Once the door has been opened by someone powerful enough, anyone else could accompany them inside. And once they're down here, it wouldn't be a good idea to let just anyone have access to the power in the storage crystal. Because if they did and they drained it and the lattices it's connected to . . ."

"It makes me wonder if the crystal *was* somehow drained when Aiar Shattered," Kor said. "I don't know how or why, but I do know that's *when* most of the Desalinator stopped functioning."

"Since I don't know of anyone powerful enough to scry two hundred years into the past, I doubt we'll ever know." Danau sighed, skimming her fingers over the thin, clear skin coating the crystal.

Kor chuckled at that. "Then don't bring up the subject with my sister-in-law Serina. I *know* she's powerful enough to scry back that far, and farther. In fact, she's working on a project that's over eight hundred years old."

Lifting one hand to her shoulder, the other still holding the lightglobe, he started to guide her away. Danau sucked in a sharp breath as the film, warmer than a true crystal should have been, chilled suddenly. Normally it was when she touched things on her *own* that they grew cold beneath her fingertips. He removed his hands quickly, and she shook her head. "Touch me again!"

Somehow, he didn't think she meant sexually, which was a disappointing prospect. Lifting his palm to her shoulder, he settled it lightly, carefully. She nodded slowly.

"Yes . . . the barrier's dissolved. I can . . . Yes, I *can* sense the energy. There's not much left . . ." Closing her eyes, Danau focused on the minute amount of power still contained within the oval, faceted orb. She probed the energy, comparing it to her own power, which in turn was automatically compared to the thread-of-copper runes lining the hems of her clothes as a standard baseline . . . and realized her sense of *power* was now skewed. Snapping her eyes open, she twisted, peering up at the man standing at her back. "*We* are more powerful. Together."

"Beg your pardon?" Koranen asked, bemused. He'd been expecting a comment on how much energy was left, not whatever this new conversation was.

"There's a trick in the Guild," she explained. "You compare the energy of whatever it is you're studying against your own energy, and against whatever enchanted object you may have with you—often, it's a pair of dowsing rods, like the ones I used to trace the ley lines empowering the outbuildings, because those are things enchanted with a specific amount of energy nearly every single time. It allows us to be more accurate in our estimates for various repairs and other services around the city.

"In this case, I used my anti-freezing embroidery as my baseline, since it's a constant in my life," she said. "But instead of being Rank 10 . . . I feel more like . . . like a Rank 15. Or close to it. I'm not completely sure, because the only person stronger than me is Guardian Sheren, and Sheren's a Rank 16, but she's not here right now to compare myself to. Or rather, *our*selves."

You are very much like Serina, my charming little bride, Koranen thought, but wisely kept that amused thought to himself. Instead, he flexed his fingers gently on her shoulder. "Focus. How much power does the crystal still hold?"

"Not much . . ." Refocusing her attention, Danau gauged the

amount of power in the crystal, then withdrew her hands and muttered a command.

Once her first two fingers started glowing, she carefully traced glowing runes in the air, adding in the necessary numbers. It was the sort of spell that cost a mage in energy, but she didn't have a greaseboard at hand. Within a few minutes, the glowing mathemagical symbols allowed her to compute the result.

"I can't say for absolute certain, because I don't know how much the freshwater influx is affecting all of this . . . but I think the minimum time we have is about two weeks before there isn't enough power to make the system work."

Mathemagics was just about the only magical language that was consistent from nation to nation, but then, it was based on logic and the cooperation of generations of Arithmancers and mathemagicians. Koranen had been trained in the basics and even the intermediates of the art, the same as his brothers. If her numbers were right . . . that looked like the bottom-line projection to him, too. "So what do we do?"

"The *first* thing we do is divert that 'recycled water' nonsense out of the system—if you want to save drinking water, then you put it into catch-basins, and then just treat it like a plebeian water source. If the Healers say it's safe to drink, you drink it. And if not, you boil it, and maybe even evaporate and condense it, until it's safe to drink."

"What about the sewers?" Koranen asked. "They're contributing to the diluting of the salt water, aren't they?"

"Sewage is designed to be recycled into the system. In fact, I'd guess that's why a little extra energy has to be recharged into the system now and again. The Healers say there are tiny living organisms that survive the trip through the body from one end to the other, so that would contribute a small amount to the system, but it's only a small amount," Danau admitted. "It's adding in all that extra water on top of what the sewers contribute, with no amelioration from extra bits of life, that is causing the drain."

"Can we give it a bit of energy?" he inquired. "Right now?"

"Good question . . . but I'd rather not risk it tonight," Danau said, dropping her hands from the power-node. "If we tried to add energy to the system right now, we would be forcing energy into dry-as-dust lattices. Because it would be priming them to start drawing energy from tiny sea life, without seawater already lurking in the latticeways, that could actually potentially damage them."

"The important thing is, the system isn't going to collapse overnight. Soon, maybe, but not in the next few days." Kor reminded her.

"Hopefully we'll have time to figure out whether this thing empowers all four tanks simultaneously, or if it can be directed to just one set," she agreed. "Whether we'll need to flood all the tanks first, or just the other seven sluices in the one functional pair of outbuildings . . . though I'd rather do all of them at once, if we have enough power. The way the subtunnels are interlaced, I suspect the system requires a balanced approach of all four sets working simultaneously to function at its most efficient."

This time, when Koranen nudged her away from the crystal-topped spire, she allowed herself to be moved. "That's all and good, but since we know we can access the crystal, and that we need to spend some time studying the system first, we *do* need to be going back up to that door now. Both of us are hungry, and while I can turn that ball of dust into food well enough to fool our palates, it wouldn't fool our stomachs in the long run."

"Yes, and only fools think they can successfully live on love." Danau winced in the next moment, realizing how *un*romantic that sounded. She flushed and reminded herself she *wasn't* a sexless worker, or a failure as a female. *And I have every right under the green blue sea to want a normal life.* She amended her words as best she could. "Not that I wouldn't like to *try* living on love . . ."

"But you have almost a decade of bad habits to overcome," he agreed. He might not be able to read her thoughts, but Koranen was shrewd enough to guess just how much she would have to struggle to overcome those habits. Unfortunately, his choice of words weren't quite delicate enough.

"They weren't *bad* habits—they were self-defense mechanisms!" Danau argued, frowning up at him. "*You* try living in a society that tells you you're a failure as an adult, over and over again, and not need a way to push that all aside!"

"My apologies," Koranen muttered, chastised. *I really must remember how sensitive she is on this point . . . and reassure it right out of her.* He cheered up in the next moment and shared the accompanying thought. "At least on the bright side, you don't *need* those habits anymore. In fact, you could acquire a whole *new* set of socially unacceptable habits."

"How do you mean?" Danau asked, suspicious of his sudden good humor. She *had* almost yelled at him just now. *I must remember not to yell at him; he hasn't swum a league in my clothes, so he doesn't know how hard a struggle it's been.* "What new habits?"

"Well, if we're both still plagued by our thermal problems when we're *not* touching, you're going to be stuck practicing the 'bad habit' of monogamy," Kor quipped, shifting his free hand from her shoulder to her back. The other palm balanced the lightglobe, illuminating their way to the door and the staircase beyond. "And— with any luck—we'll need lots and lots of 'practice.'"

Danau laughed ruefully. "You have a one-track mind."

"You are the only woman in my life I can touch. I want to practice *everything* about having a relationship with you, arguments and agreements alike. Lovemaking and laughter. All of it," he asserted, gesturing lightly with the hand still holding the lightglobe.

His words made her smile. "Then I'm glad we have something in common."

The barrier vanished at a touch, provided they were touching each other. It didn't matter if Danau pressed her hand to the wall, or if Koranen did, so long as they also pressed some part of themselves together, though both of them touching the wall individually at the same time did nothing to the spell. Satisfied they could open the door, Koranen gently set the lightglobe on the floor, double-rapped it to shut it off, and groped for Danau.

She jumped a little when his hand bumped into her backside, then jumped again when he switched from a fumbling touch to a deliberate squeeze, but it didn't prevent her from opening the wall. After the oppressive, true black of the unlit stairwell, the empty chambers leading to the rest of the warehouse were dark but not impossible to navigate. Catching Koranen's hand, Danau laced their fingers together and grinned.

Their paces didn't match; she had to take three strides for every two or so of his. But they were holding hands, and the air felt warm instead of cold. Actually, it felt rather warm. Curious, Danau freed her hand . . . and felt instantly cooler. Koranen gave her a bemused look and caught her fingers again, then stopped and frowned softly.

"Do you feel different when we touch?" he asked her. "Or rather, does the temperature of the air feel . . . different?"

"It's warmer," Danau agreed. "Normally, I never quite feel warm enough, unless it's *very* warm, like near a forge-fire, or on the surface with a Wavescout patrol on a hot summer's day. What about you?"

"I feel cooler when I'm touching you. Which is actually a good thing, since I'm wearing velvet," he muttered. Then flushed, remembering her dress. "Sorry . . . I didn't mean to . . . I'll buy you a new dress," Kor promised impulsively. "All of it velvet. *Two* dresses."

As much as his extravagant promise touched her, it was still extravagant. Danau eyed him askance. "Kor, I know velvet isn't considered quite as *priceless* on the surface as it is in Menomon, but I do know it still costs a lot! You do not have to beggar yourself for something which, by rights, one or both of those two missing imbeciles should pay to replace."

"And if I want to clothe my wife in the finest of clothes, it is *my* choice! Besides, I'm not a pauper. I have plenty of wealth at my disposal."

"You do?" Danau asked. It occurred to her belatedly that she didn't know much about *what* he did to earn his way in the world, other than make various objects from glass. "From the sales of all those glass things you made?"

"I work in several mediums," Kor told her, catching her hand in his again and gesturing with his free arm for them to continue walking. "Glass, metal, ceramic, faience . . . I've made most of the lightglobes in Harbor City and made or repaired half the ones in the palace. Not to mention kilned all of the roof tiles in the whole of the city, and pressed the panes for the windows, and fired the bricks for the hearths.

"Of course, for most of the latter, I haven't actually been *paid* for all the work I've done," honesty prompted Kor to add, "but I have a tally sheet with each shopowner and craftsman; I can use the amount on the tally sheet to 'purchase' whatever I want from them, up to the total estimated cost of their windows and roof tiles and so forth.

"Saber and Serina came up with the system, since *he* wanted to make sure each of us got paid for the work we've been doing to settle everyone in the new city, but *she* pointed out that most people couldn't afford to pay for the quality of buildings we've been constructing . . . and that it would encourage people to be more generous in 'giving' us goods, if the funds on the tally sheets were considered tax exempt, so they wouldn't have to lose even more money in transactions with us."

"By 'us,' you mean . . . ?" Danau prompted him as they reached the barn-sized doorway.

"My family, my brothers and sisters-in-law. We're still doing the majority of the construction work, since a lot of it has to be done by magic—the stone beams of the buildings and their water-cooling-and-heating systems have to be grown and sealed magically to prevent leaks, for example. But the cost is reduced proportionately by how much work each new resident puts into his or her future home," he said. Movement off to the side distracted him before he could continue. Someone had just stumbled through the entrance to the holding tank building, a familiar someone. "Morg? What's he doing here?"

Danau followed the line of his stare. She spotted Lord Morganen, and watched as he swayed. "He doesn't look well."

With an unspoken agreement, both of them hurried toward the mage. Koranen dropped Danau's hand, allowing his longer legs to close the distance to his sibling more rapidly. When he came close enough, he realized the brown smears on Morg's wrist and opposite hand weren't dirt, but rather were dried blood. Alarm quickened his steps. "Morg!"

"What? Kor." Blinking, looking tired and a little dazed, Morganen focused his aquamarine eyes on his twin. "Good. I need you. I need the others, too . . ."

Catching his twin's arm, Koranen lifted that bloodied wrist into view. The skin was reddish pink in a line along the inside—the implications were staggering. "Morg . . . *blood*-magic? No . . . no, not *you* . . ."

"What? *No!*" Morg gave his brother a dirty look. He gestured with his other hand at the building behind him, explaining even as Danau caught up to them. "I found . . . Baroness Teretha was murdered, and the . . . the parts tossed into the bay. Some of them . . . well, it's a good thing we already know that the desalination system thoroughly scours the water we drink."

Koranen blanched at the thought of what his brother implied he had found.

Morganen closed his eyes. "No, I had to cast a past-scrying, a time-sensitive one since she was killed at some point between this morning and now, and the quickest . . . the quickest way to do it required a blood-mirror."

"Are you all right? Do you need to sit down?" Danau asked, more concerned with how pale the Nightfaller male looked than the wheres and whys of some spell.

Morg shook his head. "I *need* to find her killer. It's *my* fault I didn't track down the baroness earlier this morning—I thought something *else* was more important, and it . . . I might have been able to prevent her death if I'd tracked her down . . . but I didn't."

"You are *not* the one who *put* her in danger," Koranen told his twin. He caught Morg by the shoulders, holding his brother's slightly unfocused gaze. "Even if you *had* tracked her down, you *might not have been in time*. Or worse, the murderer might have tried to kill *you*."

That snapped some of the dazed look out of Morganen's gaze. He snorted, giving his brother a scoffing look. "As if anyone could! They'd be a toad before they could croak a single word!"

"You're *not* infallible, Morg. Even you can't protect yourself all of the time, never mind all the other people living here—and if you made a mirror out of your own blood, you're in desperate need of food and water. Or even a transfusion spell," Kor added. "Remember what Kelly said when she gave her blood to Trevan?"

"I've only lost some of my blood and my magical energies, not my wits. I don't need a transfusion from her. What I *need* are my brothers to support and energize me. I need to cast a locator spell large enough to cover the whole of the city and some of the outlying land beyond. There was only *one* ship that left the island today, the ship that *bastard* swore he saw Teretha step onto . . . !"

"Bastard?" Danau asked, a sinking feeling churning in her stomach. "Not . . . Yarrin? The blond Mornai mage we brought here?"

Morg nodded again. "He's . . . insane. I cast the past-scrying twice, far enough back to figure out *how* he'd enchanted her. He wasn't just holding hands with her last night. He was *tracing runes* on her skin. It's some form of almost Mendhite magic, but not quite. Possibly something he came up with himself," the youngest of the brothers muttered. "But that wasn't all.

"When she came back to him this morning, after you saw her," he added to Danau, "he expressed his disappointment in his 'creation,' as if she were some *thing* he had made. Then he painted some sort of spell on her skin and carefully coached her to go through a conversation with him, which then took place on the dock."

"On the dock?" Kor asked, confused. "Why the dock?"

"Because that's where the trade ship from Katan was moored," Morg explained. "Like a pre-enchanted spell, she publicly expressed feelings of stress, and the need to get away from the island and all her work, and had a genteel parting with Yarrin. The ship set sail . . . and the moment it was out from the dock and none of the crew were looking her way . . . she stepped over the railing and dropped into the water. And . . . that's when the painted spell took place.

"Apparently it required salt water to trigger it . . . and it severed her body into several pieces. Instantly. A quick death, at least."

Koranen felt sick, staggered by the implications. "If he can do that to Teretha, a fellow mage, he can do it to *anyone*. No one on the Isle is safe!"

"Worse, he's *trapped* here, because he doesn't have a way off the island," Danau pointed out, looking pale herself.

"Exactly. Which is why I *have* to find him—no, Kor, it *has* to be me," Morg stated, cutting off his twin. "The only other person who knows the Locutus spell is Dominor, and *he's* never even seen the man. You have to know your target, and I'm the one who knows him."

"You? You can hardly stand without swaying!" Koranen scoffed, glancing briefly at Danau for support. Inside, he was apprehensive at how tired his twin looked, but he didn't want to show it in front of either of them.

"I have enough power left to channel my brothers' energies. At least to locate the man." Morg hesitated, then admitted quietly, "I don't know if I have enough power left to take him down, though."

"Now I *know* you're exhausted," Kor muttered. Slipping his arm under his brother's, he gave Morg his support. "Come on. Kelly called just a little while ago, long enough that they should be at the concert hall. I'll drive. You'll rest. You need it."

"That much, I know I can do. I left my cart by yours," Morg added, leaning on his twin. "The spell's fresher, and the steering's better. Coming, Danau?"

"Of course," she retorted. "If you're going to need Koranen's strength, then you're going to need mine, too."

Morg eyed the two of them, curiosity bringing some color back to his tired features. He waited until Koranen had helped him up into the back of the wagon, though, before asking, "Is there something about the two of you I should know?"

"Is there something you *don't*?" Kor retorted dryly, finding and releasing the brake lever as soon as Danau had settled herself on the driver's bench next to him. "You know, you could have *told* me you knew she was the woman for me, rather than letting me waste my time in ignorance—and you *lied* to me when you said she wasn't Destined for me."

"I said I couldn't *say*. I made a mistake with Rydan and Rora by forcing them together against their consent. I wasn't about to autocratically decree that the two of you were perfect for each other before you'd come to that conclusion yourselves," Morganen asserted, holding on to the edge of the wagon as his brother backed it up and turned it around, aiming for the road into the city. "Even if you *are*."

"I'm missing something, here," Danau said, twisting to glance between the two men, one auburn and handsome, the other light brown and wan. "How *could* you have known?"

"The dress, for one. Why else would a Seer in a whole other universe bother with buying and sending across a fancy dress?" Morg asked rhetorically. "For another . . . I *am* the Matchmaker in the family."

"That's *his* Destiny, to match-make us all," Koranen told her. "And now that we've acknowledged our match, it's *his* turn to claim his Destined bride."

"Not yet!" Morg protested. "Gods, I'll barely have enough strength to cast the Locutus and lead *you* to our murderer. She'd *better* not ask me to open a Gate to her world!"

"Reluctant to see yourself dragged into the eight altars, Brother?" Kor quipped.

"If I weren't in the presence of a lady, I'd tell you in excruciating anatomical detail what you could do with yourself—and with that, I can tell I'm getting my energy back," Morg added. "Since I can now *think* of such things. I think it was the extraction and cremation that drained me the most—the dealing with the remains, not the rest of it. I think I'm getting a second wind . . ."

Twisting a little farther, Danau studied the young mage. Her brow quirked up skeptically. "I'd believe you . . . if I couldn't see you sweating. You look like a Rank 3 Guildmember trying to convince me he can handle an *udrefong*, a kind of special air bubble we place around our bodies when diving to particularly deep depths. It's something which requires the power of a Rank 5 or higher."

"I'm sweating because it's still very hot out, even if it's almost night," he retorted, flicking his hand at the increasingly deep shadows cast by the buildings around them. The sun still shone brightly from the bay side of the city, but it had sunk close to the horizon. "Today has been very warm, even for summer . . . and I daren't spare any energy to cast a cooling spell on myself."

"It *is* rather warm," Kor agreed, steering the cart onto a new street with a careful turn of the rudder-wheel. "The rest of us don't have your in-built advantage when it comes to summer heat, Danau. I can endure it like I can endure a forge-fire, but that doesn't mean I automatically enjoy a hot summer day."

"Oh, like you'll be sounding so cheerful about my temperature when it's storm season, and I put my icy-cold feet on your calves in the middle of the night," Danau muttered.

"But if you're touching me, they won't be ice-cold for very long—and if you're in bed with me, you'll already be touching me. All night long, so your feet *wouldn't* get cold in the middle of it," Kor pointed out. He glanced backward quickly before returning his attention to the streets of Harbor City, which were thickening with pedestrians and other wagons the closer they came to the concert hall.

It was just long enough to confirm that, yes, his insufferable twin *was* grinning.

THIRTEEN

⋅❋⋅

"Morganen! Thank goodness you're here!"

Darting forward, the green-clad incipient Queen grabbed Morganen by the hand, dragging him away from his twin. Saber was with her, and as soon as he saw she had hold of his youngest brother, he turned and started forging a path for them. Koranen and Danau hurried to follow them, not wanting to get lost or stuck in the crowd gathered in the foyer. The opulently dressed crowd. Compared to his rumpled velvets and her plain blue leathers, both standing out in the mixture of brightly dyed styles, most had opted to wear finespun linens and cottons, though a few daring souls wore silk, their faces flushed with heat.

It *was* hot, despite the visible presence of fluted stone arches, the same sort of smooth, seamless arches that both supported and cooled all of the other buildings around the city. Then again, anyone who was important on Nightfall Isle—or who wanted to *think* of themselves as someone important—had bought tickets to this first performance. The babble of Katani, Natallian, and even a few voices raised in Gucheran made Kor's ears twitch repeatedly, as Ultra Tongue tried to catch up with the constant influx of languages.

It was with a relief visible on all their faces that they managed to make their way up one of the two sets of steps flanking the entrance, across the upper balcony of the foyer, and into a large, private seating area centered on the upper level of the concert hall. Danau recognized Wolfer and Alys, though there was another man present, one with dark brown hair and bright blue eyes, whom she didn't know. Even though the lightglobe sconces spaced around the edges of the balcony cast more light into the center of the room than into the private boxes, she could see how he looked like Wolfer, Saber, and Koranen, so she guessed him to be the missing thirdborn sibling, Dominor.

But there wasn't a chance for introductions. Kelly pulled Morg straight over to one of the other women in the seating booth, barely allowing time for the heavy blue curtain to fall into place behind Danau, affording them an illusion of privacy, though the open air over the balcony and the murmur of hundreds of voices reminded them they were definitely not private at the moment.

The others shifted position, revealing which sister-in-law. *Who* that was shocked both Kor and Danau. It was Amara, tied by magical bonds to one of the padded, carved chairs arranged across the shallow tiers of the viewing box. It was alarming to see her bound like a criminal, but worse . . . she was *smiling*. Politely, pleasantly, congenially, and quite friendly looking, despite her incarceration.

She had dressed in a sleeveless, black variation of a Natallian gown in some sort of supple cotton, slit up the sides to mid thigh to reveal legs encased in pale golden hose, matching the pale golden sash tied around her waist, and the pale golden ribbons threaded through her long black braid. Danau, envious of the woman's immaculate appearance, thought the mayor looked quite lovely in black and gold.

But it was the glittering, mantle-like mass draped over her shoulders and breasts, hanging almost to her waist, that caught and held the Aquamancer's eye. Row after row after row of thumbnail-sized medallions had been linked together like scale armor, each one cast in gold and many of them set with colorful carved gemstones. Each row depicted a tiny animal shape, each one meant to represent one of the animal forms the shapeshifter could assume. Danau had never seen anything so intricate or expensive before. She'd *heard* of the pectoral, since it was a part of the salvage reports, and of course had been there when Amara had described it, but this was her first viewing of the piece.

"What's going on, here?" Morg asked, eyeing the bound yet obviously happy mayor. "Why is Amara tied up?"

"That's what *we* want to know," Saber told him, gesturing at Amara. "She's *not* herself."

"Like Teretha was, only not quite like the baroness," Kelly added. "Teretha was manic. Amara is . . . She's being *nice*."

"What's wrong with being nice?" Amara asked lightly, still smiling. "I like being nice! It feels good. I should do it more often."

Behind her stood her copper-haired husband, who looked like he was struggling with a dilemma. "She's been like this ever since she got dressed for the concert. Completely pleasant and agreeable. Not a single cross word out of her and acting very helpful. It's not a *bad* thing, and *she* isn't bad, even normally . . ."

"But it's *unnatural* for her to be this pleasant for this long," Kelly finished for him. "One of the things I admire about her—in a twisted way—is that she *isn't* afraid to tell me when she thinks I'm being an idiot."

"I'm very glad you admire me, Your Majesty . . . but I apologize most sincerely if I hurt your feelings in the past," Amara added politely. "I shouldn't have done that. And there's nothing wrong with me. I feel perfectly fine!"

Trevan shook his head. "I have to agree. This is wrong. *If* my wife wants to be pleasant, that's one thing—and she *has* been pleasant in the past—but a complete personality change? No. There's something wrong with her. Something that happened while I was taking a rain-shower. I checked her over for potions and spells and didn't find anything, but I *could* have missed something. You're the best mage in the family, Morg. *You* look at her."

"I can't make any promises that I'll find something amiss, either," Morganen warned his fifthborn brother. "Just because I have a little more in the way of power and training doesn't guarantee anything."

"Just do what you can, Morg," Kelly urged him. "First the baroness goes mad, and now Amara. I don't know if these two things are connected, but they do spend a lot of time together—is it possible for a mage to contract a spell like they would a common cold? Some sort of hex-virus?" she asked.

"Baroness Teretha didn't go mad. Nor was she magically ill. She was spell-controlled . . . and . . . and killed by her controller," Morg confessed, keeping his voice low in mindfulness of their semi-exposed location. Even the pleasant-looking Amara managed to look concerned by his words, though she didn't look nearly as shocked as the others. "If I hadn't been so busy with Hope's shipment . . .

"I failed her, and I failed you," he added to Kelly, who had covered her mouth, eyes wide. "I'll see what I can do about Amara, but I *also* have to find Teretha's killer."

"Who killed her? And why?" Saber demanded. The curtain rustled, heralding the arrival of more family members. One of them was Mariel, the other her young son, Mikor. Trevan quickly stepped between the newcomers and his wife, shielding the sight of the glowing spell-shackles holding her wrists to the armrests of her chair.

The adults already in the royal booth fell awkwardly silent, until Alys cleared her throat. "Mikor, I think I saw a shaved-ice merchant down in the foyer, tucked under one of the stairs. But I can't remember which stairs it was. Would you like to come with me, and help me buy and carry some back for all of us to enjoy?"

"Sure! I saw her under the right-hand stairs, near the refreshing room the blue lady used!" the ten-year-old returned enthusiastically.

Checking himself before taking more than a step, Mikor faced his mother. "Mother . . . may I?"

"Yes, you may. And the 'blue lady' is called Ama-ti," Mariel reminded her son. "Actually, I'd like a *toska*-flavored ice, if the vendor has one. If not, then a cherry or a *cinnin*. Anyone else interested?"

The others quickly placed their orders, and within moments, the curly-haired woman and the curly-haired boy had vanished beyond the curtain. Her husband, the large, broad-shouldered Wolfer, followed the two of them out. As the curtain fell, Danau could see the secondborn brother settling into a patient stance just beyond its folds, suggesting that he intended to play curtain guard to ensure they had some privacy.

"Alright, what's going on?" the Healer demanded.

"Aside from a pay raise for Alys, for knowing exactly how to distract your son?" Kelly quipped in a low tone, freckled face pale and pinched. "I don't even know where to begin. My land reclamation advisor is dead, my mayor is unnaturally nice, and the concert is scheduled to begin in just over a quarter of an hour. The last thing I need is to panic the populace with rumors of a murderer running around . . . and yet that's exactly what we have, if Morg is right."

"Unfortunately, it's true," he confirmed, lifting his hand to forestall any questions. "But hold those thoughts while I attend to this one. Trevan—you said Amara changed at some point while she was getting dressed, right?"

"Yes. I didn't realize it until the trip down here, because she *can* be nice," the fifthborn brother added candidly, "and she's been looking forward to this evening. But she was *too* nice. Too agreeable and polite."

"My point is, something happened when she *got dressed*. And given she's currently wearing an object given to her by that woman Zella . . . a woman who admitted she's been chasing after a certain someone all this time . . . then I suspect there *might* be a subtle spell on the pectoral," Morg said. "Nothing overt, and nothing strong. It might even be covered by a layer of ward spells to hide the fact that it's been enchanted; the Amazai mage struck me as strong and clever enough to be able to do so.

"If your wife is being so very agreeable, as you say . . . then it's quite possible that, under the pectoral's influence, she'd be *agreeable* about leading Zella straight to her quarry."

Trevan turned and peered at his wife's back. "I don't see any sort of clasp." Lifting his hand, he hesitated, then flicked it, muttering. The bands holding her wrists to the chair vanished. "Amara, could you please take off your pectoral?"

"No . . . no, I don't want to. Now that I finally have it back, I finally feel like myself again. A Princess of the People," she stated firmly.

"Amara, you only have to take it off for a couple of minutes," Kelly pointed out. "You can put it back on as soon as Morg gets through looking at it."

"No!" Her hands lifted to cover the interlinked medallions. "No, I can't . . . I *won't* take it off."

"What, do you plan on *sleeping* in it?" Trevan retorted skeptically, hands shifting to his cream-clad hips.

"Why not?" Amara asked him.

"It's hexed," Mariel confirmed dryly. "No woman in her right mind would want to sleep in something *that* lumpy."

"It is *not* hexed. It is visible proof of my heritage and is worth a considerable amount of money," Amara asserted, hands still covering what they could of the pectoral. "Any Family, within or without Clan Deer, that could possibly claim even the remotest of kinship ties to me contributed the gold and gemstones to make my pectoral! I will not be parted from it!"

"Hush, you don't have to be," Morganen soothed her as her voice rose. "Actually, I'm curious about how it was made. Were there any spells woven into its construction?"

"Of course not," Amara scoffed. "The few mages that live on the Plains wouldn't waste their energies on something like this. No, it was made by a team of the finest jewelers and goldsmiths living in Shifting City, working with just their tools and their hands."

"Excellent. That's all I needed to know." Stepping around Trevan, Morganen placed his hands on Amara's shoulders. Her own shifted to grasp his wrists, to protect her bejeweled drape, but it was too late. In the low lighting of the royal box, a faint glow could be seen. It lifted and flowed through the linked segments, draining up into the mage's forearms.

Amara's frown shifted to a puzzled look, then a blank, blinking stare . . . and then a quickly deepening scowl. Her fingers clenched the ends of the armrests, but she held her tongue until the last of the glow was gone and Morg had lifted her hands. Only then did she speak, using quiet, clipped tones.

"Tossing her into the bay is too *good* for her! I'm going to grow to my biggest size, and *squish* her under my feet! I'll *rend* her with claws as long as her arms! And *then* I'll get *mad* at her . . ."

Grinning, Trevan bent and dropped a kiss on her head. "*That's* my normal, natural, virago-minded wife."

"Set aside your personal aggravations, Amara," Kelly ordered her sister-in-law. "We have bigger fish to fry."

Amara narrowed her amber gold eyes. "What do you mean?"

Standing off to the side by Koranen, forgotten by the others in this turn of events, Danau was once again reminded of the back-and-forth of a *panka* game. The sensation mingled with her increasing hunger, melding into an urge for something tasty and snackish. *Speaking of bigger fish . . . what I wouldn't give for a basket of fried squid strips right about now . . .*

"I *mean*, Zella is no doubt planning on coming back here, encountering you, ensuring that you wear the pectoral in her presence . . . and ordering you to sweetly and nicely agree to hand her that certain someone she's been looking for, neatly wrapped up in gift-wrap paper and a satin bow," Kelly said.

"Well, at least you realized I was being *too* agreeable," the mayor muttered. "That's all I *could* do, locked in that thing."

"You'll want to keep wearing that pectoral, too," Morg told Amara. "I dismantled the compulsion part of the spell, but there's a subtle tracking cantrip still embedded in it. I suspect it's to let Zella know when you've put it on, so she'll know you're under her control."

"As far as I'm concerned, manipulating someone magically into doing something against her free will is a crime . . . but we cannot *pin* that crime on Zella until she *does* come back and attempts to take advantage of your spell-enforced congeniality," Kelly told Amara. "For that matter, we don't know for certain if Zella *was* the one who enchanted your pectoral to make you unnaturally agreeable," the freckled redhead said, giving Morg and Amara both a firm look. "It *could* have been someone else. Innocent until proven guilty, and all that."

"Who else could it have been?" Amara challenged, looking and sounding very much like herself as she arched one of her black brows skeptically.

"The other Aian mage, for one," Kor offered. "The blond man from Morna, Yarrin. Morg says that's who he saw in a past-scrying, backtracking what happened to the baroness. Yarrin killed her."

"Is this true?" Kelly asked, turning to the youngest of the brothers.

Behind her, Danau felt her stomach grumble, though the noise of the Nightfallers gathering in the concert hall around them drowned out most of the actual sound. The verbal *panka* game of the others was still going strong, but so was her hunger. *Once we get this matter taken care of, I think I'm going to go find something to eat, even if I have to personally catch, slice, and fry a squid!*

"I saw Yarrin deliberately enchanting Teretha with a delayed severing spell and then instructing her under his mental control to fulfill the conditions that caused the spell to activate, murdering her secondhand," Morg told his sister-in-law. "I'll swear it on a Truth Stone if you need me to."

Kelly waved off that idea with a flip of her hand. "I'll believe you. You've never lied to me when it was something important, and only stretched the truth a few times over littler things."

That made Morg flush and clear his throat. "Yes, well . . . now that we have the puzzle of Amara solved for the time being, I need a power-boost to cast the Locutus spell," he told the others. "I exhausted myself by attending to a personal project this morning, and again with a complex temporal scrying just now, reviewing the immediate past for Teretha's killer. I know for a fact I talked to the man *after* today's scheduled boat left, so he's bound to still be on the island, but I have no idea where."

"If you're that tired, I can cast it," Dominor offered. "I have an entire Fountain at my disposal."

"Yes, but you haven't *met* the man," Morg reminded him. "That makes it vastly harder to focus the spell."

"I don't need to have met Yarrin, Brother," Dom countered. "All I have to do is assert a quest to find a murderer. We're a brand-new nation; there can't be *that* many murderers hiding on the whole of the Isle—and if there are, better we find out now, while we have the manpower to throw them off the island. And, as the Guardian of Nightfall, I can blanket the *whole* island, not just this city."

"—I'm not normally one to interrupt a war council," Saber interjected, sweeping his hand at the space beyond the balcony railing behind him, "but I can hear the musicians tuning their instruments out there. The concert is about to begin, and people are looking up at this booth, wanting to know what we're doing."

"And *I* need to get back down below to join my husband," Mariel agreed. "Not to mention, my son and our sister Alys are going to come back at any moment."

"Alright—Dom, you cast the spell, but in tandem with me," Morganen compromised. "That way we'll have the boost of your Guardianship and my personal knowledge of the man. And then . . . Koranen, Danau, and I can go looking for him. That should be enough to bring him to justice, or at least bring him down. You can't go, Dominor, or you'll miss the concert; you can only afford this one night away from your wife. The rest of you . . . well, you'll need to fill the box, so people aren't too curious."

"That includes *you*," Trevan stated as his wife started to rise. "People would notice if their Mayor was missing."

"But, just the three of them, to capture a murderous criminal?" she asked, one hand absently touching the carved stones on her pectoral.

"If you'll remember, we both watched through the looking glass as Danau destroyed that other mage, Xenos, back when he was trying to take over both the Menomon and Nightfall Fountains," Kelly told her. "Two spells, and he was dead. I'm quite sure she'd be willing to lend her combat expertise to Nightfall as a diplomatic favor . . . since if Yarrin killed here, he could have killed there, too."

"Oh . . . right. I forgot about that," Amara muttered, flushing. "Sorry."

"Between her, Kor, and Morg, the three of them should be able to stop this Yarrin fellow cold—pun fully intended," Kelly added, giving Danau and her cozy proximity to Kor a wry smile before looking at her brothers-in-law. "Go on, cast your spells, and get going. I do *not* want any murderers on my island, so while I'd prefer to have him brought back alive for questioning and trial . . . feel free to make an unpleasant example of him, should he resist arrest, or attempt to compound his crimes in some other way."

"I'll go tell Evanor we're almost ready," Mariel offered, and slipped her plump frame past the deep blue curtains hanging at the back of the royal box. The sound of a quick greeting from the Healer was followed a few moments later by Alys and Mikor entering the booth, each of them doing their best to balance several orders of shaved ices in their baked wafer-pastry cups. Ama-ti was with them, carrying a couple of the cups herself, which the blue-haired woman helped distribute.

Dominor rose from his chair, tipping his head at the back of the booth; Morganen moved to join him, pausing only long enough to accept a greenish-tinted ice from Mikor, giving him a smile and a nod. Danau accepted the purplish red ice the young boy handed her. Normally she avoided cold foods, but all she had to do was sidle up next to Koranen so that their elbows bumped. That was all it took to increase her awareness of the summer heat infusing the concert hall, and increase her appreciation of the frozen treat.

The flavored ball of ice wasn't large, barely the size of an egg, but it was drenched thoroughly with a thick, fruity sauce. She suspected the person who made the shaved ice most likely was a minor mage, maybe a Rank 1 or 2, given how difficult it would be for a non-mage to maintain a supply of ice in the middle of summer. A minor mage, but a talented baker all the same; the "cup" it came in was hard-baked and stiff, designed to withstand a certain amount of melting, yet still be edible.

She could also see why the serving of ice was so small: Any larger in heat like this, and the melting water and lingering sauce would definitely turn the pastry cup soggy. It had to be devoured within a mere dozen bites to avoid that.

On the one hand, the serving size is perfect to cool the tongue and throat, and take the edge off a person's normal hunger. On the other hand . . . my hunger isn't normal; I'm starving. I could eat two or three of these, easily . . . especially with such a lovely, spicy-sweet sauce! I wonder if I could work up an equitable trade, of say, packets of purple dye from sea spine shellfish in exchange for crates of this toska *fruit stuff . . .*

Magic pulsed against her skin, washing over her from the direction of the huddled figures of Morganen, Dominor, Trevan, and Koranen. Danau blinked, then frowned. If *she* could feel it, odds were that the Mornai mage, Yarrin, could feel it also. *Then again, I* know *what they're trying to do. Otherwise . . . well, I suppose it just feels like a random spell going off.*

Chimes rang, startling everyone. Hastily devouring the last bite of her pastry cup, Danau blinked and stared at the lightglobes affixed to the support columns ringing the hall. They were dimming at regular, pulsed intervals. Moving closer, she made out the mechanism, a clever, enchanted, felt-padded hammer, which struck the surface of its globe with increasing gentleness every few heartbeats. All of the lightglobes had them, though the two at the back of the royal booth didn't move, just the ones illuminating the main chamber. Around them, the citizens of Nightfall hushed themselves and hurried to reach and settle into their seats.

If things had gone differently today . . . she would be clad in that beautiful blue green gown, sitting at Koranen's side, and ready to enjoy an evening of the local music. *And also still under the impression that a velvet dress is all I could ever have*, she acknowledged, slipping between the seats to reach the curtain. *I may have lost a dress, but I've gained a far greater prize.*

A last glance behind her showed cleverly focused lights springing to life, pre-aimed at the stage where the performers were to appear. Then Kor caught her hand in his. She almost flinched away out of habit before reminding herself it was okay to entwine her fingers with his. Letting him pull her out of the booth, she ignored the rising sound of applause as the first entertainer of the evening undoubtedly came into view.

The balcony and the foyer were both nearly empty. A few figures clad in uniforms—blue trimmed with yellow—were still moving about, tidying up crumbs from the shaved-ice merchant, checking ticket slips and directing people to the curtained doorways that would lead to their seats. Koranen waited until they had stepped outside and were heading for something Kelly had called a "parking lot," a square specifically designed for the parking of wagons and built with amenities for the watering, sheltering, and feeding of horses and other draft animals pulling the nonmagical vehicles on the island.

"So . . . where are we going?" he asked.

"The Green Block Inn." Once again, Morganen looked pale and exhausted, though not shaken this time. His body looked tired, but his voice was firm. "Third floor, room thirty-eight."

"That's the one right next to the Desalinator," Kor said, frowning. "We usually host the salt and algae block buyers there—we were *that* close to him?"

"More to the point, it's *not* the inn he was staying at earlier,"

Morg returned. "Something made him move. Something I do not like."

"What?" Danau asked defensively when Morg looked down at her.

"He has new prey. However he convinced them to go with him, they are now in his new room with him . . . and when Dominor and I Saw them through the Locutus spell, he had just finished gagging and binding them."

It didn't take a genius to put everything together. "You mean, he has Reuen and Chana."

"Yes."

Danau eyed him. "You know, you *did* promise all those months ago that it 'wouldn't be dangerous' to us if we came here. This doesn't exactly strike me as danger free."

"Sorry. But in my defense, *you* brought him here," Morganen said.

"No arguing, you two," Koranen ordered them.

Morganen went back to the topic at hand. "Regardless of good intentions . . . my guess is, he rushed with Teretha, wasn't careful or thorough enough. And that if he has two agents, one might slip by unnoticed while the other is making a scene." They reached the wagon, Morg grunting as he pulled himself up into the back. "The problem with mind-control spells is that they're really not *mind*-controlling spells. They're body-controlling spells. The person inside can still think for themselves—certain medicines can take away thought, but even they aren't permanent.

"Even if the subject isn't strong enough to break the compulsions with brute force of will, they can do other things, exaggerate other behaviors, to warn their friends and family that Something Is Wrong. The spell on Amara's pectoral was a refined version of what I saw of Teretha's behavior in the past-scrying I did, but then, Zella had a lot more time to cast her spells on the necklace than Yarrin had with the baroness," Morg said.

"Months of time, while she was biding her time in a closed city," Danau agreed dryly. "No wonder Yarrin longed to go elsewhere."

"Come again?" Morg asked.

"He was trapped in Menomon, the same as the others," she reminded him. "Until the Council realized there were no other city traitors lurking and suffered the error of its ways through the loss of the freshwater the Fountain had been bringing in until it was closed off, no one was allowed to leave. If he's smart enough to figure out how to control the actions of others, he's smart enough to know that he might get caught and need an escape route. But there was no way to escape in Menomon. At least, no way to escape and get himself to land quickly and safely."

"Even if he's on an island with a limited number of ships coming and going each day, his quarry is *here*," Koranen pointed out. "He's after a certain someone. It could be for the same reasons as Zella, or it could be for reasons of his own, but he wants to get her under his control."

"Well, we'll just have to stop him, won't we?" Danau replied as lightly as she could.

"I don't know how much help I'll be."

Kor glanced back at his twin, before jerking his attention back to the wagon and the Nightfallers still using the city streets. Morg had slouched on his bench seat, pinching the bridge of his nose. Despite the golden glow of the low-hanging sun, he looked very pale, almost gray under the eyes and at the corners of his mouth. Alarmed, Koranen stopped the wagon in front of a cobbler's shop. "Morg—"

"—I'll be fine! Or at least, I'll live." Managing a wry smile, he added, "I also have a sudden craving for a lot of fruit and raw vegetables."

"We'll get you some," Danau promised him. Mages were the same everywhere, and she had seen a few of her own fellow Menomonites falling ill from magical exhaustion. To be physically healthy, a person had to eat a reasonably balanced diet of meat, fish, fruit, vegetables, and grains; to be magically healthy, a mage needed to eat more fruits and vegetables than meat or grain. The more raw the food was, the more energy it imparted, replenishing a mage's reserves, though most vegetables tasted better cooked.

"Do it after we've caught him," Morg instructed. "I don't know what system of spells and runes he's using, so the sooner we can stop him, the less we'll have to figure out when it comes to undoing his efforts on the ladies."

"We'll do it now. It's not that big of a detour to swing by the north market square," Kor decided. "Besides, you can eat while we go inside, and you can monitor my cryslet; I'll activate it before we confront him. If anything goes wrong, you'll still have the strength to call for the others and be free of any spells he might try to cast on *us*."

Nodding, Morg flicked his hand out from his brow, indicating his twin should drive.

In the middle of climbing the stairs at the Green Block Inn, Danau slapped her forehead. Koranen glanced at her. "What?"

"I forgot to bring a weapon. When I usually do these things—boarding pirate ships, and that incident with Xenos—we usually bring along a few crossbows. Most mages either expect a physical attack or a magical attack, but not both. If he's warded himself against my fellow Aquamancers, he might not have thought about physical shields."

"And pain distracts a mage—yes, I know. Don't worry; I have a dagger I can summon and throw—Saber makes summonable blades, swords, daggers, that sort of thing. We all got them as birthing-day presents at one point or another," he added. "Even Kelly has a dagger, though not a sword; she refused one, since she's not comfortable with sword work. The same with Alys, though Serina and the others haven't made up their minds about what they'd like. Once they do, they'll get one."

"Even Mikor?" Danau asked.

Kor grinned ruefully. "His mother has said he can have a knife when he turns twelve, and a sword at sixteen. *If* he proves himself responsible enough to handle them safely. He's not had enough training yet to wield even a pot-metal blade, though he does show some promise."

"Well, you'd better get your own knife ready. I managed to get through the basic Wavescout combat training, as all Aquamancers are required to do, but that was more than a decade ago, and it didn't include throwing lessons. You don't throw a weapon at a shark," she told him, before gesturing at the hallway beyond the stairwell. "I'll check the door for wardings. I had plenty of practice breaking into the Fountain Hall, thanks to Xenos."

"Be my guest," Kor agreed. "The ones who saw you in action against Xenos said you were pretty impressive with your offensive spells. If you like, I'll do the physical attacking and the shielding, since I'm used to practicing spell-combat with my brothers."

"Both of us should be ready to attack, though he should be taken alive if possible," Danau countered. "The baroness said she moved here with a number of her old retainers; they'll want to see him answer for his crimes in person, for closure."

Nodding, Koranen fell silent. They walked down the hall together, stopping when they reached the eighth door. Spreading her hands, Danau ghosted them several inches from the surface, gradually moving them closer. She swept the edges of the doorframe three times, then focused the last of her attention on the lever-like doorknob, and in particular its lock. Stepping back, she nodded.

"He has a very stout sound-warding spell put up, something to prevent noise coming in or out, but only noise." She spoke quietly, but didn't bother to whisper the words. "Other than that, there's a sealing spell on the lock. It's strong enough to foil most unlocking charms and completely shut out physical things, like lockpicks and even keys. It's going to take a bit to break the spell, and he will notice us doing it."

Touching her shoulder, Kor stopped her the moment she started to reach for the door. He flashed her a smile at her bemused look. "One of the ironworkers I studied with as a youth also crafted locks on the side. He taught me most of what he knew, including the secret of unlocking enchantment-sealed locks."

"So what's the secret?" Danau asked, curious.

"Don't bother with the lock." Squatting, Koranen extended his hand to the side of the doorframe opposite the lock. Then stopped, rolled his eyes, and muttered, "Firefang!"

A slightly S-curved, double-edged dagger snapped into his left hand, appearing out of nowhere. Reaching out again with his right hand, he concentrated his power. Within moments, he rose from his crouch to a stoop, hand at hip level, then straightened, palm shifting slightly higher than his head.

Danau sniffed, wrinkling her nose. She thought she could smell burning wood. In the next moment, she jumped in startlement, for Koranen snapped up his foot and kicked the door hard on the hinge side without warning. Something snapped, sparks flew from the latch side, and the door spun wide before toppling at an awkward, soundless angle off to the right. The scent of heated metal and charred wood filled the air, and the sight of a startled blond man and two wide-eyed, bound, short-haired women in chairs filled the doorway.

Sound, however, didn't exist. Koranen only had the movement of Yarrin's lips to warn him. Throwing up his right arm in a shieldward, he blocked the incoming spell and snapped his left arm forward. The dagger spun through the air—and bounced off to the side with a flare of magic. Kor cursed under his breath; the man *had* warded himself against a physical attack.

Worried the Mornai man might attempt to ward the doorway against more than sound, Danau slipped inside, already forming the words of a caging spell. "*Papaitha sussoda!*"

With a twist of her hand, Yarrin's arms and hands snapped up and together, fingers and palms pressed flat and helpless as they pointed at her. A snarled word from the blond mage, however, and the spell flung itself off of him, splitting apart and hitting his captives, one seated on the bed, the other on a chair, ankles and wrists already bound together by glowing ropes. Silk gags had been knotted and stuffed into their mouths, then tied tight enough to crease their cheeks, blocking their ability to form coherent speech. But at least she could hear again, for she heard Chana grunt, brown eyes wide with fear.

Danau watched out of the corner of her eye as Reuen's hands paled, then reddened from the pressure of two binding spells, and knew she had to tread more carefully. The rich brown of Chana's hands made it difficult to see what effect the averted spell had on her flesh, but her eyes did widen and blink, accompanied by a grunt of pain.

"Don't bother trying to contain me," Yarrin dismissed, mouth curling up on one side in unpleasant humor. "You'll only tighten the bonds on your two friends. And don't bother trying to kill me, either. Those spells will also drain off to *them* instead. You know what I want—or rather, *who*. The girl, the one who was with your mayor. I know she is here.

"Give me *her*, and you can have these—a two-for-one bargain," he added, smiling slightly. It was easy to see why he could charm a woman well enough to get close for contact; with those green eyes, that long nose, and the dimple that appeared on one side of his lips, he was quite handsome. "Any merchant would tell you that's a fair price. Any moralist, for that matter."

"*Stall!*"

Koranen almost missed the word; it wasn't loudly spoken . . . but it was in his twin's voice, and it did come from the slightly open lid of the cryslet on his wrist.

Hearing it as well, though she didn't know what the third member of their rescue party meant, Danau shifted her hands to her hips. Yarrin tensed, but the gesture wasn't magical, and wasn't threatening. Her words, however, made him frown in confusion. They also made his two prisoners tense and stare.

"What makes you think I care whether these two *ladies* live or die?"

"You *don't* care?"

"No." Pacing her words with slow and clear diction, Danau stalled for time. "Don't get me wrong. Reuen *is* my cousin, and both are my colleagues and fellow Guildmembers . . . but both of them have been more like a couple of lampreys in my life, sucking the blood out of me and holding me back."

Chana's wide brown eyes satisfied something unpleasant inside of Danau. *She* was scared of what her fellow Aquamancer was saying. Reuen scowled. Danau continued, speaking from her heart. Just not from all of it.

"Neither of them has done anything to endear themselves to me, aside from maybe being competent as Aquamancers. But—as they have reminded me so many, many times in the past—how *good* one is at one's work doesn't *begin* to compensate for one's social failings.

"Like being backstabbing, lying, dress-destroying, gossipmongering, reputation-shredding, two-faced, shark-toothed, slimy *sea witches*." Flicking a pointed gaze at her cousin, Danau looked back at the mage holding her kinswoman captive and added, "Menos be my witness . . . the way I feel about both of them right now, I would *not* cry at their funerals. I have no reason to, and *several* to stay dry-eyed."

Yarrin studied her with a shrewd look, then chuckled softly. "I do believe you mean every word."

"I do."

"Then their lives mean little to you. But you aren't beholden in any way to the other girl . . . and the Gods *do* frown on the betrayal of one's own kin. Better to sacrifice the life of a stranger than one with whom you share blood ties. And it's not as if I *want* to kill anyone," the blond mage added smoothly. "I much prefer my pretties to stay alive and be healthy and happy in my care. Only *you* could make them die."

"Oh, I have not yet betrayed my kinswoman," Danau pointed out, picking the first part of his argument apart. "*She* did that, and has done that for eight whole years of public scorn and mockery. Chana . . . I don't care about one way or another, other than that she is an annoyance as well as a competent worker."

"Then this isn't much of an impasse. If you truly don't *care* whether or not they die—" Yarrin stiffened, staring past her shoulder.

Danau didn't turn. She did, however, hear a faint but distinct sound of a dish breaking in the distance and the rattle of wagon wheels outside. She also saw a hand stretching past her shoulder, pale and trembling, and *felt* the magic in the room swirling into the newcomer.

How Morganen of Nightfall was absorbing the other man's spells, she didn't know, but she didn't *need* to know. It was enough that he was destroying Yarrin's wards. Thrusting out her hand, Danau yanked it back in again in a snatching motion. "*Freliliko!*"

Bracing herself for an influx of body heat from her foe, she gasped and staggered, suddenly colder—a *lot* colder—than she could remember. The air rippled between them, shimmering with heat . . . but not from him to her. Instead, it flowed the other way, from her to him. Clamping down on her magic slowed the outward flow, but didn't stop it.

Yarrin grinned. "Don't counterattack, gentlemen, or *she* dies— did you think I would forget all the rumors spread across the city about how you killed that fool Xenos, with your little heat-theft spell? Did you think I wouldn't come up with a counter to it?"

"Danau!" Koranen lifted his hand, racking his brain for a spell to break whatever was happening. "You will release her—"

"—Ah, ah!" the Mornai mage warned him. "She might not care about *them*, but you might care about *her*. I can slow this spell, or I can stop it . . . *or* I can speed it up, if you attack."

Stall for time, Koranen thought, warily lowering his arm. "What do you want?"

"All my life I've dreamed of controlling power greater than mine, power too great to be used up and discarded. Power like hers will not frustrate me into breaking her . . . and her power *will* be mine."

"Bl-blood-mage!" Danau scorned.

"No—I never take their life force, no," Yarrin corrected her. "I'm not stupid; that way lies madness and the curse of the Nether-hells whispering in your head. No, I am *very* clever. With my toys still alive, I'm not stealing their powers. I'm not *ripping* them from their origins. I'm just controlling them."

"What do you want?" Koranen repeated. "You want Danau's powers?"

"Her?" the blond mage snorted. "Hardly. But I'll give you half an hour to bring the mayor's sister here, or the little icicle woman dies."

Shuddering with cold, Danau strained to keep her magic from betraying her body. It was no good; whatever counterspell he had used, it was literally sucking the warmth and the power from her bones. There was just one thing: The light shining in through the west-facing window had turned everything golden orange, but she didn't miss the reddening of his face, or the sweat beginning to bead on his brow.

This was the *opposite* of her spell. A flash of insight made her grope for Koranen's wrist. She managed to catch his bare elbow, and with it, embraced the warmth of his power, easing some of her trembling. "Y-Y-You w-wan-t-t *m-m-my* hea-at-t? *T-T-Take-ke* it!"

Instinct alone made Koranen open himself to her, despite his worry and fear. It was the right decision, for without his resistance, his fire poured out of him and channeled itself through her, searing straight through the spell connecting her to Yarrin.

The result was immediate, though not quite as spectacular as the literal shattering of Xenos months ago. Squinting through the sudden, violent blurring of the air between them, Danau watched Yarrin's green eyes widen and brighten with a yellowish glow. His face reddened to an alarming degree, then his mouth parted on a cough, belching a puff of smoke. In the next moment, the spell tying them together broke. His knees buckled, and his body collapsed; chest bouncing off Chana's shoulder, Yarrin Del Ya of the distant land of Morna slumped into the space between bed and chair. Dead.

The smell of roasted meat joined the lingering wisps of overheated wood, churning Danau's stomach. From the grimace on Koranen's face, he was suffering from the stench, too. Twisting to look behind her, she found Morganen leaning against the doorframe, his forehead braced on his arm, though he looked gray enough to be more ill from magic depletion than from the fact she had just used his twin's power to literally cook their foe.

"Mmfffau!"

Dragging her attention back to her cousin, Danau steeled her nerves and moved up to the bed, ignoring the body on the floor and the smell in the air. The glow was fading from the ropes, but they were still holding Reuen's wrists and ankles tightly together. Before she reached for her cousin's bonds, however, she again planted her hands on her hips. "I want to make something perfectly clear. If you *had* died just now, I would not have cried at your funeral.

"I did not save you because you are my cousin. I did not save you because you are a fellow Guildmember, or even a fellow Menomonite. I didn't even save you because you are 'a good person' . . . because we both know you are not, for all that you pretend to be superior to me.

"I saved you because it was the *right* thing to do. Just as it is the *right* thing not to trash someone else's reputation for something they were *born* to be . . . and just as it is the *right* thing not to damage someone else's property. I think that's why you hate me so much," Danau added, finally shifting to start unpicking the knots on the other woman's limbs. "Because I *do* the right thing. You may say that you're a better woman than me, but you hate me because you *know* it isn't true. You'll never admit it . . . but it *is* true.

"Worse, I don't think you'll ever have what it takes to appreciate my saving your life. You'll just resent me all the more."

Behind her, Koranen snapped his cryslet shut to close its link to his twin's, then opened it again. Tapping a new set of numbers on the base, he called Kelly's cryslet. The first person to reassure that the threat was now over was their Queen. Kor knew Kelly wouldn't be able to truly enjoy the concert they were missing until she knew everything had turned out alright.

He got the message-taking spell, and remembered Kelly making some sort of fuss when the idea of a concert was first broached, something about ensuring that everyone with cryslets turned them off in the concert hall, so as not to spoil the performance with an unexpected ringing. Staring into the pulsing shades of blue, he kept his message simple.

"We found Reuen and Chana bound and gagged in Yarrin's possession. He attacked us with the intent to kill Danau, and was killed in her counterattack. We'll free the Aquamancers and secure the body for burial. Call Morg after the performance, and he'll tell you all about it."

"Ugh . . . if I'm not busy being sick, that is," Morg muttered from the doorway.

Ending the call, Koranen held out his left hand. "Firefang." Dagger snapping instantly into his hand, he approached Chana and crouched, sawing through her ankle bonds. "I'm not sure if I should free either of you. *One* of you destroyed a certain dress, after all. A precious, rare, expensive, velvet dress. My *wife's* dress."

"*Wfff?*" Chana repeated, lips still creased with the knotted gag Yarrin had bound around her head. "Whn fid fee mehomm yurr *wfff?*"

Straightening once Chana's legs were free, Koranen looked into the Aquamancer's eyes. "A thousand years ago, when the Seer Draganna spoke her Prophecy, compelled by the Gods Themselves to declare that Water would control the Flame. Which Danau has done just now, marking her as my Destined bride. Be advised that you *will* be questioned by Truth Stone, and that I will recommend to Her Majesty that, whichever one—or both—of you destroyed Danau's dress, be fined double the cost of that dress. At the *Menomonite* value."

Chana flinched, and Reuen paled. Koranen finished cutting the dark-skinned, blond-haired woman free, then moved over to the bed to help Danau release her cousin's bonds. The smell of the corpse on the floor churned his stomach further.

Danau stepped aside, letting him work on the knots that had eluded her fingernails. "I think, after this ... and much, much later ... the only thing I could stomach for my supper would be raw fruits and vegetables, too."

"Agreed. How did you know you could draw upon my primal fire like that?" Kor asked, curious.

"You drew upon my own affinity for water, when you opened the control room door. The door was attuned specifically to the touch of a powerful Aquamancer, yet it opened when only your hand touched it ... so long as you also touched me. That meant you were accessing my power as if it were your own," she explained, trying not to breathe too deeply this close to the body. "I didn't think of it that way consciously, but I did know that the idiot had opened up a channel into *himself*, the exact mirror of my own heat-theft spell.

"I'm built to withstand a lot of heat as well as need it, but it's rare that I *get* enough heat to feel warm. The moment I saw his face flushing from the heat, I knew it was affecting him, so I poured as much pure thermal energy into him as I could. Unlike me, he couldn't contain it—I think I need to open the window," she added, fighting back the urge to gag. "The smell is getting ... rather ..."

"*Aeromundic!*" The word was accompanied by a groan, but the spell used by the mage by the door did clear the air. "One of these days," Morg muttered, barely loud enough for the others to hear, "just *one* of these days ... I'd love to have a confrontation that *doesn't* end in a death."

"Is something wrong?" a female voice asked. Morganen quickly rolled away from the doorframe, blocking the opening with his body so that the maidservant couldn't see inside. She still tried to peer past him. "What's wrong with the door?"

"Official government business," the youngest of the brothers managed to say. "We have stopped a crime from happening and will send someone to repair the door in the next day or so. In the meantime . . . go about your business. All the excitement is over. Go on."

Knowing the woman would undoubtedly rush down to the kitchen and tell the rest of the inn's staff about the excitement upstairs, Koranen handed Danau his dagger and gritted his teeth. There was no way they'd be able to get Yarrin's body outside without a dozen gawkers and a thousand rumors, so the only recourse was to turn it into a mass of far less conspicuous ash.

Reminding himself that once a spirit had departed for the Afterlife, a body was nothing more than an empty shell—and trying very hard not to think of it by any other, less innocuous word than that—Koranen wrapped the body in a containment ward and began the incineration spell.

FOURTEEN

❦

"You'll probably catch a cold," Mariel pronounced, taking her palm away from Morganen's forehead. Traces of magic tingled in the wake of her fingers. "But other than having your natural reserves deeply depleted, you didn't do any real damage to yourself.

"So my recommendation is for you to get plenty of rest and wash your hands frequently over the next few days. Particularly after touching other people, or handling shared-use objects, such as doorknobs and juice pitchers, thoroughly after you've used the refreshing room, before you eat anything, and before you touch your mouth, nose, or eyes."

Quite willing to heed her advice, given how badly he felt, Morganen nodded. He relaxed into his pillows as she gave him a friendly, motherly pat on his shoulder and left the side of his bed. The bedding was light, the air temperature comfortably cool—Danau had assisted with that, at his twin's prodding—and his family was safe and sound for the night. Sleep and fresh food were the two best cures for an exhausted mage.

Naturally, his mirror chimed.

Wincing, Morg thought about ignoring it, but forced himself to summon enough physical energy to throw back the sheets and rise. *I swear, the Gods are like Hope and her friends, watching our lives unfold in one of those illusion-box plays she likes to watch. No doubt They even eat bowls of that fluffy stuff,* popcorn, *too . . .*

Whoever it was, they'd have to take him shirtless and clad only in undertrousers. Clean ones, but an undergarment nonetheless. Tapping the frame of the mirror, Morganen blinked and frowned, recognizing the face of the man his image melded into. "Lord Consus?"

The middle-aged mage looked no balder or grayer than before, though his age-streaked light brown hair was tangled, and there were shadows visible under his eyes. Stranger still, he was half muttering, half babbling. At least what looked like his office door was closed, maybe even spell-locked, since the first words out of his mouth weren't reassuring ones.

"Treason. I'm being forced to commit treason! Defy my Gods, or defy my king—what kind of a sick world is this, when we're forced to make that kind of a choice? I am a *loyal* subject of Katan, you know! And yet the Gods Themselves demand that I tell you! Or at least, the Laws of God and Man do so . . .

"I hope you *appreciate* what I am about to do for you," the Councilor for Sea Commerce added darkly.

Morg blinked. "Do . . . what? Are you feeling alright, milord?"

"No, I am not. I have a knot in my stomach the size of a ship's rigging and a conscience that's an even more unpleasantly vocal nag than your soon-to-be queen," Consus snapped.

Conceding the other man's point with a tip of his head, Morg merely said, "What can I do for you?"

"You can listen. And so you know that I speak the truth in this matter . . ." Lifting a silver-wrapped rod tipped with a crystal, the Katani muttered a word, then raised his hand and held the rod in his fingers so that the now-glowing point dangled over his palm.

"My name is Kelly, and I am the Queen of Nightfall." The glow winked out. After a moment, it came back. "I am Consus of Kairides, a government official of Katan."

The glow remained steady. Without preamble, the Councilor delivered the unwavering truth.

"I have learned—through a means I refuse to divulge—that a group of Mendhite warriors is being sent in disguise to infiltrate Nightfall Island with the expressed intent of kidnapping some female they call a 'living host,' to kill anyone that tries to get in their way, including any Guardian protecting said female . . . and to assassinate your impending queen if at all possible. They have a fleet of ships strung out at intervals all the way from the shores of Mendhi, ships which are carrying multiple mirrors," he continued as Morg stared in shock. "They are prepared to mirror-Gate their captive all the way back to the capital of Mendhi as soon as she is in their hands.

"Now, I was *forbidden* by my King from actively helping you Nightfallers. By the right of your Ringing the Bell, I could impose no sanctions against you, and had to lift those already imposed. I *was* ordered to increase tariffs, and was free to do so, which I have dutifully done," Consus stated stiffly. "But to *tell* you that enemies are headed for your shores is *helping* you actively. It would therefore be against a direct order of King Taurin, my liege, to tell you all of this.

"Yet to *not* tell you, I would be aiding and condoning the actions of these impending would-be murderers, which is against the Laws of God and Man. I have therefore committed treason to help you . . . because my conscience is a pookrah-sized bitch who has bitten me by the undershorts and will *not* let go until I do," the Councilor finished grimly, the wand still brightly lit. "Which I have done. Hopefully, the Gods will now give me some peace over the matter, as I have had none for the past few hours."

"You, ah . . . have my sympathies for the agony of your decision," Morganen managed to say, scrambling to gather his exhausted wits. "That you chose to side with your conscience proves you to be a better man than His Majesty . . . and I will make sure Her Majesty knows and is suitably appreciative."

"I'd rather hold the fact that I have potentially saved her life in *discreet* reserve, if you please," Consus muttered, swiping his free hand through his hair. "Any overt change in the way your people react to the Empire, and *my* Department in particular, will cause too much curiosity. Besides, I *have* been a bureaucrat for almost as many years as you've been alive. It's wiser to hold such a huge favor in reserve for when it's *really* needed.

"For your sake . . . I hope it's not. I never wanted anything to do with you, if you'll recall."

"Considering you're the one who said Katan wants nothing to do with us . . . yes, I do recall," Morganen replied, amused.

"Keep *that* to yourself, as well," Consus ordered him. "My life has become too complicated as it is, and I'd appreciate it if things were allowed to settle down." He paused, then grimaced and rumpled his hair again. "One more thing . . . the bit about the assassination of your impending sovereign . . . it *isn't* a Mendhite order. It was requested by someone here in the Empire—do not ask me who; I have too many enemies lurking in the shadows just from what I have already told you."

"Your discretion is understandable," Morg allowed. "I'll warn my side of things about the impending attack and tell only Her Majesty herself that you were the one who gave the warning. The favor you have done Nightfall is far greater than you may know—if you ever need me, call on me. Just . . . not in the next few days. I'm a little tired, right now."

"You look like you were dragged backward through a Netherhell. Is there anything the Empire should know about?" Consus asked.

"Nothing that will affect the Empire; I just cast far too much magic in a single day. You don't look too good, either," Morg offered.

"You try realizing you have to betray your oaths to your Queen, and see how you'd feel."

"Point taken. If you'll excuse me, I have a report to make to that queen," Morganen said.

"And I have reports for my Department to file. I've been away from my work far too long." Nodding, the Councilor for Sea Commerce reached up and touched the edge of his mirror. His image winked out, replaced by Morganen's reflection.

Ugh. I do look like hell, Morg thought, staring at his pale face. Like Consus, he had shadows under his eyes. He lifted a hand to his light brown hair. *At least I'm not graying and going bald. Yet. If I do . . . well, I hope Hope doesn't mind. Hair-restoration potions are only temporary, and long-term usage isn't healthy . . .*

Returning to his bed to fetch his cryslet, Morganen realized he was too tired to dress and confront the people who needed most to hear Lord Consus' message. Drawing the covers over his legs, he activated the communications bracelet. First, he would call Kelly to his bedchamber. Saber would no doubt come with her, but that was alright; he'd just whisper whom the message was from into his sister-in-law's ear.

Then he'd have to call Rydan and Rora to his chambers, too . . . because this was the most compelling reason of all for Rydan to permit his wife's Fountain to be extracted, even if it meant having to kill and then attempt to revive her.

They're not going to stop coming after her. Yarrin may be dead, but Zella will return, and the Mendhites will come—and Gods forbid the Empire finds out about this. They don't have to string who knows how many ships from here to some far-flung shore just to be able to multiply mirror-Gate Rora out of our protection. Not when dear Uncle Broger— may he rot in his Netherhell forever—sent his monsters to us with just the one set of mirrors. And the wards around the palace only protect the palace grounds. Not the rest of the island.

Gods . . . I'm going to need protection from Rydan's temper. He might not want to rile the aether, but he did accidentally try to zap Kelly the last time this subject came up . . . which means contacting, uh . . . no, Dominor's gone back to his wife. Trevan, I guess. He's the next most powerful of us. And his wife, Amara, is Rora's twin; she'll want to know what has to be done. Gods, that'll be fun to witness . . .

So much for resting and relaxing, he thought wryly, settling on the bed and punching in the number for Kelly's cryslet. *Let's hope I can play up how horrible I look, to the point where they'll all shut up and co-operate, so as not to further stress the "poor invalid" I've temporarily become . . .*

Reuen and Chana stood in the space between the two legs of the V-shaped table in the Nightfall Council Chamber. Flanking the pair were Koranen and Danau, ensuring they couldn't flee. Opposite the Aquamancers, and seated at the point of that V—which was actually a flat section of table edge—Kelly scribbled on a piece of paper with a charcoal pencil. Next to her sat her husband, Saber, arms folded across his muscular chest, fixing the two Menomonite women with a hard, steel gray stare.

"Let's see . . . the cost of the dress and the undergarments in outworlder funds, converted into the equivalent purchasing power in Nightfall currency, plus the cost of goods sent back through the Veil to balance the equity of mass and energy between the two universes, plus the cost in material components for opening the Veil between worlds, *plus* Morganen's labor and personal energy spent in opening said Veil . . . and figuring in the cost of materials and labor in Nightfaller terms to *replace* the dress with local materials—and this, mind you, does *not* take into account the fact that there are no *zippers* in this universe; the fasteners are not truly equivalent, so I'll have to triple that figure . . . all of it double-checked to make sure I haven't made a mistake in the math and accidentally over- or under-charged you . . ."

She scribbled a bit more, then nodded in satisfaction at the calculations she had made.

"And so we come to a total of . . . one thousand nine hundred sixty-four gold. Though it should be rounded up to two thousand, for convenience's sake—let's call it a stupidity tax."

Reuen choked. Kelly looked up from her numbers, pinning the red-and-brown-haired woman with a hard, aqua glare. She glanced at Chana, who fidgeted and looked elsewhere.

"Of course, that's just the *base* cost. There is also the mental anguish and emotional trauma that your victim suffered upon finding her beautiful, rare, and costly dress shredded beyond repair. Where I come from, there is a saying that you harvest three times what you sow. It means that, if you are kind to someone, you'll receive three times that kindness in the near future. If you are cruel, however, you will suffer three times as much cruelty.

"So, three times two thousand is . . . ? Can either of you tell me?" Kelly asked mock sweetly when neither woman moved.

Chana licked her lips, hesitating, then mumbled, "Six thousand . . . Your Majesty."

"Correct. Now add two thousand to it one more time for tax, and what do you get?"

"Eight thousand."

"Very good. Six of that eight will be paid to the victim. The remaining two thousand will be paid to the government of Nightfall, for the inconvenience this crime has caused us.

"Now, according to Truth Stone testimony, *your* only crime was reporting the existence of the dress to Reuen, here. You're not the one who invaded Danau's privacy, nor did you demolish her dress. However . . . it wasn't your business to tell Reuen about Danau's dress," Kelly chided the blond-dyed Aquamancer. "And, knowing of Reuen's dislike of her cousin, it should have occurred to you that Reuen would react adversely to the thought of her rival receiving such a precious gift. If you hadn't told her about the dress, she wouldn't have been able to damage it before Danau got to wear it.

"Therefore you will be fined five percent of the cost of the dress. Four hundred gold . . . or at least the equivalent in Menomonite gold as compared to the weight of four hundred Katani gilders. You, Reuen," Kelly said, looking at the other woman, "bear the brunt of responsibility for your irresponsible, asinine actions. You will pay the remaining ninety-five percent, seven thousand six hundred gilders. And we'd prefer both of you to make your payments in cash."

"*Cash?*" Chana gasped.

"I don't *have* that kind of money!" Reuen protested tightly.

"You should have thought of that before you wrecked someone else's very expensive personal property," Saber told them. "And don't think of skipping out on your payment. You won't be beyond our reach if you try to return to Menomon; Guardian Sheren will be informed within the hour of your crime and your restitution, and she owes us too much—literally, her life—to allow the Council to shelter you. *Everyone* back home will know of your crime.

"To encourage further compliance, your government will be fined *triple* this amount in your absence if you try to flee elsewhere. You are Menomonite citizens here on official Menomonite business, after all, and everything you do while you are here reflects back upon the government that sent you," the Consort of Nightfall reminded them. "We believe this should encourage you to comply. If not, it will encourage them to assist us in tracking you down, as well as cover our own expenses for the chase.

"Considering my youngest brother has the power to reach into other *worlds* . . . don't presume you'll get very far in fleeing across this one."

Reuen blanched. It was harder to tell Chana's reaction because of her dusky brown face, but she did swallow visibly.

"As it is, since you claim you don't have the cash on hand, your government *will* be requested to make the full payment in cash for you . . . and the suggestion made that your wages from the Aquamancy Guild will be garnished to recoup their losses," Saber told her. "They will ensure that a suitable percentage is deducted automatically before you receive a single copper of each wage payment, until the whole amount is paid off. You *can* lessen the length of time that will take by selling various personal possessions, of course," Saber allowed mock generously.

"Which would be ironically fitting, really," Kelly added dryly. "The loss of your personal property, in exchange for the loss of Danau's . . . We would keep you here beyond the needs of the Desalinator, so that your labors benefited Nightfall more directly, but for one, we'd far rather have the actual cash while we're getting our economy under way, and for another . . . we don't need any more snakes on Nightfall. Particularly vipers.

"As it is, we're stuck with you until the Desalinator is fixed."

"I have news on that, Your Majesty," Danau spoke up. "Lord Koranen and I found the entrance to the monitoring chamber and the central power unit. We know the basics of how to restart the system, once the repairs to the pipeways have been finished and some catch-basins established. However, there is a problem."

"What problem?" Saber asked.

Koranen answered for her. "The recycling of the water from the house pipes is actually *draining* what's left of the system's power reserves. It was designed specifically to get its energy from seawater, not from freshwater. That energy is augmented by a storage crystal that needs to be recharged every four to five decades. With almost all of the Desalinator shut down, the reserves were enough to continue to power the thin trickle that has existed from the one sluice for more than two centuries . . . but only because the system was still getting most of its energy from unadulterated ocean water."

"Gauging from what's left in the crystal, you have maybe two weeks before the system collapses," Danau said. "It can be extended a little bit if the freshwater is rerouted to catch-basins, but not by much."

"Catch-basins?" Saber asked. "Why not let it dump into the bay, like it was before?"

"I haven't had enough time to study the whole system in depth, but it looks like it will need to have all the latticeways restarted at once," Danau explained. "In order to do so, you'll have to flood *all* of the tunnels with seawater before starting. Unfortunately, the filtration system works over a set distance as water flows past the runed lattices. One end starts out salty and filled with minuscule sea life; the other end finishes fresh, clean, and drinkable."

"But if the *whole* system starts out salty, that means no one will be able to drink out of the taps for, what, a whole day? Longer?" Kelly asked, catching on to what the auburn-haired woman was saying.

"Accounting for the fact that the water currently going into the one active channel is diluted, versus the undiluted stuff at the time of the system restart . . . I'd say somewhere between one and two days. Possibly three, given the limited number of outlets for the desalinated water at this time, but that's presuming all taps on the island are opened and allowed to run at full volume," Danau said. "It might be smartest to run the system for two to three days.

"Once the lattices have been activated, each channel can be restricted down to a certain minimum flow without shutting off their empowerment . . . but you will still be processing around twelve times the salt and algae you're producing now. And that's *not* including the sheer masses of blocks that will be produced during those two to three days that the whole system is running at its fullest capacity."

Kelly and Saber glanced at each other. The magesmith sighed. "I'll get to work on processing the backlog of immigration permits. Thankfully it's summer; people can live in tents if they have to, at this time of year. And they can bring drinking water from the mainland . . . maybe a tax cut . . ."

"I'll figure out how to word a mandatory-labor draft that won't make everyone carp and complain." The freckled ruler started to say more, but the silver and gold bracelet on her wrist chimed. "Since we're done for now, the two of you can go back to your quarters. Remember what we said about running away, and remember that it was *your* choice to hate Danau," she told each woman over the ringing of her cryslet. "*Your* choice, Chana, to gossip about the good fortune of her dress, and *your* choice, Reuen, to destroy it.

"If you had made different choices, you would not have been fined. You are merely harvesting what *you* decided to sow. Dismissed."

Not waiting for them to leave, Kelly flipped up the white crystal top of her bracelet, answering her caller. Koranen gestured with mock courtesy toward the open end of the table and followed behind Reuen and Chana as they filed out. Danau joined him, tucking her hand into his.

Part of her hoped the pair ahead of them would glance back. She *wanted* them to see her touching a handsome man with no thermal repercussions. But part of her mulled over the incipient Queen's words. *You harvest what you plant. If I flaunt my ability to have a relationship in their faces, Reuen and Chana—particularly my cousin—will only hate me all the more.*

Right now . . . they might *have a chance at admitting to themselves that what they did was beyond wrong, and they might consider trying to be better women in the future. But if I rub my new status in their faces, it'd be like that old saying about trying to make love on a beach: It may sound like fun, but in the end, it's just an unnecessary irritation of sensitive anatomy.*

Of course, once we get back to my quarters, or his . . . then *I can pounce on him,* she decided, allowing herself a tiny little smile. *Last time, we were on a cold, hard floor. Next time, I want to try a bed. Or a chair. I liked it when I was straddling his lap . . .*

Plotting what she might do to him once they were alone, Danau smiled all the way back to the southeast wing. Occasionally, Kor would glance down at her, and after the second time catching her smile, he smiled back. He even squeezed her fingers lightly.

Just as they reached Reuen's door, Ama-ti's flew open. The blue-haired Aquamancer peered out into the corridor, then hurried to join them. "There you are! Where were you? You missed an utterly *gorgeous* performance! I haven't heard music that good since . . . since the Sea of Lights Festival three years back! Luckily for you, they've decided to hold a third concert, and Her Majesty has generously ordered four more tickets, since the lot of you were missing. Where did you go, anyway?"

Exchanging only brief, subdued looks, Reuen and Chana ignored her, heading for their separate rooms. That left Ama-ti staring at their retreating backs, before turning to Kor and Danau. Her green eyes dropped to their joined hands, and her light brown brows rose.

"I see. What *else* did I miss, while you were missing the concert?" she asked guilelessly.

Grateful that Ama-ti, at least, had always been kind to her, Danau returned the kindness with a quick explanation. "Chana overheard me telling Koranen that I had a velvet dress to wear to the concert. She told Reuen, who snuck into my room and destroyed it. After that, at some point the two of them ran into that Mornai mage, Yarrin, and he somehow convinced them to go to a room at an inn with him . . . where he subdued, bound, and gagged them, and planned to control their bodies with some system of rune-spells. Just like he did the Baroness Teretha. I'd worry that he managed some form of preliminary control, but he's quite firmly dead, negating his spells."

"Yarrin? A spell-controller?" Ama-ti asked doubtfully. "Are you sure?"

"He controlled, and then murdered, Baroness Teretha," Koranen confirmed. "And he was willing to kill Reuen and Chana, too, in order to get his hands on . . . the Fountain of Nightfall."

"You have a Fountain?" the blue-haired Aquamancer asked, distracted for a moment. Then scowled in the next. "A murderer? *Yarrin?* But . . . but he seemed so *nice*! So charming. If he hadn't been so blatant about wanting to leave Menomon, I might've asked him to stay and be one of my husbands."

"My guess is, he wanted to leave Menomon so that he could go back to preying on lady-mages, and have options for escape, should he be caught," Danau told her. "If he'd tried any of his tricks in Menomon, he would've had no easy way to flee. Especially after seeing what we did to Xenos when he tried to take over *our* Fountain."

"Well, I suppose that makes sense," Ama-ti allowed with a tip of her head. Then shook it slowly. "But he just seemed so *nice* . . ."

"There's more," Danau said, distracting her colleague. "Because Reuen committed a crime on Nightfall Isle, and Chana was her accomplice, they've both been fined by Her Majesty for the destruction of my dress. Since neither brought that kind of money with them, the Council will be petitioned to send the money, and their Guild wages will be garnished accordingly, afterward."

Ama-ti grimaced. "The Council is *not* going to like that."

"No, they're not. But we did come here specifically to *help* these people and are being hosted at Nightfall's expense. It's implied that, in return for their hospitality, we'd be good little law abiders . . . and Reuen broke the law. I'm not so sure about Chana . . . but I'm not going to protest her punishment," Danau admitted wryly. "It's not nice of me, but then she wasn't nice, either. Oh, and if they try to escape, or default on payment, Menomon will be fined with an even bigger payment, since they're Menomonite citizens here on official Menomonite business."

"Ah. I appreciate the warning," Ama-ti added, giving Danau a slight bow. "I wouldn't want to fall into the trap of helping them, making me an accomplice in the Council's eyes, however unwitting. So . . . the two of you, huh?" She grinned as she said it, eyeing Koranen from head to foot before smirking at Danau. "Finally landed one—and a big one at that, you sly hook master!"

"Thank you," Danau returned, bowing politely in return. From Koranen's frown, she'd have to explain the Menomonite joke later, though she didn't know how he'd react to being compared to a sport-fish. "And thank you for being a good colleague all these years."

Ama-ti shrugged blithely. "Well, you can't help being the way

Menos made you. But, um . . . if it *doesn't* work out between you two . . ."

"It *will*," Koranen stated flatly. The last thing he wanted was to be one of several men married to a woman with blue nether-hair. Not that he could; the only woman he could touch with impunity was Danau. Squeezing Danau's hand, he gave Ama-ti a polite nod. "Good night."

"Get some rest," Danau advised her. "We'll have a lot of work getting the Desalinator ready for resurrection—that's the other thing that happened. We found the control chamber. I'll need all three of you ready to take measurements, bright and early in the morning."

"Not *too* early," Koranen protested, giving the short Aquamancer a pointed look.

Ama-ti giggled and fluttered her fingers at them. She backed up to her door, opened it, and then—just before disappearing behind it—offered cheekily, "Don't forget to get *some* sleep tonight!"

The door shutting firmly between them cut off the embarrassed retort Danau wanted to make. Unsure where to look, cheeks heating to the point where their breaths would have been frosting, if he hadn't still been holding her hand, Danau cleared her throat. "Well. I suppose we should . . . um . . ."

"Clean up the mess in your suite?" Kor offered, taking pity on her. At the wrinkling of her nose, he changed his offer. "On second thought, let's let the servants do that. You can sleep in my quarters, tonight."

Tugging gently on her fingers, he guided her to the other side of the hall. Opening the door, he ushered his impending bride into his sitting room. Danau blinked at what she saw. Very little in his front chamber was made from wood; most of it seemed to be constructed from slabs of stone. "Stone furniture? Oh . . . right. Heat resistant. But why the all-white pillows? Is that your favorite color?"

"It's stonefiber cloth, actually. Naturally heat resistant. And I like greens and purples. I don't think I look good in purple," he

THE FLAME...

added lightly, "but I do like looking at it. I picked these rooms out of all the ones in the southeast wing because the floor and three of the walls were stone, reducing the chance I'd accidentally scorch something just from walking around. Other suites have more amenities and room, but this one is safest.

"This door over here leads to the bedchamber, and the door opposite it is the refreshing room. Considering all that we've been through, you might feel better after you've had a bath. Or a rainshower. I find I like them—it's a Natallian innovation," he added. "Water rains down from above, instead of having to submerge oneself in a bath."

"We bathe in waterfall-fed pools," Danau admitted. Then amended, "Or we did, before freshwater rationing came into play."

"Well, a single shower right now isn't going to make that much of an impact on the waning energies of the Desalinator. Come!" he added, grinning and tugging on their joined hands. "I've always wanted to bathe with a lover! Trevan makes it sound like a lot of fun."

"Trevan? Your brother?" Danau asked, uncertain of what he meant.

"Trevan is *the* authority in the family on male-female matters," Kor explained, leading her into the refreshing room. "He used to court a *lot* of women, back before we were exiled here. And since it became rather obvious I couldn't actually *touch* a real woman, all I had left were lessons in the theory of touching one. So I listened to just about everything he had to say on the subject."

"Ah. I suppose that makes sense," Danau allowed. "We have sexuality education classes in Menomon, but it's all pure theory in the classroom, from biology to technique. And of course, I was too busy focusing on my studies and my powers to try the practical application side of things, until . . ."

"Yes, Ama-ti told me there was an idiot who reacted badly and ruined your reputation," Kor admitted lightly when she trailed off. "That's the other reason why I'd rather not travel to Menomon."

"We *agreed* to go to Menomon!" Danau protested, hands going to her hips. "That Desalinator is *important* to the future of my people—and if you and I compound each others' powers when we touch, then *we* are the most likely candidates to take over the Guardianship of Menomon from Sheren. The Council knows I am loyal to the City, and Sheren knows I am *not* impressed by political maneuverings. And *you* are an honorable man, so *I* have every confidence you'd hold the City's best interest in your heart!"

"Danau, I *meant*, if I ever met this so-called man, I'm afraid I'd want to torch him on the spot for what he did to you. My father taught my brothers and me that a *real* gentleman is *gentle* with another person's reputation—particularly a former lover!" Kor argued, spreading his hands. "But while we're on the subject, *why* are you loyal to a City where everyone mocks you?"

"They don't *all* mock me," Danau muttered, folding her arms across her chest. "At least, Ama-ti doesn't. And Guardian Sheren. *And* a handful of others, within and without the Guild. And . . . I just *am*. You might have broken away from your birth land, but *they* abandoned you first, exiling you here. Menomon never abandoned me. I might not have a social life, but I have a career where I'm both respected and *needed*. You *don't* stop protecting and helping people just because they mock you."

Koranen studied the petite mage in his refreshing room for a long moment, then folded his arms. Lifting one hand to his chin, he rubbed thoughtfully at it.

"What?" Danau asked defensively.

"Do you think this counts as our first argument?" the redhead asked her. At her confused look, Kor smirked slightly. "I've heard that post-argument lovemaking is often worth having the fight."

His suggestion was so absurd, she couldn't help chuckling. Shaking her head, Danau stooped and started unlacing her boots. "Just get the water ready. I'm sure we'll have a *real* argument soon enough."

"But I wanted to have a making-up romp!"

Tugging off one of her boots, Danau peered up at him. "Koranen, before we progress to such an advanced stage in our relationship . . . shouldn't we practice the *regular* sort of sex? Neither of us has had much in the way of hands-on experience, you realize. And there's only so much that theory can teach, before you have to actually *try* something."

"Good point," he conceded, and hurried to strip off his own clothes.

By the time he finished removing his loincloth, she had worked her way out of everything but her leather undergarments. Catching her hand, Kor tugged Danau close, stooping for a brief kiss. Letting her go, he turned to the shower, throwing one lever to the far left, and making sure the other was still to the far right. When he turned back, she was naked and desirable. Mindful that they both needed a rain-shower, Kor gestured at the tub.

"Ladies first . . ."

Danau approached the stone basin. Something about the water streaming from the perforated pipe overhead made her pause, however. Bemused and unsure what it was, she extended her hand, touching the spray. And yelped, snatching her hand back.

"What's wrong?" Kor asked.

"It's *cold*!" she protested.

"So?"

"Koranen, I am *not* getting into a *cold* shower! I'd be covered in ice within twenty breaths," she added tartly.

"It's not *that* cold—the heat of the day hasn't dissipated," Kor argued, sticking his hand into the spray. "See? Perfectly comfortable."

Danau hooked her hand around his other elbow. It took the Pyromancer only a moment to wince and withdraw his hand. "See? Even *shared*, with our powers cancelling each other, it's too cold!"

"Fine; I'll just work the heating lever." Shifting his left arm so that their hands were clasped, Koranen reached for the lever in question with his right hand and nodded at the spray. "Stick your hand in and tell me when it's the right temperature."

Wary, Danau leaned over the rim of the tub and let the falling
water splatter over her fingertips. It wasn't nearly as cold as it had
been before, but it was still quite chilly. After a few seconds, she
glanced at him. "Well? Turn the lever!"

"I did; it's all the way over," he told her. Sticking his free hand
into the spray, Koranen frowned. Then winced and slapped his
forehead. "Of course! I only use heated water in the middle of winter, and this spring, the thermal spell wore off the lever. I didn't do
anything about it because I knew I wouldn't *need* to do anything
about it until late autumn or early winter . . .

"I do *not* want to stop and take the time to re-enchant the
damned thing," he muttered, freeing his left hand from her grasp.
Leaning over, he switched the flow lever from the shower to the
faucet setting and crouched so he could tuck a piece of cork into the
drain. "So instead of a shower, we'll just take a bath."

"Koranen, you do realize that a pool of cold water isn't any better than a drizzle of cold water?" Danau pointed out.

Kor gave her a dry look. "I'm a Pyromancer, remember? All I
have to do is climb in first, heat things up for a few moments, and
then you'll be able to join me."

"Good point," she admitted, though her attention wasn't on his
face. "Why don't you climb in now and get things started while the
basin is filling?"

Twisting, Koranen peered over his shoulder to see what she was
looking at. It took him a few moments to realize she was staring at
his backside. Rather than waste the heat of his flush, he climbed
into the tub. He took his time settling down into the hollowed
stone basin, though, not wanting to spoil her view. *If she likes my
body . . . who am I to deny her the pleasure of it? She is my Destined bride,
after all.*

Yes, my wife. Or rather, my wife-to-be, he thought, smiling at her.
They hadn't formally married yet, but it was as inevitable as the fall
of night. No one else could touch him, and no one else could touch
her; the odds of anyone else suiting them were even lower than the

usual odds of the matchmaking quest for happiness. *It won't be easy—we'll* have *to learn to get along—but she is smart, and pretty, and very alluring. And she has a truly alluring backside* . . .

The view of her stooped over, investigating the shelving next to the sink counter for its collection of softsoap pots, was enough to steam the water within a dozen heartbeats. Long enough for her to dip her knees, wriggle her hips, display hints of her dark reddish brown nether-curls with a lower stoop, and straighten again, washcloth and softsoap jar in her hands. Elbow braced on the edge of the basin, jaw resting on the backs of his knuckles, Koranen continued to admire the view as she turned to face him.

Danau, seeing the smile quirking the corner of his mouth, realized he had been staring at her. She flushed and tried to shrug it off as nothing, since plenty of men had admired her from a distance in the past—then reminded herself firmly that this *wasn't* a man who had to stay in the distance. Setting the jar on the broad ledge behind his head, she cleared her throat.

"Enjoying the view?"

"*Very* much. Thank you. Um, you'd better test the water before you get in, just in case I made it too hot," Kor warned her. "I suffer from excess outside heat only up to a point, then my innate defenses take over, and I just don't really feel it anymore. I'm not allowed to heat water for anyone else without casting a thermal gauging spell, but since you absorb heat naturally . . ."

Nodding, she bent over and tested the water with her fingertips. "Mm . . . perfect. Hot enough to last just long enough for me to bathe. Which means too hot for anyone else."

Lifting his hand, Koranen offered it to her, to help her step into the tub. The moment their fingers met, however, he hissed and jumped violently. The contact broke their touch; the moment they let go, the burning heat faded. Danau blinked at him.

"What was *that* for?"

Flapping his hand in front of his face, Kor nodded at the water. "*Too* hot. I lost my ability to block it out—from surprise, if nothing else. I could probably block it out consciously instead of instinctively," he added as she frowned, "but . . . why don't you just climb in without touching me, absorb some of the excess heat, and *then* we'll touch?"

Sighing, Danau climbed carefully into the tub, avoiding his stretched-out legs as he swept them to either side, making space for her between his calves. "This relationship is going to take a lot of experimentation and compromise, isn't it?"

"I was thinking the same thing. But I *want* to try—wait," Kor interrupted himself. At her bemused look, he gestured at her with his hand. "Would you do something for me? Please?"

"What should I do?" she asked.

Koranen flushed and rubbed the back of his neck. "Well . . . I have this fantasy . . . regarding you."

Danau felt herself blushing, too. She couldn't even remember if Jiore had ever mentioned harboring any fantasies where she was concerned. Desires, yes, but nothing specifically dreamed about. "A fantasy regarding me?"

In for a coppera, in for a gilder . . . "Yes," he repeated firmly. "Um . . . if you're willing . . . could you stand over me and, you know . . . touch yourself? All over, while I watch?"

She blushed again at the suggestion. Koranen felt the water turn chilly around her calves in response. Complying, Danau carefully stepped over his thighs. In return, he shifted his legs together, then lifted his hands, gingerly touching her shins. Both sighed in relief as the water shifted to a comfortably warm temperature. Letting his hands settle against her ankles under the water, he nodded at her.

"Now . . . touch yourself. Do whatever arouses you. I want to see *everything* that excites you," he directed her.

Intimidated and yet aroused, Danau lifted her hands. She didn't quite feel ready to touch her breasts, so she bypassed them, sliding her cool fingers up over her heated cheeks. Stroking her skin, she closed her eyes and just *felt* how smooth and soft it was. Moving her hands up over her hair, she ruffled and raked them through her short, auburn locks, and imagined what it might feel like to run her hands through *his* hair. Not just the brief, distracted explorations of earlier, but over and over. Long, sensual, exotic strands, all hers for the exploring.

Opening her eyes, Danau looked down at Koranen. Though the slope at the back of the tub was designed for lounging, he wasn't relaxed. She could see the tension in his muscles. Only his hazel eyes moved, though, flicking from her hands and hair to her breasts, belly, hips, and knees, before returning back to her face for another circuit.

Sliding her hands down to her shoulders, she snared his gaze, dragging it down around her breasts, following the paths of her fingertips. She teased her ribs for a few moments, then splayed her hands across her abdomen and slid them slowly down. The bathwater grew warmer around her ankles as she bent over, palms caressing her thighs.

Just knowing she had the power to excite him, to arouse him, without either of them harming each other, made Danau feel both confident and nervous. Confident, in that she *was* desirable and could act on that desire. Nervous, in that she was sorely out of practice in the art of acting on her desires.

Except he's asked me to show him what I like. What I know of pleasuring myself. Glancing at the water-covered waist between her feet, she could just see the head of his arousal breaching the surface of the bath. *And he's very much interested in my answer . . .*

This, I can do.

Straightening slowly, she dragged her hands up the insides of her thighs and detoured teasingly around their apex. Circling the dimple of her navel, she swept her fingertips out and around her breasts, down and in, spiraling inward along their soft curves until she could play with just her nipples. She took her time, too, rubbing and plucking gently until he groaned and shifted. Fingers tightening on her ankles, he wordlessly encouraged her to do more.

Aroused, Danau trailed her right forefinger down the centerline of her torso, deviating only long enough to swirl it around her belly button. From there, it slid straight into her nether-lips. If her self-ministrations were a dialogue, all of the preamble had been up at her breasts. This, however, was the crux of passion's argument. With her left hand still playing around her breasts, she used her right to stroke the stiff little peak of nerves.

When her hips started rocking in time with her touch, another groan escaped Kor. As did the heat of such a stimulating view, but her ankles were still cool under his touch, not blistering, but welcoming and absorbing his passion. But to watch wasn't enough. This wasn't an illusion hovering over his body as he lounged on the cinders of his forge hearth; this was the real woman. His woman.

Sitting up, Koranen skimmed his hands up her thighs. Her legs could only part so far without some awkward contortions, but she didn't seem to understand the tugging of his fingers. "Here," he verbalized, tugging again on one thigh. "Put your leg over my shoulder."

How did *Trevan manage all those seductions he boasted about, without having to awkwardly ask for cooperation?* Kor wondered wryly as she hesitantly lifted her leg, bracing one hand on the wall next to her. The tub was broad, almost wide enough for two to have bathed side by side comfortably, and she had to lean over a bit to catch her balance. *Or any other awkwardness . . . Ah, that's perfect. Even if I do get a crick in my neck from it . . .*

Draping her thigh over his shoulder opened her loins to him. The scent wasn't quite as strong as before, but the taste was just as sweet. Within just a few licks, he was entranced, the same as before. *This* had to be the food of the Gods—or at least the God Jinga, happily wed to the Goddess Kata.

Danau shuddered, struggling to maintain her balance. It wasn't easy, caught with only one leg for support, the other too awkwardly draped for control, and her strength being suckled from her flesh. She shuddered again, right hand braced against the wall, and clutched at the back of his head with her left.

Long, soft, slightly damp strands met her delving touch; they entwined around her digits, as much from the nuzzling of his head as from the explorations of her fingers. She could feel more locks brushing against her thighs, their ends wet and cool, but not cold. *Not* cold.

Nothing about the man loving her body was cold. Not the palms cupping her buttocks, not the shoulder supporting her thigh, and not the tongue laving her folds. The heat of his breath as he groaned, shifting to suckle her once more, was enough to tip her into a shuddering orgasm. It almost toppled her, but she managed to avert a fall with the hand braced against the granite blocks that formed the wall.

As pleasurable as that was, she had to tug gently on his hair to get him to stop. Not because she insisted they move on to other things, but simply because her leg literally wouldn't have stood for another round. The disappointed noise he made pleased her; she *was* a real woman, attractive enough to snare the passion of a real man.

Wanting to appease his disappointment over the change in her position, Danau adjusted her legs and sank to her knees, straddling his lap. It didn't take much to find his hardened flesh, though the way he hissed made her extra careful in aiming it. That, and her inexperience. Finding the right spot, she sank slowly onto his shaft, filling herself with his unwavering heat.

Once fully seated, Danau cupped his face, bringing their mouths together. She didn't flinch from the taste of herself—salt and musk, the perfume of the sea—but instead devoured it in slow, suckling kisses. When he wrapped his arms around her, holding her tenderly close, it completed her pleasure in a way that not even a climax could have managed. *This* was what she wanted most, to be held lovingly by someone she could not possibly hurt.

With the water lapping around her hips, she rode him slowly, lazily, making their pleasure last as long as possible. Their seated position gave Koranen more control over himself than their previous session, permitting him to enjoy the slower rise of passion between them. Or perhaps it was simply that this was his third climax in almost as many hours. It didn't matter; whatever gave him control gave him enough time to guide her hips in a circular grinding that pleased both of them.

The difference in their heights was negated by her straddling his lap, too, allowing him to kiss her back without any stooping or scooping or seeking out a stair step. Not that they'd done that yet, but he knew they would, sooner or later. For now, it was enough to kiss her, and kiss her thoroughly. Even when they finally moved on to a more vigorous pace, making the bathwater slosh, he didn't want to stop kissing her. This was what he needed; his woman, his very own woman, to hold and to love in all ways possible.

He didn't ever want to stop.

FIFTEEN

❧❧❧

Sleeping with another person in the bed was a different experience for both of them.

Danau, used to feeling cold and needing to huddle completely under the covers, naturally gravitated toward the greatest source of heat. That meant plastering herself against Koranen's side . . . but every time she did so, either she'd start with surprise, or he would twitch, waking both of them. Eventually they settled into a quiet repose, but it was still strange to be touching someone, as if he were some sort of giant, flesh-covered heating rune. She had to keep reminding herself she *wasn't* going to give him frostbite just by cuddling with him under the covers.

Koranen, used to feeling overly warm and needing to sprawl, usually kicking off the covers in the summer, found it sort of cloying to be clung to by more than just bedsheets. On the other hand, just by touching him, she cooled him. The feel of the sheet might be annoying—she insisted on hiking it up to her chin, which meant up over most of his chest—but with her hugging his side, he wasn't overheated. It was just . . . strange . . . to have someone sharing his bed and not have to worry about burning them.

Half the time she moved, he would wake with a jolt of worry that he might hurt her. Half the time, he woke from a jolt of hers, no doubt from her own fears of harming him. It would take them time to get over these instincts. And time to get used to the presence of another person while they slept.

Despite the lack of solid sleep, Koranen greeted the gray light of dawn with a lighter heart than he could ever remember. Because she *was* snugged against his side, keeping him partly awake with her unfamiliar proximity. Some parts of him more than others.

He knew the moment she awakened, too, by her deep inhalation, and by her sudden stillness. Tentatively, her hand slid from his waist to his ribs, feeling the rise and fall of his breath, the thump of his heart, and most important, the warmth of his skin. He knew she would do that, because she had done it half a dozen times through the night.

Danau exhaled in a sigh, snuggling closer. *Still warm, alive, and mine . . .* Because she could touch him, she did, rubbing her palm gently back down his torso from ribs to hips. *Gods*, why *did I say we'd get to work bright and early this morning? What kind of an idiot am I, wanting to rush off when I could stay in bed? Wait . . . what's this?*

His breath caught, the moment her wrist bumped into a certain part of his flesh. Smiling to herself, Danau encircled his shaft and rippled her fingers along its length. Koranen grunted, then twisted onto his side, squirming a little lower on the bed until his lips could brush her forehead. Liking that, she encouraged him with firmer ripples, then sighed a second time when he caressed her own curves from shoulder to hip. Obliging the path of his hand, she lifted her knee, giving his fingers better access to her femininity.

That earned her another kiss on her forehead. Tilting her head back, Danau nipped his chin and stroked the velvet skin of his hardened shaft. It coaxed Koranen to scoot just a little bit lower so their mouths could meet. Even the slight staleness of morning breath couldn't ruin the sweet bliss of lying side by side with her, arousing each other.

When she tugged gently on his manhood, squirming to hook her upraised leg over his hip and bring them a lot closer, Kor was more than ready to assist her. Mindful of the dryness of his flesh, he didn't let her align them just yet, sliding his shaft between her folds instead of into them. She moaned softly, hitching her hips into a better angle for rubbing against him. That aroused him further, knowing *his* touch was giving her nothing but pleasure. It was a mixed blessing that he needed to use the refreshing room, since the mild discomfort from the pressure gave him an extra incentive for self-control.

As delicious as it felt to rub herself along his shaft, Danau wanted more. Fingers slick with her own desire groped his passion-heated skin. This time, positioning him just so, she managed to ease them together. Unfortunately, lying on her side didn't give her a good angle to do anything more. Debating which one of them should climb over the other, she gave up and twisted halfway onto her back, tugging on his arm.

Catching on, Koranen shifted over her, settling his hips between her parted thighs. He had to reposition himself, but the feeling of sinking into her snug, wet, unscorched warmth was well worth the effort. More than worth the effort; even grinding his teeth together didn't quell the urge to thrust.

Most of his recent fantasies took place with him lying on his back, since lying facedown on forge-fire cinders wasn't exactly comfortable. By default, his imagined self was also on his back. But this ... this was an old fantasy, the kind that used to literally set his sheets on fire if they weren't properly spell-stitched. A half-forgotten longing finally being fulfilled.

Between the splayed welcome of her body and the clutching of her hands, the soft, encouraging moans and hungry little nips from her mouth, Koranen couldn't have stopped himself, even if Prophecy had demanded it. Driving his hips with increasing vigor, he surrendered to his need. It didn't take long for the fire building within him to burn down his spine and spill through his skin, pouring into her in shuddering, panting moans.

Two things kept him from slumping bonelessly on her as his orgasm subsided: One, he didn't want to crush her slender, smaller form; and two, his bladder was still very much in need of the refreshing room. Bracing himself on unsteady elbows and knees, Koranen struggled to regain his breath.

That's it? He's done? Panting, Danau clutched at her lover's shoulders. She had been so *close* to her own climax . . . and then he had finished, and slowed, and stopped. All that momentum toward her peak, wasted. Dismayed, she asked bluntly, "Is that it? You're not finished, are you?"

"Uh . . ." Gathering his wits, Koranen wondered dazedly how she could have missed him climaxing. Her next complaint clarified the matter.

"I was so close! And then you . . . you *finished* without me!" She didn't mean to sound like a petulant child, but really—was it too much to ask a man to ensure his partner had her fun, too? Everyone back in Menomon agreed that a wise husband pleased his wife, so that she would not neglect him for the better considerations found in the arms of her other spouses. *One would think a one-man-one-woman culture would insist on it even more strongly, so that one's partner doesn't stray outside the laws of marriage, looking for satisfaction!*

Jinga's Sacred Ass . . . which I don't *mean to resemble,* Kor thought, wincing. Pulling out of her, he moved down her body. "No, no . . . I'm not done. Or, rather, *you're* not done—shh, let me . . ."

Two fingers slipped into her slick core. Koranen curled them upward, bringing down his mouth to meet her flesh from the outside even as he stroked from the inside. Giving her fluttering, circling little rubs with his digits, and some lapping and suckling with his tongue and lips, he focused on reviving her pleasure. The scent of his spilled essence was only marginally better than the occasional taste of it, but the more he stroked and lapped, the more of *her* filled his senses.

He knew he was near his goal—her goal—when she dug her fingers into his sleep-mussed hair, pushing on the back of his head to encourage more. Some of his own excitement returned, particularly when she stiffened and bucked, choking on his name . . . but most of him was simply relieved that she had climaxed. Mindful of Trevan's lectures on women and their post-orgasmic needs, he gentled his touch, eased his fingers free, and kissed his way slowly, thoroughly, back up her torso.

He was rewarded by the caress of her hands, stroking his hair back from his face as he reached her lips. Sharing a slow, sweet kiss, Koranen finally pulled back, smiling at her. "*Good* morning . . . yes?"

"Very," Danau agreed. Her voice was a little husky, but he had made her shout hoarsely at the end there. At the very considerate end. Grateful that Kor had been willing to sate her arousal, Danau smiled back at him.

Before she could thank him, however, he rolled off the bed and padded toward a door. It took her a moment to orient herself in the new room, his bedroom. It was a mirror image of her own, which meant he had just vanished into the refreshing room. *Mm, I'll need to use it, too. A bath wouldn't be amiss; I never got to experience just how* messy *lovemaking is before . . .*

An oath escaped her as realization hit. Danau thumped the bedding, struggling to contain the frost that crept across the bedcovers. "*Drown* it! Sodden, soaking seas, I cannot believe we did it *again!*"

The refreshing room door opened a moment later, auburn hair swinging forward as Koranen popped his head into the chamber. "What? What's wrong?"

"We forgot the sodden contraception again!" Scrubbing her face with her palms, she mumbled a belated, "Pardon my language."

Koranen didn't know what was so awful about the word *sodden* to render it in need of a pardon, but he managed to grunt something appropriate. Withdrawing his head, he returned to his task, thinking.

I know she wants to wait, and I know it's wise to wait, but . . . part of me wants to start a family. Except I suppose we really should wed, first, and establish ourselves in a home, somewhere. Menomon, given how strongly she feels about serving her people. Even if they don't respect her nearly as much as they should . . .

His father had lectured him thoroughly, back when a much younger Koranen had burned a comely young maiden. He'd been underage that first time, and his handprints made it very obvious where he'd burned her on her chest, but it was Saveno's lecture on the responsibilities of being a physically mature man that came back to Kor now. *A real man doesn't beget bastards. He takes care with the women he shares pleasure with, so that they don't create an unexpected new life. He makes sure any child of his will be wanted, and will be cared for . . . and will be born within the eight altars of marriage.*

Of course, we don't have the eight altars of marriage, anymore, Kor acknowledged, moving on to wash his hands. *The ceremony that Evanor and Mariel came up with for their wedding is a good replacement, though I'll feel better about using it for my marriage to Danau once we're an official kingdom, and thus blessed by the Gods.*

Neither he nor his brothers were particularly religious. Spiritual, yes. Reverent . . . mostly, though having lived as eight bachelors in exile for three years, they had let their reverence slide along with their observances. Mostly, their attitudes had slid in the direction of taking the boisterous Jinga's name in vain. The male God of Katan was considered to be more lenient about such things than their Goddess, so it wasn't entirely blasphemous, just rather irreverent of them.

But marriage was sacred, recognized everywhere by the Laws of God and Man. *These Menomonites may insist on multiple husbands, but they do insist on marriage. Ama-ti more or less said Danau's unmarriageable state was a social embarrassment. In wedding her, I would do more than heed Prophecy; I would restore some of her worth in the eyes of her people.*

He grimaced at his reflection. *But I can't say that. Even if Danau prefers, or rather, is used to a work-like approach to her life,* he amended, *Trevan was very clear on the feminine need for romance in a relationship. For a declaration of love. So . . . do I love her? Not just for Prophecy's sake, but . . . do I love her?*

Koranen stared at his reflection in the scrying-warded mirror over his sink, weighing how he felt. No answer came immediately to his mind, save that he simply did not know yet. A knock at the door broke his contemplation, as did her light-voiced query. "Did you drown in there?"

An amused thought made him smile as he opened the door. "Only if it'll get you to breathe life back into me with a kiss."

"Maybe. After I've scrubbed my teeth," she compromised. Then held up a glass marble. "I found this on your bedside table. It looks like it has a little woman trapped inside. What is it?"

Paling at the sight of the sphere, Koranen snatched it from her hand. Burying it in his fist, he quickly tucked his arm behind his back. "Uh . . . nothing! Nothing at all. Refreshing room's free . . ."

A hand on his naked chest stopped him from edging around her and making an escape. Blue eyes pinned him in place, though at least the corner of her mouth was curled up in amusement. "What *is* it? Surely not some deep, dark secret?"

"Uh . . . a birthing-day present. I don't need it anymore, so I'll just, um, put it away in a drawer."

"Koranen, I am not a fool," Danau chided him, holding him in place with her hand on his bare chest. "It embarrasses you enough to suggest it *is* important. Don't make this our second argument."

Trapped, Kor flushed and brought the marble back into view. The only thing that could possibly have made this worse would have been for his own departed mother to have returned from the Afterlife to find it, instead of Danau. "It's . . . it's an illusion-woman. A sophisticated enchantment that, upon command, projects sight, sound, and touch, though not taste or smell."

One of her auburn brows quirked up. "I take it from your awkwardness that it's enchanted to behave in a specific way? Such as a lascivious way?"

"Well . . . it's not like I could practice on a *real* woman," Koranen defended himself. He fell back on the technical explanation, trying to treat it like just another Artifact. "Trevan convinced one of the women at the Companionship Guild to pose for the recording spells. She did so with the help of a fellow, male Guildmember to instill in it a set of accurate female responses to pleasurable interactions. And he put the enchantment spell into one of my heat-tempered, illusion-anchoring crystals, so that I could interact with the illusion and safely practice how to be a good lover—skills which *you* have benefited from."

Wrapping her hand around his, enclosing the crystal as well as his fingers, Danau managed a reassuring smile. "It's alright; I understand. If I could have done the same thing, and had thought of it, I probably would have. I haven't been celibate by *choice*, after all . . . and I'm a bit envious that you had even this much, when I've had nothing. But I'd rather you practiced your techniques on *me*, since even I know that what works for arousing one woman doesn't necessarily work for another."

"I'll put it away," Koranen promised quickly. "In fact, I should probably return it to the Guild, so they can have it as an instruction aid, or something. Though it is my birthing-day gift . . ."

"Well, you can keep it, but you *could* always practice on me, instead," Danau reminded him. "After all, I could use the practice, too."

"Good point," Koranen agreed, and stooped for a kiss. A brief one; they did have to dress and find something to eat, after all.

"Now . . . could I please use the refreshing room?" she asked plaintively when the kiss ended.

Grateful she wasn't going to make any more of a fuss over the sphere, Koranen nodded and traded places with her. Not that he *needed* it, now that he had her. *Maybe I could save it for a future son?*

We'll have to remember to visit Mariel about contraceptive measures. And I should schedule some time to craft a pair of wedding torcs—I wonder what Menomonites use to mark their marriage bonds?

"And we should have the pipes ready for the cooling-system water to be diverted into the first of the city reservoirs here by about sunset," Danau finished, gesturing at the large, deep, empty pool. Well, mostly empty; bushes, dirt, and even a few trees had found a way to grow in the deep basin, though almost half of it had been cleared already, spell-lifted out of the tank and into a growing pile of debris off to one side.

Reuen was down there, using her magic to remove the grime and plant growth that had collected in the tank over the last two hundred years. It pleased Danau to see her cousin grubby and sweating, attending to such an unglamorous job, but it was even more pleasant that Reuen hadn't protested the assignment. The brown-and-red-haired Aquamancer hadn't said much of anything to Danau, period. At least she hadn't gone so far as to ignore the shorter mage. Danau decided that was a good thing; it hinted that her cousin *was* sorry she had messed with that precious, triply expensive dress.

Chana hadn't protested her assignment, either, but then, it was the blond-dyed woman's job to muck out the pipes that led to this reservoir tank. There wasn't as much in the way of grime, but the pipes had to be scoured clean and any cracks found solidly patched. She would be just as clay-covered by the end of her task as Danau had been yesterday, if not more so; the blond-dyed mage didn't have a Pyromancer to help quicken the setting of the mortar.

Of the other three, Ama-ti had the easiest job; Koranen and Danau had let her into the underground control chamber so that she could start measuring and testing the function of the various quality-sampling Artifacts down there. Danau was determined to re-create the Desalinator, and that required the sort of meticulous attention to detail that the blue-haired Aquamancer was good at observing.

She would still be down there with Ama-ti, if Amara hadn't contacted her via Koranen. The mayor was ready to discuss her rough estimate of daily household water usage for the city and the volume of freshwater that would need to be reserved for the day or days it would take to restart the whole Desalinator. Koranen had excused himself after making sure a small handheld mirror found in the desk of that alcove-room was capable of contacting one of his twin's scrying mirrors, should either Aquamancer run into trouble. He claimed he needed to go shopping, though for what, he wouldn't say.

Amara, using a scrap of chalk to mark numbers on a slateboard, slowly nodded. The movement made her pectoral glitter, which in turn made Danau squint. "Given the volume . . . I *think* this one tank can fulfill our needs. If we fill it to capacity."

"It's a huge tank; even halfway to capacity should be enough," Danau pointed out. "There are only, what, three thousand people on the Isle?"

"Three thousand three hundred sixty-four . . . sixty-two, rather, though we'll be bringing in hundreds more to handle the Desalinator's increased output," Amara amended, brow pinching unhappily. "At least the baroness was good at long-range planning and in writing down those plans clearly. Until we can find someone good enough at land reclamation to replace her, we'll have to manage the outlying farms based on her notes. I know how to oversee the needs of established fields, rotating crops and such, but those are for preestablished fields on flat terrain. I wouldn't have thought of the terracing system she suggested for retaining irrigation water on all these hills, preventing runoff and soil erosion."

"She did seem very competent, from what little I knew of her," Danau agreed. Unbidden, memory resurfaced of Yarrin's reddened face, and the puff of smoke escaping his lungs. It made her uncomfortable. She didn't like killing, but sometimes it was necessary.

Not all the sailors whose ships sank in the waters of the Sun's Belt Reefs were honest citizens. Some were pirates blown from their usual hunting grounds by storms, or who ran afoul of the shoals around Menomon in the pursuit of the rare reef-crossing barges, laden with treasures bound for Katan or Aiar. Some of those sea pillagers proved to be too dangerous to allow to stay in the city . . . and too greedy to be allowed to leave. Memory modification spells did exist, but like most spells, they could be broken if one was determined enough.

"I wish Yarrin could have suffered more for the crime of her death," Danau offered quietly. "But I've found a quick, clean death is best when you do have to kill someone, even if they're evil."

"Same here," the black-haired shapeshifter agreed. She started to say something else, but turned her head, looking off to the side.

Danau glanced that way, seeing a youth of about fourteen or so loping in their direction. It was a tired jog, the kind that said he'd been running for a while. The Aquamancer didn't know who the boy was, but the mayor did.

"Paulen, son of Sharlindra and Betany, the soap makers . . . Am I right?"

"Yes, milady," the youth agreed, catching his breath between words. "I'm honored you remembered me." Digging into the small pouch slung on his belt, he offered her a folded scrap of parchment. "Someone on the new ship wanted this sent to you. She paid a lot, so I figured it was important. I've been looking since midmorning."

Taking the note, Amara unfolded it. Her frown came back as she read the contents. Finally, she snorted.

"Do you need me to carry back a reply?" Paulen asked, his curiosity visible.

"No . . . no reply. Thank you for bringing this to me," the mayor added. "You said the sender was on a new ship?"

"The *Neap Tide*. It's moored at the north dock, across from the fish ship," he added, sneaking a glance at Danau.

"Technically, it's an *udrejhong*, a very specific type of vessel that can travel both on the surface and under water," Danau corrected. Then smiled wryly. "Though sometimes we do call them 'fish ships.'"

"Here, go get yourself a shaved ice; it's a hot day, and you could probably use it by now," Amara said, digging a few coins from her own pouch. The youth grinned and sketched her a bow as soon as he had the coppers in hand, before turning and trotting off again.

Curious, Danau asked quietly, "What's in the note? If it's not prying too much, that is . . ."

"It's not. Actually, I wouldn't mind your opinion. Here, let's see what you think this means," she added, passing over the paper.

Taking it, Danau unfolded the missive. It was only a couple lines long. It also *seemed* innocuous . . . except it wasn't.

I had a wonderful visit with you the other night; you were radiant, even resplendent, in your finery. Would you grace me with your witty, golden company once more? Head straight to the Neap Tide, *as soon as you are free to come alone, without fuss or accompaniment.*

~An Admirer

Danau lifted one brow. "Zella?"

"Zella," Amara confirmed. "Not that I'd know her handwriting on sight, but honestly, who else could it be?"

"I'm not an expert on controlling charms, but I suspect the spells she laid on your collar may have contained extra compulsion spells. Ones that would force you to comply with anything following a specific phrase or sentence," Danau said, nodding at the paper. "Those first two sentences are overly flattering, even obsequious. Most people don't talk like that."

"Sometimes they do, if they want something from someone in a position of great power and authority. I used to get flatteries like this all the time, back when I was Queen Aitava's apprentice. Well, all the time in the winter months, when the Clans and Families would come back for shelter against the winter storms," the taller woman amended.

"What do you plan to do?" Danau asked.

"What I *want* to do is tie a big rock to her feet and hurl her out into the bay," Amara quipped. "But for one, she's a mage, and that wouldn't be more than a temporary solution. For another . . . Her Majesty wants to confront the woman personally. Which makes me wonder if she's insane, since she has no magic and Zella does."

Glancing to the side as another half-grown tree sailed up from the depths of the holding tank, Danau smiled wryly. "I think I'll come along. I owe Her Majesty a small debt for handling my colleagues so adroitly last night."

"Oh? What did she do?" Amara asked, snapping open the lid of her cryslet.

"She fined both of them for the destruction of my property. Steeply. My cousin in particular will have to work for at least a decade to pay off her debt . . . which is a very satisfying thought," Danau added.

"You sound like you dislike her, and yet you're still very polite around her," the mayor observed.

Danau shrugged again. "I don't let anything interfere with my work. It's not productive."

Amara smirked. "So says the woman who was late to breakfast, and who arrived in the company of a certain redhead, with a certain glow of relaxed happiness about both of you . . ."

Blushing, Danau defended herself stiffly. "There are exceptions to every rule, save only the Laws of God and Man. Last I checked, my *personal* life wasn't a matter of international importance."

"Well, no, but gossip *is* universal . . . and if he's even half as talented as my Trevan, I'd say it's a very plausible and understanding exception—I am not blind," Amara added, cutting off Danau's next protest. "I may have been enchanted for most of the time, but I saw the way you two looked at each other last night at the concert hall. And I approve. I've come to know Koranen as a younger brother over the last few turns of Sister Moon, and I know he deserves someone who is smart, ambitious, and can make him happy. Someone who can truly love him. I think that woman could be you."

Clearing her throat, Danau nodded at the woman's communication bracelet, returning their attention to a more important subject than her love life. Even if she did finally have one, she still didn't know if it was love yet. "You'd better call the others and let them know the Amazai mage is back."

"Easy!" Morganen chided his brother, though he didn't move from where he slouched on a tall stool he had brought into the suite. He winced as the padded chair bumped into the wall before Koranen managed to correct its drift. "Watch it!"

"I *told* you I was a little rusty on my levitation spells. I keep forgetting to compensate more for the greater inertia of the larger items. You'll note I didn't damage it, though." Setting the chair down, Kor ended the spell with a snap of his fingers.

Turning back to the cheval mirror, he peered into the other universe, looking for the next piece to come across. Hope had marked the items she wanted transported with fanciful, multilooped bows made out of some sort of shiny yet flexible, bright red metal unique to her realm, something she called her *larr*. The next bow he spotted was affixed to the top of a stack of colorful, squarish, leatherbound tomes bigger than dinner plates. They sat piled along a long, low, two-layered table.

"I take it she wants all of the stacks of books. Do you think she wants the table, as well?"

"Might as well grab it. Better for her to have it and not want it, than the other way around," Morg agreed. He waved at a slateboard set up to one side of the sitting room, one covered in white and blue markings. It wasn't his sitting room, just one of the spare rooms in the northeast spur of the eastern palace wing, but then, there wasn't enough room in his own quarters to put everything she was sending across. "Just keep an eye on the calculations. The bottom line of the mass transference tally will turn pink, then red, if we get close to the exchange limit."

"And just how much wheat have you stolen from our stores for future plantings, just to pay for all this?" Koranen quipped.

"Don't ask." Changing the subject, Morg eyed his twin. "So . . . how goes your own courtship?"

"Not too badly. In fact, I'm hoping to upgrade it to 'rather well,'" the redhead added, bringing across the stacked tomes and their underlying table with a mutter and a flex of his fingers. On the other side of the looking glass, Hope came into the room, strange, handled objects dangling from her hands. She set them down—each black-sided, rounded box had a red bow affixed to its narrow upper edge—and waved in the direction of the mirror before departing again.

Morg waved back, though she couldn't have seen it. "How do you plan to do that?"

"Last night's courting was spoiled by the ruining of her dress. We missed dinner because of it, and the concert because of that murderer. So . . . I went into town and arranged to have another meal at the Giggling Pear for tomorrow night, and then arranged for flowers to be delivered to our table. Thankfully, Kelly bought those tickets to the third performance for us, or it would be hard to re-create the missed concert part of the night." He grimaced in distaste. "Of course, Reuen and Chana will be there, as well . . ."

"I'll make sure to sit between you and them if they're seated in the same area," Morg promised. "Since I'm getting a ticket of my own, but won't be needed as a chaperone, I might as well make myself useful as a shield-ward to buffer you."

"Your great and terrible sacrifice will be duly appreciated," Kor quipped, floating across the black cases. "When do you think you'll be back at full strength? And was it wise to open the Veil between here and there so soon after depleting yourself?"

"I promised her I would," his twin replied, shrugging. He sat up a little as Hope came back. This time, the curly-haired woman was carrying a white paper box embossed with some sort of symbol. "I know that box . . ."

"You do?" Kor asked, curious.

"Yes, it's the same box the velvet dress came across in," Morg said. He squinted. "Look, there's a note on this one."

However she managed it in a world with virtually no magic, Hope had found and faced the intersection plane of the mirror. She held up the box, tilting it toward her unseen audience, so that both of them could read the note clearly.

Kor's eyes twitched, translating the foreign characters. *For Koranen's Lady.* Exchanging a bemused look with his brother, he snapped his fingers and muttered the levitation charm, targeting the box the moment she shifted her hands from grasping to merely supporting.

The moment it came across, Morganen left his stool, grabbing the container. Kor ended the levitation charm so that he could grasp the lid, and the two brothers cooperated, easing off the tight-fitting lid. Layers of thin, crinkly paper hid the contents, until the auburn-haired mage batted it impatiently aside. Deep blue green velvet met their gazes.

Morg chuckled. "I see she's replaced the dress—here, let me take this."

"It is for *my* lady," Kor retorted, shifting one hand to clutch at the box. "I should give this to her tonight . . . after warding it with several protective spells, of course. Just in case."

"You can do that later. *I* need to resize it. Hope says dresses like these are made to a standardized pattern in a range of general sizes, and *not* to an individual body like our clothes are made, so it has to be tailored just a little bit before it's perfect." Tugging the box gently but firmly out of his twin's grasp, Morg returned to his stool. "You just keep bringing across anything and everything *my* lady wants, while I take care of perfecting *your* lady's gift."

"Fine—but that's *all* we're sharing. I am *not* going to let her get a second or a third husband. I don't care *what* the Menomonite custom is," Kor added firmly.

Morg gave his sibling a mild, amused look. "Jealous?"

"I would need an actual rival to be jealous . . . but yes. She is mine," Koranen said, nodding to confirm that fact. "The Gods Themselves decreed it."

"So, you love her," Morg prodded.

Once again, he was reminded of that word. Destiny was one thing, but love . . . love was something else. Pausing in his survey of the other universe, Koranen mulled over that possibility. His uncertainty puzzled him. Glancing over his shoulder, he eyed his twin. "How do you *know* when you're in love? I mean, how do you tell?"

"Do you respect her?" Morg asked his brother.

"Of course! She's competent and intelligent. She may seem a little cold on the surface, but she is willing to look past her difficulties with others and not let those problems interfere with whatever she needs to do," Kor said. "Not everyone can look past an insult and continue to work with the person who slights them. She has great strength of character—I think Mother and Father would have been proud to know her."

"I see. Do you enjoy talking with her?" Morg asked next.

"Yes—more so, now that she's no longer trying to deny her right to be courted. Now that she *can* be courted," Kor amended. "We've discovered we can use each others' affinity for fire or water, too, so when we weren't focused on the Desalinator control chamber, we were exchanging tips and tricks of each other's magical trade this morning. It was rather interesting, because she was taught in an even more formal education system than we were. Katani students are schooled until the age of sixteen, when they either go straight to work, become an apprentice, or pay for extra schooling.

"In Menomon, they also train until sixteen, then are sorted into a Guild and are apprenticed for another two to four years, depending on their talents and aptitudes. Sometimes someone is admitted into a Guild a year or two early, and Danau was one of them," Kor related. "Her fellow apprentices were a year older than her, so she felt like she had to study extra hard to make up for her lack of experience."

Morg nodded. "You studied hard in your own way, too, going from craftsman to craftsman, learning all the crafting aspects of fire, kiln, and forge."

"Yes, and she's been very interested in all that I know. They have metalsmiths in the City, but most of them are descended from shipmakers and weaponsmiths, and a random smattering of whoever else fell overboard. Their Smithy Guild is an eclectic collection of skills, very knowledgeable in some areas, but not nearly as well learned in others. From the sound of things, no single Guildmember has the same wide range of knowledge that I have, either," Kor told his twin.

"Good. So you not only get along in conversations; she respects you like you respect her. That's very good. Next question. Not to pry into intimate details or anything, but . . . do you find her attractive?" Morg asked lightly.

Kor smirked, thinking of what they had done before breakfast. "Very. At first, I was a bit taken aback by her short hair . . . and her short height makes it awkward to kiss her . . . but she's very pretty, once I got past that. Especially when she blushes."

"That's good. Attraction isn't everything, or even the most important ingredient in a long-lasting relationship, but it does have some importance. Now for the two most important questions," Morg cautioned his twin. "Think carefully about this one: Can you picture yourself still living with her, and still liking her, eight years from now?"

Koranen ignored the reappearance of Hope, though she was carrying the next bow-decorated item. Eight years was a long time . . . and if Danau had her way, they'd still be living in her far-flung, underwater home. She would expect them to still be down there, protecting and defending the people of Menomon as paired Guardians.

"I can't picture what life would be like in Menomon, if we moved there permanently," he admitted slowly, honestly. "I haven't actually been there, so I couldn't say. I do know she needs to return and construct their own desalination plant. And I know she wants me to join her in becoming Guardian Sheren's replacement for when that lady retires, since together, we seem to have enough power to control a singularity. But . . . I *can* picture myself still at her side."

"Alright. Now for the other important question. What if there was a way that, oh . . . say, that someone could remove your Curses of Fire and Ice?" Morganen asked. "Would you still want to be with her, even if you could move on and have any other woman?"

Blinking at his twin, Kor asked the uppermost question on his mind. "*Can* you do that?"

Balancing the paper box on his lap, Morg gave his sibling a solemn look. "We *are* going to resurrect the Convocation, Brother. Rora once mentioned to me that there were old records of similar petitions being brought before the Gods, and that some of the petitioners *were* unCursed."

For one moment, Koranen enjoyed the wild hope of doing just that, of going before the Gods as soon as his family opened the Convocation and They had confirmed Nightfall as its own kingdom. He easily pictured himself asking the Gods Themselves to remove . . . and that was where his daydream fell apart. As painfully lonely as it had been to be a fire-afflicted Pyromancer, Kor *liked* being a Pyromancer. He had worked long and hard to explore and exploit his skills, most of which depended to some degree on the manipulation of his Curse.

Take that away . . . and I'd be a shell of what I was. I'd have to work hard, probably for years, to relearn how to do all that I did through different applications of magic. Presuming the Gods left me still a mage and didn't remove that as well as my affinity for fire . . . No, he decided, shaking his head silently. *I'd not change myself. I'd not change any of my past, or drastically alter the possibilities of my future. Compared to losing what makes me uniquely me, moving to a distant underwater city and having to adjust to a whole new culture is a mere inconvenience ...*

The flip side of that coin occurred to him. If *he* could petition the Gods, so could Danau ... and she had more reason to loathe her abilities than he did his. Kor had enjoyed the loving support of his family, in spite of his magical affliction. She had known too many years of discomfort and isolation because of hers.

If she chose to petition the Gods ... there would go the only woman I could touch. But ... I couldn't demand that she not petition them. I like her, and I want to be with her, but I don't want to limit her like that. Which begets a new question. If she feels like I do, that her powers are worth it in spite of her suffering ... then I would stay with her. But if she wants her Curse gone, and the Gods grant her request ... would I be willing to give up mine, too? And would she still want me, if neither of us were limited to just each other by our Curses?

Gods ... if neither of us were limited to just each other ... she would have her pick of husbands, not just me. In fact, she'd have to marry several men, just to comply with that damnable Menomonite law. But ... would she want other men? Fear roiled up in his stomach at that possibility. So did jealousy. *I want her to want me! No one is better suited than me!*

That thought rang very true. Koranen realized why after only a moment of consideration. *Because ... because erasing our affinities wouldn't erase our pasts. Who else would understand why she'd still be leery of casually touching another person, except for me? Who else would understand me, for that matter, other than her and my family? And I'm not going to try to marry someone in my family, Gods forefend ...*

Even if she gave up her power and I gave up mine ... I'd be giving it up for her, to stay with her, not for the hope of finding some other woman. He nodded again, if slowly this time. At an inquiring noise from his brother, Koranen refocused on Morg's face. "I think I have a very important question to ask her, tomorrow night."

"If she'll marry you?"

A wry smile twisted the redhead's lips. "That, too. But I am neglecting *your* lady . . . and *you* have a dress to alter. Try not to hurt yourself."

"I may not be as good at tailoring spells as Evanor, but I'm no Wolfer, either," Morg retorted.

Koranen chuckled at that. Wolfer was good enough at plying a needle through leather, but when it came to stitching anything finer, he was hopeless. Kor had meant magically injure, not physically, but he couldn't deny handing his twin the opening for the jest, either. Morg, at least, wouldn't bleed all over the fabric. Returning his attention to the mirror, the Pyromancer sighed and searched for yet another bow-decorated item to float across the Veil.

SIXTEEN

❧

Not wanting to disrupt the illusion spell that the eldest of the brothers had cast on her by bumping into the other two with her, Danau boarded the *Neap Tide* carefully. She had two narrow misses with crew members once she reached the mid-deck, but she managed to stay out of their way. Thankfully, she had seen her target from the dock; the middle-aged mage was standing at the starboard rail of the aft deck, staring thoughtfully at the island through the rigging of the ship.

The older woman had taken care to change her clothes from her Menomonite leathers to what looked like Katani clothes, a bodice laced over a blouse and skirt. The garments were a light cotton in deference to the day's heat, and they softened her frame, made her seem more feminine. Even her hair was down, tangling in the occasional onshore breeze, and definitely would have fooled most people at a casual glance . . . but she was still the same black-haired, tanned-skin mage. The tight pinch of her mouth was proof of that.

Danau was there to provide magical support, if needed. The plan, however, was to avoid a mage-battle. Yarrin's death had turned out to be unavoidable, but he had been an insane killer. His death had been necessary to protect the others. Zella was power-mad, but otherwise sane, and a bit more law abiding.

Dodging an unaware crewman, Danau mounted the ladder-like set of steps to the aft deck, wanting to flank the Amazai mage. She couldn't see the others, but knew they were aboard when she heard the mayor hailing the ship, requesting permission for a government official to come aboard. The Katani crew didn't hesitate, welcoming her with a friendly wave up the same ramp which Danau had just climbed.

As earlier, the pectoral she wore glittered in the sun. Danau belatedly realized there were other dangers than just Zella. That was a *lot* of wealth to be wearing onto the deck of a foreign ship. Most everyone on the Isle knew that their lady mayor was a shapeshifter; even Danau had heard rumors of how Mayor Amara had grown herself as tall as a mast and heaved an unwelcome Katani ship and its officious tax collector out of the harbor. But this was a Katani vessel. They might not know her reputation, or even that she was the mayor of this particular port, but they would know she seemed to be all alone.

Zella stiffened when she spotted the younger woman and her eye-catching wealth. She turned slowly as Amara picked her way across the ship, watched the younger woman mount the ladder, and nodded politely when she reached the aft deck. Danau, attention split between the curious glances from the crewman and the two women, strained her ears to catch their exchange of greetings.

Thankfully, Amara proved herself to be a good actress; though her rib-length decoration was no longer enchanted to control her, she acted as though it still did. Danau heard the words *bring* and *sister* from the older woman, and saw Amara nodding and smiling in reply. And then a figure flickered into view between the Aquamancer and the two Aian women.

Zella started, but it was too late; a shift of Kelly's half-visible body, and Danau could see a rune-carved manacle clamped on the older woman's wrist. Amara caught her other hand, holding it firmly while Kelly quickly snapped a matching metal band around Zella's other wrist. The touch of the manacles finished draining away the rest of Kelly's protective illusion, leaving her fully visible. Closing the distance to the knot of females, Danau caught and steadied Kelly when the older woman shoved her back, ensuring the incipient Queen stayed on her feet and letting her know she wasn't alone.

"How dare you! I am an envoy of Amaz! You will remove these things *at once!*" the ambushed mage demanded.

"How dare *I?*" the freckled Queen retorted. "*You* broke the law on Nightfall soil. You used a set of spells to control one of my subjects against her will . . . and you did so in order to kidnap *another* of my subjects!"

"That subject is an Aian citizen by birth! She belongs to her people, not to some upstart nation," Zella retorted, then reined in her temper with a tight smile. "But it is *nice* to know you acknowledge that she's still alive."

"I *acknowledge* it because she is no longer valuable to you," Kelly returned, freckled hands planting on her hips. Like Zella— ironically enough—she had chosen to wear garments dyed a light, dusty pink, but she had selected trousers to go with her blouse and bodice, not a skirt. The contrasts between the two women were sharp.

Zella narrowed her dark brown eyes. "What do you mean?"

"I mean, the ceremony to extract the Fountain has already taken place . . . and *you* are clad in anti-magic cuffs. Even if you could get past me and my guards, from what I've been told, you couldn't touch the unleashed Fountain even if you tried . . . because all that power would drain straight into your manacles and literally burn off your hands. Unless you plan on changing your name to Stumpy, . . . you've lost. Give in gracefully, and accept your penance for breaking the law," Kelly told her.

"You lie—you haven't extracted her Fountain!" Zella challenged.

Amara held out her hand. In it was clasped a white marble disc. "My sister, who *was* a Living Host, has had her Fountain successfully extracted . . . and that Fountain has been secured against all possible theft. Anyone who tries to breach the deadly wards erected to protect it before the precise release date of the coming Convocation will simply die . . . and believe me, you're *welcome* to try."

Uncurling her fingers, she displayed the unblemished surface of the stone. Zella stared at it, then blinked at the younger woman. "You aren't . . . but those spells were well hidden! How did you know there was an enchantment?"

"You crafted your hexes to make Amara, here, pleasant and agreeable," Kelly enlightened Zella. "That was your biggest mistake."

"Yes, but the spells were set to render her no more agreeable than she would be normally!" Zella protested, lifting her chin with a touch of pride. "No one should have noticed a deviation in her behavior—and the spells themselves were hidden from magesight!"

Amara smirked. "*Normally* doesn't take into account the fact that Her Majesty and I get along about as well as a brick of sandstone scraped against tender skin."

"You know, I think I am actually glad you hate me," Kelly quipped.

"I don't *hate* you. I just find you annoying and irritating," Amara retorted lightly.

Once again, Danau felt like she was at a *panka* game. Unfortunately, this was not the right moment for this particular exchange. Lifting her hand, she gently tapped the incipient Queen on her back, silently reminding her to get back to her task.

"Right. Enough of this banter," Kelly said, catching the hidden Aquamancer's meaning. "For the crime of conspiring to kidnap a citizen of Nightfall, and the crime of magically controlling and manipulating *another* citizen of Nightfall, you are hereby fined five thousand gilders, or the equivalent weight, pound for pound, in Aian coin.

"You will be sent away from Nightfall and given three months to sail home, gather the funds, and return the money to Nightfall, either in person or through a courier. Personally, I'd suggest a courier, because I *really* don't care to see you anywhere near here again. Or make use of . . . What's the name of your Guardian in Amaz . . . ? Torlau? Teral? Whoever it is, you can ship the payment from him to Guardian Sheren through the Fountainway, and she can then forward it to us."

Zella started to say something, then compressed her mouth in a taut line.

Kelly wasn't a fool, and proved it by her next words. "Don't think to skip out on payment. Your crime was motivated by the desire to re-create the Convocation of the Gods on Amazai soil. Your punishment is therefore highly appropriate to your crime, because of this: Should you fail to deliver your fine by the end of one full turn of Sister Moon from today . . . the Patron Deity of Amaz will *not* be Named at the next Convocation. Your people will have no voice with which to make petitions, no chance to question old versions or propose new ones when it comes time to review the Laws of God and Man, and your people will have no say in the shaping of the new world that is to come."

"You're bluffing," Zella said, staring skeptically at the shorter woman. "You don't even know the name of the Amazai Patron—and I *know* you cannot resurrect the Convocation without naming *all* of the current Gods. You'll *have* to name our Patron, or fail. Your threat is empty."

"Oh, I have all the Names of the Gods," Kelly corrected her. "I haven't yet *memorized* them, but I do have them, and the list is both current and complete. The Patron Deity of Amaz *will* be named the first time around, as is required to reconvene the Convocation. No, I'm talking about the *next* time. The first Convocation will only have a few pieces of business on the petitions docket. Just a quick peek through the Gateway to Heaven, if you will. The second one . . . *that* Convocation will hold your kingdom's chance at influencing the world.

"*If* you pay your fine on time, your Deity will be named again at that time . . . which is only appropriate, since the whole reason why you committed your crimes was to steal that power for your people." Stepping to the side, Kelly leaned partway over the railing and called out to the sailors on the mid-deck. "Ahoy, there! Get your captain on deck; the Queen of Nightfall has something to tell him!"

Facing Zella again, she addressed the older woman.

"I'll be kind and request the captain of this ship sail you straight back to mainland Katan, at Nightfall's expense. And that he consider offering you the names of any ships and captains he might know that might willing to cross the Sun's Belt Reefs and get you home all the faster. Mostly because I don't want you lingering here any longer than absolutely necessary. May you have a safe trip home . . . and may you stay there. Amara, shall we go?" she asked politely, gesturing at the ladderway closest to the gangplank.

"After you, Aikelly," the mayor returned equally politely, giving her Queen a graceful bow.

Danau watched the other two leave, pausing only long enough to have a short conversation with the *Neap Tide*'s captain. She didn't bother to move closer to hear their exchange; her attention was focused on the Amazai woman standing stiffly at the aft deck rail, between the rail and the rudder-wheel. Nor did she leave as the captain gave orders to round up the crew that had gone ashore and prepare the ship for departure.

In fact, she stayed onboard all the way through the casting off of the mooring lines and the raising of a couple sails. Danau stayed onboard to keep an eye on Zella Fin Rin, wanting to make sure the ship was well under way and the mage being carried away before she could enact some sort of revenge.

A few minutes after the ship pulled away from the dock, the Amazai mage caught the arm of a passing sailor and inquired tersely if any of them knew how to pick a lock, since it seemed Her Majesty had neglected to provide a key to her manacles. The man answered in the negative; Zella's visible disgust when he said she'd have to wait to reach a locksmith at the nearest Katani port pleased Danau. Satisfied the mage wouldn't be able to cause trouble for Nightfall, the Aquamancer slipped silently to the back railing. Waiting until the crew's attention was on the full unfurling of the ship's remaining sails, she dove neatly, quietly into the bay and began the swim back to the city.

When she finished climbing the ladder at the end of the north dock, Amara, Kelly, and Saber were waiting for her. Or rather, they were waiting to make sure the *Neap Tide* left the island with only one person "lost" overboard. Dismissing the illusion spell he had cast on her, Saber offered her a scrap of nubbly fabric to wipe the salt water from her face.

"Any problems from her?" he asked.

"Only that it'll take her until the next port city to get those manacles off," Danau reported. "As for your threats . . . I'd say she swallowed them, worm, hook, line, and rod."

Amara grinned and flipped the disc in her hand, before clutching it again. "My name is Petri, and I am Queen Kelly's absolute best friend!" Flipping it again flashed the unblemished sides. The gold-laden woman smirked. "I should get *this* back to my sister, so she can put it back into the 'to be enchanted' pile."

"And I have to get ready to talk to Rydan yet again about the need to go through with the extraction process," Kelly agreed. "Morg's news about the coming Mendhites has almost convinced him, but almost convinced isn't the same as fully committed."

"I'll drive the wagon," Saber offered, glancing at Danau. "You can ride along, if you want to go back to the palace to bathe and change. If not, we can drop you off at the Desalinator."

"The Desalinator," Danau chose. "I need to get back to work, to ensure your source of drinking water doesn't collapse."

Saber offered Kelly his elbow. For a moment, Danau felt the same wistful envy that had plagued her every other time she had seen a loving couple touch. But it died within two or three heartbeats; Saber was the firstborn of eight in his family, which was a roundabout reminder that Koranen was the seventhborn. And the seventhborn of the brothers, she *could* touch as much as she wanted.

"How is your meal?" Koranen inquired politely.

"Very tasty. We don't grow these kinds of beans in Menomon," Danau admitted. "And I've never had venison before. It's sort of like lamb, only different, isn't it?"

"You have room to raise lamb in Menomon?" Kor asked, surprised.

"No—a ship came down just outside the salvage zone of the city, about six years ago. A Wavescout patrol managed to save five of the crew, but the rest . . . It was carrying a flock of sheep, among other things. The patrol salvaged most of the bodies, but the sheep had to be eaten quickly, so there was a welcoming feast when they returned to the City," she explained. "I was already advanced to Rank 8 by then, so I was invited to partake, and I managed to get a bite of lamb. I understand mutton tastes a lot stronger, but that was served to those with more seniority."

Kor chuckled. "On land, lamb is considered the tastier meat."

"Well, yes, but it was the *novelty* of the new meat," she pointed out. "As it was, I didn't get more than half a dozen bites of it. I was wondering why you didn't pick venison yourself. I thought it was considered a rare treat by Aians and Katani alike."

"Normally it is, but for more than three years, the only animals my brothers and I had to eat were chickens, game birds, fish, shellfish, and deer . . . unless you counted salt-preserved meats, which we couldn't always get reliably from the traders. I chose the pork because we only got pigs on the island a few months ago, and I like the way it tastes," he explained.

"Pork is the most common meal made from the larger land animals in Menomon," Danau related. "Cattle are reserved for their milk, so it's pigs that get slaughtered first. They also breed faster, because pigs will eat almost anything, including random plate scrapings . . . and to me, they *taste* like it. I much prefer fish."

"Fish is good," he agreed. "I prefer the free-swimming sort over the bottom-feeders, since the bottom-feeders taste like the mud they eat."

"Some bottom-feeders aren't that—oh! Oh, *no*," Danau groaned, hastily setting down her fork and grabbing for her napkin. Wetting it in her water cup, she dabbed gingerly at the drops of sauce that had fallen on her lap, grimacing as it started to smear. "Oh, please, please come out . . . !"

Seeing her fuss over her velvet dress, Koranen shook his head. "Danau, *relax*. It's just a dress."

"That's like saying Amara's pectoral is 'just' a necklace, instead of an overblown display of blatant wealth," she muttered, dabbing a clean corner of the napkin in her water cup. That helped ease the rest of the smear, though it did leave her with a damp blotch on her lap. He had given it to her yesterday afternoon, telling her it was a replacement for the one she had lost . . . and that the whole rest of their aborted date was being replaced, dress, dinner, and concert. "And it's not just *a* velvet dress; it's the *second* velvet dress your family has given me."

"And I'd *gladly* give you several more, if wearing them gives you pleasure. You could even have one for every day of the month, if you liked," Koranen reassured her. It was the best opening he had for the questions he wanted to ask, the questions Morganen had asked him. "Danau . . . speaking of more . . ."

Shaking out her napkin, Danau set it beside her plate and gave him her attention. "Yes?"

"If you think about it, can you imagine the two of us still getting along and liking each other eight years from now?" Only after he asked the question did Koranen realize the significance of that number for her. Eight years ago, that other man had humiliated her. He'd picked eight years, because eight was the preferred number back on the mainland, where he had been raised. But aside from a brief, questioning look, she didn't seem upset by the reference.

It was a good question. Danau cast her thoughts into the future, mulling over the possibilities. *Eight years from now . . . hopefully the Desalinator will be fully functional long before then, but it would still need the occasional maintenance check . . . And there'd be Aquamancy Guild tasks, and his Pyromantic efforts. The Smithy Guild would certainly try to claim his time. Sheren would probably have retired, and together we'd get to deal with all the same, unending, headachy little requests that have plagued her . . . but we'd have each other for support, and for conversation, and for lovemaking. Which of course might lead to a child or two . . .*

A child or two. I think I'd like that. Now that I'm over the shock of being able to beget children. Of course, we'd both have to be very careful when caring for our children, if we weren't touching each other as well while doing so . . .

"Yes," she confirmed. "I can see us getting along quite well together."

"Alright . . . Here's another question," he offered. "It is said that those who were Cursed used to be able to go to the Convocation and petition the Gods to remove their Curse. If this is true . . . would you petition the Gods at the Convocation to remove your affinity for absorbing heat and inducing cold in everything around you?"

Danau blinked, taken by surprise. *If that were possible . . . ! I could stop being a danger to others whenever I was agitated. I could feel comfortable about cuddling a child, or . . .* The thought, *taking a lover,* faltered as she stared at him. *If I petitioned, and my Curse was removed . . . it's not just my Curse that would have to be considered.*

If I petitioned and he didn't . . . he wouldn't have a woman he could make love to anymore. The converse would apply, if he petitioned, and I didn't; I would have to go back to being celibate and untouched.

That wasn't a happy thought. There was a part of her that was starved for contact, though she had done her best to ignore it over the years. Though she still had half of her venison left on her plate, Danau needed to think more than she needed to eat. This wasn't a question about what *she* wanted, but what *they* could have.

Of course, he wouldn't offer the suggestion unless he'd considered it for both of us. The best solution would be for both of us to ask for our Curses to be lifted. If mine were lifted, I could not only touch any man I wanted; I'd be expected to take on at least three husbands as soon as possible. But Koranen isn't a Menomonite; most land-born men express a clear distaste for the thought of sharing a wife with other men.

But that's assuming he'd want to stay with me. The biggest reason he's sitting across from me is that he can *court me. Perhaps . . . the* main *reason he's still here with me.*

That thought put a lump in her throat. It was a good thing she wasn't trying to eat at the moment; the rare deer meat would have been wasted on a tight throat and a mouth turned dry with dismay. Picking up her cup, she took a sip, trying to ease the knot of anxiety tightened by that possibility. The lump didn't go away, but it did allow her to speak.

"What would be *your* choice?"

He shook his head, his auburn hair sliding across his shoulders. The blue velvet of two days ago had been laundered and looked even better now than it had then. "I don't want to influence your decision either way. Choose whatever is best for *you*."

Best for me? But he's *what's best,* part of her protested.

Since he wanted her to make up her own mind, Danau pursued that thought. *Why is he what's best? It isn't the long hair or the handsome face; that's just surface attraction. He's a witty conversationalist, but*

I've met men just as witty. And charming, and persistent, and smart, and well educated . . .

But it isn't any of those things, is it? she admitted to herself. *This is a man—the only man—who knows even a fraction of what it means to be Cursed. To be isolated, even when surrounded by others. This is the only man who pursued me, even when he wasn't sure if he should, and he did so on pure faith. A faith that the Gods had arranged for the perfect woman to show up in his life, the woman who would be his Destiny . . . and when he realized I was his opposite . . . he pursued me.*

I am the best woman for him . . . and if I choose to petition, he would have to petition as well, because I would no longer be his woman. He would have no one. But it isn't fair to force him to give up his powers if he's happy being a thermally influenced Pyromancer. Nor is it right for me to say, "No, I want to keep my own powers," if he wants to be free of his . . . in case he feels obligated to give up his own.

Shaking her head, she set down her cup. "No. I cannot make this decision on my own. Not this one. I can only make it with you, by mutual agreement."

"Why?" He meant to ask it more diplomatically than that, but Koranen had to know. His blunt question drew an equally blunt answer from her.

"You complete me." She hadn't meant to put it quite like that; she *meant* to let him know she would respect his preference and any reasons for it, but Danau didn't take back the words. They were truthful, after all. "Whatever you choose, I'll respect you for it. Even if . . . even if you want to choose someone other than me, or at least be free to choose. Petitioning the Gods could grant both of us that kind of freedom. But . . ."

"But?" he prompted.

"Your life and mine are meant to intertwine. If you *want* to remove your powers, I'd remove mine, too, because otherwise I'd have no one left to touch . . . but though I'd be free to seek others once they were removed, I don't think I'd *want* to. I want *you*. You didn't hesitate to pursue me, even when I flatly refused to be pursued."

Koranen carefully buried the memory of his twin whacking him on the back of his head to get him to actively pursue her. She didn't ever need to know his reluctance on that point. And, frankly, he had deserved the blow, just for being a blind fool where Danau had been concerned. Her answers were certainly encouraging; even if she hadn't *said* it in so many words, it *was* clear that she cared about him.

"If you wanted to keep your powers," she continued, "well, I'm used to being an *udrezero*, but I'd also have you in my life. It's only been a few days, but you understand me. And you don't let me discourage you. More than that, I understand *you*. For the first time in my adult life, or at least the last eight years of it . . . I am good *for* someone."

Nodding, letting her know he did understand what she was trying to say, Koranen forced himself to press his point. "I know . . . but what would *you* choose?"

"Koranen—"

"—Danau, *I* cannot make this kind of a decision without *you*. But . . . suspend the you-and-me, just for a moment," he urged her. "Ask yourself what *you* want."

Danau felt her heart thump in her chest and her cheeks begin to burn with a blush of blended hope and distress. Out of the corner of her eye, she could see frost beginning to form on the edge of her plate. Reaching across the table, he covered her hand with his. The frost immediately faded, melting in the warmth of the restaurant.

"Just *ask*, do you want to get rid of your ice power? Or would you prefer to keep it? Is it a burden you can no longer bear? Or is it a part of you that you would rather not remove? Just you, and you alone. No consideration of anything else." Giving her hand a gentle squeeze, he released it, leaving her to her thoughts. "Would you prefer to keep it? Or would you prefer to live without it?"

The way he worded his query sunk into her.

It is *a part of me, isn't it? I don't like being* isolated *because of it . . . but when he touches me, I'm no longer isolated. I'm not even isolated from*

*others, so long as Kor is near—and maybe this joint-power thing is some-
thing we can learn to wield even when we're not touching directly. I mean,
it's not as if we have to be touching flesh to flesh to use it, not if I could
shove at him with my sleeve-covered forearm and open up the barrier-door,
particularly without either of us even knowing what we were doing . . .*

To give up her affinity for cold . . . it might make her more socially effective, but it would ruin some of her effectiveness as an
Aquamancer. Danau prided herself on her work. *I've spent the last
eight years defining myself by it. I may have a new way to gain a sense of
self-worth,* she acknowledged, eyeing the man across from her, *but
that doesn't stop me from being the best Aquamancer in the Guild. Only
the removal of some of my magic would do that.*

*And if I keep my power, he would have to keep his, and I wouldn't have
to force him to share me with other husbands because we would still be
dangerous to others. Menos . . . I sincerely hope You will grant our children a certain thermal insensitivity.*

Mind made up, Danau reached across the table, covering his
hand with her own. "I don't want to limit you, if you have chosen
otherwise . . . but if it's alright with *you* . . . I think I'd like to keep
mine. Which I hope means you'd be willing to keep yours. It hasn't
always made me happy, but it has made me what I am . . . and it has
made you what you are, too. We *are* perfect for each other, or as
perfect as mere mortals can get."

Turning his palm up, Koranen held her hand in his. "I would
prefer not to petition the Gods, either. I like who I am, and what I
can do. And I like you. More than that . . ." He forced himself to go
on, because it needed to be said. "More than that, I'm falling in love
with you. Frost or no frost, you complete *me* . . . but I'd prefer to
know and love *all* of you."

There it was, the blush that made her look charmingly feminine,
despite her short hair and short stature and short temper. Koranen
wanted to press a kiss to her knuckles, but the table was just a little
too wide to do anything more than merely hold hands. Now there
were only two more things he needed to know.

"Okay . . . two more questions. The first one is important," he cautioned her. She gave him an inquiring look, and he smiled in reassurance, though the question itself made him nervous. "Do you . . . or could you . . . possibly love me, too? Or at least learn to?"

Of all the soul-searching she had just done, this one was the easiest to resolve. Danau shook her head. And realized her mistake as his expression fell. Tightening her grip on his hand, she held his hazel gaze steadily. "No—sorry—I meant . . . no, I couldn't *just* possibly learn to love you. It'd be very hard to *learn* to love you, because I already do. I mean, I'm not very . . . Well, it just occurred to me right now that I do . . . but I *do*.

"Am I making any sense?" she asked him plaintively. He blinked at her. Danau tried again. "Kor, I am *not* very good at this. I told you, I don't date! I don't have any practice at this sort of thing."

"No, you don't," he agreed candidly. Cradling her palm in his, he squeezed gently. "But then, the only 'practice' *I've* had has involved two disasterous attempts at courtship from too many years ago, an illusion-woman created for pleasure, which isn't the same as companionship, and a lot of in-theory lectures from my brothers. We will learn *together*, you and I. And practice on each other."

"A lot?" Danau asked, hope creeping into her tone.

"A lot," Koranen promised. He squeezed her fingers once more, then let go. "But first, we finish supper. And then we enjoy the concert. Because that's what people do when they court. Even I know that much. And afterward . . . well, we'll get to practice that part, too. A lot."

"Good," she agreed, picking up her fork. Only to drip another blotch of venison gravy on her dress. Setting down the implement, she braced her elbow on the table and buried her face in her palm. "I am having *no* luck with velvet, am I?"

"Considering the destruction of the last dress brought us together, and discussing this one led to us admitting we're falling in love with each other, I'd say you're having *good* luck with it," Kor said, picking up his own fork.

Rolling her cheek onto her palm, Danau eyed him skeptically. She changed the subject, wanting to get through his questions so that she could ask one of her own . . . now that she knew how both of them felt about each other. "So what was your last question?"

"Yes, that. Bear in mind that I have as little practice in dating as you do," Kor prefaced his words. "But with that in mind, and forgiving me my bluntness . . . will you marry me?"

She buried her face back in her palm. A moment later, a giggle escaped her.

Setting down his fork, Kor gave her a firm look. "Danau, that isn't meant to be humorous."

Shaking her head, she straightened and picked up her damp napkin, dabbing at her dress again. "No, it's not that. It's just that, in Menomon, it's the *woman* who asks the man. I was just thinking about asking *you*, when you asked *me*."

"If we get married by non-Menomonite custom, that's one more layer of protection against you being ordered to wed a second husband," Koranen pointed out. "Call it selfish by your people's standards, but I really don't want to share you with another man."

"And I don't want to share you with another woman. So, will you marry me?" Danau wanted to know.

"I asked you first," he insisted.

She arched an auburn brow at him, and he lifted his own in return. Another laugh escaped her, this one a rueful chuckle. "Is this going to be argument number three?"

"No; this one is too easily solved," Kor dismissed. "We just count to three, and say *yes* simultaneously. Ready? One . . . two . . ."

"Yes," Danau stated firmly, before he could get to *three*. "I will marry you. By Nightfaller custom, too . . . because it'll be an extra layer of protection to keep the Council from insisting that, if I can marry *one* man, I should be able—and thus required—to marry three."

"Good point. But I'm saying *yes*, too," Kor told her. "I don't want you to have any doubt in your mind that I want you as my wife."

"Good. But we're still moving to Menomon, once we're through here," she said, picking up her fork—with extra care this time, so she wouldn't spatter her dress again. Even if he did buy her a dozen more, it was still velvet. "We'll stay for the Convocation, but the City needs us even more than the Isle does."

"Alright, fine. But you're growing out your hair," he reminded her. "Now, what would you like for dessert, once you've finished your venison?"

"Kelly? Where's Kelly?" Morganen demanded, twisting to peer around the garden. "Saber, where did that wife of yours go?"

"She went to use the refreshing room. She'll be right back," the blond magesmith told him. "Now, would you calm down?"

"No. Wolfer, tell me you are *not* wearing that," Morg chided his next brother. "I don't care if you came straight from milking the cows. You were not born in a barn—and get that hay out of your wife's hair! Trevan, stop fiddling with that . . . whatever it is . . . and pay attention! Evanor—"

"Koranen, could you *please* calm your sibling down?" Saber demanded.

"*Him?* He has lovemaking on his brain!" Morg protested, jerking his thumb at his twin. "Not that I blame him, but he's hardly going to be of any help."

Koranen was sitting on the stone bench at the stone gaming table in the stone-paved center of the garden, directly across from the cheval mirror Morganen had brought out of his workroom, a pot of powder next to the elbow he had braced on the table. Danau was cuddled on Koranen's lap, though in deference to the public location, they were merely holding each other, not making love. Morg didn't let a mere technicality slow him down.

"I have the most important spell of my life to cast in the next few minutes, the fulfillment of a thousand-year-old Prophecy, less than an hour's notice that it's time to bring across the woman of my dreams, and to bring her across safely, half my family isn't even here to give her a proper greeting, and you want me to *calm down*?"

Slipping behind his youngest sibling, Evanor cupped his hands over Morganen's ears and hummed. Morg's aqua eyes glazed within moments, and some of the frenetic tension drained from his body. Taking his hands away, the blond Voice mage shook his head. "If I didn't know better, I wouldn't have guessed that just four days ago he was bedridden from spellshock. Where Morg gets his energy, I have *no* clue—he even beats out my son!"

"You're lucky your son isn't here to resemble that remark," Kelly quipped, approaching from the nearest wing of the palace.

Morg blinked and shook off his brother's calming spell. At least, the dazed portion of it. "It's about time you got here, Ev. I want her to be surrounded by friendly, familiar faces. The *best* reception possible, so she'll feel utterly welcome."

"She *will*," Kelly reassured him. "And, unlike me, she already knows what she'll be getting into. At least, as much as anyone from my old world can."

"I see movement in the mirror," Alys warned Morg, finger-combing a last piece of straw from her dark gold curls.

Morg faced the cheval glass, then spun, glancing worriedly around the garden. "My powder—where is my powder?"

"Exactly where you left it, Brother, safe in my keeping," Koranen reassured him, holding up the pot of Gating powder with the hand not busy holding Danau on his lap. A cloud slid across the sun, dimming and cooling the garden a little. The heat wave had broken with a rainstorm the previous night. Kor suspected his sixthborn brother had grown tired of the oppressive, excessive sunlight and had done something with the weather, but it was only a suspicion. Rydan wasn't in a very talkative mood, of late.

Plucking the jar from his twin's grip, Morg faced the mirror.

"Cover your ears," Koranen quickly warned Danau, muffling his

own with his palms. As did everyone else in proximity to the mirror. She followed suit, just in time to protect herself from the
strong-voiced, magic-backed spell Morganen cast. Literally cast, for
he grabbed a handful of the special powder and flung it at the surface of the mirror. The surface seemed to flex and ripple, then it
stilled again.

Noise came through the fully opened mirror-Gate, a strange
rushing, rumbling noise. It resolved an image of a wall with what
looked like one of the Menomonite greaseboards spread across the
wall, and a woman with tanned skin and wavy dark brown hair. A
clutch of canvas bags was slung over her shoulder by one hand. The
other one was empty as she lifted it, aiming it with remarkable accuracy at the invisible point where the mirror intersected her world.

Koranen had seen Hope before, and had seen how Morganen
greeted her. As his twin moved to do so, one hand touching his
chest, the other reaching into the mirror, she smiled, but it was a
strained smile. And rather than touching her palm to his, she
grabbed his wrist, speaking up over the roar of noise in her world.
Her voice wasn't very loud, though it was clear she was shouting . . .
which meant whatever that noise was, it was very loud.

"You can bring me across now!"

Startled by the deviation, Morg blinked at her.

"Now, Morganen—" Her head whipped to the side, her eyes
widening into a ring of white around brown. *"NOW!"*

Koranen reacted instinctively to her fear, pushing to his feet. It
dumped Danau off his lap, though she caught her balance quickly
with only a brief stumble. Thankfully, his twin's reflexes were faster
than his own; with a hard yank, Morganen pulled Hope O'Niell
from her world to his. It helped that the outworlder woman leaped
even as he pulled, allowing her to clear the mirror's frame without
touching the edge of the intersection plane.

The moment she landed, she whirled to face the mirror. "Close
it! *Close* it!"

Some of the powder had spilled from the jar still clutched in his hand, thanks to the force of his pull, but there was enough for Morg to grab a handful and cast it at the mirror. Another string of shouted syllables echoed off the granite walls of the castle-like palace. The mirror flexed, settled . . . and madness consumed the view of her world.

The wall cracked, bowed, and flung itself backward. Wood and plaster exploded and whirled. The white-and-metal box that Koranen vaguely recalled as some sort of food-heating device tumbled right through the edge of the intersection plane—and if the Veil between their worlds hadn't been closed, it would have destroyed the mirror. Any of the debris whirling through the shocking view would have destroyed the mirror, quite probably in an unpleasantly powerful explosion. Even without sound to accompany the destruction of what had once been Hope's home, it was an eerie, frightening view.

A bare moment later, a misty haze covered the view, occasionally peppered with bits of debris. It lasted maybe a dozen heartbeats, then retreated. It left behind stubs of wooden studs, torn floor tiles and bared mortar, rubble-strewn grass . . . and the view of a retreating wall of water, wind, and wreckage that tore bits of roof and chunks of wall off the other outworlder buildings it passed.

"That . . . that was a *tornado*," Kelly muttered, aqua eyes as wide as Morganen's. "Or rather, *another* tornado. You already escaped one of them, several years ago, didn't . . . ?" Turning from the mirror to her friend, she trailed off as she saw the other woman's expression. "Hope?"

The outworlder wasn't staring at the mirror. The others looked away from the cheval-framed destruction, though the view was disturbingly compelling in its carnage. Morg touched her shoulder, but she didn't even glance at him. All of her attention was focused on the heart of the palace, and its distinctive, blue-domed donjon. It *was* distinctive, but surely it wasn't anything worthy of the awe-filled look Hope was giving it.

"Hope?" Morganen asked her gently. "Is everything all right?"

"All *right*?" she asked faintly, still staring at the palace. Tears welled in her brown eyes, one spilling down her cheek. "I'm home . . .

"I'm finally *home*!"

Song of the Sons of Destiny

The Eldest Son shall bear this
    weight:
If ever true love he should feel
Disaster shall come at her heel
And Katan will fail to aid
When Sword in sheath is claimed by
    Maid

The Second Son shall know this
    fate:
He who hunts is not alone
When claw would strike and cut to
    bone
A chain of Silk shall bind his hand
So Wolf is caught in marriage-band

The Third of Sons shall meet his
    match:
Strong of will and strong of mind
You seek she who is your kind
Set your trap and be your fate
When Lady is the Master's mate

The Fourth of Sons shall find his
    catch:
The purest note shall turn to sour
And weep in silence for the hour
But listen to the lonely Heart
And Song shall bind the two apart

The Fifth Son shall seek the sign:
Prowl the woods and through the
    trees
Before you in the woods she flees
Catch her quick and hold her fast
The Cat will find his Home at last

The Sixth Son shall draw the line:
Shun the day and rule the night
Your reign's end shall come at light
When Dawn steals into your hall
Bride of Storm shall be your fall

The Seventh Son shall he decree:
Burning bright and searing hot
You shall seek that which is not
Mastered by desire's name
Water shall control the Flame

The Eighth Son shall set them free:
Act in Hope and act in love
Draw down your powers from above
Set your Brothers to their call
When Mage has wed, you will be all.

—THE SEER DRAGANNA